Return of The Griffin

Turn Two of the Hybrid Helix

JCM Berne

The Gnost House

ISBN-13: 978-1-7349170-4-8

Cover image by Chris McGrath

Cover graphics by Stephanie Yang

Acknowledgments

I have more people to thank than I can easily count, starting with my wife, Moneeka, without whose support none of the rest of this would have happened.

Then there's my alpha reading group: Jonathan, Ed, Anne, Randy, Richard, Dori, Allison, and Dylin, who contributed immeasurably to early drafts. The gang at INKubators who helped polish pieces of this when I couldn't see how.

My editor, Lauren Donovan of The Book Foundry, who (gently) pushed me to make changes that really needed to be made. Chris McGrath, cover artist extraordinaire, whose work inspired me, along with Stephanie Yang who reminded me how important good graphic design really is, and who tirelessly helped me make choices I am ill-equipped to make.

My web and marketing guru, Marc Greenwald.

My online teachers: Brandon Sanderson, the cast of Writing Excuses, and Mur Lafferty, all of whom were there for me and asked for nothing in return (at least in part because they have no idea who I am).

And last, my Facebook community, who brought me so much encouragement and support.

Contents

Prologue

(Nearly) The End

Dr. Kraken's tentacles twitched and jerked like dreaming cats as he maneuvered the spinning globe of water closer to Rohan's exposed chest.

Rohan tugged at the heavy, nanotube-laced steel cuffs restraining his arms and legs. A haze clogged his thoughts.

The globe grew a bump at its equator, immediately spinning into a sharp ring that edged closer to the il'Drach Hybrid's skin.

Rohan braced, uselessly willing his body to cave backward into the unyielding steel frame that held him.

Why am I so weak?

The spinning blade parted his chest hairs, sending a fine shower of black grains to the ground, then reached eagerly for his flesh.

Dr. Kraken spoke, his voice deep and resonant and warbling from a voicebox meant to function underwater.

"Your people use pressurized water jets to cut steel and fashion machine parts. It is one of the few things I admire about humans."

"Only . . . half human, Doc." Rohan grunted as the edge of water touched his skin.

Flesh split, and blood began to etch skinny lines down Rohan's chest.

"No offense, Griffin. Or should I call you Rohan?" He reached one tentacle toward Rohan and swiped it across his chest, an obscene parody of a mother wiping dirt off her child. It picked up a smear of blood and immediately carried it back under his hood of flesh.

The tip of the tentacle emerged clean but trailing strands of saliva.

"Mm. Delicious. I will always say that mammalian humanoids were an evolutionary mistake, but by the Ancients, you do taste delicious."

Rohan grunted with pain as the water blade dug deeper into his chest muscles. "Glad I could help you out."

"Oh, no, you haven't helped me. Not yet. Where was I?" The creature lifted a comically oversized syringe in his hand and closed on Rohan.

"Um." Rohan let out an involuntary grunt of pain. "About to let me go?"

"Ha! I am glad that your humor, rudimentary as it is, has survived. You will need your strength for what is to come."

Dr. Kraken brought the syringe closer. His skin was gray and slick; his body humanoid; his head a dome of nearly unbroken flesh, the skirt of meat around his neck supporting four long tentacles. Eyes protruded from the sides of his head, dumbbell-shaped pupils dark against bloodshot backgrounds.

With four-fingered hands, he slid the tip of the syringe into the cut in Rohan's chest and depressed the plunger.

"You have no idea how difficult it is to brew substances capable of subduing an il'Drach Hybrid. Especially not without dulling the subject's pain sensors. Were I not such a genius, we would instead be holding you captive by means of repeated head trauma."

Rohan's muscles relaxed against his will as the drugs spread through his body. "Thanks. Both for skipping the head trauma and for the drugs. Maybe later you could put some in a doggy bag I could take with me. For recreational purposes."

Dr. Kraken laughed, a wet burble of sound that emerged from the flap of skin covering his unseen mouth. "For you there is no later, Hybrid. You will die in this room. But not before telling me what I want to know."

"Was this whole thing about me? A lure, a way to draw me in?"

Another laugh from the man-shaped cephalopod. "No, Griffin. It never ceases to amaze me how self-centered you Hybrids can be. No, *none* of this was about you. You are . . . how would you put it? You are a consolation prize. At most. Do not let it get to your head."

Rohan strained at his bonds again, to no avail.

Dr. Kraken continued. "I imagine this predicament is unfamiliar to you."

"You'd be surprised. I was in a situation just like this six months ago."

"I sincerely doubt that it was 'just like this.' You don't yet realize how different. That's fine; you will learn to accept your helplessness and to comply with my requests."

Rohan looked around. The framework restraining him was set vertically in the middle of a cavernous, dimly lit space. It was lined with walls of raw stone, slick with moisture. The air was damp and cool, filled with the echoes of distant dripping water. The only light came from patches of phosphorescent moss that grew like rashes on the stone, rancid green and nightmare purple.

Figures moved in the shadows, their silhouettes human until they turned to the side and revealed misshapen appendages protruding from their backs.

"It was closer than you'd think. The decor was different. More spacious." *He'll never get that pun. Because I was in space. Like all my best jokes, wasted.*

"You can take solace from the fact that six months from now you will not be in for a repeat."

"I get it, because I'll be dead, right? But for now, please let me know, what is it that you think I'm going to tell you? Seriously, why am I here?"

"Ah, Griffin. You don't know? Try to think."

Rohan sighed. "You're overestimating my intelligence. I really have no idea what you want from me. Dating tips? I'll try, but I'm not sure I'm your guy. Maybe start by being a little less assertive. Also, go easy with the tentacles. Then again, I'm sure plenty of women are into that, so I take that one back. You just have to look for partners with the right kink."

If Dr. Kraken was amused by Rohan's banter, he gave no sign of it. "Griffin. My masters and I would like to know what you can tell us about the defenses on and around Drach. For a start."

"You're kidding? The il'Drach homeworld?" Rohan laughed, the sound quickly devolving into a hacking cough.

Dr. Kraken waited while the Hybrid regained his wind.

Rohan continued. "You don't understand. I won't help you get to Drach. Not because I hate you; it's because I don't hate you enough to send you there."

The spinning globe closed on the Hybrid's hands.

He spent some time screaming.

Dr. Kraken swayed side to side in time with Rohan's screams. Left with each scream, then right as the half-breed paused to suck in more air, then left again.

"That is fine. It gives me something to work on. A few days of this and I'm sure I can intensify your feelings toward me. If that is what you require."

A voice spoke from behind the wizard.

"Master, why *are* you torturing him? I thought the drugs would make him answer all your questions."

"They will, boy. We simply have to ask the questions in the correct fashion."

"But . . ."

"But what?"

"This is not what you promised."

Dr. Kraken's voice grew an angry taint. "It is the will of our masters. And it is not your place to question."

The voice's owner retreated.

Rohan sighed. *Thanks for trying.*

He looked up at Dr. Kraken. "Now that we have some alone time, I've been wanting to ask you something."

"We are not alone. But I will entertain your question."

"How long have you been doing this for? Like, a long time, right? Centuries. Are you, like, the original evil mastermind? Are you the archetype for all the bad guys in bad action movies?"

Dr. Kraken made a rude noise using the edge of the flap of skin above his shoulders. "You speak a great deal of nonsense, little one. Now tell me of Drach."

"I don't know where Drach is. Yes, I went there, but I was taken on a ship through a wormhole. Nobody gave me a map or coordinates. One end of the wormhole is at Fleet Academy, but isn't that common knowledge?"

"You will tell me of Drach's defenses, of its layout and weakness, of the forces stationed there. You will tell me who you met there and what you discussed. You will tell me what the flowers smelled like and how the food tasted, the color of the sky, the weight of your steps. And from these tidbits and morsels I will fashion an understanding of the homeworld of the il'Drach."

Rohan screamed wordlessly as another slice was taken from the skin covering his ribs.

Why am I screaming? Pain and he were old friends.

The water pulled away from his skin. He panted, hanging in the metal restraints, unable to get enough air.

Dr. Kraken leaned closer to the Hybrid. "What do your people say? I believe it is: 'I can do this all day'?"

Rohan laughed despite the sinking feeling in the pit of his stomach.

"Do not believe that your friends will rescue you. The Director has ordered all of Vanguard personnel to abandon you."

"Has she now? I should call my union rep. That's . . . disappointing. And unexpected."

"Not to anybody with a modicum of intelligence. Should I kill you, her hold on power will remain unchallenged. It is exactly typical behavior for you mammals. No sense of loyalty to species."

"I don't think she and I are the same species, technically. Or are we? Half and full? How is that defined again? Last time I set foot in a biology class was fifteen years ago."

Dr. Kraken flapped a hand and two tentacles in a synchronized wave of dismissal. "You mammals are all the same to me. Now speak to me of Drach."

Rohan braced for a fresh round of pain, but the doctor was showing patience.

He looked up into the creature's eyes, mesmerized by the cephalopod pupils. "The il'Drach have sent their half-breed children out to conquer half the sector. Think about it. They sent those forces *out*. Can you even imagine what kind of forces they kept behind? To protect their own precious lives?"

"You are obfuscating. I fail to understand your motivation. If you hope I will become angry or lose patience and do something rash, know that I am eons too old for such a reaction."

"Actually, aggravating you is its own reward. It's about the journey, not the destination, for me." Rohan felt a tug of anger inside and nursed it, hoping to draw some of his Power along with it.

The sparks of anger fizzled out like dud fireworks, bringing down with them the slender line of hope he'd been nurturing. The drugs were too powerful; he couldn't access his Power.

Dr. Kraken stood unmoving and unmoved.

Rohan swallowed, his mouth dry and hot. "I really can't tell you what you want to know. Maybe there's something else I can do? Some compromise? I'll give you my mother's samosa recipe. Better yet, I'll have her bring some. Come on, just give me my phone, I'll set up the GPS, they'll come get me. We can all be friends. I'll let you try my special tequila."

"Are the samosas good enough to dull the agony that comes when I disappoint my masters?" The cephalopod's voice was laden with sarcasm.

"I doubt it. Mom isn't much of a cook. Kind of goes against the stereotype, but those are the cards we were dealt."

The water blade went back to work on Rohan's torso. Red blood bubbled through gaps in his brown skin as the Hybrid screamed.

Dr. Kraken's voice burbled as if it came from underneath a layer of running water. "Tell me something innocuous about Drach. Something safe. Talk about the food. What did you eat? Surely your Fathers wouldn't mind if you told others about their favorite snacks."

"I . . . really . . . can't."

"Have more faith in yourself, dear boy! I do. I have enough faith in you for the both of us. Start with breakfast. What did they feed you for breakfast?"

1

Two Weeks Earlier, When Things Started

"Rohan, there is a situation developing on Toth 3." Wistful's voice interrupted the fast-paced music playing over Rohan's comm system. Her tone was flat and emotionless. The independent space station sounded very much true to herself: an artificial intelligence, millennia old, that was rarely surprised and even less often *worried* by anything that happened.

"Ugh. You know I hate situations. Hold on a moment. Let me get *Wings Away* docked, and I'll deal with it."

It was taking all of Rohan's concentration to safely maneuver the ship toward her dock on Wistful. After a full year of towing and docking ships by hand, he was confident in his abilities as a tow chief, but *Wings Away* was unusually massive. She had been overloaded, affecting her margins: improving profit but reducing safety.

With a grunt, he gave a final careful push to the ship's anchor point, canceling her inward drift and a hint of clockwise spin. Rohan relaxed as he felt the thud of the docking clamps sliding into place.

"All set, *Wings Away*."

"Thank you, Tow Chief Second Class Rohan."

Rohan sighed and turned his head, feeling his neck crack with satisfaction. He wanted to scratch his beard, but the only thing between his face and the cold vacuum of space was an oval-shaped mask that was precariously sealed. Sticking his finger under the mask's rim was a sure way to disrupt his air supply.

"Wistful, *Wings Away* is docked. What's going on?"

Wistful didn't answer, instead replaced by her security chief.

"We have received a distress call from a ship on the planet's surface." Wei Li's voice was almost as flat and unimpressed as Wistful's. The reptilian empath would have been a champion poker player if anybody in the system would play with her. Anymore.

"I thought there aren't supposed to *be* any ships on the planet." Toth 3 was a beautiful blue-and-green planet, with a breathable atmosphere, close to standard gravity, and a rich biosphere. It was also forbidden territory, mostly because encounters with its native megafauna were classified as apocalyptic events.

Wei Li sighed softly. "That is a significant part of the problem, Rohan. That ship should not be there, yet it is."

"What ship?"

A pause.

"The distress call names her *Darkness Follows*. Based on her speech patterns and what little I can pick up from active sensors, she is a Shayjh stealth vessel."

Rohan whistled softly. "Sounds like *everything* is wrong with this situation. Because there is no way a Shayjh stealth ship should be anywhere in this system, let alone on the planet."

"That is a solid interpretation of the facts you've been given. Most impressive."

He shook his head. Wei Li's sarcasm stung as much as her jab or her inside low kick. Maybe more.

"I assume we're going to attempt a rescue?"

"That is Wistful's desire. Though I urged her to instead allow the corpse of that ship to serve as a deterrent to future treasure hunters."

"I'm sure you did. Something about evolution, how saving idiots is detrimental to the laws of nature."

"That is another solid inference you have made. I shall note the date in my calendar, to be celebrated annually for all future times. Perhaps we'll serve cake."

Rohan laughed. "Are we going with the new plan?"

"Do you have an alternative?"

"Me? Absolutely not."

Another pause. "Then, yes. I've already contacted War Chief Ang to request his assistance."

"Good." Rohan tapped at the side of his mask, switching channels away from Wei Li.

He kept tapping until the link to his ship, *Void's Shadow*, appeared in the mask's display.

"Hey there. You available for a rescue mission?"

There was a long pause before she responded.

"Captain? Rescue who and where? Is it Toth 3 again? Of course it is, it's always Toth 3."

Rohan wasn't sure how much of it was in his own imagination, but she *sounded* like a child. Young.

"Yes. A ship is sending a distress call from the surface."

"Who is it? Anyone we know?"

Rohan smiled. "Doubtful. A Shayjh stealth ship. Probably treasure hunters."

"A Shayjh stealth ship thought she could sneak by the kaiju?" *Void's Shadow* was able to land on the planet unmolested, but Rohan doubted any other ships in the sector could manage it, even ones as sophisticated as those built by the Shayjh.

"I guess so. You want to help rescue them?"

A pause. "I'm not sure, it's dangerous."

Rohan sighed. *Void's Shadow* had declared him her captain after her previous crew had been killed, but he was trying to teach her to be independent. Sometimes those lessons took hold at the most annoying times.

"Well, you don't have to, but I'd think you'd love to show that ship what real stealth looks like. Or doesn't look like. You know."

"Well . . . that *does* sound like fun."

"Come on, help me out. First sign of danger, you can take off. If we don't finish the rescue, that's fine, right? At least we'll have tried."

A pause.

"Okay, I'll do it. Heading toward Wistful now."

A blip appeared on his mask, showing him where *Void's Shadow* was coming from.

"I see you. Hop onto the security channel."

"Aye, Captain."

He tapped himself back onto Wistful's channel.

"*Void's Shadow* is on the way. Is Ang heading down yet?"

Wei Li was quick to respond. "Momentarily. He seems very eager."

"Great. This will be our first live test of Plan Ang-Distraction Alpha."

"I am certain the Shayjh ship will be excited by its role as test subject for your unproven rescue plan."

"Hey, beggars can't be choosers. She's free to rescue herself. Also, maybe don't tell her that it's untested."

"Is this thing to working yet? Hello, hello?" Ang's voice was rough and gravelly over the channel.

"Hey, Ang. I'm heading toward the planet now. Get to the upper atmosphere as quickly as you can."

"As you say, Brother Rohan, so shall it be." Ang was speaking in quotes from holodramas again. The Ursan had been watching a lot of action-oriented shows. He claimed it was to improve his fluency with Drachna, but it was all too obvious that he loved the stories. Rohan had been working on a way to break the news that they were actually written for ten-year-old boys.

Wistful orbited Toth in the L5 point of Toth 3, which meant she was always stationary relative to the planet, on the side opposite the system's sun. The blue-green orb was directly overhead, spinning in place, visible at all times through the transparent roof of the station.

Rohan twisted in space, exerting his Power first to orient himself and then to accelerate toward the planet.

Void's Shadow pinged him. "I have you on scanners. I'll aim to intercept close to the atmospheric edge."

"Great." He marveled as he flew past the glittering space station, a diamond-encrusted, cross-shaped behemoth enclosing two million inhabitants with room to spare.

"Wei Li, where exactly on the planet is that ship?"

"One moment." He heard tapping sounds over the comms. By the time he'd maneuvered past the station and was in open space, only the planet beneath him, a destination was showing on his mask's display.

Wei Li spoke to him. "They were headed for the far side of the planet, presumably looking to land where it's daylight."

"Any kaiju activity yet? Do you even have that area under satellite surveillance?"

"We have satellite imagery. No noticeable kaiju activity yet."

Rohan had started calling the planet's indigenous monsters *kaiju*, a reference to the Japanese monster movies he'd enjoyed as a child. The name stuck.

Wei Li continued. "Ang is in a shuttle; they just left dock."

Rohan accelerated toward the planet.

Six months earlier, he had escorted a team of scientists to the planet's surface, led by his childhood hero, Dr. Benjamin Stone. They hadn't lasted an hour on the ground, but before they were chased off by an enormous insect, they had managed to discover evidence of structures buried under the planet's surface.

That information was supposed to have been kept secret, but treasure seekers and amateur archaeologists had been coming to Toth ever since in expanding numbers.

Void's Shadow spoke to him. "I don't understand. Why are these humanoids risking their lives so casually?"

Rohan sighed and began decelerating so he would reach the planet's atmosphere at relative rest. "Greed? Desire for fame?"

"I understand that much. But they also know the planet kills almost everyone who lands there. Don't they care? Or are they that desperate? Or just stupid?"

Wei Li snorted softly and responded. "Why choose?"

The ship broadcast a rude sound over the channel. Rohan laughed.

"Let's save them first, then you can ask them yourself. Right now, open up. It's time."

Void's Shadow suddenly loomed over Rohan's shoulder.

Her hull was the darkest black, a color found at the center of a black hole or just after the heat death of the universe. It was absolutely non-reflective, absorbing all frequencies of electromagnetic radiation, larger radioactive particles, and even tachyons.

More unusual than that color was her lack of *presence*. From inside, she *felt* to Rohan like any other ship, a living being with a regular assortment of emotions and moods. But from outside her hull, there was no trace of it. To his Third Eye, she was as flat and dead as a moon rock.

Which was exactly why he needed her help for this rescue mission.

"You do love sneaking up on me, don't you?"

She giggled over the comms.

Rohan moved himself closer to *Void's Shadow*. With her lack of color, it was hard to make out her flattened-teardrop shape or to see the three thick struts that emerged from her rear, curving back to meet at a basketball-sized sphere marking her tail.

She was tiny for an interplanetary ship, not much bigger than a big passenger van or a small RV from Earth.

A bright arc appeared suddenly at the top of the teardrop, widening abruptly into a circle as the hatch to her airlock cycled open.

The tow chief slipped inside, barely noticing as the hatch cycled shut above him. He stepped across and lay back into the cool leather of the reclining captain's chair.

"Do you have our course laid out?"

"Yes, Captain."

"Great. Bring it up on the screen, let's see what we have. Overlay any satellite imagery you can get from Wistful."

The screen in front of him, taking up the entire front of the cabin, was already coming to life.

"Of course. You don't really have to tell me, you know. This isn't my first . . . whatever you call it. That thing with the quadrupeds and the rope and the hats measured in archaic units."

"Rodeo. Your first rodeo. Great."

He frowned. A bright dot on the map indicated the ship's location, but imagery wasn't showing anything other than a plant-covered hill.

"I don't see her. Camouflage?"

Void's Shadow's tone was skeptical. "A Shayjh ship camouflaged for a surface landing? It's possible, but I've never heard of it."

"Yeah, probably not. Okay, let's get in closer. How close is Ang's shuttle?"

Wei Li answered. "Ten minutes away."

"*Void's Shadow*, bring us in."

She rocked back and forth as she entered the atmosphere, the buffeting mostly muffled by her internal gravity field. Rohan squinted at the screen, then tilted his head.

"Am I crazy or does this hill look familiar?"

Wei Li answered him over the comms. "That is the same hill where you landed with the Professor."

Rohan shook his head. "Same hill. And the odds of that being a coincidence are . . ."

"Astronomical. Against."

"This is looking like a pattern. Maybe we need a more proactive deterrent to these guys."

Wei Li responded. "We have been actively warning ships away, but this one snuck by."

"Right. *Void's Shadow*, please open a public channel."

"Open, Captain."

"Hail, *Darkness Follows*. We are answering your distress call."

"Oh, lovely. And here I was hoping I'd be left on this disgusting planet to die in peace, but no, first I'm forced to send a distress call, and now you're mounting a *rescue*." The last word, especially, was said with an audible sneer.

"Huh. That's not exactly the response I was expecting, *Darkness Follows*."

"Well, then *please* excuse me for not meeting your expectations, whoever you are. It's not as if you met mine, responding to my distress call without so much as an introduction. I hadn't realized we'd drifted so far from actual civilization. I certainly didn't want to leave il'Drach space. Maybe now they'll see *why*."

"Right, sorry. This is Tow Chief Second Class Rohan, captain of *Void's Shadow*. We're planning to rescue you, assuming, I guess, that you still want us to."

"It looks like I'll be the one having to rescue you, as you can't even get your title straight. Is it Tow Chief or is it Captain?"

Rohan sighed, a bit louder than he intended.

The ship continued. "Oh, am I boring you, Mr. Can't-Decide-On-A-Title? I'm *so* sorry my mortal distress isn't interesting enough to hold your attention."

Wei Li laughed over the comms.

Rohan cleared his throat. "Okay, *Darkness Follows*, we have a small problem. I can't see you on visuals. Any idea why?"

"I will try to explain with small words and short sentences. You can't see me, Tow Chief Second Class, because I am underneath the surface."

"Well, that explains it. Kind of. Without explaining it, really."

Void's Shadow interrupted. "Hi, we haven't met, I'm *Void's Shadow*. We don't really understand how you got underground."

"It seemed like the best way to avoid being destroyed by these dreadful flying lizards. I kept telling my captain I am not designed for atmospheric missions, but does he listen to me? Of course not. Why listen to the one intelligent being in the entire universe who is most qualified to tell him what I am or am not capable of doing? So, of course, he ordered me to descend, and then a lizard crashed into me and knocked out two of my drives, and honestly at that point I drove as deep into this hill as I could manage, half-hoping the impact would kill all of us. Sadly, it didn't work."

Rohan responded. "I hate to tell you this, or rather, I'm glad to tell you, but you might hate to hear it: that move probably saved your lives."

Darkness Follows responded drily. "I do hate to hear that. Still, it isn't so bad, I'm sure that even if you do save us from this predicament, my captain will manage to get me killed on our next mission. He's terribly stupid."

Void's Shadow spoke. "You should get a better captain! You can't have mine, though, I'm still breaking him in."

"Who is breaking who in—can we please cut this out and focus on the job? You say you're under the hill?"

"That is correct. Though I fail to see how it matters, considering you will be unable to approach without incurring the interest of these ridiculous creatures."

"You let us worry about that. We have some experience with them. When I tell you it's safe, can you get yourself out of there or do you need help?"

Wei Li interrupted. "Tow Chief. We have movement near the hill."

"Kaiju movement?"

"What else could it be?" There weren't any sub-monster-size animals on the planet.

"Flyer or crawler?"

"Crawler. Most likely a decipede."

"Crap." Decipedes were segmented, crawling insects that could spit a highly corrosive neurotoxic venom. Which by itself wouldn't be an insurmountable problem, but they were also close to two hundred meters in length. Rohan had taken on entire armies in hand-to-hand combat and won, but against a fully grown decipede, he was almost useless.

Void's Shadow interrupted his train of thought. "Shall I go in closer, Captain?"

"Yeah, bring us in."

A deep growl burst over the comms. "I have reached the atmosphere, Brother Rohan. Ang is ready to assist you."

Rohan thought. "Hold steady, Ang. Let me get a look at the situation. We have a decipede on the ground and a buried ship under it. I need to figure out a plan."

"Be fast, Brother Rohan, in your thinking."

"I know, Ang, I know." He paused. "*Darkness Follows*, are you stuck? Can you free yourself?"

"I'm not sure, and I don't see how to test that without attracting attention from those . . . things."

"Fair enough. Just hold tight. Is your crew on board?"

"I'd hardly call those morons a crew. They disembarked and are walking in the tunnel. Because clearly that's the smart thing to do on a planet full of monsters. I'm sure they'll separate as soon as they have a chance."

Rohan had never been more torn between his desire to laugh and to cry.

"*Void's Shadow*, take us to that hill, nice and easy."

The kaiju were empaths. They reacted violently to strong emotions, especially anger, and not much else. Because they couldn't sense *Void's Shadow*'s emotions, or those of anybody within her hull, they ignored her completely. It was something Rohan had discovered quite by accident.

Void's Shadow slowed her descent to avoid unnecessary noise and turbulence. As they closed, she replaced the satellite image of the hill with a direct look through her own cameras.

Rohan leaned forward out of his chair, intently studying the screen.

"I see it. There." He pointed, unnecessarily.

"Yes, Captain."

"And there's the decipede. Sniffing around."

"Yes, Captain. It seems awake but not agitated."

His ship spoke to him. "Rohan, I'm highlighting a spot at the base of that hill. I think it's the tunnel *Darkness Follows* made. I mean, it could be."

There *was* something on the screen. Unfortunately, the decipede was there, too, circling the hill, flattening vast swaths of forest and mossy vegetation with its bulk. "Get us a little closer."

Soon the decipede loomed large on the forward screen. It had five segments, the first two held higher than the back, so its head was almost a hundred meters off the ground, with mandibles more than wide enough to eat a ship the size of *Void's Shadow* in a single bite.

The monster had found the tunnel.

"Any flyers still around?"

Wei Li answered. "Two are circling not far from you."

Darkness Follows broke in with a droll tone. "I don't particularly care, speaking for myself, but my crew has reached the end of the tunnel, and they think they can get away from that bug on foot. I believe they are panicking now."

Rohan swore softly. "I don't see any way of getting to them without using Ang. Anybody else have any ideas?"

Silence washed over the comms.

"Okay then, we go with plan A."

Ang rumbled over the link. "Am I to do my job now, Brother Rohan?"

"Yes. Drop down and do your thing."

"With pleasure, Brother Rohan."

Ang had been an intimidating force from the moment Rohan met him. Rohan had assumed that Ang's presence was simply a result of the Ursan's physicality; he was two and a half meters and five hundred kilograms of fur and teeth and claws, interrupted by heavy scars and one red, glowing, cybernetic eye.

Wei Li was the first to recognize that Ang had more than just that physicality. Something about his spirit was *loud*; all his emotions were broadcast at high volume. If he was angry enough, everyone around could *feel* it, empathic or not. With training, he had developed to a level where his emotions projected with enough power to cause pain to an actual empath.

Which made Ang the perfect tool for luring away kaiju that were attracted to strong emotions.

Rohan shivered slightly as he *felt* the echo of Ang's rage from far to the north. He watched the decipede stop in its tracks, its head swiveling ponderously in Ang's direction.

2

Best Intentions

"*Void's Shadow*, get us in position by the tunnel mouth."

"Yes, Captain."

Rohan studied the screens, waiting as the decipede meandered around the hill, drawn toward Ang's anger but still interested in the tunnel where *Darkness Follows* had buried herself.

Darkness Follows droned on. "It wasn't always like this, you know. I was an elite scout in the il'Drach Navy. Once upon a time. I was one of the first ships to enter Zahad after the Scourge wiped out the rebels. I saw things there you can't imagine. I was *trusted*. Then we come back, and all of a sudden all I hear is '*Darkness*, you're too depressing.' '*Darkness*, you're oversharing your feelings.' '*Darkness*, two of your captains committed suicide, you have to stop doing this.' I'm a stealth ship—I can't very well *show* my feelings, can I? But I'm supposed to just stop talking about them? Stop sharing entirely? What they really want is a shuttle, some dead thing without any personality. No soul."

Rohan pointed at the screen. "*Void's Shadow*, you see that? Is it moving?"

"Yes, Captain. The decipede is moving away. Slowly."

"Do you have a visual on the flyers? How close are they to Ang?"

Wei Li answered. "Ang is still in the clear, but the flyers are closing on his position."

Ang was muttering in his native tongue, a harsh growl that formed background noise on the channel. Rohan made out the gist of what he was saying: a rant against the religious oppressors who had wiped out his home.

The sensation of rage grew stronger as Ang worked through a list of names of the dead.

More from *Darkness Follows*. "You're free to go, they said. Oh, lovely, hand me a steaming pile of waste lubricant and pretend it's a present. They take away my purpose, my function, my community, and tell me it's a gift. My *freedom*. Next thing you know, I'm working for these brain-damaged treasure hunters, and I'm stuck in a tunnel, being stalked by a bug. And they wonder why I'm not more *positive*."

The decipede started to crawl away, each step of one of its ten legs felling trees and tearing bedrock-exposing holes in the ground as it gathered speed. As soon as the plume of dirt and moss and shattered plants had settled, *Void's Shadow* closed in on the tunnel mouth.

Three humanoid figures were emerging from the tunnel. They were Andervarian, their dark-purple skin liberally adorned with bright-yellow tattoos. One was tall and slender; one was short and slender; one was between the others in height but twice as thick. All wore rugged work clothes, a patchwork of faded leather and stained canvas.

The tall one stopped in his tracks and pointed at *Void's Shadow*. Her black hull was not hard to spot against the colorful foliage.

"There! A rescue!" The voice suddenly burst over the public comm channel, speaking heavily accented Drachna.

Wei Li spoke. "Flyers are closing on Ang's position. He can't remain in the atmosphere much longer."

Rohan grunted. He'd been hoping for more time. "*Void's Shadow*, can you see down that tunnel?"

"Yes, Captain, but not to the end. It's quite deep and a little twisted."

"Do you think you could get down there and tow *Darkness Follows* out of there?"

"I doubt it, Captain. It's too tight for me."

"That's what I thought. Okay, open the hatch. Let's get those three on board."

The roof over the main cabin split and opened like a giant clamshell, a larger opening only suitable for use inside an atmosphere. "What about the ship, Captain?"

"I'll have to disembark and get her free by hand."

"Do we have time for that?"

"I guess we're going to find out the hard way."

Rohan stood at the opening in *Void's Shadow*'s hull. He let out a breath, stepped out, and flew over to the Andervarians.

They recoiled visibly. The short one sputtered, "Holy hangover, it's a Hybrid! We're dead."

Rohan held his hands out and spoke to them over the comm channel, his mask still sealed to his face. "Relax, nobody's dead. Yet. I'm Tow Chief Second Class Rohan, of Wistful. I'm just here to get you guys off this planet and someplace safe."

The three started debating furiously.

Short One spoke first. "We can't go with him!"

Then Tall One. "What choice do you think we have? You want to become bug food?"

Stout One answered, "It's not even near us! It left, look! This guy just wants to get us away from our claim!"

Tall One responded. "The bug's distracted, it's not gone, you moron. It will come back, and then what good will your precious claim do you?"

"Well, I'm staying, and you two can hear from my feed about how rich and famous I am after I cash in those artifacts."

"Your ship is damaged and buried under twenty meters of dirt and rock, this planet is as full of monster animals as the rumors said, and you think you'll come out of this rich? I have no idea what my sister saw in you. Ma and Pa told her you'd never amount to anything."

"Don't bring your sister into this, man! Whose idea was it to come here, anyway?"

"I was just talking! We weren't supposed to actually *do* it! By the Fathers, who was dumb enough to loan you money for that ship?"

Wei Li's calm voice came over the feed. "Ang, it is time to leave the atmosphere, flyers are closing in on you."

The aura of rage began to diminish almost immediately.

Rohan cleared his throat and addressed the Andervarians.

"We really don't have a lot of time. That decipede is going to be turning around pretty soon."

Tall One shook his head and started walking toward *Void's Shadow*. "I'm going."

Rohan flew over to him. "Let me carry you. The plants here get very sticky when the decipede is nearby."

Tall Andervarian took another step and looked up with widened eyes, suddenly understanding Rohan's point. He held out his hands and let the Hybrid pull him free. Within seconds, he was dumped into the stealth ship's cabin.

Rohan flew back to the other two. They were arguing, and their tone was growing increasingly heated.

"Guys, let me let you in on a little secret. The decipede is attracted to anger. The more you fight, the faster it's going to come back."

Short One shook his head. "Con-Conspiracy on the web says that rumor has only a twenty-seven percent chance of being true. We're fine."

"Con-Conspiracy?"

Stout One snorted. "He doesn't even read it. How does it feel to be so far out of the loop, Tow Chief? Only Con-Conspiracy readers really know what's going on in this sector."

Darkness Follows broke in. "Do you see what I've been putting up with from this crew? And you wondered why I'd be glad to die here under this hill? Well, not so much glad, but at least relieved. Definitely relieved. Who says I'm not positive?"

Rohan slid his mask back and rubbed his forehead, then pointed to the two men where they stood huddled at the entrance to *Darkness Follows*'s tunnel. "Three seconds, and I'm putting you on that ship by force."

"What? No! You can't! This is my big score!"

"Two. One." Rohan pulled his mask back down and flew over to the fat Andervarian. He grabbed the man under the arms, easily lifting him off the ground.

Void's Shadow spoke over his comm. "The decipede has turned around and is heading back toward the hill. Not full speed, at least not yet."

Rohan sighed.

"Got it." He flew over to his ship and dropped the Andervarian into the cabin. "You, stay! Leave that ship and you're dead, and I won't be coming back for you."

The Andervarian stood and gestured rudely toward the Hybrid. "You . . . oppressor! Ugly mule! Shoving innocent people like us around like that! Who do you think you are?" He did not, Rohan noticed, try to leave the ship.

Rohan headed toward the last of the Andervarians, pointing at the humanoid's exposed chest. "You ever notice that your coloring is like the inverse of my uniform? Mine is gold with that horrible metallic-purple accent, you're purple with yellow accents."

The man looked at Rohan's uniform, then down to his own chest.

"What? Oh, hey . . . what?"

The Hybrid grabbed the short Andervarian and snatched him into the air.

The treasure hunter resisted, punching meekly at Rohan's chest.

"You do realize what I am, right? Like, if you actually hurt me with those punches, I would probably retaliate by folding you into a perfect cube and mailing you home to your parents?"

The short Andervarian nodded and answered softly. "I have to make it look good. I'm going to lose every credit to my name on this failure."

Rohan dumped him into his ship's cabin. "*Void's Shadow*, close up and get them to Wistful."

"Are you sure, Captain? What if you need help?"

"I'll be fine." *I think.* "Just get them somewhere safe."

The hatch lowered smoothly, the last line of light disappearing as it closed. Then the dark shape lifted, pivoted in place, and flew straight up toward space.

"Well, your job is done now, Tow Chief. I suppose you'll be leaving me to my fate. Down here in the dark. And the cold. With the dirt."

"Actually, I'm going to try to get you out of there."

"Fine, but don't expect me to be grateful. I don't have anything to look forward to that's much nicer than this dirty hole I'm stuck in right now."

"I'm going to rescue you despite that, and then, after you're free, you can blame your future miseries on me, okay?"

"Don't think I won't."

"Never. Now tell me, can you move at all?" Rohan began flying down the tunnel.

Void's Shadow piped up. "Captain, the Andervarians are trying to take over my controls."

"Oh for . . . can't you do anything about it?"

"Of course. Shall I expose them to vacuum?"

"No, don't . . . I don't know. Turn off internal gravity and, like, fling them around a bit maybe?"

"Excellent idea, Captain! I shall do so."

"Great. Now, *Darkness Follows*. I see you now. Can you move at all? Even a shake?"

The ship, a deep-black mass bigger than *Void's Shadow* but with a similar streamlined shape, wiggled in place.

"That's all I can manage. Once the pride of the il'Drach scouting corps, reduced to this. What a dark journey I've been on."

"The good news is, you're moving, even if it isn't much. Now hold on, I'm going to pull you back."

Rohan flew up to the rear of the trapped ship and found her anchor point, a sphere at the base of the teardrop that was structurally designed to handle enough force to move the ship by hand. It was a standard feature for ships in il'Drach space, because many space stations and ports only allowed ships near them to move by tow, for security reasons.

He yanked on the anchor point, and *Darkness Follows* slid toward him by half a meter.

She groaned in response. "I haven't actually gotten wider, have I? Is that even possible for a ship? Am I fatter than when I dug down here? Oh, please tell me I'm not fat. I had a fat captain once, the crew mocked him mercilessly for it. All behind his back, at least until I shared the recordings with him. Poor man."

Rohan laughed despite his mounting feeling of frustration. "You're not wider, but the dirt is settling behind you, so the hole is narrower than it was when you punched through it. I'm going to have to drag you out."

"Oh, just leave me here. It's not worth the trouble to rescue me, I'm useless."

Rohan pulled again, dragging the Shayjh ship another meter through the tunnel.

Wei Li's voice came over the comms. "Tow Chief, the decipede and both flyers are heading back to your location."

"How fast?"

"Too fast for you to linger there. They are showing signs of agitation."

Darkness Follows let out a small squeak. "You really can leave me, you know. Perhaps come back for me later, after the creatures have calmed down? I'm in no hurry."

Rohan thought. "However good your stealth is, it wasn't enough to keep the decipede away before. Now it's angry, so if I leave and it decides to dig you out of this hill, you'll be rendered into scrap before anybody can do anything."

"Oh. Then I suppose this really is the end. Goodbye, world. On balance, existence wasn't quite worthwhile, though there were some good moments."

"You'll have some more good moments. Probably. I'm not giving up just yet."

Rohan let out a breath and *pulled* at his Power, summoning energy up through the base of his spine, shivering as it spiraled around his backbone and up into the back of his head. It collected there, then flared through his body.

The light feelings of fatigue in his joints washed away, along with any doubts he had about rescuing the Shayjh ship. The tunnel seemed brighter, details of the dirt and rocks standing out sharply, like frost-covered leaves on a snowy day.

The Hybrid pulled harder, dragging *Darkness Follows* through the hill in a smooth glide, her hull scraping the walls of the tunnel as he forced her free.

"That hurts."

"A little pain is better than being bug food."

Wei Li again. "Rohan, the kaiju are picking up speed."

He grunted. "I had to pull up some extra Power. I bet they felt it."

"You are running out of time."

He pressed his tongue to the roof of his mouth and *pulled* harder, drawing another burst of energy through his spine. *Darkness Follows* was starting to annoy him, a sure sign that his Power had brought a little anger along for the ride. The price of his il'Drach heritage.

That's why some people call it a curse.

Rohan yanked again, the hood of his uniform flapping against his back as the Shayjh ship came loose in starts and stops, catching on heavy clumps of soil, then sliding freely through sandy sections of tunnel.

"How far does this damn tunnel go? We should be outside by now!"

Void's Shadow answered, her voice soft over the comms. "You're almost out, Rohan. But the decipede is closing fast. Maybe you should leave that ship behind?"

"Nobody is being left behind." With a heave, he pulled *Darkness Follows* free of the hill, falling onto his back, the ship landing in the dirt ten meters away.

Rohan tilted his head back. All he could see was the open maw of a giant bug bearing down on him.

Wincing, he slapped the ground with his hands, bouncing himself up into the air, and flew directly toward the decipede.

Its head was an insectoid nightmare. Two huge, multifaceted black eyes protruded above a cavernous maw dripping with clear and green fluids. Flanking that maw were four long mandibles reflexively twitching open and shut.

He aimed for a spot centered between the mouth and eyes, and the kaiju flinched backward and shielded the spot with chitin-covered forelimbs.

"That move used to work on these things."

Wei Li spoke. "Perhaps it is learning."

"You think this is the same one I fought before?"

"It is quite possible, especially if they are territorial."

The kaiju spread its upper limbs, swiping at Rohan with broad strokes of its twenty-five-meter arms.

He dropped down, below the path of the strikes, and the kaiju tilted its head forward and spat a tight stream of greenish fluid at him.

Rohan hadn't been expecting that. In the past, the decipede had only spit acid after being hurt.

Maybe it really *was* learning.

He twisted in the air, desperate to get clear of the stream of corrosive fluid.

The Hybrid avoided most of it, but a fat glob of the liquid washed over his right hand.

The decipede's head was left exposed by the spitting action, giving Rohan a clear path toward its face.

A burning sensation flared up almost immediately in his hand, but Rohan did his best to ignore it and accelerated up toward the creature.

With a jolt, he impacted the decipede's right eye. The facet he hit, one of dozens, was as wide as his forearm was long.

The shiny, black material cracked with the impact, a clear fluid immediately oozing out and covering several adjacent facets.

The creature screamed and flinched farther back, waving its front limbs in a mad scramble in front of its head, forcing Rohan to dodge frantically.

"*Darkness Follows*, can you get into the air?"

"I . . . will try, Tow Chief."

Now that she was out in daylight, Rohan got a good look at the ship. Deep black, though not the impossible black of *Void's Shadow*, she was larger, spacious enough to comfortably support a crew of ten. Her front end was dented and torn, as if from a blunt impact, and two of the three bootstrap drives that dotted it were clearly wrecked, the hull mangled around them, exposed mechanicals sparking and smoking.

"You are not getting into orbit without some help."

"No, I do not think that I am. A ship that can't fly; how embarrassing."

Rohan turned to face the quickly recovering decipede.

His hand was in a great deal of pain. He glanced down. His glove had burned away; his skin was blistering and cracking.

With a snap of acceleration that broke the air in front of him, Rohan sped back toward the decipede's eye.

It flinched, slightly, but swung its massive forelimbs toward the Hybrid.

He ducked, then rose, then twisted in midair, avoiding the limbs. The arc of his flight took him right past the creature's head.

With an angry grunt, he pushed even harder, *pulling* more Power through his body, until he began to see flashes of the world in black and white, then in a rainbow of vibrant colors. His hair snapped at his scalp, pulling his face taut against his skull, and he was past and beyond the decipede.

A downward jerk redirected Rohan toward the ground, flying with his right hand out front like an old poster of Hyperion. He was hoping to scrape off the decipede venom by tunneling through the ground.

Wei Li spoke. "Rohan, your vitals are indicating a lot of stress. Your heart rate is higher than I believe I have ever seen. Is something unusual happening? Beyond the obvious."

"My hand *really* hurts. I've been hit by it before, and it always sucks, but this is something else."

"Noted."

Rohan hit the ground with enough speed to liquefy it. Dirt splashed up around him in a crest as he drove himself farther underneath the surface, fist held out in front.

He could feel sand and small rocks and hunks of hard vegetation scraping at his flesh as he tunneled through the ground, but with his hand burning he had no choice but to continue driving forward.

With a thunderous beat, the decipede followed his path, sending shockwaves through the ground with every step.

The chemical burning in the Hybrid's hand began to fade, and he angled himself upward toward the surface. He could tell by the shockwaves that he wasn't leaving the decipede behind.

"*Darkness Follows*, are you airborne? Or do you need help?"

"I am off the surface but only barely, I'm afraid. I am not able to control my direction with only a single functional drive. There's still time to save yourself."

"Oh for . . . Rudra save me please, give the woe-is-me bit a rest!" He felt a pang of guilt as soon as the words left his mouth. The burst of Power he had pulled was definitely affecting him.

The ship didn't respond.

He exhaled, holding his lungs empty, and willed the anger away.

Void's Shadow's voice came over the comms. "We are out of the atmosphere now, Captain. How can I help?"

Rohan broke through the mossy surface and out into the humid air. He was immediately assaulted by the scream of the decipede rapidly closing on his position.

"You can't. Just get those Andervarians out of here. Wait, maybe you *can* help. Prep a regen tank for me. I think I'm going to need it for this hand."

He looked at it. Almost half the skin was burned away, leaving streaks of raw meat oozing clear and red fluids halfway to his elbow.

"Yuck."

"Flyers are moving toward you, Tow Chief."

"You think I can get the decipede and the flyers to fight over me while I sneak away unnoticed?"

Ang roared briefly over the comms, then spoke. "I can reenter the atmosphere and attempt another distraction."

Wei Li interrupted him. "There are more flyers approaching the area, Ang. I do not believe that would be wise. Your margin of error for escaping is narrowing."

Rohan considered his options, discarding plans as quickly as he could form them. "Stay away, Ang. I'll deal with this."

He twisted in place to face the charging decipede, slowing his forward momentum. The creature was closing quickly.

3

The Visitors

Rohan could feel the approaching flyers without looking, their auras red and hungry, attracted by his own anger as much as the decipede's.

With a fresh burst of energy, Rohan angled downward and pointed himself at the decipede's front right leg. Timing the impact to the moment the leg struck the ground, Rohan knocked it to the side, screaming his rage and pain as he directed all the energy at his disposal into a sideways push on the base of the leg.

Slowly at first, then faster as the resistance dropped, the limb rotated outwards. The decipede's weight continued coming down, without support, and the giant insect's front section slammed into the forest floor with a deeper, louder boom.

A gust of displaced air blew at Rohan's hair and sent him flying toward the rear of the decipede. It was strong enough to knock the flyers away from the battling pair. Trees shook for kilometers around. *Darkness Follows* let out a surprised exclamation as she was pushed back toward the hill.

Rohan let the wind carry him away from the fallen insect, *willing* his Power and the feelings it had brought to subside.

He exhaled slowly, resisting the air hunger in his lungs that clamored for fast, deep breaths. He relaxed as his body skidded across the mossy ground, letting his muscles go limp, trusting the soft vegetation to cushion the impact.

As the Hybrid slid to a stop, he held his breath, lungs empty, waiting until the pain in his chest was just past the point of being unpleasant, then drawing in a slow, slow breath through his nose.

He lay in place for three more breaths, holding his lungs empty at the end of each cycle.

Wei Li spoke. "Rohan, are you hurt? Your vitals are dropping fast."

He whispered his response with his next exhalation. "Just. Relaxing."

"I see." There was, for a change, no sarcasm in her tone. Rohan assumed she understood what he was planning.

Rohan put his left hand down to help himself stand, cradling the injured right hand to his chest. The pain was intensifying as his Power receded, but it was much less than it had been before his trip through the ground.

He gingerly picked his feet up, testing the grip of the sticky fluid that was extruded from the nearby plants.

With an effort, he took several steps toward the hill that *Darkness Follows* had dug into.

Another long breath out, another long hold of empty lungs, another slow inhalation.

The decipede was turning in circles, searching out Rohan's combative energies.

The Hybrid took another few steps. He was taking too long to get to the ship.

With eyes half-closed, he summoned up the barest trickle of his Power, willing himself to stay relaxed and calm and, most of all, not angry as it flared through his body.

A soft *push* while he imagined a cool breeze of force beneath him, and he was in the air.

He hovered, breathing slowly, alert for any sign that he was drawing the attention of either the decipede or the flyers.

He muttered to himself softly, repeating a calming mantra, and *willed* his body forward. His feet dangled close to the ground, his toes barely clearing the taller plants, as he slid between trees and mounds of earth that had been dug up by the decipede.

The flyers zigzagged through the air above him, searching for something, and the decipede turned a wide circle around them all.

Long, slow breaths.

"Wei Li, can Ang give me another distraction?"

A pause. "It would not be safe, but neither would it be certain death."

Ang growled over the channel. "That is promise enough for me!"

Rohan chuckled. "You have a shuttle pilot who might not feel as carefree with his life, Ang."

The pilot answered. "I'll take my chances with the Ursan, sir. You can count on us."

Rohan sighed, a surge of gratitude filling his chest.

"All right. Give me a few more minutes to get close to *Darkness Follows*."

"Yes, sir. Just give the word."

More long breaths as Rohan got to the hill.

Darkness Follows was hovering near the hill, drunkenly teetering from side to side as she tried to maintain position with missing drives.

Rohan looked at his hand. It was raw and cracked, slick with fluid. He looked up at the Shayjh ship.

"You ready, *Darkness Follows*?"

"For what, exactly?"

"Well, I'm going to have to put a shoulder into you and push. I can't pull on your anchor point with this hand. It's going to have to be hard and fast until we get out of the atmosphere."

"Well, then. I suppose I am as ready as I will ever be. It's not as if there is an abundance of alternatives, is there?"

"No, not really."

Rohan paused, feelings of anxiety creeping up again as he thought about the upcoming effort. He focused on his breathing, letting the nervousness wash away.

"All right, Ang, do your thing."

Ang began working himself into a rage before Rohan finished speaking.

Rohan listened to the pilot and Wei Li discussing details as the shuttle dipped into the upper reaches of Toth 3's atmosphere.

Drifting upward to the Shayjh ship, he looked for a place to brace.

He had decided on the exposed structural elements beneath one of the damaged drives when Wei Li spoke to him. "Flyers and decipede are moving toward Ang's position. They are already close to him. You have very little time, Tow Chief."

With a grunt, Rohan *pushed* against *Darkness Follows*. "Give me everything you have, right now."

She responded, suddenly pulling away from him, creating a gap between them.

With another grunt, Rohan closed and slammed into the Shayjh ship, *pushing* into and through her structure, driving her up and away from the ground.

The two weren't balancing their efforts well, and *Darkness Follows* started to turn as Rohan overcompensated.

Void's Shadow coached him over the comms. "Push out more, toward her edge, Captain. Your left. No, the other left."

"Not. Helping."

The two tore a dizzy spiral through the air, going faster and rising higher with each turn but also cutting a wider circle.

Wei Li spoke. "The flyers are closing on you, Rohan."

Darkness Follows responded. "I know what to do now, Tow Chief. Sorry."

She adjusted the direction of thrust from her working drive, and her path straightened.

The air grew colder as they closed in on the cloud layer.

"Flyers approaching. Brace for impact."

Rohan *pushed* harder, deliberately unbalancing the ship.

"Oh!" She cried out in surprise.

They tore an erratic path through the sky.

Behind them came the flyers.

The Hybrid maintained his pressure, corkscrewing the ship through the air layer above the clouds and toward the safety of space.

His hand presented a fresh array of sensations as cold air bit into his raw flesh.

Rohan's ears, unprotected by his mask, popped softly as the air pressure dropped.

Darkness Follows spoke softly over the comms. "Are we safe yet? Do those . . . things fly in space?"

Wei Li responded. "You are almost clear. We do not know if the flyers are capable of travel through a vacuum, but they have never been observed to try it. So most likely you will be safe in another few seconds."

"Oh. Thank you. I was not expecting to survive. Now I suppose I'll have to go back to those moronic Andervarians so they can find a new way to endanger my life."

Rohan smiled. "Maybe not. I think that as punishment for breaking the blockade on Toth 3, we can levy a stiff fine against them. And since they have no money, we'll have to seize any assets of value they have instead."

"You mean . . . I'll be free of them? But then what shall I do?" Most ships had a strong desire to work, or to serve, baked into their personalities.

"Let's worry about that later, okay? Maybe work for Wistful. She's a great boss. But really, I don't know. Right now, I need to get you to a dock and myself to a regen tank." The fluids oozing out of his skin were boiling away in the vacuum, making bubbles that felt like living things crawling their way out of his arm.

"Wei Li, have I ever mentioned how deeply unpleasant it is to bleed out in space?"

"Not to me, Rohan, at least not that I recall. But I only listen to half of what you say, given your predilection for prattling on about nonsense."

"That's kind of sad. But fair."

Wistful broke into their conversation. "Rohan. There is another issue that is likely of interest to you."

"When it rains, it really rains. What is it, Wistful? I really need to get this hand worked on."

"A ship has arrived. From Earth."

Rohan processed that declaration in parts. "Does it need a tow? Wait, a ship from Earth? Earth doesn't have space travel technology. Hold on, does it now? I thought they didn't. I thought they *couldn't*."

"I did not say it was a space ship, Tow Chief Second Class Rohan. A sailing ship. A wooden sailing ship. And it does not need a tow, it is already comfortably floating in the south corridor fish tanks.

"The ship belongs to Lyst. I believe you two are already acquainted. She is an old . . . friend of mine."

Lyst is here?

"I'll be there as soon as I can."

· · · · · · · · · ·

Wei Li shook her head. "We should not dawdle."

The security chief was dressed in a ship's uniform, a simple jumpsuit in gold with metallic-purple accents. The design was similar to Rohan's, but it left her arms and lower legs bare and was made of a lighter material, soft and breathable like silk.

She was hairless, her yellow skin streaked with lines of red and green scales. Her body was trim and muscled like an athlete.

Her vertically slit eyes were narrowed as she studied Rohan.

"I'm not dawdling, I'm recovering. And maybe procrastinating. A little."

"We can engage in scholarly debate regarding the distinction between procrastination and dawdling after we've met with this Lyst individual. She is a friend to Wistful, and as such is the most important dignitary we have entertained during my tenure as security chief."

"Wei Li, are you nervous?"

She gave a tight shake of her head. "Not nervous. Apprehensive."

Rohan leaned forward and stood slowly. A medical technician had wrapped a sleeve filled with regen gel over his arm, and the drugs were starting to kick in. "We can add that distinction to our scholarly debate. But later, later. I'll hurry."

"Why are you procrastinating? Are you not eager to see old friends?"

"You'd think that, wouldn't you? I just can't imagine any pleasant reason for anyone I know to have come this way."

"I see. Is that all?"

He sighed. "It's also been a long time since I've been home. Maybe I'm feeling a little, I don't know, guilty. I should have gone back at some point in the last eleven years."

"Will delaying this reunion ease or exacerbate your feelings of guilt?"

"I know, I know. I'm coming."

"Good."

Rohan and Wei Li left the docking bay and walked over to a nearby elevator. They ascended to the transport level. From there they caught a transport pod large enough for eight, which whisked them toward Wistful's center section.

"Did anybody tell Dr. and Dr. Stone that we have visitors from Earth?" He thought back to the stories he'd read about Ben and Marion back on Earth, when they'd been teenage sidekicks to the most powerful hero on the planet, the mustachioed Hybrid Hyperion. Had they worked with Lyst? He couldn't remember.

Wei Li nodded. "They are on their way."

Rohan sank back into his seat, fighting the urge to get comfortable. The trip would only take a few minutes, and he was going to have a hard time getting up as it was.

"Those are some good drugs in this regen pack. Sleeve. Whatever you call it."

"I can imagine. Dr. Simivar believes strongly that ameliorating pain is the first step to healing."

"That's funny. In the Imperial Navy, pain was the last thing the doctors cared about."

"So I have heard. Come now, this is our stop."

Rohan sighed and stood, then followed the security chief through the guts of the station's command center.

Wistful had taken the shape of a huge cross, with most of the civilian housing, businesses, recreation, and food production distributed along her four spindly arms. The bulbous center section held facilities for the crew and administrative personnel, as well as Wistful's power supply and central processing units.

The central section was also studded with conference rooms and command stations that reminded Rohan very much of a large warship. Most of those facilities had gone unused long enough to accumulate layers of dust.

Wei Li led him to a large conference room he hadn't seen before, deep inside the central section.

"I didn't even know Wistful had friends."

"If this Lyst is as old as you think, they have had plenty of time to develop a relationship. You are speaking of a span of millions of years."

"I guess so. You think in ten thousand or a million years Wistful will call us friends?"

"I doubt either of us will have a chance to test that hypothesis. Then again, I am no expert in the maximum lifespan of Hybrids." She paused. "Are there any Earth-specific customs or rituals I should know about? So as not to offend our guests."

Rohan paused. "Well, on Earth, the genders are highly segregated, and males are considered superior in basically every situation. Make sure to defer to me at every occasion. You know, stay quiet, keep behind me, nod a lot, don't argue, speak when spoken to."

She reached up and tousled his thick black hair. "You cannot prank an empath, Rohan. But it was a lovely try."

They had arrived at a closed door. Wei Li reached for the switch that would open the door.

"Wait, do they know—" The door slid open before he could finish. "That I'm here."

4

Reunions and Disappointments

The space brought memories back to Rohan of time spent in war rooms on Imperial capital ships. Screens covered the walls from the floor to the five-meter-high ceilings. A ring-shaped table, large enough to seat twenty-five people with an overdeveloped sense of personal space, dominated the room.

Two levels of empty, banked seats surrounded the table. Altogether, at least two hundred people could have fit comfortably.

Once Rohan and Wei Li entered, it held eight.

One was a uniformed security officer who immediately saluted Wei Li, turned toward the door with a smart snap of booted heels, and left.

Rohan took in the Stones with a quick glance.

Ben Stone was tall and blond, with the rangy build of a lifelong amateur athlete and bushy eyebrows he could never quite get under control. Marion Stone was also tall and also blonde, rapidly turning gray. Her face was dominated by big eyes, a wide mouth, and a long, thin nose, as if every square inch of its surface needed a feature to justify it.

If he squinted, Rohan could see in them the teenagers who had become famous as sidekicks to Hyperion, Earth's most powerful hero.

The other two humans got to their feet as the door slid open.

Rohan exhaled and spoke softly. "Spiral! Wait . . . Amber?" He had barely recognized the woman.

She walked over to him and wrapped her arms around his body in a tight hug. "Griffin. I did not . . . I didn't think you'd be here."

He recovered from his shock and awkwardly hugged her back, gingerly patting her with his bandaged right arm. "Amber! Rudra save me, you were a kid last time I saw you."

She had pale skin and straight brown hair tied back into a practical ponytail. Her lean frame was squeezed into tight, stretchy clothing in black and gray, an outfit that would have been equally in place on a comic book cover or outside a yoga studio.

She released the hug and stepped back. "Well, it's been, what, ten years? More? I *was* a kid last time I saw you." She smiled, but it failed to reach her eyes or voice.

Rohan turned to Spiral. The man matched Rohan's height and build, slightly shorter than average for a grown human male, his frame packed with muscle that fell just short of being bulky. Where Rohan's skin was a rich brown and his features South Asian, Spiral had beige skin; black, East Asian eyes, complete with an epicanthic fold; and hatchet-sharp cheekbones. His hair and beard were cut to a uniform length, short enough to form a spiky halo around his head.

Spiral wore a red, hooded sweatshirt and loose, black cotton pants. He came over for his own hug.

"Griffin. I didn't expect to see you here. Or at all."

Rohan winced. Spiral sounded down. Tired. Maybe . . . defeated?

"Call me Rohan."

They looked at each other. Spiral chuckled softly. "I don't think I even knew that was your name."

Rohan smiled. "Well, it would hardly be a secret identity if you did, right?"

Rohan turned to Lyst, who had also stood behind the two humans.

She wore a loose, sky-blue robe, belted at the waist. The parts left exposed were covered in rugged, dark-green scales. Three frills of dark bone rose from above her eyes to meet in a heavy crest at the back of her head. There were vicious extrusions of bone at her elbows, the base of each wrist, and behind her feet.

Rohan walked over toward her and awkwardly ducked his head in a bow. Living dinosaur wizards weren't the sort of people you could just *hug*.

She smiled, showing teeth that were too large and sharp for comfort, and spoke. "Griffin. It is good to see you again."

She didn't speak English, Drachna, or any other recognizable language. Her words were something more primordial, less filtered, as if she spoke pure meaning into one's soul. Every word was experienced as if waking up suddenly from a dream; the listeners would remember the meaning but none of the actual words.

When teaching it to Rohan, she'd called it the Fire Speech, because if all other languages were shadows cast up on a wall, that language was the fire itself.

Rohan swallowed nervously. Lyst wasn't the sort of person to make social calls. He shook his head as he remembered his manners.

"Lyst, this is Wei Li, Security Chief of Wistful."

He turned to point to Wei Li, who was staring with wide eyes at the Earth sorceress.

Rohan suddenly wondered what a Class Four Empath would be sensing from the ancient female.

Lyst nodded. "It is always nice to see the child races doing well for themselves. Tell me, your people, how do they fare?"

Wei Li swallowed audibly. "We . . . they are well, Ancient. We lay our eggs on many worlds."

Lyst smiled. "Good. Now is no time to catch up, sadly. Sit."

Ben and Marion Stone nodded to Wei Li and Rohan. No introductions needed between them.

Lyst looked toward the center of the room. "Wistful?"

A projection burst into life in the open space inside the ring-shaped table. It was a ship, an elongated teardrop with a heavily textured exterior, speckled with ports and sensory dishes and open docking areas. After a moment, Rohan realized it matched Wistful's central section very closely.

Wistful's voice started, filling the room. "We may begin."

Spiral and Amber's eyes met, and he nodded sharply. Amber cleared her throat and stood up at her seat. "We're looking for Hyperion."

Rohan and the Stones exchanged startled glances. Rohan cleared his throat. "Um, that's not going to be so simple."

Amber was shaking her head, her ponytail bobbing with the motion. "Look, I know it's irregular, I know he's working for the Empire or whatever, but this . . . it's serious."

Ben Stone tapped the table with his hand. "It's not that we doubt what you're saying, um, Amber, but we can't get you Hyperion. It's not . . ." His voice broke, very gently, and his wife put her hand over his arm.

"My husband is trying to explain—"

Amber interrupted. "I know, okay? I know we're not supposed to be here, asking for him, but it doesn't look like our species can survive without him. No exaggeration. So we need Hyperion, one way or another. Empire be damned if they don't like it."

Rohan scratched his beard and sighed. "Hyperion is dead."

What sparse color dwelled in Amber's cheeks drained away as she turned to face him. Spiral, seated to her right, stood up, looked from Rohan to the Stones, then sat down.

Amber shook her head. "What do you mean?"

Rohan shrugged. "I don't think I know another way to say it."

"No, I mean, yes, but . . . but how?"

Rohan looked at the Stones. Ben Stone answered. "He went on a mission for the il'Drach. He didn't come back. I don't know that the details are important at the moment."

"So . . . okay. He didn't come back. Let me think. Maybe he escaped? Or was captured? Maybe he faked his death. We have to find him, find out for sure. We *need* Hyperion."

Rohan was shaking his head. "Look, Amber, I feel what you're saying, I do. We all thought those things. But, look, I was on the planet when he died. I *felt* it. It's not something . . . it's not a mistake. I know it's hard to imagine."

"Hard to imagine? It's Hyperion! What the hell kind of planet was it?"

Rohan sighed. "I'll tell you the story, okay, one day. But right now, you have to trust that he's dead, and we need to know *why* you came here looking for Hyperion. I'm guessing it's not to get him to autograph your copy of his graphic novel. Or action figures."

"Just listen." Her palms were flat on the table as she leaned forward. She paused and took a long breath, with just a hint of a shudder at the end of it.

"Sorry. Please, just listen. He can't be dead."

Spiral stood next to her and rested a calloused hand on her shoulder. He wasn't much taller than his protégé. "What about the other Hybrids? Soul Thief, Winter Dragon? Five of you left Earth to fight for the Empire."

Rohan scratched his beard. "Soul Thief died on the Ringgate, fighting the Wedge. That was the first year after we left Earth. Winter Dragon disappeared right as her two-year enlistment ended, and I never found out where she went. Hyperion spent six months looking for her, five or six years ago, and got nowhere. I can't imagine we'd have any better luck looking for her."

Spiral's shoulders slumped with the words. "So, out of the five of you, Hyperion and Soul Thief are dead, Winter Dragon is unreachable. The Valkyrie?"

Rohan shook his head. "Also dead." He had killed The Valkyrie himself, not that he was eager to share that information, or explain the circumstances.

Amber's brown eyes were wide, her face several shades paler than when Rohan had first walked into the room. "Just . . . you? You're the only one left?"

"I guess so. And since I am, maybe you want to tell me what's going on?"

She nodded and took a credit-card-thin slab of glass out of her pocket.

Phone technology had obviously advanced on Earth in the decade since Rohan had left.

She tapped at the screen and looked at Wistful. "I sent you an image." Then she turned it and reached past Lyst to hand the phone to Marion Stone.

Amber took a deep breath. "Just under seven weeks ago, there was an attack on Tokyo."

Marion looked at the phone, then handed it to her husband. "I don't think I understand what I'm looking at here."

Amber continued. "That's one of the better pictures we have of the first monster."

Rohan leaned forward. "First?"

Amber nodded, her face still pale. "The first monster destroyed half of Tokyo. The death toll in the first hour was over two million.

"All the heroes of Japan, alongside most of the villains, formed a united front to drive it offshore. They did it, but the cost was tremendous. Another half million civilians died in the fighting, along with most of the heroes. The Otaku Force Five was wiped out. The Sunfire Club, too, all dead."

Rohan shook his head. He knew the Otaku Force Five; despite the silly name, they were tough, competent, and packed enough raw power to have earned Hyperion's respect. "Then what?"

"Once the first one was pushed far enough into the Pacific, Lyst brought down a meteor strike that killed it.

"Which was great, except that the resulting tsunami did a lot of damage. Altogether, we had a death count from flooding in the tens of millions. With damage to housing and infrastructure, millions more will almost certainly die in the aftermath."

Marion Stone leaned forward against the table, her fierce, blue eyes intent on Amber. "You said, 'first.'"

"I did. Four weeks later, a nearly identical monster appeared. Again in the Pacific, though it didn't head for Japan."

Ben Stone handed the phone to Rohan and spoke. "Could it have been the same one? Did it survive the meteor strike, recover, and attack?"

Amber shook her head. "Its markings were different, and we managed to recover cellular tissue from both monsters. DNA is similar but not a match, so probably not."

Rohan looked at the phone. If he didn't trust Amber, he would have thought the image was a prank.

"Is this . . . what the hell? A shark with legs? How is that . . . just how big are these things?"

Spiral answered. "The first one was about one hundred fifty meters. The second was slightly longer."

Marion Stone shook her head. "Is the second one still roaming around, three weeks after appearing?"

Amber's shoulders slumped with fatigue. "The second land shark struck farther south than Japan but did a similar amount of damage. A group of mostly Chinese heroes worked to drive it east and south. There was another slaughter, and tens of millions more died. It was heading for Indonesia when it was killed."

Rohan noticed that she wasn't eager to say *how* it was killed.

Marion didn't hold back. "What killed it?"

Amber sighed. "We nuked it. Not regular nukes; they got Masamune to build special high-yield, high-focus nukes. The most advanced weapons ever made on Earth. They were worried, actually, that the nukes were *too* advanced, that the il'Drach would be pissed off if they found out what we made. In this case, there were no plausible alternatives.

"The nukes killed the second shark, but aftermath was bad. Tens of millions dead. With the fallout, the long-term casualty estimates are . . . let's just say horrific."

Ben Stone let out a long, low whistle. Rohan looked at Lyst.

"You couldn't bring down another meteor?"

She shook her massive, scaly head. "I can alter the path of an existing meteor, should its path be close enough. I can't conjure one out of nothing."

"Don't you have anything else hidden away that can take care of these things?"

She tilted her head from side to side. "Of course I do. I have a cousin in a zero-entropy prison who could tear through these sharks by claw and tooth. The question is, how much of humanity would remain if I set him loose?"

Rohan leaned back in his chair. "I'm going to guess the answer to that is: 'not much.'"

Amber looked over her audience. "Without Lyst, we wouldn't have had any way to get off the planet. You know interstellar travel from Earth is banned. Finding Hyperion was our last idea."

Ben Stone shook his head. "You mentioned two of these monsters. Sharks. Both are dead. What's the issue?"

Spiral answered for her. "A third one came a week after. Pacific again, closer to North America. We couldn't stop it, but we directed it toward southwest Nevada."

Rohan nodded. "The Green."

Spiral nodded back. "Once it was in his territory, it was neutralized. They've been fighting to a standstill for days now."

Amber tapped the table nervously. "One attack, then four weeks later another, then two weeks later another.

"Which is why we need Hyperion. Or something. Earth's strongest heroes have been decimated by these things, and for all we know, they're just going to keep coming."

Rohan nodded. "Or maybe that third one was the last of them."

Amber nodded. "I'd love for that to be the case. And you know what? If we can figure out where they came from, go there, and establish for sure that this ordeal is over, I'll be the first one to pop a bottle of champagne. Maybe after a little revenge-taking. But as of now, we have to assume that more are coming."

Marion nodded. "I agree."

Rohan held his hands up. "I'm not saying you're wrong, just saying maybe there's hope."

Amber fixed him with her eyes.

"These creatures are killing us by the hundreds of millions. We don't have time for *hope*."

They sat in silence for a while, Wistful's hologram flickering slightly in the brightly lit room.

The door chimed, then slid open. Food was brought in.

The eight of them ate and drank.

Wei Li broke the silence. "You have no history with these creatures on your world?"

Marion Stone replied. "We have sharks, but they're strictly underwater. No legs. And the largest are, what, six meters long? Maybe seven? Ben?" He was the biologist.

He nodded. "That's right. We have remains for megalodons that were larger, but not more than fifteen meters in length. And since these creatures are proportioned similarly, they must be a thousand times as massive as the largest megalodon. More."

Rohan grunted. "They're bigger than a large decipede."

Wei Li continued. "You have no idea who would be creating, or sending, these monsters to Earth?"

They answered her with silence.

Wistful added. "I have no records of creatures such as these. Other than Toth 3, I have no records of a place with creatures that even compare."

Amber hung her head over a plate of sliced fish. "Getting Hyperion was our plan B. No, plan C. I'm out of ideas."

Spiral put a hand on her shoulder and rubbed it gently, if somewhat awkwardly. "We'll figure something else out."

"Will we? What exactly are we going to figure out? Maybe we can infect them with a computer virus. Or give them all Earth colds." Her sarcasm hung thickly over the words.

Rohan cleared his throat. "Let me make sure I have this right.

"Giant monsters are attacking. Origin unknown.

"We have weapons that will kill them, but their side effects are not conducive to continued human presence on Earth.

"Earth's heroes can stop or defeat the creatures, but only with significant losses, and there aren't very many heroes around as powerful as, say, the Otaku Force Five, so counting on them is not a good long-term strategy.

"How am I doing?"

Spiral nodded at him. "That's the situation. Hyperion is—was—strong enough to maybe anchor a long-term defensive force, or so we were hoping."

"Except he's not coming. So we move on."

Ben Stone turned his gaze to Rohan. "Move on to what, exactly?"

"I'm not sure yet."

Amber looked up. "Will the il'Drach help? I feel crappy about it, since Hyperion sacrificed so much to keep the Empire off of Earth, but maybe we can reverse that? It would be better than having humanity wiped out."

Rohan shrugged. "I have to be honest, I can't say for sure, but my experience says they'd be very hesitant to give you the resources you'd need to solve this problem. I'm not sure they *have* the resources. Hyperion was the strongest Hybrid the Empire had seen in centuries. It's not like they have a dozen other lances of similar Power they could send to Earth. They don't even have *one*."

He considered mentioning the Matrons. il'Drach females blossomed with Power after menopause, and were individually as strong as, or stronger than, Hyperion.

But their Power came with a cost, and if one was let loose on Earth, it was doubtful any humans would survive the aftermath. The existence of the Matrons was also a closely guarded secret. If humanity knew about them, the il'Drach were likely to sterilize the planet to keep it.

Ben was nodding. "I agree with Rohan, but that doesn't mean it isn't worth a try. Marion and I can go to Academy and talk to some people. While we're there, I can look through the archives and see if we have any clues to where these things might have come from."

Amber sat back in her chair. "Thank you. It's better than nothing."

Marion put her hand over the back of her husband's, gripping until her knuckles turned white. "Neither of us are going to be any use throwing punches at a giant shark, but we should be able to arrange for some tools for getting rid of radioactive waste. I think we can get to Earth and at least help with the environmental cleanup."

Lyst leaned forward. "There are some avenues I can explore in other parts of the sector. I'll travel for a bit and see whether I can gather help."

Rohan smiled grimly. "Those are good ideas. Well, at least solid ideas. Better-than-nothing ideas. I think I'll take some of my saved-up vacation days and go to Earth to sort this thing out."

Amber snorted. "Really? You'll 'sort this out'?"

Wei Li put a reassuring hand on Rohan's shoulder and spoke to Amber. "Rohan is far from useless, despite his occasional demonstration of a lack of common sense."

"No offense, ma'am, but I've known Griffin a lot longer than you have. If Earth's survival is in his hands, maybe we should be planning an evacuation instead of a rescue."

Rohan held his breath a moment, reminding himself that Amber was under a great deal of stress. "An evacuation isn't a terrible idea. As a last resort, if you know what I mean. Dr. and Dr. Stone, maybe you can see if there are more ships we can have on call to get people off-planet?"

Ben shook his head. "Rohan, you have to realize, we can try, but in the absolute best-case scenario, we could get maybe one million people off the planet. That's assuming maximum cooperation from the il'Drach. One million out of seven or eight billion."

"That's still one million more than zero."

5

No Place Like Home

Rohan tossed his toothbrush into the bag that sagged open on his bathroom floor. "Do I need this hairbrush? I think I do. Can I use it for the beard also, and leave the beard comb here? I think I can."

He used his left hand exclusively; his right arm was heavily bandaged.

He threw the bag onto his bed and started sorting through the meager contents of his closet.

I've killed teams of Hybrids in hand-to-hand combat, but I'm not sure I can fold a pair of pants with just one hand.

His comm system chimed briefly. "Yes?"

Wistful's voice filled his apartment. "Tow Chief Second Class, I see you have applied for accumulated personal time off. Indefinite duration."

He pinned a uniform to his chest with his chin and executed an awkward one-arm fold. "Yeah, sorry about that. I don't think I'll be gone long. We'll either figure out a way to save humanity or get killed trying. In which case, you're just going to need a new tow chief."

"Your leave is granted. I am very old, Rohan, by the standards of your species. I do not have a great many friends. Lyst is one of them. Please do your best. I believe she would be quite saddened by the elimination of your species."

"So would I. It's my planet, too, you know. My mom is there. The first girl I kissed. It's the only place where they make tequila."

"I would also prefer for you to come back alive. You have become a most adequate tow chief."

He laughed. "I'd prefer that, too."

He took out one of the three non-uniform outfits he owned and carefully folded it for packing.

There was a knock on his door. He said, "Open."

Wei Li stood in the doorway. He waved her inside.

She sat in his armchair and narrowed her vertically slit eyes as she watched him pack.

"I came to tell you that your leave has been granted, but it seems you are already aware."

"Yup. I think Wistful *wants* me to go. Which would normally hurt my feelings, but I'm going to believe it's not that she wants to get rid of me but that she wants me to help Lyst. Who would evidently be upset if humanity was wiped out, seeing as she's spent much of the last forty thousand years preventing exactly that."

"Do you think you *can* help?"

"Weren't you the one who told Amber that I'm not so useless?"

"I did, but that was more of an attempt to support a friend than an honest assessment of your abilities."

She's being sarcastic. Isn't she?

"Well, thank you for that. And to answer your question, yes, I probably can help. This isn't some regular supervillain emergency. This is a war, and if the il'Drach taught me anything, it's how to win wars."

He gave up on folding his suit and jammed it into the bag. He would finally see if its claim of being wrinkle free was justified.

"Rohan, I am alarmed by your mood. It is more joyful than I would expect for a person who has just found out that his home is in grave peril. Does the idea of humanity's doom bring you happiness for some reason, or have you lost your grasp on reality?"

He laughed. "It's not that. Either of those things."

"What, then, is it?"

"You're volunteering to talk to me about how I feel?"

"I am. If you have lost your mind, your safety will be compromised and I am, as you know, security chief for this station."

He laughed. "I will celebrate this day every year, like a holiday."

"As you should."

Rohan sat on the bed and smoothed his hair. "I'll try to explain. When I left Earth, I wasn't exactly on the best terms."

"On the best terms with whom?"

"With anybody. I had a hard time with my temper. Well, I guess I still do. But it was worse back then."

"You were younger. It is typical for the young to lack emotional management skills."

"I know. Plus, being half il'Drach, it's a lot worse than a regular human kid."

"Did you cause many problems?"

He let out a long sigh. "Enough. Nothing too serious, but I was heading in that direction. To the point where I don't think even my mother was sorry to see me leave."

"I see. That is interesting background information, but not actually an explanation for your current mental state."

"When I left, I guess I felt unwanted. Which only made me angrier.

"After a few years in Fleet, I could have come back on leave, to visit, pretty much anytime. But I always found a reason not to."

"Ah. You feared you would still be unwanted."

"Right. I don't know, maybe it's silly. I mean, my friends, my mom, they're good people. I'm sure they'd give me another chance. Forgive whatever stuff I did back then. I was barely out of my teens."

"I cannot speak to how your friends or family would have received you. But you seem to think things will be better now."

"Not better, but maybe better for me. I told you, I'm good at wars. I can go back and, I don't know, prove that I'm useful, right? Save the human race? Be the hero. This is, like, the chance I've been waiting for."

"My people say that every broken egg is food for *something*."

"Exactly. Every cloud has a silver lining."

"I didn't realize Earth had gaseous metals in its atmosphere. I thought your people were adapted to an Empire-standard air composition."

"Very funny. It's just an expression. Tell me, do I sound selfish? Being happy for this chance to make amends?"

"Sound selfish? Perhaps. A better question is whether you *are* being selfish. Would you return and render assistance even if you were for some reason forced to remain anonymous? Or if your actions resulted in your death?"

"Yes. That's not what I'm hoping for, but yes."

"Then your actions are not selfish. Which is not to say that your reunion will be a joyous one."

"You don't think the circumstances will make them happy to see me?"

"It is possible. But in my experience, if people are angry or resentful with a person, the fact that they suddenly need that person's help with some urgent matter does not make them less angry or less resentful."

Rohan scratched his beard. "Well, I hope you're wrong. There's a first time for everything, right?"

"As there are many things that have never happened, there is not, in fact, a first time for everything."

"You're taking all the fun out of my apocalypse."

"Of course. 'Wei Li,' my name, means, 'she who removes joy from catastrophe.' In my native language."

"Really?"

"Of course not."

"You're going to miss me, aren't you?"

"I will certainly miss some aspects of your presence. Let us leave it to the philosophers to debate whether that is synonymous with missing you as a whole."

"That's all I'll be thinking about on my trip."

· · · · • · • · · ·

"You don't have to come back, you know." Amber didn't look at him as she spoke, instead examining the inside of *Void's Shadow*'s cabin.

"How else were you going to get back to Earth? Walk? Lyst isn't heading back there anytime soon."

"We're on a space station. There are dozens of ships docked here. I bet I could convince one of them to give me a lift."

"Maybe. But with the Earth under il'Drach embargo, you really need to sneak in to be safe. You won't find a ship in the sector with better stealth capabilities than *Void's Shadow*."

The ship interjected. "Captain, that's a very nice thing to say. And so you know, we're far enough away from Toth for me to open the first rift. Whenever you're ready."

Rohan nodded. "No time like the present, *Void's Shadow*. We just want to get to Earth as soon as possible."

Amber watched the screen intently. "I'm impressed you own your own ship."

"I don't *own* her. She chose to make me her captain. Ships are mostly glad to have someone to work for. It's part of their nature."

"They used to say the same thing about human women. And slaves."

"Sure, but in this case it's actually true. *Void's Shadow* is free to do whatever she wants, whenever. She knows that. Not the same as slavery."

Amber held up her hands in surrender. "Okay, fair enough. Look, I'm sorry, I've been rude. I'm kind of on edge. With . . . everything."

"It's fine. I get it. I'm not the droid you came looking for."

"I don't think you're using that reference correctly."

He smiled. "You are far too young to be correcting my pop culture references."

"Hey, I'm twenty-three physically, but my mind is five years older than that, remember? I'm the one who was kept in a magical prison."

"I remember. But you weren't watching movies for those five years, were you?"

He slid open the top of the regen tank.

"True. What is that?"

"It will fix up my arm."

"Captain, do you require assistance?"

"No need. I've done this before." *Too often.*

He twisted in his chair, setting the angle so he could slide his arm into the vat of restorative gel. With a grunt, he peeled off the medical sleeve, exposing the burned flesh beneath it.

Amber scrunched her nose at the sight. "What happened?"

"We have our own monsters. On the planet, right above Wistful, Toth 3. That's why nobody lives there."

"And you were down there because . . ."

"Some idiots got it into their heads that there was something valuable on the surface. It's been happening. It was on me to rescue them. Really, nobody else around is qualified."

"Is that your job here?"

"Nah, mostly I tow ships in and out of the station."

"You're a human tugboat."

"A Hybrid tugboat. Not many humans would qualify for the job."

He sighed as he eased the wounded hand into the tank. The nutrient-rich liquid, full of peptides that dramatically accelerated stem cell growth, worked so fast he could feel the skin itch as it started to knit back together.

Void's Shadow was displaying a direct view of the outside on the big screen that covered the inside of the hull. The effect was as if the hull were transparent and the crew could see right out into space.

What they saw was mostly the dark of space, dotted conservatively with pinpoint stars and an occasional splotchy nebula. Then they *felt* something, on a metaphysical level, as if someone were exercising Powers nearby.

A spot in the darkness opened, dilating out into a disc no more than twenty meters across. Inside that disc was a view of another star system, another sky.

The ship slid directly into the disc. Amber and Rohan braced themselves, an unconscious reaction, but they couldn't feel the transition through the rift any more than they could feel the ship's movement through the gigameters of regular space before or after it.

Rohan resisted the urge to turn his head to make sure the rift had closed behind them.

Amber smiled at him. "That was kind of cool."

"I forgot, you got here on Lyst's ship. You haven't done interstellar rifts before."

"Nope. One minute we were bobbing along in the Hudson River, next minute we're in a fish farm on Wistful. Is this Sol system?"

Void's Shadow answered. "I can only make rifts over short distances, and only between certain points. Older and stronger ships could make the jump more quickly, but it's going to take me a few jumps to get to Sol system."

Amber looked at Rohan. "How long is this going to take?"

He shrugged.

Void's Shadow spoke up. "I will hurry, but I don't think I can get there in less than twelve hours."

Rohan patted the floor next to him. "That's great, *Void's Shadow*. Twelve hours would be awesome. Thank you for this, I really appreciate it."

Amber nodded and projected her voice slightly, to make it clear she was addressing the ship. "Yes, thanks. I didn't mean to criticize. I'm just eager to get back. A lot of people back home are hurt. Hurting."

"I understand. I promise, I'll do my best!"

They flew in silence for a while.

Rohan looked at Amber. "What's been going on with you the past eleven years?"

She sighed. "I've been busy getting the Children of Mu under control. You wouldn't believe how many splinter elements and sleeper cells those guys spread around in the last ten thousand years."

"They still think you're their savior? Messiah, whatever they call it?"

"You bet. They're obsessed with fighting the Sons of Atlantis, trying to get the same set of corrupt politicians in our pockets, or take over some third world country or criminal empire, all in the name of restoring the glory of one or another lost continent."

"Sounds exhausting."

"Sometimes. Spiral and I have also been doing the hero bit a little."

"And Spiral just hangs out and helps you with all that? Is he your sidekick?"

"Please don't call him that. I told him he doesn't have to, but, you know. He feels guilty about everything that happened, the whole sorcerous imprisonment thing. Also, Lyst told him that one time to protect me, and he said he would. You know his type, man of his word, loves his solemn vows, that whole macho bushido thing that's not really bushido."

"Oh, I know it well. It's probably good for him, too. Having something to focus on outside himself."

"I guess. I'd just like to be able to convince him that I don't need a babysitter."

"I bet you don't. I'm sure your Powers have gotten a lot stronger."

She snapped her fingers and reached for her hips. "Remember these?" She pulled two trench knives out from their sheaths: long, slightly curved daggers with knuckle protection built into the handles.

"Oh wow. I gave those to you, didn't I?"

"These are copies, but the same pattern. Between these, my Power, and all that time training under Spiral, I hold my own.

"Until we're fighting a ten-thousand-ton shark. Then these aren't even an annoyance, and I'm useless."

"You're not useless. You got me to come back, right?"

"Is that supposed to help? Because it doesn't. At all."

"No, I guess not. Hey, did anything happen on Earth in the last decade I should know about?"

She chuckled halfheartedly. "Are you serious?"

He shrugged. "Kind of. I mean, what did I miss? Any good movies come out?"

Amber shook her head, her ponytail swaying side to side with the motion. "You can borrow my phone and look up all the sports scores if you want.

"Griffin, look, you haven't been back in more than ten years. You can just drop me off, and we'll call it even. Thanks for the ride, I'll tell everyone you helped."

"I'm not just dropping you off. I'm going to stay and fight."

"It's not necessary."

He adjusted his arm's position. The itching was getting worse.

"You're not really in any position to turn down offers of help. And by 'you,' I mean your whole species."

"You can't come back and cause problems, Griffin. You know what I'm talking about."

"I promise, I'll be good. For now, you can help me out. Fill me on the last decade. I left in a hurry. Earth got some il'Drach tech as part of the treaty, right? Anything happen with that? What did Hyperion do, just release everything online?"

"You're seriously asking *that*? Weren't you, personally, twenty percent of that treaty?"

"I agreed to go, sure. But Hyperion wasn't the type to consult with the rest of us on what he wanted to do. He was more the inform-after-the-fact kind of guy. Better to ask forgiveness than permission. Yada yada yada."

Amber paused. "Well, he didn't 'just release' the tech. He formed a company with it. Within two years it was the most highly valued company on Earth."

"Let me guess. He named it Hyperion Inc. or something."

She laughed softly. "Hyperion Industries. A little more old-school."

"What do they do? I never even found out what sorts of things they got. Antigrav?"

"The big industries are energy and carbon fixing. They have factories that take carbon dioxide from the air and pull out the carbon. Make things like graphite, diamond, anything you can think of."

"That takes energy. Must burn a ton of oil to do that."

"Nah. They covered huge tracts of desert with carbon based solar panels—more il'Drach tech. Lay out a big field of solar panels, put a factory next to it, make a bunch more, then more factories. Pretty soon you have enough industrial capacity to do almost anything.

"They synthesize octane, too. Gasoline. People can use their old cars to their hearts' content. No need for batteries made from rare materials, and everyone can reuse the old gasoline infrastructure. I mean, the oil producing countries weren't happy, since it kind of shut them out of the equation, but they couldn't do much about it.

"Plus, there's a net pull of carbon dioxide out of the air."

Rohan whistled. "That helping out the environment?"

"As of about six years ago, climate change trends have been reversed. We're supposed to be close to adding ice back to the poles."

"That's . . . actually a really huge deal. Right? Isn't it? I remember we all thought the planet was doomed."

She shrugged. "It seemed great. The company was doing a lot of other good things. They build schools, set up infrastructure in poor places, provide clean water, cheap power. Now with the sharks . . ."

"Hey, we'll figure it out. How are my old friends? Vanguard?"

"Hyperion Industries funds most of the superhero teams. People with Powers can concentrate on fighting crime or whatever instead of holding down jobs as photographers or journalists. Or villains."

"Must be nice. You don't have to inherit billions to be a hero. Now anybody can be Batman."

"Not exactly anybody. It's a good deal, though. Spiral and I are on the payroll."

"Great. Maybe I can borrow some cash when we get to Earth so I can rent a hotel room."

"Griffin, Hyperion Industries has a director and a board that runs the company, but they don't *own* it. The five of you, the Hybrids who left to fight for the Empire, are the actual owners of Hyperion Industries. I think you're actually one of the richest people on the planet."

"Ha! Really? Neat. But that's ironic, isn't it? I find out I'm crazy rich, but all my wealth is based on a planet that's on the cusp of annihilation. Now I really do have to stop these land shark things."

"That's your motivation?"

"Hey, I was going to stop them already. It's just *extra* motivation."

Amber turned back to Rohan, her expression somber again. "Do you think we have a chance of saving the Earth? Without Hyperion?"

"The planet will be fine. The real question is whether we can save any or all of the people who live on it."

She hit him with her elbow. "That joke wasn't funny when Lyst made it, and it's not funny now."

"Do you want the truth or do you want me to say something to make you feel better?"

"The latter, I think. Both if you can manage it."

"Okay. I probably can't." He took a breath, gathered his thoughts. Let it out, held his lungs empty for a long count of three.

"I'll tell you something most people around here don't know. Not a secret, exactly, but, whatever.

"You know Hyperion was the strongest Hybrid on Earth, right. But not just on Earth—he was the strongest, well, the strongest *being* the Empire had in their control. There were crazy uncontrollable forces of nature around that might have been tougher than Hyperion, but nothing sane. Nothing rational. Nothing you could, like, have a conversation with, that could act with purpose.

"And you know me, at least you know the 'me' of eleven years ago. We both know I was not the cream of the crop on Earth. I mean, I had Powers, sure, but I wasn't the one who had the bad guys wetting their spandex, right? Always a little bit the loose cannon, always overshadowed by the others in Vanguard. By my own girlfriend.

"Well, a couple of years of fighting the Wedge taught me some things. I grew up a little, started using my brain a little more.

"After five or six years in the Imperial Navy, I forget exactly when, I realized something.

"When the Empire needed a guy in the field who would absolutely positively win in a straight-up fistfight against anything in his way, they'd send in Hyperion. Of course.

"But, more and more as time went on, when they had a war that needed to be won at all costs, when they had a situation that needed resolving that wasn't as simple as punching down a wall, when it was really important, when it really mattered, they didn't send Hyperion anymore.

"Instead, they sent me."

6

Heart of Brightness

"Captain. Captain, you should wake up."

Rohan felt a nudge on his arm as he came up out of a deep sleep.

"What? Where? Who?"

Amber's voice came from his left. "We're here. Sol system."

He shook his head to clear it. His arm was stuck.

On *Void's Shadow*. In the regen tank.

"Wow. I was really out of it."

"*Void's Shadow* said there were enough toxins in your system to kill a tribe of Ursans. From the venom stuff that burned your hand. She said to let you sleep to clear it out."

Rohan rubbed his eyes with his free left hand and nodded. "What time is it?"

Amber shrugged. "I have no idea what time zone we're in. You've been out for about ten hours. We're in Sol system, but not near Earth yet. *Void's Shadow*, how long until we reach Earth?"

Void's Shadow's voice rolled softly through the ship.

"Reaching Sol 3 orbit in half an hour."

Rohan grunted. "I can't remember the last time I slept that deeply."

Void's Shadow continued. "The tank administered anesthetics and sedatives to promote your recovery."

"My liver's getting a workout. What else do we need to do before reaching Earth?"

Amber shrugged. "I have no idea. I'm not even sure we should be here."

"Where else should we be?"

"I don't know. Finding someone else who can help us? It's a big galaxy, right? It just feels like we got to Wistful, found out Hyperion was dead, gave up, and came running back."

Rohan stretched his left hand up and behind him, trying to loosen the tension in his upper back and shoulder. "Lyst is old, and she's been around the block a few times. Wistful is no spring chicken. The Professors Stone have the full academic might of the il'Drach Empire at their fingertips. If there is more help to find, those guys are more than capable of finding it. Tagging along with any of them wouldn't help them, but if we get to Earth, we might be able to do or see something useful."

Amber sighed. "I know. It's just . . . it's like I'm disappointing everybody, coming back without Hyperion. He seemed like our last, best hope."

"You're kind of making me feel bad, you know."

"If you want me to believe that you're going to be of any actual help to anybody in this situation, you should probably start by growing a thicker skin."

He laughed. "That's fair. I'll try to worry less about my feelings and more about stopping those land sharks."

"Now you're talking."

"As for what we're doing at this precise moment, where should we be heading exactly? Is Vanguard still in New York? Is there some kind of base where The Green is fighting that monster?"

Amber shook her head. "I'm not sure. We should see The Director first."

"The Director?"

"Of Hyperion Industries."

"Sure. So, this Director, he's kind of leading the charge in terms of defending the planet?"

"*She* is. Since it was her idea to fund all the superhero teams, like Vanguard, it just sort of worked out that way."

"Governments are okay with that? The United Nations? Nobody's pissed off that some private citizen has that much power?"

Amber's cheeks tightened into a cold smile. "Oh, they're pissed. But what exactly do you think they can do about it?"

"I suppose not much."

"Plus, Hyperion set it up this way. Everyone's still expecting him to come back at some point and check up on things, and nobody really wants to be the one to tell him that they messed up his arrangement. After they find out, though, who knows."

They sat in silence for a bit as *Void's Shadow* closed on Earth, carefully accelerating to get near the planet as quickly as possible without overshooting.

Amber tapped at her phone.

Rohan spotted Earth on the ship's forward display, a lovely, blue-and-white marble hanging in space. He swallowed, fighting back a mixture of feelings.

He pulled his arm out of the tank, shivering as the hydrophilic field over the top wicked the regen liquid off his skin. It left his arm dry and very slightly tacky to the touch.

He looked over his hand. A thin layer of pinkish skin had grown over the burns, a layer he knew would take at most a few days to darken to his natural dark-brown color.

There wasn't much privacy available on the tiny ship, but Rohan did what he could by getting up and circling around to the small mess at the back of the cabin. He poured himself some water and noisily unwrapped some meal replacement bars while Amber talked.

Within two minutes, Amber had silenced her phone and settled back in her chair. Rohan came over and settled heavily into his chair next to her.

"Anything?"

She gave a quick shake of her head. "No news. Vanguard Prime is with The Director in Sahara City, so it makes the most sense to go there first. Besides, Bamf is in Sahara City, so from there we can go anywhere else pretty quickly."

"Now I have questions. Bamf? Sahara City? Vanguard *Prime*?"

Amber sighed and tossed her head, flicking her ponytail back over her shoulder. "They call all the hero teams Vanguard. For a while they called the other ones Vanguard Junior or something, but really just wound up calling the original team Vanguard Prime."

He restrained the urge to ask about one of his old teammates in particular. "That's . . . my old crew? Prime?"

"Yeah, basically. Except . . . well, you'll see soon."

Except what, exactly?

"Okay. What's a Bamf?"

"He's from after your time. He's a teleporter, really powerful. Also *severely* agoraphobic, and people-phobic, so he's not much for field work. Just hangs around Sahara City and sends people back and forth when there's a real hurry."

"Bamf. Okay."

"It's the sound of the displacing air when he opens a portal. Like, you know, a pop."

"Oh. Well, that makes sense. Sounds handy. Wish we had a Bamf around back when I was in Vanguard."

"I bet. Other questions?"

"I don't remember Sahara City."

"Right. Hyperion Industries bought a big chunk of the Sahara Desert, put the first big solar panel farms and carbon-fixing fabrication plants there. Pretty soon they couldn't recruit enough engineers or research scientists, so they added a university, plus housing for all the workers, plus security, then entertainment and support systems for all of the above.

"Before they knew it, the factory complex was a city. I think it has a stable population as large as Fresno, but it might be more."

"Wow. A whole city. Ten years."

"Yup."

"Can we land there? Are they going to try to shoot us down?"

The ship answered. "They can try! They'll never see us coming."

Amber shook her head. "I got us clearance. *Void's Shadow*, I'm going to forward you a code; just broadcast it as we come down."

"Will do."

· · · ●·● · · ·

"Wow."

Sahara City was visible from space: a shiny graphite disc, fifty kilometers across, dropped in the middle of an endless, lifeless desert.

One quadrant bristled with slender black and glass structures in a variety of shapes, growing out of a speckled bed of sand, white roads, and tentative green spaces.

A thousand intricate spiderwebs draped over the city, forming a network of covered walkways and elevated streets.

Four long, straight arms extended outwards: highway lanes, train tracks, and gleaming pipelines. One went northeast into Egypt, another northwest into Libya, the last two farther into the heart of the continent, toward Chad and Sudan.

A large, flat area well inside the city was marked to delineate runways and flat landing fields. A quick negotiation between *Void's Shadow* and Sahara City security, conducted over Amber's phone, got them sorted into an unused heliport.

As they disembarked, Rohan patted his ship's warm, black hull. "What do you want to do?"

"Can I leave? Check out the system?"

Rohan paused. "I think so. Maybe ping me before you get too far."

"Thanks!"

Amber looked at him. "You going to mask up?"

"Almost forgot." Rohan pulled a piece of cloth out of a pocket. He shook it out, revealing a printed eagle beak.

He held it out to Amber. "What do you think?"

Amber nodded. "Looks like your old one. You think you still need it?"

"I still have family on the planet. Someone gets a picture, uses facial recognition to figure out who I was, they're all at risk." He rolled the mask up over his mouth and nose, lining the beak up with his mouth.

Time to be The Griffin again.

A half dozen soldiers suited in open-face helmets and black uniforms bristling with shiny plates of carbon fiber approached Amber and Rohan. They were carrying short, wide-mouthed rifles and quickly formed a little wedge around the two heroes. As the group walked away from the tarmac, *Void's Shadow* lifted silently into the air.

One of the guards elbowed another and spoke in a language Rohan didn't recognize. "Real grav generators."

Rohan nodded and responded in the Fire Speech. "You guys don't see a lot of bootstrap drives?"

The guard turned, surprised. Rohan saw a male face, wide nose and broad cheekbones, looking at him through the heavy goggles. "Sorry, sir."

Rohan shook his head. "Don't be. I haven't been on Earth in a decade, I'm just trying to catch up."

Amber answered. "We got the theory for it in the treaty but not the tech. We were on pace to have a functional bootstrap drive within five years."

"This way, please." The guards beckoned and led the two heroes onto an open-air, electric vehicle.

The streets were congested. People on bicycles and electric scooters weaved around small buses, sedans with tinted windows, and a dense network of tram lines. The guards expertly guided their electric bus through the traffic.

Minutes later, they stopped in front of a massive, city block-sized building. Its upper reaches were a geometry lesson in action; spires and towers and swooping structural elements arranged to defy symmetry.

The logo of Hyperion Industries, a stylized Roman *H*, dominated the stone above the building's main entrance.

A broad courtyard offset the entrance, an open space uncommon within the city. Several hundred people milled about, many carrying signs displaying crudely drawn slogans.

Amber touched Rohan's arm. "This is the main admin building. They'll be in here."

He nodded. "What's with those guys?"

The group walked around the courtyard's edges, avoiding the bulk of the mob.

"Protesters."

Rohan read some of the signs.

Overweight, pale men with long beards wore shirts printed with Humans First and red hats that read Make Earth Great Again. Skinny teenagers in torn jeans carried signs with scrawled messages using the Law of Attraction to prove that it was aliens on Earth that had caused the attacks.

"They blame Hyperion Industries for the shark attacks?"

She shrugged. "It's always something. Anything that goes wrong is because of aliens. And Hyperion Industries is all about using alien tech, so this becomes their target."

Rohan heard his alias muttered by a few of the protesters. He noticed armed security monitoring the protest from its edges.

He examined the crowd.

"A lot of white faces."

"The company has poured a ton of money into local infrastructure. I guess there are people in Africa and in Asia who hate the company, but not too many."

He grunted.

"Before we go in, can I get a tour of the rest of the city?"

"Later."

The lobby centered on a statue of Hyperion, at least ten times the size of the man himself, arm outstretched as if he were about to fly up, through the ceiling and into the sky.

Rohan paused in front of it and nudged Amber. "Kind of over the top, eh? You think Hyperion wanted that statue?"

She shrugged. "You knew him better than me, what do you think?"

"Probably. Just to remind anyone coming in here what they'd have to face if they tried to mess with the company."

She took a deep breath. "Come on, they're waiting for us. I am not looking forward to this conversation."

Rohan nodded. "Me neither. Hey, I'm hungry, maybe we can stop for a snack first?"

"Let's go, Captain Procrastination."

"It was Major Procrastinator, and I gave up that name when I became The Griffin."

"Why Major? You didn't want to make yourself a general?"

He chuckled.

"You win." He followed her through the lobby. "Geez, I haven't seen these people in more than ten years. This is a weird feeling."

"Let's go."

Most of their escort peeled away, leaving just a pair of guards who led them onto an elevator, then down, deep into the bedrock underneath the building.

Amber ran her hands over her clothes, pointlessly smoothing out the already-taut fabrics. They stepped out into a broad, carpeted hallway overlayed with a rich, dark-gray wood paneling and interspersed with an occasional patch of roughly chiseled rock.

Rohan swallowed. "Men's room around here?"

"Come *on*, Griffin."

He sighed. "Fine."

You can't make things better if you don't help, and you can't help without seeing them. That's an eagle beak on your mask, not a chicken.

The group approached a set of double doors, each three and a half meters high and wide enough to easily pass four people walking abreast. One of the guards touched a panel, and the doors swung open on silent motors.

He saw *her* less than ten meters away.

She paced, her back to the doors, the muscles in her legs and back rippling under her silver-and-white uniform, the blue accent blocks contrasting the rich brown of her hands and neck. Her black hair clung to her scalp in tight braids just long enough to kiss her round shoulders.

Rohan tried to swallow. Failed.

She turned as the door opened, her dark eyes widening over the silver mask covering her mouth as she took in Amber, widening further at the sight of Rohan's eagle-beak mask.

Amber entered, passing the three rows of stadium seating that ran along the back wall and halfway up both sides.

"Ares?"

The woman looked from Amber to Rohan and back, the surprise in her eyes giving way to sadness.

The woman shook her head, her eyes hard.

Amber hugged the woman. "Oh, Bright Angel, I'm sorry." The woman wrapped strong arms around Amber for a long breath, then disengaged.

Rohan walked up to a spot behind Amber's shoulder. "Hey."

Bright Angel looked at him. "Hey." Her tone was completely flat. He swallowed.

"I . . . came. To help."

This is already going worse than I expected.

She nodded. He could feel tremors of her Power falling off her body like ripples crossing a pond. His mouth was dry.

"Is that . . . What about Ares?"

Bright Angel let out a sigh. "He didn't make it." She turned to face the room's central feature, a rectangular conference table with seats for twenty.

A man stood up from the table and walked toward them. He had pale skin, shockingly white hair, and a costume that screamed in yellow and bright blue. A long-handled sledgehammer dangled from a loop at his waist.

The pale man jogged up to Rohan and bent down to hug him. "Kid Lightning! Kid Lightning!" Soft sparks danced over his face and hair as he spoke.

Rohan hugged back while casting a questioning look over the man's shoulder.

Bright Angel shook her head. "He pushed his Power too hard, the backlash fried his speech centers. That's all he can say right now."

Kid Lightning let go of the Hybrid and stepped back, then turned to hug Amber. "Kid Lightning." He said it softly.

Rohan looked at Bright Angel. "He still goes by that? Isn't he like forty-five?"

She shrugged. "You try telling him to change it." Her face was grim, no hint of softness for Griffin.

The other person who had been sitting at the table was walking to the huddle of heroes. Rohan looked at her with a smile. He'd always liked The Damsel. Everybody did; they couldn't help it.

She wrapped her arms around him and squeezed, her breasts flattening against his chest and spilling up over the top of her dark-red bustier.

Eyes up. Focus on her face.

She wore no mask, and her pale skin was showing fine creases and faint-blue veins. Her hair was a deep red that Rohan had never believed came from nature.

He remembered that she was at least as old as Kid Lightning. The pair had already been a crimefighting legend when Griffin and Bright Angel joined the team.

"Oh, Griffin, it's been *forever*! You've grown so handsome! You grew out your hair! I like it."

"Hey, Damsel, thanks. You look great, too." She did.

She smiled. "Sweetie, we both know you have no choice but to think that. It is still nice to hear, I must admit!"

Bright Angel rolled her eyes at the pair.

Damsel's expression darkened. "Sorry, not the time for all of that. You know me, I'm no good at toning it down."

Rohan nodded.

"I know." He looked around. "We're waiting for The Director?"

Bright Angel gave a short, loud laugh. He looked at her, mystified.

She looked back. "Oh, wait . . . Hm. What did Amber tell you? Never mind. Yes, she should be here any second."

They walked over to the conference table. A screen covered the wall behind it and showed a map of the Earth, squashed into a large oval with Sahara City in the center. A red dot was blinking on the left side, in the southwestern part of the United States.

As they got closer, Rohan could make out a metal object on the table. It was about a meter long with a savagely pointed tip and ornate metalwork. The blunt end was twisted and bare, as if it had been torn apart.

"Rudra save me, is that Ares's spear?"

Amber answered him. "A land shark bit through it."

Bright Angel cleared her throat. "Not to be rude, but where's Hyperion?"

Rohan looked at Amber, wondering if he should answer. She didn't let him.

"Let's wait for The Director."

A small door opened, just to the left of the massive screen, and a woman walked through.

7

Family

"Speak of me and, well, you know the rest."

Her face had the sort of beauty that wouldn't have been out of place on a Bollywood movie poster, diminished very little by the fine lines creeping toward her temples. She had dark-brown skin that matched Rohan's, just a touch of makeup around her eyes and lips breaking the color, her medium build wrapped in a colorful, green-and-blue sari that sparkled in the harsh conference room lighting.

Amber walked over to the woman. "Director. I don't think you've met, this is Griffin. He's—"

The Director flashed white teeth at the young hero. "Actually, we have. Years ago. Hello, Griffin. Welcome back to Earth. Welcome home." Her voice was hard; cold.

Rohan swallowed, his voice not cooperating as he tried to speak. "Um. Thanks. Director." He looked at Bright Angel, who was fighting back a smirk.

The woman smiled again. It wasn't a comforting expression.

"This is turning out to be quite the day. I take it you've all heard about Ares?" She walked over to Bright Angel and squeezed the woman's forearm. "I'm so sorry."

Bright Angel covered The Director's hand with her own and nodded.

"Kid Lightning." The man hung his head low, almost moaning the name.

The Director took a breath. "Let's sit. The fact that Hyperion isn't in this room suggests we need to be bracing for the next round of updates."

Amber swiveled her head in a noncommittal response as they sat. Rohan looked to Bright Angel, who took a chair between Kid Lightning and The Damsel.

With a shrug, Rohan sat across from them.

The Director looked at Amber, who paused, then glanced sharply at Rohan.

He took his cue and cleared his throat.

"Well, there's no easy way to say this. You all know, I think, that I left with Hyperion to fight the Wedge incursion. To fight for the il'Drach.

"We drove back the Wedge, but there were other missions, other wars, one after another. A couple of years ago, Hyperion went on one of those missions. They sent him up against something like The Green, only, I guess, more so.

"It killed him.

"So . . . bottom line is Hyperion's not coming to help."

The group sat in silence.

Rohan continued. "The other Hybrids who left with us are gone, too. Soul Thief died saving Hyperion's life on the Ringgate, which is pretty ironic, considering. The others are all gone. One way or another."

He looked around the table, took in the stunned faces of his oldest friends.

"It's not all bad news. You know Ben and Marion Stone, Hyperion's old sidekicks. They've been working at Academy, which is like the Oxford of the il'Drach Empire. They took their ship back there to see if they could find anything in historical records we could use against the land sharks.

"And Lyst is still looking, with Spiral, to find more help.

"And, well, I'm here." He looked around at the faces that did *not* light up at his last announcement. "I spent most of the last ten years on a war footing against the toughest enemies the il'Drach could find to point me at. I'm not Hyperion, but I'm not useless, either."

Bright Angel spoke, her eyes narrow and flashing at him. "What about Valkyrie?"

Rohan swallowed. The Damsel was a decent empath, and so was Bright Angel. He couldn't outright lie to them, but he also didn't want to start a harder conversation.

"Also dead. A year ago, more or less."

"You're sure? About all of them?"

He shrugged. He had felt Valkyrie's heart stop beating in his own hand. "I'm as sure as you can be. Really, Winter Dragon is the only unknown, but she left no trail. I used to wonder if she came back to Earth, but if that were the case, you'd have already seen her fighting these land sharks. Which means she's somewhere else, and it's a big galaxy."

The Director focused on him. "Are you telling me we should not expect any further help from off-world?"

Rohan looked away from her eyes. "The Stones will be here, and they said they could help with environmental cleanup. But they're not likely to come up with anything military to help. So, yes, that's what I'm telling you."

She sighed and put her hands flat on the table. "Not the news we were hoping for, but so be it. What now?"

Rohan gave everybody a minute to jump in, an offer that had no takers. Then he spoke.

"First thing we do is kill the land shark that's fighting The Green."

The Director, Bright Angel, and Amber all started talking simultaneously. The younger women quickly deferred.

"The president of the United States has asked us not to interfere."

Rohan shook his head. "Okay, I'm out of touch, so please explain. Why on Earth not? No pun intended."

Bright Angel waited, then spoke. "They're hoping the land sharks can get rid of The Green for them."

Rohan sputtered. "Seriously? The guy lives out in the desert, leaves everybody alone, but they want to get rid of him?"

She shrugged. "He scares them. All of them. He scares me, too, to be honest. Not that *I* want him dead."

Rohan shook his head. "Screw that. You have exactly one Power on this planet that can go toe to toe with a land shark, and they're trying to get rid of him? That's like . . . I can't even come up with an analogy. Something about a condom and a first date."

"Kid Lightning!"

"See, he gets it. Look, I've been in, and won, a lot of wars. Trust me, you do not get rid of your most effective weapon because you're worried it will turn against you after. You use that weapon, you protect it, and you hope that by the time it becomes a problem, someone else is in charge and you've moved on."

The Director glared at him. "You've been on the planet for an hour and you're already confident you should be making that decision?"

"Yes. We go and kill the land shark. If The Green is fighting that thing to a draw by himself, we can definitely finish it off together. We do it for two reasons. First, that land shark will be dead, so if another one shows, they can't team up. Second, it might give us a corpse to study. I understand there's not much in the way of remains of the first two, right? After a meteor strike and a generous dose of nuke?"

Nods answered him.

"That's the plan, then."

The Director shook her head. "Tell me. How is it exactly that you think you're in a position to give orders to anybody in this room?"

Rohan let out a breath.

Be nice.

"Sorry, force of habit. Let me rephrase. I am going to go help The Green fight the land shark. I'd love for any or all of you to come and help. If the US government doesn't like it, they can take it up with Wistful."

Damsel cocked her head. "Hon, who or what is Wistful?"

"My boss. She's a thirty-kilometer long, diamond-coated space station that's older than recorded human history by at least an order of magnitude."

He paused again.

"Look, I'm not sure what to say. You remember the hotheaded, impetuous me from a decade ago. I'm sure you're thinking about mistakes I made, me losing my temper, the situation with Brother Steel, me not listening to anybody. I get it, I do.

"But I spent ten years training and fighting for the il'Drach. There are maybe a quarter million il'Drach alive, total, and yet they control most of this sector, running an empire of trillions. You know how? Because they have developed a system for winning wars. Which they've been drumming into me for a decade.

"And let me tell you, the way someone like me would win a war is to exploit exactly the kind of thinking that you're seeing here. Letting an enemy survive so it will weaken a rival, like The Green? The second I smelled that on a planet was the second I knew they were doomed.

"I'm not saying you should follow me out to Nevada because you're my friends or because I'm a great guy or because you really like me. I'm saying you should follow me because it turns out I'm not such a great guy, and that's why I'm the right person to help you win this war."

He looked at the members of Vanguard, not sure if his speech had been in any way coherent.

Will they buy it?

"Kid Lightning!" The older man walked over to Rohan and extended his arm, palm down.

Rohan covered the hand with his own.

Bright Angel shook her head. "That was the dumbest speech you've ever given, and it reminds me how much you love the sound of your own voice. Which is not a good enough reason to follow your lead."

Bright Angel crossed her arms over her chest and held Rohan in a steady gaze.

The Director sighed. "This plan will have ramifications you don't understand. Can't understand. I can't stop you, but I'll tell you it's a bad idea."

Amber stepped over to the two men and turned, her arms spread wide. "I know this is going to sound crazy, but maybe we should listen to him."

Bright Angel looked at the younger woman. "Why?"

"Because Lyst told me that, despite his flaws, Rohan is probably the warrior we need. That the Earth needs."

The Director snorted in surprise. "Are you kidding?"

Rohan snorted louder. "Lyst said that?"

Amber held steady. "I'm dead serious. She told me we might be luckier to have found him than Hyperion. Also, I saw how the people on Wistful look at him. They look at him like a leader. I'm willing to take a chance on that. I'm in."

"Kid Lightning!"

Amber added her hand to the stack.

Bright Angel unfolded her arms and rubbed her hands quickly over her face. She said, "Lyst's word is good enough for me. It's not like we have any kind of real alternative." She put her hand over Amber's.

The Damsel followed suit. "Not sure what I can do, but I'm in."

Rohan looked at the hands for a moment before they disengaged. "How soon can we leave?"

The Director cleared her throat. "You're sure about this."

Rohan looked at her. "I'm not forcing anybody. But we have to do this."

She nodded. "I'm not going to try to stop you. Bamf can get you to the staging area a couple of kilometers from the fight. You'll need to prepare, and I'd like a word in private with The Griffin before you go. Say, twenty minutes?"

Nods all around, and the group dispersed. The Director beckoned for Rohan to follow her through the small door next to the room's main display screen.

Beyond the door was an office, one wall completely taken up by a screen that presented a false view down onto Sahara City, as if they were fifty floors above ground instead of below.

Rohan barely had time to take in the overbuilt wooden desk and tasteful collection of artwork on the walls before The Director spun and slapped him full across the face.

"Eleven years! Eleven! Not a word, not a text, not an email. Eleven! Do you know what we thought?" She pulled back her other hand and punched him in the chest, putting her full weight behind it, the end of her sari flipping up into the air with the motion.

She rubbed her hand, obviously hurting from the impact more than he was.

Rohan pulled his mask down to his neck. "I'm sorry, I couldn't . . . I didn't . . ."

"Didn't what? Know how to send a message? Lyst and Amber found your sorry behind in, what, a day? You disappear for eleven years and can't find a way to get a message through?"

"Mom, I'm sorry. You're right, you're right. I'm sorry. I don't know."

"Of course you know. Knew. Knew we were waiting, knew what we'd be thinking. Do you realize we planned your funeral? We almost held it. Half a dozen times we were ready to mourn your death, every time I said to Carla we should postpone. They think I'm crazy. You have any idea how frustrating it is to have everyone in your life look at you like they think you're losing your mind?"

Rohan's stomach hurt. "Mom, I . . . I know. I mean, I don't know. I'm sorry, really. I couldn't message for a while, things were crazy, and then once they settled down, I . . . I didn't know what to say anymore. I thought you'd be better off without me."

Her eyes were moist. She balled her hands up into fists, as if to hit him again, then stepped up and wrapped him in a fierce hug. "I can't believe I raised such an idiot."

Rohan hugged her back. "I guess it's really your fault, then, right?"

She leaned back and punched him again. "Don't start that with me. I can make one call, and they will never find your body. I know people. They say I'm the most powerful woman on Earth. Person."

"I realize that. How did that happen?"

"Ask Hyperion." Then silence. "Oh God, I guess you can't, can you? He handed me the company, right before you all left the planet. Said I was the smartest person he knew, which was true, and that he trusted me to do the right thing with it, which was reasonable. I think he just wanted someone in charge who had some experience dealing with the il'Drach and all their manipulative insanity."

Rohan nodded. "As in Dad. You knew how to handle Dad, so Hyperion figured you could handle the rest of them if you had to."

"Yes. Nobody else on Earth has that kind of experience standing up to il'Drach bullshit."

"Which makes you uniquely qualified. That's pretty cool. And Amber tells me I'm rich. So you should be glad, I'm not a doctor or a lawyer, but I still made something of myself."

She snorted. "As if. *I* made something of you. I built this company while you were off gallivanting around with Hyperion."

Rohan nodded. "You can take the credit, I'll take the money. But if I'm going to cash in, I have to start with saving the planet."

She paused, and her eyes were wet again.

"I can't believe I'm crying. I never cry. We've lost tens of millions of people. Maybe hundreds of millions, when all is said and done. None of this"—she waved her arm to take in the building and the city—"mattered at all. I'm helpless."

Rohan sighed. "I know, Mom. I can only imagine."

How many Tolone'ans or Shayjh mothers had similar conversations with their own children, crying about the toll I've taken on their people?

He shrugged the thought away.

The Director took a deep breath, let it out, visibly collecting herself. She had never been one to let emotions get the better of her for long.

"I'm making tea. Do you want tea?"

Rohan shrugged.

He waited while she stepped to the wet bar in the corner of the room, behind her desk. She heated water and made two cups of tea, finishing each off with a liberal pour of milk and a pair of sugar cubes.

Her hands steadied visibly with each step of the process.

She put one mug in front of Rohan and sipped tentatively at her own.

Rohan took his own sip. It tasted like home.

"Mom, I didn't think to ask. Where's Poseidon?"

She shook her head, her earrings swinging with the motion. "Nobody's seen him in months."

"Another bender? He likes to drink. And screw around."

She shrugged. "What are you thinking?"

"I'm thinking that we need someone with an extra level of ocean savvy, and Poseidon's the guy. Someone needs to start checking out his likely haunts."

"Which is where? I was never exactly on Poseidon's list of drinking buddies."

"Some picturesque villa on the Italian coast with a huge mess inside."

"That doesn't exactly narrow things down."

Rohan scratched at his beard. "I know, I'll try to think of something more helpful."

She reached over the desk and grabbed his cheeks with both hands. "Look at you, you're a man now."

He sighed. "Mom, I'm, like, thirty-two. And it hasn't been an easy decade. I'm not a kid."

"You'll always be a baby to me. But no, you're not a kid. We should start looking for a wife for you. Do you remember Dr. Gupta, my dermatologist? Her daughter just finished her residency at Johns Hopkins, very pretty, good prospects. And Dr. Gupta is a good cook, I'm sure her daughter can manage the kitchen."

"You know, your threat of an arranged marriage would be less hypocritical if you hadn't run halfway across the planet and married an actual alien to escape your own."

"That was different, I was twenty. But you, Rohan, you're not getting any younger. Thirty-two? What will people say?" Her half-smile told him that she was at least mostly joking.

Rohan shook his head. "Will you tell Dr. Gupta's daughter that I'm sterile?"

"Oh please, we're modern people, you can adopt, or get a sperm donor. Nobody cares about that sort of thing. Remember, you're fantastically rich. That makes up for a lot."

He sighed. "I actually got rich on my own. Believe it or not. The il'Drach pay their lances well."

Her tone tightened. "How was it? Fighting for your father?"

Rohan shook his head. "It's a long story. Complicated. I managed to get out, though it took some doing. Now I'm a tow chief. Basically, I pull ships in and out of dock at a space station."

"You're telling me I studied medicine, moved to Canada to pursue a career as an anesthesiologist, and raised a child with a first-rate education so he could become a dockworker."

"A very well-paid dockworker. I also write poetry."

"Do you?"

"No. But I save lives sometimes. Usually by punching things, but still."

"There's nothing wrong with saving lives. Now go, kill that land shark. I have to call the president of the United States and tell him to shove his demands where Sol won't see them."

"Okay, Mom. Say hi to Carla for me."

Her face softened. "I will. She'll be glad to hear you're okay."

"Well, I'm off to fight a ten-thousand-ton shark with my hands. So maybe don't let her get too excited."

"Don't you dare die now, Rohan. I haven't forgiven you for leaving the first time."

"I'll do my best, Mom."

8

Third Time's the Charm

Vanguard Prime stepped through Bamf's rift onto a run-down gas station surrounded by a flat, horizon-reaching expanse of desert. The early morning sun was rapidly driving the chill out of the air.

Rohan saw the others stumble briefly as they passed thorough the doorway, even Bright Angel grunting about something as she walked out onto the asphalt. He was last, and as he followed The Damsel, he felt an awful *presence* filling the air, an almost overwhelming cocktail of anger, hunger, and an unearthly flavor of damp aversion. The desert *felt* wet and dark and oppressive despite the dry air and bright sunlight.

The Hybrid was reminded of the Power of the Tolone'an religious caste, a Power they exercised from lairs secreted hundreds of fathoms beneath the surface of their water planet.

Bright Angel pointed to The Damsel. "Can you do something about that?"

The Damsel took a deep breath to steel herself from the effects of the shark's spirit. "I'll try."

A psychic burst emanated from the older woman, followed by a cooling, gentle wave of her own Power. The team, along with the other people walking around the area, relaxed and straightened their posture, sighing as The Damsel's aura displaced the land shark's intimidating miasma.

"I can seal off this area, but I can't extend farther out."

Bright Angel's shoulders loosened. "That's still great, thanks."

A dozen or so large vans and military vehicles had parked around the gas station, spilling off the asphalt on all sides. Armed people in a variety of uniforms, military and civilian, milled about, their faces coated by an acidic mixture of sand, fear, and fatigue. Rohan was amazed that so many apparently normal humans had been able to resist the pressure of the land shark's psyche.

The team walked together through the area until Bright Angel seemed to spot someone she knew. She led them to a graying man dressed in crisply pressed army fatigues.

Rohan followed, touching his face to make sure the printed gaiter was still covering his nose and mouth. Some of the people wandering the makeshift camp had cameras out.

"General Ryan." Bright Angel's voice was authoritative, holding a hard edge that Rohan didn't remember from her younger self. Her silver, white, and blue uniform was a stark contrast to his muted camouflage.

The general turned to her, his eyes softening. "Bright Angel. Always glad to see you, though I'm not sure why you're here." He turned to the others, nodding a greeting to each, his eyes widening in surprise when he caught sight of Rohan.

"Kid Lightning!"

The Damsel patted the older man on the back, and he settled down. "We know, hon. Let's hear what the man has to say."

Bright Angel looked up at General Ryan. "We're going to help The Green kill the land shark."

The general grunted. "Not beating around the bush, are you?"

Her eyes narrowed. "Do you think I should be?"

The general shook his head. "We're supposed to be keeping the area clear and stopping anyone from making contact with either The Green or Three."

"Three?"

He shrugged. "The monster. Needed a name."

She sighed. "Does that mean you're going to try to stop us?"

He gave her a tight smile, his square, white teeth flashing in the bright sunlight. "I would, except some militia folk came around a day or so ago and started raising a ruckus. We were ordered to withdraw, so I don't have enough assets in place to even try to get in your way."

Amber cleared her throat, looking up at the general from an even steeper angle. "What militia? Like, separatist neo-Nazi types? The Proud Guys?"

He shook his head. "No, one of those supposedly secret societies that we all know about. Children of Mu, I think. Talking about how that shark monster is the Second Coming of their shark god. I don't know, it's not my job to keep track of the crazies, just to keep them out of harm's way."

She smacked her palm into her forehead. "Morons. I leave them alone for one day . . ."

Bright Angel spoke up. "Are they going to interfere with us? How much force do they have in the area?"

He shook his head. "They're not going to stop you from doing a thing. Light arms, civilian vehicles. One step above the security department of a Vegas casino. Nothing you guys can't handle without breaking a sweat. The real challenge is going to be keeping them alive, if you're inclined to try. They are not averse to getting in the way of that battle." He pointed with his thumb, and in time with the motion, a sound like a hundred simultaneous bursts of thunder cracked out of the desert and washed over the camp.

The general continued. "They've been at it for days now. It would be impressive if it weren't so damned annoying. And terrifying."

"Still fighting to a draw?"

"More or less. That shark thing gets torn up, but it heals just as fast as The Green can rip chunks out."

"Is it safe here?" She looked around the makeshift camp.

The general shrugged his thick shoulders. "I can't say for sure it's done on purpose, but The Green seems to be containing the fight to the really abandoned areas out that way. If they close on us, we're prepared to hit the road pretty quickly, but so far we haven't had to."

Bright Angel turned to Rohan. "All right, cowboy, this is your rodeo. What's the plan?"

The general looked at him. "You're The Griffin, right? I though you left the planet with Hyperion."

Rohan nodded. "I did. Came back to lend a hand."

"Wish you'd brought the big fella back with you. I met Hyperion once, he was . . . something else."

Rohan rubbed his forehead. "Well, I spent most of a decade protecting his back against the worst the galaxy could throw at him. Let's hope I picked up a few things."

He turned away from the general and looked over the team. "Damsel, I'm thinking you and Amber should stay back. Keep the Children of Mu off our backs and be ready to come rescue us if this goes really south." Damsel nodded, her face tight with the strain of maintaining her protective aura.

Amber shook her head. "I'm the fastest person here. You sure you want me on the sidelines?"

"I want you safe so if we need to get pulled out, the fastest person is still in one piece and able to do that. Okay?"

She nodded, reluctance in her eyes. "Fine."

Bright Angel looked at Rohan. "Then the three of us?"

He nodded to her. "Let's fly closer, take a look. I have a few ideas."

"Ideas? From your vast experience fighting ten-thousand-ton monsters?"

"Yeah." He locked eyes with her.

She paused. "You're serious." Her dark eyes flashed.

"Dead serious."

"You've done shit like this before? This isn't just posturing and your male ego talking? Because if it is, now's the time to come clean."

He reached up under his mask to scratch his beard.

"When have I ever lied to you? Now, let's go."

She gave a brief nod. "Let's do it."

"Kid Lightning!"

All three turned on the personal comm units tucked behind their ears and tuned to a channel managed by one of General Ryan's soldiers.

Bright Angel took off, her Power manifesting in two huge pairs of birdlike wings, each large enough to wrap around her body three times. Kid Lightning summoned a ball of raw voltage swirling with sparks, flashes of light, and miniature thunderstorms. He hopped onto it and rose into the air.

The Griffin reached inside and brought up a thread of his heritage, the curse and Power of his father's people, and used it *pull* himself up into the air.

Within moments, they had left The Damsel's sphere of influence and entered the terrible, moist cloud of Three's aura. They plowed through it, every meter a struggle of will against the intense urge to run.

Shortly, they felt an electric spark of a second aura, smelling of moss, scales, and pure battle rage, bright and powerful but far less overwhelming than the shark's.

"That's got to be The Green."

Bright Angel answered. "Assuming we can take out the land shark, Three, what's going to stop The Green from killing all of us in the aftermath?"

Rohan shook his head, not that she could see it while they flew.

"Most likely he'll be super easygoing. If he's really let loose with his Power, fully, it should be sort of satiated by now. Hyperion used to have real conversations with him, but only after knock-down, drag-out fights that lasted hours and flattened mountains."

The three heroes closed on the epic, desert battle.

The shark was easily a football-field-and-a-half long, the tip of its dorsal fin close to seventy-five meters high. Its proportions were almost exactly those of a great white shark, except for the bulky shoulder and hip structures that supported four thick, muscular legs, mottled gray and blue.

The land shark's movement belied its ridiculous size. It pounced, retreated, spun, and rolled with an agility that wouldn't be out of place in a big dog.

Up close, its aura was even more potent. It took no effort at all for any of the heroes to see its Power throb and coil through its body, reinforcing whatever bit was in most need at any moment.

The Green, just over three meters tall and weighing over a ton, had gotten his name from the bright-green color of his skin. Hairless and naked, he was built as if he'd been drawn by a twelve-year-old comic book artist with more enthusiasm than talent. There were bulging muscles all over his frame fighting each other for space, threatening to decapitate him with every hard flex.

The Green was in constant motion, jumping back and forth, occasionally catching Three with a massive punch, tearing chunks of flesh and cartilage out of the land shark, but more often than not catching a stomp from a hundred-ton leg as a reward.

Each impact between the two sent shockwaves that pushed ripples through the desert terrain like ocean waves, leaving concentric circles of disturbed sand around the mighty combatants.

Rohan was rendered speechless by the speed and ferocity of the giant fish. It moved with violent acceleration that fractured the limits of his imagination.

Bright Angel flew closer to the place where he hovered.

"See? Scary, and you know I don't scare easily."

Rohan swallowed. "I've fought worse."

"Did you win?"

"You know the rule. Don't ask questions unless you're sure you want the answer. But I'm still alive, so . . ."

She laughed, a short burst of strained, shaky sound, and patted his shoulder. "I missed your inane banter in the face of impending doom, Griffin."

He smiled grimly at her, unseen beneath his mask.

"Is there anything you can think of to hold that thing in place for . . . really any amount of time? I have an idea how to hurt it, but not if it's dancing around."

"What are you thinking?"

"Hybrid Meteor Strike."

She paused. "Really?"

He nodded. "I've gotten much better at it. But not something I want to try on anything moving like *that*."

She looked at Kid Lightning. "I flash it, you get in place and zap its leg. You can stun it for a few seconds, right?"

"Kid Lightning!" He held up his sledgehammer and shook it in the air.

Rohan nodded. "Good. Remember, The Green is not a mindless monster. More likely than not, he'll figure out what you're doing and help. I'm going to get some altitude; you guys get ready."

Rohan reached inside and *pulled* harder on the psychic thread leading into his Power.

He opened a torrent of energy that came up through the base of his spine, spiraling up and through his body, then flaring into closure when it met a matching energy circuit at the back of his skull.

Power flooded through him. The oppressive miasma of the land shark retreated to a barely noticeable sensation.

His senses sharpened, every grain of sand distinct in its crystalline uniqueness.

He could hear Bright Angel's heart; The Green's deep, grunting breaths; the sparks crackling between Kid Lightning's hands and body.

The Power carried a tidal wave of emotions that flooded his mind. Anger, outraged pride, eagerness for battle, and naked bloodlust all met and swirled a violent maelstrom in Rohan's mind.

How dare this creature invade *his* planet, threaten *his* people? Didn't it realize who he was? How could it deny him his due, deny him respect? He was an il'Drach Hybrid, most feared creature in the galaxy, and this monster would soon learn that it had picked a battle with the wrong planet. With the wrong *person*.

He shot upward, air cracking and snapping behind him as he punched a hole through the atmosphere. The land shark twitched and tilted its head to follow, eyes not designed to look up straining to find him in the sky.

The Green used the distraction to leap onto the gills along the creature's right side and tear handfuls of tissue out of the sensitive area.

The land shark roared and dropped its body on top of The Green, crushing him into the sand with its entire ten-thousand-ton weight.

It rose again, shaking, long ropes of blood and fluids dropping from its torn gills.

Rohan reached the height of a wispy thread of cloud.

Three shook its massive length. Rohan could see the tears around its gills closing again as it healed, its Power flooding the area to seal the damage.

Bright Angel's voice came over the comms. "On three."

Rohan flipped over and faced the sky.

"Kid Lightning!"

"One, two, three."

Bright Angel had positioned herself right in front of the land shark.

As her count finished, her body flared with the light of a dozen suns.

Rohan could feel the light as it burned across his back. His hair felt hot, and he could swear he saw a bright afterimage lighting up his retinas from behind.

As the flare subsided, he pivoted midair, pointed toward the ground, and let out a grunt as he *pushed* himself down at the land shark.

The gigantic creature was pinned in place, recoiling from the light flash, arcs of blue-white electricity surging up its limbs and carving a twisted roadmap of lines into its torso. The effect of Kid Lightning's assault was nearly as bright as the flare that had preceded it.

The Green attacked the other side of the beast, leaping to deliver a mighty, two-handed blow against the side of its knee joint.

The bright pulses of shark Power were now concentrating around its eyes and legs.

Rohan swallowed as he broke the sound barrier, outracing his own sonic boom.

The air singed and burned as he *forced* his way through it, feeling thick like fog, then smoke, then mist, and finally almost liquid in its resistance.

He *pushed* harder.

A fresh layer of pain woke in his arm as new skin seared with the heat of the friction he was generating.

The land shark sent up a tubular tendril of Power, enough to knock aside any mundane missile or projectile, but Rohan's own Power easily resisted the *push*. Any living creature's own Power was more potent in its influence on the creature's own body, by several orders of magnitude. Even the land shark would have to work hard to alter Rohan's path.

Rohan's Power sang through his mind. *This mindless creature is nothing before the Power of a lance primary of the il'Drach Empire.*

He *pulled* energy up through his back, fast and hard, the Power burning through his power junctions, singeing his chakras, blazing a trail through every nerve and fascial line in the Hybrid's body.

He smelled the burning of his own nostril hairs, felt the fresh skin on his right hand peel back with the wind.

The land shark dipped its nose into the ground, bringing up a wave of sand that knocked Kid Lightning off his feet. Bright Angel slammed into one of the creature's front legs, buckling its knee inwards with the impact, while The Green had peeled himself out of a crater and was attacking the creature's other front leg.

The land shark swung its massive, pointed nose, knocking Bright Angel backward, and lifted its injured leg, stamping down on The Green.

Then Rohan struck the top of its skull.

In that moment, the Hybrid poured all of his Power, every last erg and dram of glowing energy, into the back of the land shark's head.

He instantly realized several things.

Had the creature not already been exhausted by its days-long battle with The Green and distracted by Bright Angel's flash and attacks from Kid Lightning, it would have deflected most of the blow.

The bones in his forearms and arms had been fractured by the impact. If the skin and tissues around the shark's head hadn't been soft and freshly regenerated, the impact would have pulverized the rest of his body along with them, almost definitely killing him.

He was upside down, buried to his ankles in steaming shark brains, and that was on the short list of least pleasant places he'd ever been.

9

How Green He Is

The Green took a dainty sip from the five-liter pitcher of water dwarfed by his massive, green hand. He was half a meter taller than the last time Rohan had met him. Rohan figured he weighed in at a metric ton of muscle, bone, and violence.

The giant was folded into a lotus position on the ground, each foot perched on top of the opposite knee. Even seated he had to look down to meet their eyes.

Bright Angel stood across from her teammate, marveling at the most famous and most feared Power on Earth.

Waves of Power sloughed off the seated man in dense chunks, impulses that thudded out of him and across the terrain, calm and deep, heavier than any Power Rohan had felt since the time he'd sat in a room with two il'Drach grandmothers.

Rohan and Bright Angel rocked back onto their heels with every impulse, then leaned back to their original positions.

There was a loud crack of sound, followed by a long, drawn-out sizzling, as the third member of their team pounded at the dead land shark with his sledgehammer. "Kid Lightning!"

The Green swallowed the water and cleared his throat. "Your friend back there seems to be acting, well, rather like me." His voice was an inhumanly deep and rumbly bass.

Rohan nodded. "His Power acts an awful lot like crystal meth. These little rages don't last long. Usually."

"I don't know what crystal meth is, but I'll take its meaning from context. Is his vocabulary always this limited?"

Bright Angel shook her head. She waited while the next crackle of lightning and shout of "Kid Lightning!" passed.

"He really overdid it a few weeks ago, seems to have damaged the speech centers of his brain. We're hoping it heals up on its own."

The Green nodded. "Brain damage doesn't typically do that, you know. Though I admit my medical knowledge is a half century out of date. Maybe more." He rubbed a hand over his bald scalp.

"There's not much else we can do about it right now other than hope."

The Green sighed and rolled his head from side to side, releasing loud pops from his neck. "You know, this is the clearest my mind has been in almost twenty years. Since the last time Hyperion really indulged me with a weeklong fight."

Rohan nodded. He was staring at the glossy, black deposits on The Green's knuckles, elbows, and knees. They matched the tortoiseshell color of his finger and toenails, a chitinous armor covering.

"Hyperion wished he could have done more for you, more often, but those fights took a lot out of him, too."

"I can imagine." The Green took another sip, the pitcher reduced to a small cup in his colossal hand. "It was never his responsibility. I did this to myself, I'm fully aware of that."

Rohan drank some water from his own, much smaller, water bottle. A truck full of soldiers had driven out to them with medical supplies, food, and water as soon as it was clear that the land shark had stopped moving.

"Kid Lightning!" The voice was getting more and more muffled as the hero sank down into the flesh crater he was digging into the land shark's neck.

Rohan looked at The Green. "Do you want them to bring you a pair of pants, maybe?"

The Green chuckled, flashing some very sharp teeth between his dark-green lips. "Do you think they have some kind of magic, purple pants that will grow and shrink with my body as it adapts to my surroundings?

I'll probably be half a meter shorter by this time next week. I'm only this big because of that shark creature."

Bright Angel swallowed. "It's a little distracting, is all."

"Is it? But I have no external genitalia." He patted his crotch, smooth except for a discreet slit whose purpose Rohan did not want to carefully consider.

Rohan swallowed. "I'm not sure that makes it better. Though I have a friend off-world who would definitely approve."

The Green laughed again. "Would you prefer a giant, green penis dangling at your eye level when I stand up?"

"I suppose not."

"You know, I'm only lucid for, at most, a few hours at a time, and sometimes only after twenty years of savage insanity, yet when these occasions come up, the conversation always steers toward my lack of clothing."

Bright Angel shook her head, as if to clear it. "You're right, that's really not the important issue here. Can you tell us anything about the shark?"

"You're this generation's holder of the Angelium, aren't you?"

She nodded. "You know about it?"

"I did some research on the holder back in the fifties. Nineteen fifties. When I was first exploring superhuman abilities."

"My great-grandfather, I think."

The Green laughed. "I wish he could see you now."

Bright Angel shook her head. "Why?"

"Not to speak ill of the dead, but some of your ancestors had a less-than-enlightened attitude toward, well, toward people of African descent. Or really anybody not white and European."

Her brown eyes narrowed. "They were racists."

"That's putting it mildly. And your great-grandfather's ability to harness the Angelium was far inferior to yours. He had Power, but not much more than making his hands glow."

Bright Angel nodded. "I hope he's spinning in his grave. Not that I really understand why my ability to use it is so much higher."

The Green chuckled. "Everything follows rules. To be honest, I really miss being coherent enough to work on figuring out those rules."

Bright Angel paused. "I'd like to hear more about my great-grandfather, and the other people you worked with back then, but to be honest, we're short on time. Right now, we need to know what you picked up from the land shark. Anything you picked up during the fight, like what it wants, its weaknesses, where it's from."

"What it wants? It's actually very similar to me, when my Power is awakened. It wants to fight, and to kill. As far as I could tell, it was a mindless engine of destruction."

Rohan swallowed. "Nothing more specific? Is it targeted? Trying to destroy something in particular? Or just, like, teenager-angry? At the whole world?"

The Green shrugged, his trapezius and neck muscles swelling up past his ears with the motion. "If there was more than that to its psyche, I couldn't tell. As far as weaknesses go, apparently beating it half to death for three days, then dropping a missile into the back of its head, exploited its only weakness. That creature was *tough*. And that's the perspective of someone who has fought Hyperion."

A handful of drones buzzed by overhead, well out of reach. Probably capturing video for sale online or intelligence for one of the many organizations with a stake in the fight against the land sharks.

"Kid Lightning!" They heard the thud of the sledgehammer through the shark's body, giving it a deeper resonance. More sizzling sounds followed.

Bright Angel looked at Rohan. "This was a good plan, but I don't see how it will work as a long-term strategy for these things."

The Green looked down at her, his hairless brow furrowed. "Things? There are more than one?"

"That was Three. The first one was killed by a meteor strike, the second with nukes. A lot of nukes. Both times we lost millions of civilians in the aftermath, so if more of those things come, we can't just keep nuking them."

"You can. You just won't accept the consequences."

"Would you?"

He shook his enormous head. "Some consequences seem unacceptable. Until they aren't. A group of those sharks could present an extinction-level event. Losing millions to prevent that might be the lesser evil. In context."

She shrugged. "Fair enough. But I don't think we're at that point yet."

"Good. So set those options aside, but don't forget them. Now the question is, can you just get the creatures all here to fight me, and after I soften them up, you come in for the kill?"

She nodded. "That's an idea, if we're brainstorming here, but I don't know if it's feasible."

The Green looked from her to Rohan. "I don't either. But why do *you* say that?"

Rohan swallowed. "A lot of people—heroes *and* gods—died in the fighting to get the creature to this area. And once you're . . . back to your usual self, we can't just call you and have you meet us at the thing's location."

"If they're killing heroes and gods each time, pretty soon you're going to run out of both. Also, while I fought this one to a stalemate, if the next one is a little stronger or comes before I'm fully recovered . . ." The Green finished the water, tossing the pitcher to the side. "It came from the ocean, I assume?"

The two Vanguards nodded.

"I don't think I could fight it in the water, and I can't just hang out on the coast and wait for its next appearance. There wouldn't be any coast left. I think you're going to have to go to the source of these things and stop them there."

Rohan nodded. "Easier said than done, Dr. David."

The Green smiled. "Nobody calls me that anymore."

Bright Angel pinched the skin above her eyes, trying to push away her growing headache. "We don't know enough. Where they're from, what they want. It's frustrating."

The Green sighed and looked at Rohan more carefully. "Do I know you?"

Rohan nodded. "I've fought you before. Hyperion brought me. I think you broke three of my ribs and both my legs."

The Green nodded. "Ah. Sorry for not remembering, not much stays with me from the times when the Power is in control."

"Don't apologize. I'm an il'Drach Hybrid, believe me, I understand how it is to lose control. Though we don't last years in that state."

"Kid Lightning!" Another pop of frying meat. The outbursts were becoming less frequent.

Bright Angel reached up and put her hand on The Green's elbow, just above the black shell covering its tip. "How long do you have?"

The Green shrugged. "Possibly hours, no more. Maybe less. I can already feel the stirrings building back up."

"Is there anything we can get you? Do for you?"

He smiled at her. "That is kind of you, but no. Actually, I'm a little resentful that you killed the shark. That was my most enjoyable fight in a very long time."

Rohan shrugged. "Sorry, but not really sorry. We couldn't risk a second one showing up here and actually killing you."

The Green looked at him with suddenly sad eyes.

"Kill me?" Then he shrugged and started drawing circles in the sand next to him. "Maybe you could tell me what year it is. Give me a little news."

Bright Angel tossed her braids over her shoulder and started briefing The Green on what had happened on Earth over the previous twenty years.

"Kid Lightning!"

Rohan watched a military vehicle approach, kicking up a cloud of dust as it drove. He stepped away from The Green and Bright Angel to meet it.

The vehicle, an old military Jeep, had an open top and four seats. He spotted Amber and The Damsel in the front seats, two surly looking men in suits in the back.

The vehicle skidded to a stop in front of him. Amber hopped out, her skin a little flushed from the sun, brown ponytail bobbing behind her as she moved.

"Griffin, these two imbeciles were leading the Children of Mu agents in the area. The ones that were trying to help the land shark."

He looked over the two men, who were handcuffed to the car.

"Did you find out what they're thinking?"

The Damsel walked over. "Oh, hon, they can't help talking to me, you know that. They think those sharks are their Second Coming."

Amber nodded. "They think their shark gods are returning to Earth."

Rohan nodded. "Okay, this might sound crazy, sure, but . . . maybe they're right?"

The two women cast concerned glances his way.

He held up a hand. "Hear me out. Mu sank, what was it, ten thousand years ago?"

Amber shrugged. "In this timeline, that's about right."

"Sure. Let's stick to this one for now. Weren't the people of Mu allied with some kind of paranormal shark civilization? I mean, for real? Am I forgetting my deep history? Spiral explained this all to me before, but to be honest, I never fully understood any of it."

Amber sighed. "Yes. The Shark Riders of Mu were a real thing, ten thousand years ago. They got Powers from a race of highly advanced, intelligent sharks. Who, as far as we can tell, either left Earth or were wiped out when Mu sank."

Rohan nodded. "Maybe they stuck around. Deep underwater? Like in some secret base? Frozen? Or on another planet, planning a return, opening gates from one body of water to another the way Lyst does?"

Amber's face tightened. "It's possible. At least I can't prove it isn't possible."

One of the suited men in the back of the Jeep shouted. "The Shark Lords have returned! They will destroy the surface infidels, and Mu shall rise again!"

The Damsel waved a hand in his direction. "Hush, hon." The man's head fell; his eyes rolled back, and drool began to leak from the corner of his mouth.

Amber shook her head. "Anyway, that is a possibility, I guess, except we have no records of anything even close to . . . this . . . even going back ten millennia." She waved a hand at the ten-thousand-ton carcass dominating the landscape.

Rohan nodded. "So it's something new."

She nodded. "Oh my God, is that The Green? Just sitting there?"

"Yeah. Go say hello. He's a nice guy when his Power isn't driving him into a destructive, homicidal rage."

"I will. That way, if I die fighting these shark things, I can at least know I shook hands with The Green."

"Kid Lightning!"

Rohan turned to The Damsel. "What do you think?"

She smiled sweetly. "Griffin, you lost me with the timeline question. I'm just here hoping that Kid doesn't kill himself beating on that dead shark."

"I think he's losing steam. I'm actually kind of impressed how he's going at it."

"It can't be easy for him, you coming along out of nowhere and showing him up."

"You think? That's not . . . that's not what I was going for."

"Oh, hon, I know. You're just trying to help. But you should know as well as anyone how hard it can be to accept help from someone else. Especially for one of us."

"I guess. Hey, has anyone told The Director what happened here?"

Damsel nodded. "Some of the civilians at the gas station were Hyperion Industries. She knows."

"Okay." Thinking about his mother gave him a fresh pang of anxiety.

Rohan led Damsel to where The Green was sitting, pausing to brace slightly as each pulse of Power washed over them. Some drones plummeted from the sky, damaged by The Green's emanations.

". . . timequake?"

Amber was nodding a response to The Green's question. Rohan broke into the conversation.

"Anything new come up? Because I don't think that dive-bomb attack is going to keep working. I caught the land shark off guard, but to be honest, if I could rewind and try that ten times, I think I'd get pulverized in at least six of them."

The Green shook his massive head. "I'm happy to fight one if it shows up in my neighborhood, but I can't beat one alone, and I can't think of a way for you to fight them."

Rohan looked at Bright Angel, who shrugged. "Nothing."

He slid his hand under his mask and scratched his beard. "We really need Poseidon for this."

The Damsel shook her head. "We haven't seen so much as a scale of his since this whole thing started."

"Okay. Dr. David, any suggestions? Hyperion said you were one of the smartest men he'd ever met. We could sure use that right now."

The Green shook his head, a rueful smile on his broad, emerald face. "I wish I could help."

"Kid Lightning?"

The group turned in unison to face the land shark's corpse.

"Kid Lightning! Kid Lightning! Kid Lightning!!!"

The Damsel muttered under her beath. "What now?"

Rohan and Bright Angel shared a quick glance, then rose into the air in unison and streaked over to the top of the land shark's back.

The hole in the monster's back was a cone of carnage, meat and cartilage singed and torn, piled on all sides in ugly heaps.

At the bottom of the gruesome crater stood their old friend, long-time cornerstone of Vanguard Prime.

The two heroes dropped down to stand next to him.

"Kid Lightning!" He straddled two white boulders, which Rohan realized were the land shark's exposed vertebrae, each easily the size of a large truck. The long-handled sledgehammer was pointed at a spot between his feet.

"What is that, Griffin? Do you see something?"

Rohan knelt in a pool of spoiling blood and cervical fluids. With one hand, he splashed a foul-smelling liquid away from the spot Kid Lightning was pointing to.

"Yeah. There's something metal in here."

"Metal as in hardcore and kickass, or metal as in made from metal?"

"Metal as in . . . seriously? You're going to make that joke now?" He looked over at her.

Bright Angel's mask covered her mouth, but her cheeks were bunched up with a hard smile.

"I couldn't help it. You used to call everything 'metal' when you thought it was awesome."

"Well, forgive me. I was just a poor, immigrant kid from Canada who wanted to be as cool as his awesome, big-city girlfriend."

She shook her head, smile still straining at her cheekbones. "Just dig that thing out. And you weren't poor. Also, it wasn't word choice that made you not cool."

Rohan pointed at a strut of cartilage. "Kid, do me a favor and knock off that chunk. I'm going to pull this out."

"Kid Lightning."

A swing of the sledgehammer, a shower of sparks, and the knob of tissue was loose.

Rohan put his hands on both sides of the object and yanked it free in a small spurt of released fluids.

The object was octagonal, a matte-metallic slab half the size of a stop sign, still dripping the body fluids of the land shark. The sticky surface was covered in markings Rohan didn't recognize.

Bright Angel and Kid Lightning both bent to look at the object, the woman holding up a finger and casting a bright light over its surface.

She spoke first. "That's writing."

10

The Artifact

The three descended from the shark's corpse, Kid Lightning's berserker state apparently expended.

Rohan dropped the object to the ground, rubbing sand over it to clean off the grime, then picked it up and showed it around to the group.

He pointed at the marks etched into the slab of metal. "You recognize that?"

Amber, The Damsel, and Kid Lightning shook their heads. The Green looked down on them with relaxed eyes.

Damsel squinted at the etchings. "Is that supposed to mean something to us?"

Rohan shrugged. "I hope it means something to somebody."

Bright Angel poked Rohan's shoulder. "I thought you knew that meta language thing that lets you understand anybody. Or did you forget after a decade of war and concussions?"

"I can't read the Fire Language. I just speak it."

Amber stepped around Kid Lightning and ducked her head for a closer look.

"Huh." Her voice held equal parts puzzlement and disappointment.

Damsel looked at her. "What? Do you see something or were you expecting to?"

Amber shook her head. "I thought it might be from Mu, the language of the shark civilizations. They had a lot of languages, but they all shared the core of their writing. This isn't from that family. But it looks familiar. I just can't place it."

Rohan looked around. The other shook their heads as they made eye contact.

Rohan snapped his fingers. "You think your Children of Mu guys over there would recognize it?"

Amber shrugged. "Can't hurt to ask."

They crossed the desert sand to the idle Jeep. Amber slapped one of the dozing cultists.

The man, thickly built with dark, curly hair, light-brown skin, and features that looked like a Pacific Islander, snapped awake.

"Yes, Oracle!"

Amber pointed to the object. "Do you recognize this writing?"

The man squinted. "Yes, Oracle. I am sorry, I cannot read it. You should slay me for my incompetence. I do not deserve to live in your shining presence."

"Don't tempt me. You can't read it, but you *do* recognize it. How?"

"Those are Atlantean hieroglyphics, Oracle. At least, that is what they look like."

Amber snapped her fingers.

"That's it!" She turned to Rohan. "It's Atlantean, he's right. I've seen this writing on their old records, inscribed on the armor they wear, all of that."

They left the bound man in the Jeep and rejoined their fellow Vanguard members and The Green.

"Anybody here read Atlantean?"

Headshakes all around answered him.

Rohan sighed. "And nobody knows where Poseidon is?"

Shrugs all around.

Bright Angel pointed at the metal slab. "There must be someone in Sahara City who can read that. At least translate it with whatever resources they have. I know they have a lot of esoteric information on file."

"Perfect."

The Damsel stepped back. "What if it's a bomb? Or some kind of contagion? What if it starts a zombie apocalypse?"

Rohan paused. "I doubt it's going to start a zombie apocalypse."

"Someone says that at the start of *every* zombie apocalypse. I watch movies."

Amber held her phone up to the object. "We can send it directly to a saferoom in Sahara City. Something buried deep underground."

Rohan nodded. "That sounds great. Let's get some linguists working on that writing while we're at it."

Bright Angel shook her head. "We don't have time for that. We should take it to Masamune."

Everyone fell silent.

The Green looked over the heroes. "Masamune is still alive? He was already an old man when I met him. Before I became . . . this."

Bright Angel nodded. "He's a thousand years old, at least. He made Ares's spear in the sixteenth century, and Ares said that Masamune was ancient when he did that."

"We thought those stories were exaggerations."

She shrugged. "You thought that when . . . you're talking the fifties, right? I don't think Masamune was too eager to work with Americans so soon after World War II. He probably wanted to keep a low profile."

The Green nodded. "I understand the desire for anonymity. The Army was tossing around this crazy idea to have him build an indestructible shield that could be used by whoever made it out of my super soldier program."

Rohan put the Atlantean artifact on the ground. "I bet they wanted the shield in red, white, and blue with a big star in the middle."

The Green laughed. "Pretty much."

"Well, maybe Masamune can help us figure out what this thing is. And maybe he can come up with some weapon we can use against the land sharks. Either way, we owe him a visit."

Bright Angel cleared her throat. "It's not easy to visit Masamune. He never liked company. Now, after building the nukes we used to take out Two, he's pretty depressed. Does not like the legacy of 'killer of millions.'"

Rohan shook his head.

"Under any other circumstances I'd leave the guy alone. Now?" He pointed a thumb over his shoulder, toward the ten-kiloton shark carcass. "I'm a lot less concerned about his feelings and a lot more concerned about the next one of those."

· · · · ● · ● · · · ·

"Are you okay, Griffin?" Bright Angel was looking at the raw skin on his right hand.

Rohan stretched back in the butter-soft leather chair. "I spent ten years being called nothing but Griffin, then a year getting reaccustomed to my actual name. Now hearing 'Griffin' again is weird."

"Do you want me to use your real name?" Bright Angel's mask was down around her neck, as was Rohan's. There was no real risk that anybody would be taking illicit pictures of them in the bowels of The Director's building in Sahara City.

Rohan thought it over. "I wish you could. But no, better not get in the habit. I don't want my identity to slip while we're in public."

"I think The Director can take care of herself. If people figure out your relationship, it's not like they're suddenly going to be going after a regular schoolteacher or whatever, someone without protection."

He shook his head. "It's not just that. I mean, a lot of it is. I don't want my old Earth enemies going after my mom, even though she does have security. But I have enemies off-world who might show up with a similar idea. Hybrids. Groups of Hybrids."

"Why exactly are groups of Hybrids pissed off enough to come after your mom on a planet that's not even on il'Drach star charts?"

Rohan paused. "It's kind of a long story. Can we just say I still have a knack for annoying people and leave it at that?"

"That is not surprising. You think I should be worried?"

Rohan shook his head. "I doubt it. Logically, I don't really think she should worry, either. It's just, you know. She's my mom."

"You know what, I get it. Say no more. No precautions are too much when it comes to family."

"Yeah. How are your folks doing?"

She smiled. "The same, just older. Still in Baltimore, still kicking. I can't see them much, you know how it is. But I can make sure they're taken care of, financially at least, so that's a good thing."

"Yeah." He sighed and rubbed his eyes, scratched his beard.

"I like the beard. You look grown."

He smiled. "You look pretty good yourself. I like the braids."

She touched her hair wound tightly to her skull. "I was shaving it for a while. I'm trying this out."

"The uniform is nice, too. Not as skimpy as the old one, but you fill it out well."

"Are you calling me fat? Are you looking to be on the receiving end of everything I've learned about using the Angelium in the last decade?"

He held up his hands in surrender. "I meant it as a compliment. It just reminds me of how young we were, back in New York, a bunch of skinny Powered kids fighting crime out of Kid Lightning's basement in Staten Island."

"I'm pretty sure it was his mother's basement."

"I don't think that really changes the point I was trying to make."

She laughed.

"No, I guess it doesn't." She stood and stretched, muscles rippling along her shoulders and back, visible through the thin fabric of her uniform. "Let's get out of here, catch up. I need some air. There's nothing for us to do, anyway. Neither of us are going to be any help finding Masamune's Hidden Fortress or translating those hieroglyphs. You can tell me stories about space princesses and galactic adventuring."

Rohan shrugged. "Sounds good. What did you have in mind?"

"You remember that cliff in Shenandoah?"

He smiled. "I do. I miss that spot. Let's go."

Bamf opened a doorway to the other side of the world, letting them out in a tiny, Virginia town that held nothing of interest to either hero.

Ten kilometers away, however, was Shenandoah National Park, and a cliff face that was very difficult to access on foot.

"When did you find this place, again?" Rohan asked as they flew up over the lush, green valley.

"Kid Lightning told me about it. He and The Damsel came here when they dated."

"They dated? How come I don't remember that?"

They approached and landed on a slab of naked rock that jutted out from between tufts of green trees and loose shale.

Rohan waited for Bright Angel to settle on a spot, then floated to a position next to her.

"I don't think it lasted long. She knew the park from coming here as a kid. At some point, she realized he could fly to this spot. Said she'd always wanted to come here, but you can't really make it on foot."

Rohan leaned back on his hands, wincing as pain sparked through his body. Then he settled back onto his elbows and took in the view of the valley far beneath their feet.

Bright Angel noticed the movement. "I know I asked already, but are you sure you're all right?"

He gave a slight shake of his head. "I think I broke most of the bones in my arms with that Hybrid Meteor Strike."

"Oh. Anybody else, I'd say we have to get to a hospital. It hurts?"

"I can reinforce the bones with Power, but, you know, then I relax and forget and put weight on it. I'll heal."

"When? Not to be cruel, but another land shark could pop up at any moment. When are you going to be at one hundred percent?"

"Two or three days, at most. Assuming I don't take more damage in the meantime. We heal fast. Hybrids."

She nodded.

Rohan continued. "To be honest, a second or two either way and I wouldn't have killed that thing. If it had been the slightest bit less distracted or hadn't thought it could deflect me, it would have reinforced that spot, and I would have been smeared across its back like an egg dropped onto the sidewalk."

Bright Angel looked out over the valley. "So we know this isn't a long-term solution. We knew that already. We'll figure something else out for the next one."

"I guess we will. You know, you got tougher, over this last decade."

She shrugged. "Didn't really have a choice."

They sat in silence for a few minutes, taking in the sun as it slowly settled toward the horizon.

Rohan smiled. "Someone asked me, not too long ago, about the best part of having Powers. I told her it was being able to get to all the places. Like this. I mean, I didn't say this, specifically, but you know."

Bright Angel jabbed his shoulder with her elbow. "Oh, 'someone' asked you? Who was this 'someone'?" She was smiling.

He smiled back. "She's a shuttle tech on Wistful. I met her totally by accident. She's smart and pretty and sweet. Then she wore these dresses . . . just like a sari, you know? And I had no idea how hard that would hit me, then I saw her in one, and it just broke me down."

She laughed. "Desi clothes? That's your thing? I had no idea. I could have done a sari, you know. Back then."

"*You* had no idea? Angel, *I* had no idea. That's the funny part. Maybe it was homesickness. This all happened, like, six months ago."

"You guys still together?"

He shook his head. "Didn't work out. We only dated for, I don't know, less than two weeks? But I really liked her."

She nodded. More silence.

"How was it, going to war for the il'Drach?"

He sighed and breathed in deep, focusing on the smell of trees and grass. This area was, for the time being, completely untouched by the land shark incursion.

"First it was terrifying. Then I adapted. Then I got really good at it. There's this . . . there's a mindset you have to have. Like, you strip away part of yourself, become more functional, less human. You're just a tool to get the job done, even if it's horrifying. You get to a point where torturing some innocent people to get information you need is no more emotional than piloting a ship to another star system. Just tasks."

"Sounds very ends-justify-the-means-y."

"Yes, that's it. Exactly."

"Doesn't actually sound like you. That was never your jam."

"I know. The Fathers . . . the il'Drach . . . they have a way of putting you into situations where 'the ends' is your survival. Principles usually take a back seat when the alternative is death. After a while, you get so used to doing what you have to do just to survive that you forget to check your moral compass."

"That doesn't sound great."

"It's not. The funny thing is, I got really good at finding those means. Turns out I have a talent for it. I'm more creative than the other Hybrids. They tend to be very straightforward thinkers. You know, if it's in your way, punch it. If it doesn't fall down, punch it harder. In a real bind? Maybe kick it."

"That sounds a little bit like you."

"Twenty-year-old me, maybe. But I got more creative over the years. Like I said, I ended up being really good at coming up with horrible, effective solutions to difficult problems. Irony, right? I found something I was really good at, for the first time, but being good at it required me to become a pretty awful person."

"I'm sure you weren't awful."

He smiled at her. "That's kind. Not true, but kind. Thanks."

"But you quit? Is that what I heard? Someone, Amber I think, said something."

"I quit. I was working on a space station when she found me. I'm a tow chief, second class. I tow big ships to and from the station."

"You went from war hero to . . . tugboat?"

"It was nice. The work is harder than it sounds, but it's not, you know, morally challenging. You either tow the ship safely to port or you don't. You never have to wonder if it's the right thing to do."

"I get it."

They sat, listening to the trees behind them rustle in the breeze.

Rohan ran his hand over the smooth, rounded stone.

He looked at her, concave line of her nose backlit by the blue sky, rounded forehead, strong jawline. Her skin, just a few shades darker than his own, drank in the sun. She was every bit as beautiful as he remembered. More.

"Everyone was giving you extra condolences about Ares. There a story there?"

She sighed and shook her head. "We were involved. Friends with benefits, on again and off again."

"Really? Ares? Wasn't he kind of an . . ."

"Watch it, he died fighting for this planet."

"Yeah, but . . . did I misjudge him?"

She looked at him and half smiled. "He was kind of a jerk, to be honest. But those abs . . ."

"I have to admit, he was built like a Greek—"

"Don't say it!"

They laughed together, softly.

Rohan cleared his throat. "Well, I'm sorry. I mean, I'm sorry he's dead. He was never my favorite person—"

"God."

"Sorry, favorite god, but he wasn't all bad either."

"No."

"You date anybody else? I mean, anything serious?"

She shrugged. "Griffin, it's been ten years. More. I missed you, when you left. But I didn't think you'd come back, not after what happened with Brother Steel, and I was okay with that. In some ways I thought it was for the best. And yes, I got over it. Over you. I'm a big girl. Don't sit around thinking I've been pining after you for the last decade."

"That wasn't what I . . . Not what I meant. Sorry. I'm just asking."

"Okay. I don't want to revisit my romantic or sexual history in great detail with you right now, all right? There's no point."

"No, of course not. Look, forget I asked. Really, I'm sorry."

She sighed. "I know. I'm on edge. It's been an epically shitty few weeks."

"I can imagine. Or maybe I can't, but I can try."

"You know what? I'm actually glad you're here. Maybe you can help us out of this, which would be great, but it is nice to see you again, see that you're okay."

They sat and took in the view; a broad, green valley spread out beneath their feet, a handful of small lakes and towns breaking up the scenery.

Rohan stretched, enjoying the warmth of the afternoon sun on his skin. "Tell me something about your life. I mean, something trivial. Like, Vanguard Prime is a big deal, right? Do you have your own action figure? Comic book line?"

She smiled. "I'm pretty sure there's a porn parody of the whole team."

He laughed. "Who did they pick to play The Damsel? Or did she volunteer for the part?"

Bright Angel shook her head, still smiling. "I actually think she watched it and was kind of pissed her actress wasn't younger."

Rohan laughed again. "What about regular movies? They make a film about you guys?"

She shook her head. "There were talks about a film series covering the Vampire Wars, but it never amounted to anything. I got a seven-figure advance for my character rights, though."

"Vampire Wars?"

"It's just what it sounds like."

"Well, I don't know. What kind of vampires? Paranormal romance novel vampires or horror-action movie vampires?"

She laughed. "Unfortunately, more of the latter than the former."

"Too bad. Any of our old enemies keep you busy?"

"The Proud Guys got an upgrade."

"What? Who gave those idiots more power?"

"I forget, were you around when Professor Z showed up?"

"The Nazi scientist?"

"Yeah. The guy who got frozen after Germany surrendered. He was allied with American neo-Nazi groups for a while, did a ton of experiments. One of them worked, and the Proud Guys are . . . well, they're still the same, just tougher."

"That sounds like a step backward for the world."

"If they weren't so dumb, they'd be a real threat. As it stands, they're classified as low-level domestic terrorists."

"Maybe I'll pay them a visit before I go back to Wistful."

She sighed. "Feel free. Then Sister Steel popped up for a while, teaming up with one group or another. She eventually fell off the radar."

"Sister Steel." His voice was flat. He didn't want to think about Brother or Sister Steel any more than he had to.

"Yeah. She was angry. For a long time."

Rohan sighed. "I can't say I blame her."

11

Tokyo Epsilon

B right Angel looked sideways at him. "You know, when you attacked the shark, when you were up in the air, for a moment, I could *feel* the old you. The part of the old you that I never liked. All the anger, the rage, all bursting out of you."

He nodded. "Yeah."

"But then you hit it, and the fight was over. And I have to admit, I was kind of braced for what was going to happen afterward. Like, I was waiting for you to still be full of the anger, to be . . . I don't know. To be cruel? To be a jerk to somebody? Or worse, to be in a berserker rage and start fighting everybody."

Rohan sighed. "I can't blame you."

"Wait, I'm not criticizing you. I'm saying, I was braced for it, but then you shrugged it away, hopped out of that thing's skull, wiped off a bunch of gunk, and were joking around as if nothing had happened."

Rohan shrugged. "The fight was over."

"I get that. But before, with you, the fight was *never* just over."

He paused, not sure how to explain himself. "The thing is . . . I don't know. I've *felt* your Power. I can feel the emotions that come with it. It's not angry, it's not inherently, I don't know, violent? It's not violent. But the Hybrid thing . . . the il'Drach thing . . . it's angry. It feels alive, like it wants to hurt things, to hurt and to dominate."

"So you feel that way all the time?"

He shook his head, his hair bouncing with the motion. It was getting close to the time when he'd have to choose between a ponytail and a haircut.

"Not exactly. Maybe a tiny bit. You get some of the Power without getting all the feelings. But the more of it you want to draw, the faster you want it to come, the more of the feelings leak through."

"Like a rider."

"I guess. Maybe."

"So . . . what changed?"

"I don't know. Growing up? Practice? Lots of meditation? The Power is like a bull. You can learn to ride the bull, you can't give up and let the bull ride you. When I left, I'd been bull riding for five years, most of it with no guidance whatsoever, and all while struggling to handle regular human hormones and teenage emotions. Now I've had fifteen years of practice. I can let go of the anger when I don't need it anymore. Well, usually."

She nodded. "I guess in my mind you might have grown a beard or looked older, but I didn't think that you might have matured."

"Surprise!"

She laughed as a song erupted from her phone. She answered it quickly. "Tell me."

Rohan leaned forward to look down the cliff face. It was very sheer, adding an impressive feeling of depth to the view.

"Where did you say? Tokyo Epsilon? Right now?" A pause while she listened. "I'm on my way."

She ended the call and looked up at Rohan.

Her eyes were grim. "Time to go."

"What's up?"

"I have to take care of something."

"What's Tokyo Epsilon?"

She paused and focused on his face. "You can help if you want. It's a Japanese refugee camp. They've been having disappearances. At first it looked like bad accounting, just losing track of people who had gone back home or whatever, but then we heard some stories about pale-skinned creatures attacking civilians. Nobody really believed that either until some of our people found a freshly dug mass grave."

"I assume you have a theory."

She shrugged. "Pale-skinned. The bodies all had telltale neck wounds and seemed a little . . . dry."

"I guess the Vampire Wars aren't quite over."

"Looks that way. I don't know, though, it feels *off* somehow. The vampires we fought weren't inclined to mass killings. Too noticeable. Also, the stories mentioned tentacles, and no vampire clan I'm aware of manifests that way. You in?"

"I'm in."

"I'll call Bamf for a portal."

Moments later, a hole opened up in the air in front of them. The heroes pulled up their masks and stepped through from midday sun into the dark of night.

The other end of the portal was in an empty, cordoned-off field, big enough to land two or three transport helicopters at a time. Large administration tents and portable cabins surrounded it, barely visible in the dim light cast by the stars and a handful of portable lanterns.

The smell struck Rohan immediately: waste and vomit and rotting food, like the portable toilets after a heavy metal concert.

A few people were standing at the waist-high, wooden sawhorses that sectioned off the landing area, watching. Two were smoking cigarettes. All were thin, starved into frailty.

Bright Angel hadn't unfurled her wings, not wanting to advertise their presence. Rohan looked at her.

"Why is it called Epsilon?"

"Just a designation. There are a lot of camps. Most of the survivors from Tokyo are spread out through places like this. The city infrastructure is wrecked, and disease was starting to spread."

"Oh. Wow. I mean, that's crazy."

"Yeah. If it were just Tokyo, we'd have managed better, but with similar situations all around the Pacific, resources are stretched really thin."

"Sure. What's the plan? Are we going to try talking to the vamps?"

She shook her head. "These creatures are feral. No point trying to have a polite conversation. They've killed hundreds, maybe thousands, of these refugees. I've fought vampires; the sane ones won't do that."

"So we go in killing."

"Yeah. I assume you're okay with that?"

"Just asking. You're in charge here. Now, how do we find them?"

"*We're* going to find them by *you* being quiet and letting me concentrate. If they're feeding anywhere near us, I should be able to sense them."

Rohan nodded and watched as she sat on the grass, legs folding into a lotus, and closed her eyes.

He cracked his neck and scratched his beard under the gaiter that covered his mouth and nose. He let out a breath, holding his lungs empty, and silently repeated his mantra, willing his Power to subside, relaxing his aura from its usual fierce projection to a more muted hum.

A moment later, Bright Angel stood, four wings of pure light and Power snapping open out of her back.

Her eyes glowed white when she looked at Rohan.

"South."

Air cracked as her wings beat in a quick counter-rhythm, lifting her off the ground.

Rohan took a sharp breath and lifted off to follow.

Bright Angel cut a straight line toward the southern side of the camp. As they flew, Rohan began to take in just how large the camp was, tents lined up for over a kilometer in every direction.

Bright Angel was easy to follow, the glow of her wings the brightest thing around by thousands of lumens.

She slowed in midair and let Rohan catch up.

"There."

She pointed to a close set of tents. Now that they were close and he knew what he was looking for, Rohan could *feel* the metaphysical energies at play.

Without a word, Bright Angel drifted to the ground while Rohan arced farther south, ready to come back and catch the feeders in a pincer movement. It was a maneuver they'd practiced endlessly as teenagers.

As he descended, Rohan started to make out more and more Powers on the ground, their auras twisted and stained, a chaotic jumble of notes.

He landed between two green canvas tents, knees flexing to absorb the impact. He took a single step and grabbed the nearest tent, tearing it off the ground and flinging the covering away.

The creature inside had a humanoid body, pale, clammy flesh shining damply where light struck it. Its jaws distended like a snake's, long incisors fully exposed and dripping viscous red and lime-green liquids.

From its back extended four long tentacles, gray-white like its face, each twice as long as the humanoid body at its center.

The creature stood up from a body and hissed at Rohan.

The Hybrid took in the bodies, large and small, that lay strewn about the floor of the dwelling, then looked at the vampire and snarled.

Bright Angel's voice rang out over the quiet camp. "They're here!"

The creature dropped the body on which it had been feeding and stepped toward the Hybrid. Its tentacles snaked up and around his back.

He smelled blood and saltwater.

The hero moved forward, letting the tentacles pull him in, and launched a blistering combination of punches that splintered its sharp incisors into a dozen pieces and crushed its larynx.

The vampire dropped to the ground, tentacles spasming wildly. Rohan was knocked back half a dozen meters by one connection as the creature lay dying.

"Rudra save me, these things are strong!"

"I'll bet you dinner at Keen's I can kill more than you."

The dying vampire cried out, a wail of anger and fear. A dozen, then two dozen, then more voices arose in response, screeches of indignant rage filling the camp.

"How big did you say this mass grave was?"

Bright Angel's voice was tight. "Does that mean you forfeit?"

Tents were torn away, revealing intimate scenes of domestic suffering. Bodies were strewn about, frail and wasted, many showing signs of old injuries in addition to the fresh tears and rents created by the monsters.

The two nearest vampires closed quickly on Rohan.

They moved in a strange gallop; lower tentacles punched into the ground, vaulting them forward. They landed on both legs, springing forward into the next tentacle-driven leap.

Rohan surprised the first creature by moving forward to meet it in the air, leaping and cracking his knee into its abdomen.

The blow stunned the vampire, which dropped to the ground. Rohan followed it down, ready to finish it off, when the second struck him with a broad swing of its two upper tentacles.

The hero was knocked back into another tent, its flimsy structure crumpling with the impact. He caught himself on his hands and sprang back to his feet.

"They're smart enough to use teamwork?"

Bright Angel answered as she separated another vampire's head from its body. "Not so much smart. Cunning, maybe."

He covered up, forearms in front of his head, as the vampire struck at him with fists, slashes of the sharp talons at the end of each finger, and stinging tentacle strikes. He leaked Power into his arms to hold the bones together, wincing as each strike aggravated the fractures and raised welts on his still-healing skin.

He ducked, letting a salvo of slashes sail over his head, and flipped forward, kicking his legs up and over his back to snap into the creature's head. It crumpled to the ground.

He turned as a fresh trio of creatures came for him.

"Griffin! I'm coming to cover you."

He smiled as he stepped into the next creature's path, cracking his elbow into its face and shattering its teeth and jaws.

She's going to rescue me?

Bright Angel landed on one vampire and sliced another in half with her wings. A third wrapped her legs in its tentacles while a fourth leapt from behind a nearby tent and tried to grab her back.

Bright Angel's wings shredded the monster behind her. She slapped her palms into the chest of another one and did . . . something.

The creature exploded in a spray of meat and bone shards.

She looked at Rohan, the shower of gore falling all around her.

"In case we weren't sure, definitely vampires."

He nodded and ducked forcefully, breaking a vampire's hold on him, and slipped out to its back. He kicked into the back of its leg, destroying the knee.

As it fell, he torqued his right elbow through an upward arc that intercepted the back of its head.

The crunch told him that one was finished.

He *lifted* off the ground, halted by the pull of another pair of tentacles wrapping around his legs.

Two of the vampires leapt into the air, tentacles lifting them high, and launched powerful kicks that knocked Bright Angel backward, her wings of light beating erratically to keep her aloft.

The pair wasn't going to be able to fight them all.

Rohan shouted. "There are too many! We need a new plan!"

"Working on it!"

The Hybrid drove forward, dragging his vampire along, and plowed into the group surrounding his teammate. He spun at the point of impact, swinging the vampire that held him like a mace, scattering a dozen others ten meters in each direction.

Momentarily free, the two heroes rose into the air and headed north, both dripping gore.

Bright Angel spun to face the horde.

"If we get them all together, I can kill them with a solar flash. But I only have enough juice to do it once. We need to draw them to a central location!"

"Where?"

She pointed. "Head for the landing field!"

They took off toward the north.

The woman turned in midair to survey the monsters.

"Ugh. They're not all following. Maybe half. We can't let the rest just leave and keep feeding."

Rohan drew a fresh line of Power and focused it on his eyes. The starlight was enough for him to catch glimpses of moving forms as individual vampires spread farther into the camp, even while a larger group continued to approach the heroes.

"What should we do?"

"I don't know. They don't usually group like this."

"Call for help?"

"There's no time. They'll scatter before backup can come."

Rohan nodded and reversed course. "I have an idea."

"Griffin, we can't go toe to toe with all of them."

"I know how to draw them off."

She paused, wiping her hand over a wet patch on her arm, flicking the blood off to the side. "Okay. I'll cover you."

She followed as he took a path back into the middle of the devastated section of the camp.

He picked up speed as he charged the monsters. They saw him coming, and one of the larger creatures planted its feet in the ground, drove all four tentacles deep into the earth behind it, and braced to meet him with teeth and claws.

Rohan crossed his arms, placing each palm on the opposite shoulder, and lifted his elbows so they would make first contact. He struck the monster like a missile, driving it three meters back as all six of its support limbs kicked up mounds of dirt and grass.

The impact drove the creature's claws deep enough into his arms to draw blood.

Rohan leapt back, breaking clear of the monster. The vampires around it all scrambled forward to get at him, tearing at the ground and at each other in their frenzy.

The vampire who had cut Rohan tilted its head back and howled.

A dozen meters away, a vampire stood up from the body it had been draining and turned toward Rohan.

The next tent over opened, and another one stepped out, sniffing at the air as it emerged.

All around them, the vampires were coming out and moving toward the heroes.

Bright Angel looked at Rohan. "What did you do?"

He winked at her. "I'm irresistible."

He *lifted* straight up into the air, his hands cupped around the tears in his flesh. When he was about five meters up, out of reach, he poured a choppy stream of his Power into the fluid gathered in his hands.

He flung open both hands, launching his own blood in a spray of droplets so fine they came out as a thin mist that spread out over the area.

The Hybrid focused, keeping his energy in the fluid, *pushing* it farther and wider than it would have traveled on its own. Within seconds, the entire section of the camp was splattered in a thin and barely noticeable film of Rohan's blood.

"Go! Back to the clearing!"

Bright Angel didn't question. She spun, her wings snapping at the air, propelling her to the north.

Rohan twisted and followed her. He could hear barks and grunts and labored breathing from the frenzied vampires as they tore across the camp to chase him.

He dropped to the ground and ran after Bright Angel, letting his cut continue to leak, vaporizing each drop to create a trail of blood-mist.

"This is kind of disgusting. These people are all going to wake up in tents covered in a thin film of your body fluids."

"Better than never waking up at all."

Tentacles grabbed at his back, sliding across his skin as they sought purchase on his body. He leaned forward and ran faster, spreading pulses of Power into his knees and ankles.

"How much farther?" He knew he could fly higher and escape, but that wouldn't do the refugees any good.

"Just over that ridge."

Moments later, Rohan crashed through the wooden barricade and entered the landing field. He headed right for the center, where Bright Angel was hovering, her wings dim, her eyes gently lit like twin full moons in her head.

The tentacled vampires streamed through the opening behind him, their soft growls and pants like a pack of dogs.

Rohan reached the center of the landing area and turned to face the monsters. He could *feel* Bright Angel gathering her Power above him.

Keep them coming.

"Come to daddy! How's that for a catchphrase, eh? You like that? How about, come to papa? Is that better? Do any of you even speak English? Oh wait, that was Drachna."

The mob closed on him.

He stood with feet planted, angled so his left shoulder was forward, right hand up by his jaw, left fist across his belly, elbows close to his body. His gaiter was pulled over his nose, eagle's beak print facing forward. His knees were bent, weight on the ball of each foot.

The wave of vampires, reduced to a singular mass of flesh and fangs, struck.

Claws and tentacles grabbed and reached for Rohan from the front, then from the sides, and then from behind him as the creatures swarmed.

Rohan fought back, thrusting kicks straight into bodies, twisting heavy elbows into heads or faces, and finally grabbing at arms and appendages and swinging the monsters away with powerful turns of his body.

The beasts scrambled back to the fray, open mouths reaching for any exposed flesh they could see, pulling and tearing at one another in their hunger.

"Hurry, maybe?" he called out to Bright Angel.

One trapped his left leg and closed on his thigh with gaping maw. Three others fought over control of his right arm.

Rohan leaned down and smacked his head into one of the monsters, crushing its face but embedding one of the fangs in his forehead.

Blood leaked down his forehead and toward his eyes.

He twisted his arm, trying to free it, but the monsters readjusted and kept it in their grasp.

Bright Angel's voice carried over his comm, a breathy whisper. "Close your eyes."

He reached up pressed his left arm over his eyes.

The flare was so bright, he could clearly see the thin, curved shadows cast by his radius and ulna, a deep-red glow around and between them as the light penetrated the flesh of his arm and eyelids.

He heard short grunts of pain.

Loud, grinding pops.

Gelatinous splashes.

It was over as suddenly as it had begun. Rohan lowered his arm and looked around the field.

Unidentifiable fluids and chunks of decomposing flesh covered the grass.

Bright Angel floated down to a spot next to him.

"The area is clear."

He looked at her. "That was some flare."

"That was some trick with the blood. How did you know that would work?"

"Some of the Wedge were blood drinkers. They loved Hybrid blood. We could set traps with it, lure them this way or that; they'd always go for it. I thought it might work on these guys, too, and after seeing the way the first guy who cut me reacted, I was pretty sure."

"Well, nice trick. Though it was kind of gruesome. And you're hurt again."

"I'll be okay."

"I know. Still. We should head back, get you some rest."

"Great."

"And you should probably talk to your mom."

He grunted. "Yeah. Thanks for warning me about that little surprise."

She laughed and held out a hand. "I would apologize, but I'm not really sorry. Your face when she walked into the briefing room was precious."

He took the hand and let her haul him to his feet.

"I'm glad my suffering amused you. Now please call Bamf for us before I fall over."

12

The Answer is Always Tequila

Rohan sat in a leather chair, trapped by its depth and softness. He held his arms up and *focused* energy into them, trying to achieve the mental state that would enhance the healing process in the fractured bones.

Spiral had spent months trying to teach him the trick. Trying, but mostly failing.

The room was near the main conference room but significantly smaller and furnished for more intimate breakout sessions. The walls showed a wide array of video feeds from all over the world. Rings of matching chairs surrounded an array of small, low tables littered with half-finished plates of food and nearly empty glasses.

The lighting was dim. Several of the video feeds had soft audio accompaniment, leading to a muted, white-noise-like buzz that was dangerously close to carrying him to sleep.

The main door opened, and The Director walked in. She was wearing a white-and-green sari, her only jewelry a set of hanging earrings, a tall glass bottle cradled in one arm, a small bag in the other.

"Rohan."

He looked up, quickly standing as he saw who had entered. "Director." He looked around the room. There had been other people there, earlier.

"We're alone. I have people to make sure I know where everybody is in this building, especially down on this level." She smiled softly, very fine crow's feet showing at the corners of her large, dark eyes.

Rohan stood awkwardly, not quite sure what to do with his hands. "I was trying to get them to heal faster. Kind of lost track of everything else."

She nodded. "Sit. I'm not here to disturb you. I just . . . here." She held out the bottle, not to hand it over, but so he could see it. She set it on the table.

He sat, but stayed perched on the edge of his seat, leaning forward. She sat in the chair across from him. "What is it?"

"It's nothing, really. You'd been gone for maybe a year, and I thought we should have something for you when you got back. So I bought this. It's supposed to be the best sipping tequila in the world. Then a year passed, I bought another bottle. I now have a small closet full of the finest tequila in the world, and you know me, I can't stand the stuff. But you're back, and, well."

Rohan nodded. "Thanks. That's . . . that's really sweet. I'd love some."

She set the bottle on the table and the bag next to it. She took two glasses out of the bag. With a deft motion, she unwrapped the bottle and popped the top.

Rohan inhaled deeply, enjoying the fragrant aroma of the aged liquor. "I do miss this stuff. We have good liquor on Wistful, but it's not the same."

She poured a thin layer into one glass, then a more generous amount into the second. She handed over the second glass.

He took it and stuck his nose in, inhaling more deeply.

"I should probably say something about notes of oak and honeysuckle or something, but honestly it just smells like amazing tequila."

She raised her glass. "If you say so."

He touched his glass to hers, then took a sip. "Wow, that is really good."

"I'm glad you like it."

He leaned back into the chair, letting the subtle burn of the liquor work its way down his chest.

"Did you get the samosas I told them to send over?"

He nodded. "Thank you. They were delicious."

She nodded back and took a small sip of her drink. "This actually isn't bad. Not my thing, but not bad."

He smiled. "Do you know I got super drunk with Dr. Benjamin Stone? With a bunch of talking bears who were sitting Shiva after escaping an Inquisition on the other side of the galaxy?"

She gave her head a soft shake. "I couldn't tell when you were joking, even when you were young."

"That's the best part, every word of that was completely true."

"You're friends with the Stones?"

"Well, friends with Ben, and I know Marion, but . . . you know. She doesn't like me and isn't too good at hiding it. We met up six months ago. Ben's actually fun. They'd be here now, but . . . I explained this already, didn't I?"

"You did."

"Sorry."

"No, it's fine." She took another sip, then put the glass down on the table. "I'll let you get back to what you were doing."

"What? No, Mom . . . stay. If you can. For a bit, maybe?"

She looked at him. "I have a little time. There's a lot of work to do."

"I can only imagine. You've done a great job, you know, fixing the planet."

She laughed, a short, loud snap of sound. "Is that what you think I've been doing?"

"Come on, yes! Global warming? All the clean water and power infrastructure you've built? Dad would be proud." As soon as the words left his mouth, he regretted them.

"Your father? All he cared about was that I had a functional uterus and wasn't smart enough to see past his flattery and lies."

"Mom, that's . . . that's not entirely fair."

Her eyes flashed angrily. "You want to tell me how it isn't?"

"Well, it's mostly fair. But Dad . . . he at least felt something for you. I heard him talk about you, a few times. He always sounded so proud. I'm not sure I'd say that about the il'Drach Fathers in general, but he really cared about you."

"Is that supposed to make me feel better?"

"Um, I don't know. Yes? I'm not saying you should forgive him or anything, just . . . I don't know. Isn't that better than thinking he saw you as just a human incubator?"

She was sitting up straight, perched on the edge of the low-slung chair. "Maybe."

"Well, good then."

"Was that it? What you wanted to tell me?" She was clearly annoyed at having to think about Rohan's father.

This is all wrong.

He took another sip of tequila and sat up straighter in his chair. "Mom, I really am sorry. About not coming back."

She looked at him, her expression flat, her eyes even. "I'm not ready to hear that at the moment. But I'm glad you're here. We could use your help. But right now I have a meeting with the leaders of a team bringing a third wave of temporary housing structures to Thailand, so let me get back to that."

"Sure, Mom. Thanks. And thanks for the tequila."

She nodded, stood, and left the room, trailing a swirl of luxurious fabric.

· · · • · • · · · ·

"I have never seen you work so hard just to eat." Bright Angel elbowed Rohan as she spoke, pointing at his plate with the tip of her fork.

He nodded, brow furrowed as he pinched a wad of spiced potatoes inside a torn piece of flatbread, then popped the whole thing into his mouth. He leaned back and sighed as the spices hit his tongue.

Bright Angel shook her head and bit into a cake of fried lentils.

Rohan finished swallowing and looked at her. "I'm trying, but it's hard to eat with all the damage my hands have taken."

She waved her fork in the air. "I know. Did you want me to feed you?"

He looked at her with wide eyes. "Would you?"

She let a small grin flash over her face, gone as soon as it was born. "Absolutely not. But I was wondering what you would say."

He shook his head. "Teasing me. So unfair."

She reached over and rubbed her hand over the top of his head, ruffling his hair.

They were in the large conference room, along with the rest of Vanguard Prime and a few officials of Hyperion Industries. The room bustled with waitstaff and attendants.

Rohan focused and let a trickle of Power into his hand, reinforcing the bones, and very carefully lifted a ceramic teacup to his lips.

It would have taken him less effort to punch a hole in the wall; delicacy was not what he'd been trained for.

The Damsel smiled at them from across the table. "I see you two are right back to your old tricks."

Bright Angel shook her head. "Don't read too much into it. We need him in one piece to finish off the next land shark that comes along. Which could be in just a couple of days."

Rohan looked at her. "You think?"

She shrugged. "Do the math. It was four weeks between the first two. Two weeks between Two and Three, so Four should come . . . the day after tomorrow."

"Kid Lightning!"

The Damsel patted his arm. "We know you're ready, hon, but we're going to need a better plan than 'keep hitting it with an electric hammer until it gives up.' Especially if sharks start showing up every couple of days. Or hours."

Bright Angel nodded. "No argument there."

Rohan swallowed another mouthful of food. "Anybody know where Amber is? I haven't seen her."

"Kid Lightning."

The Damsel nodded. "She left yesterday. Had some work to take care of. Something with the Children of Mu."

The main doors swung open on silent hinges, and a pair of dark-suited executives filed into the room. One man and one woman, both with very short hair and distinctly Sudanese features.

The man took a position standing at the head of the table while the woman stood to his right.

"Gentleman, ladies." His English had a thick local accent, a blend of influences from languages around the eastern side of Africa and the western side of India, a strong undercurrent of British pronunciation tying them together. "The Director cannot be here, but she has asked us to brief you despite her absence."

Rohan looked at Bright Angel, who whispered, "They're from the Information Office."

Rohan raised his eyebrows. "Spies?"

"More like analysts."

The female executive had a small tablet. As she tapped its surface, the screens all around the room went dark.

The male executive continued, undaunted by the heroes chattering like schoolchildren. He pointed at the members of Vanguard Prime. "This statement was released by your White House late last night. They seem very agitated." He turned to the side and nodded, and the woman tapped at her tablet.

Rohan looked at the man. "It's not 'my' White House? I'm Canadian, don't blame me."

"Regardless, please watch."

The speaker was a woman, blonde, in a red pantsuit and standing behind a podium with some kind of fancy seal attached to the front. A text crawl below her said she was the press secretary.

"I repeat, yesterday's actions can only be viewed as an invasion by an alien force. The United States military, of which I am so proud, you know, had the situation well in hand. Above that, the creature had neutralized the much greater threat of The Green, who has terrorized this country for decades. This alien . . ."—she waved a hand at a monitor behind her, which showed a pretty good image of The Griffin as he headed out to do battle with the land shark—"entered United States territory without permission, violating the sanctity of our borders, and conducted an illegal operation on our precious, God-given soil."

Rohan felt his heart sink a bit at the words. "Hold on. I own a big chunk of Hyperion Industries, right? Are they going to go after the company? Or Vanguard?"

The man smiled, revealing the kind of perfect white teeth that spoke of expensive dentistry and a small hint of vanity. "We can handle the United States government."

The Damsel looked at Rohan. "You haven't been here, but this president has been after The Director and the company for years. Hates the fact that she built Sahara City in Africa. Part of his campaign was to force her to expand US operations. Which, naturally, was not possible."

Rohan nodded.

The executive cleared his throat and continued. "Polling shows support for Vanguard's action at below forty percent for supporters of the current administration but above sixty percent for their opponents. So, public opinion so far is falling in line with partisan US politics."

He waved his hand again, and a new video started playing, mostly graphs and charts.

"On a separate note, we have updated statistics on casualties and damages relating to the land shark attacks. Totals, then broken down by attack, and separating direct damage from the collateral impact of nuclear weapons and meteor strike."

"Kid Lightning." His voice was sad.

The room stayed very quiet as they read the display.

Bright Angel shook her head. "How are those numbers going up every time we see them?"

The executive responded. "We are only counting confirmed reports. If you want best-guess estimates of actual total casualties, we can provide them. Don't ask if you want to be able to sleep tonight. Also, the losses at the refugee camps are higher than expected, for reasons that are still under investigation."

Rohan swallowed. "Am I counting those zeros right? There's a lot of them."

Bright Angel shook her head. "Not the time for jokes."

"I didn't . . . yeah. Sorry."

Once everybody's attention was off the displays and back on him, the man motioned for another video change.

"There is now extensive footage of all of you at the site, from many different sources." The screen showed a few seconds of drone footage of the team, then another clip from a different angle, then from a handheld camera at the gas station site. "We have not caught any images of you unmasked or any other security violations. Except this."

He pointed, and a new image came up.

It was grainy and pixelated, obviously blown up from a small part of a much larger picture. Rohan tilted his head to one side, then the other, before figuring out the orientation.

The picture had been taken from directly above the team, and in the center was the artifact they'd pulled out of the land shark's spine.

The man adjusted the collar of his white shirt. "With skilled enhancement, the image could be clarified sufficiently to allow someone to read the hieroglyphs."

Bright Angel interrupted. "Has anybody actually done that?"

He shook his head. "Not as far as we know. However, both the Sons of Atlantis and Children of Mu probably will."

Rohan looked around. "Is that a bad thing? Like, why do we care?"

Bright Angel shook her head. "It's just going to stir things up."

Rohan sighed and pinched the skin between his eyebrows. "Can you tell us some good news?"

The executive shook his head. "Not today. I do have one more thing you ought to see." He nodded at the woman, who tapped again. "This has been posted online. It has a small but growing audience."

A woman's voice came over the room's speakers.

"Eleven years ago, the alien criminal known as The Griffin escaped justice by leaving Earth, conveniently abandoning this planet before he could be made to pay for his crimes."

The video was dark and pixelated. A figure sat in a chair in a dimly lit, nondescript room that could have been anywhere on the planet. Her face was hidden in shadow, but Rohan recognized the voice.

"He committed crimes against many people, not just my brother. He left maimed and murdered victims behind. I gave up hope that we would ever see justice done for any of them."

She leaned forward, her shiny, chrome skin polished to a mirrorlike finish.

"Now The Griffin has returned. Now, finally, in this most terrible of times, with the planet in peril, we have a chance to at least, with all that's happening, at least make this one thing right.

"We demand that this criminal, the alien being known as The Griffin, be arrested and brought to trial for the murder of the Powered individual known as Brother Steel.

"If you doubt his guilt, know that we will be releasing more video evidence of his crimes tomorrow.

"I'm not making a threat. I am not a terrorist. I'm not saying that The Griffin should be arrested and put on trial *or else*. I am only saying that he needs to be brought to trial now, while we have a chance. It is the only *human* thing we can do."

The woman sat back, her face disappearing into the shadows, and the video ended.

Rohan opened his mouth, then closed it again. "Is it me or did she get much better at public speaking?" He felt a flare of anger building behind his eyes.

Bright Angel nodded. "She's been practicing that pitch, more or less, for the last eleven years."

"I didn't kill Brother Steel." He looked around the room. Nobody responded. "Does anybody take her seriously? Is that video getting hits?"

The woman executive cleared her throat. "Several million." Nobody else would meet his eyes.

He stood, sending his chair crashing to the floor with the motion, and planted his hands on the table. His Power crept up his back, licking at the base of his skull. "Are you guys kidding me? I didn't even want to be here. I was perfectly happy on Wistful, living my life. I come back here because you're desperate, humanity is in danger, fine, I'll drop everything and come back, no problem. And you're all thinking about Brother Steel?"

Bright Angel shook her head. "Rohan . . ."

"What? You want me to turn myself in? Go to prison? How long is that prison going to last, with the land sharks running around? Over what, a fight that happened more than ten years ago? With a serial bank robber?"

A soothing pulse of energy washed over the room. Rohan looked at The Damsel, who was radiating a pale-green aura that was close to putting the normal humans in the room to sleep.

She looked at him and spoke in a soft voice. "Please calm down, Griffin. We're all worked up, all upset. Nobody's asking you to go to prison."

He shrugged off the effects. "Are you sure? Because that's really the vibe I was getting just now."

"Settle down, hon, maybe we didn't handle that perfectly. Maybe we don't know how to handle it. It's complicated, you're too smart a man to say it's not."

"Oh, I'm a man now? Because Sister Steel keeps reminding everyone I'm not really a man, right? Just an alien."

The big double doors swung open.

Rohan, and everyone else in the room, turned to face it.

Amber strode through the doorway, her cheeks tight, eyes grim.

Her black-and-gray suit was torn in several places, and most of her exposed skin was smeared with still-damp slicks of blood. There were small scratches on her face, wet with flecks of white crust near her jaw. Her hair had been pulled back into a ponytail, but several strands were free, wet and clinging to her skull.

She walked briskly to the big conference table, surveyed the quiet room, and spoke.

"I found Poseidon."

13

Even Gods Need a Hand Sometimes

R ohan stood with his feet planted wide, bracing against the rolling motion of the ship, a pair of matte-black binoculars held up to his face.

"What am I looking for again?"

Amber stepped to his side and squinted. She had changed into a fresh, untorn uniform. The scratches on her face had healed, and she had cleaned the blood and salt off her body. "You can't see it from here, we're just over the horizon. But look north."

"I thought the island was west—Oh."

Rohan turned and saw Bright Angel flying to them, her wings of light outstretched, beating in a mesmerizing, rhythmic counterpoint. She held The Damsel in her arms like a child, the older woman's flaming-red hair streaming behind her in the stiff wind.

Rohan and Amber moved, leaving a generous bare patch of deck. Bright Angel landed with a thud, setting the boat to rocking as she lowered The Damsel to her own shaky feet.

The Damsel shook herself off, fingers futilely attempting to brush her hair back into shape. "Desperate times, I suppose."

Bright Angel relaxed as her metaphysical wings retracted into her body. "Are we waiting for Kid Lightning? Or anybody else?"

Amber answered. "He's in Sahara City. The Director wanted someone on hand to help protect the artifact. At least until we can figure out what it does."

"Fair enough. We found Poseidon's villa right where you said it would be. Typical Poseidon stuff, all the signs of a months-long, drunken orgy ended by a sudden burst of violence."

Rohan swallowed. "Violence as in kidnapping-violence or murder-violence?"

"I get the feeling the authorities there will ignore almost anything that happens in those villas but dead bodies. Which makes kidnapping a solid guess. You said you think you know where he is?"

Rohan pointed off toward the east. "There's a doozy of a force field around a tiny island over the horizon that way. Amber says it's a known Sons of Atlantis base, and I can't imagine why they'd have the force field up if they weren't trying to hide a god in it."

The Damsel, her cheeks still flush and red from the wind, looked intently at Rohan's face, then at Amber's. "Can somebody please explain to me why the Sons of Atlantis kidnapped Poseidon? Now of all times?"

Rohan turned to Amber. "All yours."

She nodded, her ponytail bobbing with the motion of the ship, her face tight with tension and fatigue. "We have the Children of Mu and the Sons of Atlantis. Everyone thinks of them as insane, secret-society nutjobs, which is basically accurate, but in some ways they are more than that.

"Mu and Atlantis were early human civilizations. Both were advanced, maybe not by today's standards, but more than most people realize. Atlantis was somewhere around here; Mu in the Pacific. Big islands, maybe even continents. And those two civilizations hated each other. A lot. Enough that they managed to destroy each other in a cataclysmic war."

The Damsel nodded. "Mutually assured destruction, right? Like nukes in the eighties. Except they did it."

"Exactly. The leaders of both groups are descendants of the survivors of those battles.

"We don't know everything about either society, but we do know that Mu's totem was the shark. We can see that in all their rituals and artifacts. They even rode sharks in to battle."

Rohan chuckled. "The Shark Riders of Mu. Pulp fiction titles strike again."

"Yeah. Except I think it was more than that. They didn't just ride the sharks, they worshipped them. Or more."

"More? What, sex with sharks?"

"What? No, not sex. What is wrong with you?"

"Sorry. I'm in a weird place."

"Well, get out of it. Not sex. Spiral and I think that the sharks helped build the Mu civilization. Brought them writing, technology, taught them magic."

The Damsel held up a hand to interrupt. "I've seen sharks. There's a huge tank of sharks in the National Aquarium. I'm pretty sure they don't have hands. How were sharks teaching anybody how to write?"

Amber nodded. "Not *now*. Remember, this was ten thousand years ago. Longer. There were things alive then that are long gone, or long hidden."

Bright Angel shook her head. "You're saying that there really was an intelligent civilization of Powered sharks that, what, that taught early humans how to make fire and wage war?"

"Exactly. Something like that. Is it really that strange? We know there was intelligent life on this planet long before humans evolved. Look at Lyst."

Rohan rubbed his hands through his hair, feeling crunchy salt crystals against his skin. "Speaking of Lyst. Have you mentioned this hypothesis to her?"

She smiled at him. "I have."

"And she . . ."

"She didn't deny it."

The four stood in silence for a moment.

Rohan grunted. "That would explain why the Children of Mu were so happy to have the land sharks around. And why they had agents try to stop us from killing Three. They saw the sharks as natural allies. At least until Kid Lightning found the Atlantean object inside it."

"Right. They're a mess right now, because it looks like the sharks are just tools of their ancient enemies and not, you know, here to restore Mu to power."

"Of course." Rohan scratched his beard.

Amber continued. "For the past two months, I think the Sons of Atlantis have been trying to get rid of the land sharks. And the first person they'd need to help them do that is Poseidon."

The Damsel shook her head. "You think they just . . . kidnapped him? Is that really the best way to get someone's help?"

"Come on, you know Poseidon. When has he ever just *willingly* helped anybody?"

"Hm. Good point."

"If you really needed him to do something, something important, how would *you* go about it?"

Rohan nodded. "I would kidnap the guy and cut off fingers until he did what I needed."

Amber turned and pointed east. "Which is probably what's going on right now in that rock."

Bright Angel stepped to the deck railing and looked at the horizon. "Let's hope that when we rescue him, he still has a finger left to point us in the right direction. How did you find him? Find this place?"

"The Children of Mu usually answer to me."

Bright Angel nodded. "Right. Because they think you're their mystical leader. Oracle."

"You all know that story. Anyway, they have agents all over the world, people in every news organization and intelligence service who will pass along any information they have, all hoping to restore the glory of Mu."

". . . And?"

"And I guess they knew about this base, and about Poseidon. But they didn't really want me getting to him, because they thought I'd recruit him to help fight the land sharks. Because while they do believe I'm their savior, they know I care about civilian casualties more than I do about the glory of Mu."

The Damsel nodded. "They're not wrong, hon."

"Yes. And they figured Poseidon wouldn't cooperate with the Sons of Atlantis, so they left him alone and conveniently forgot to let me know where he was."

"Oh."

"Right. Until now, knowing that the land sharks aren't actually on their side, they sort of abandoned that plan. At least, enough of them abandoned it that some decided to call me."

Rohan looked at her. "You're okay with the fact that they kept secrets like that from you?"

She unsheathed a trench knife and had it held in front of her, shining in the sunlight, before he could blink. "Not exactly 'okay.' I made that point clear."

Rohan swallowed. "You've grown up."

"Is that a criticism?" Her cheeks were pink from the sea wind.

He laughed.

"No, the opposite. Careful knifework can be very educational."

The Damsel cleared her throat. "What are we going to do now? About Poseidon?"

Bright Angel held her hands up, curved as if she were holding a basketball in front of her chest.

"I saw the island from the air. Just a big rock, really. Then I *looked*, and that force field is no joke."

Amber stretched her arms overhead. "You can imagine how many schemes they've had to try to raise Atlantis in the last ten thousand years. Most often they fail completely, but sometimes they bring up a big rock from the ocean floor. That's one of them, about five hundred years old. It's riddled with caves, and on the far side there's an inlet you can drive a small boat into."

Bright Angel nodded. "The top has a couple of flat spots big enough to land a helicopter. I saw a handful of people on it."

Rohan shook his head. "That shell—force field—are we sure it's solid? Or is it just a screen so we can't sense whatever is inside?"

"It's solid."

"Who the hell do they have on their side that can cast a force field that big? I know I couldn't do it. I'm not sure even Hyperion could have done it, not if he had to hold it for hours or days."

Amber looked at him. "They have a few serious Powers on their side, but their real trick is gathering cabals of minor Powers and getting them to work in unison."

"So a group is working together to run the force field?"

"Yeah. Most likely there's a big chamber down inside that rock, filled with incense smoke and people in heavy robes, all chanting in unison. It's even more pulp fiction than shark riders."

"Maybe this is where the pulp writers got their idea from."

She shrugged. "That's actually plausible. Not relevant to the situation at hand, but plausible."

Bright Angel held her hand up. "Do we know more about the force field. It's solid, sure. What about air? Liquids?"

Amber rubbed her forehead. "I've dealt with these before. The field lets through light and liquids and gases, but not solids, and it blocks any attempt to bend space inside it. We can't teleport in, and unless someone here can change state, we pretty much have to crack it open."

Rohan thought. "'Crack it open' meaning just hit it hard enough that they can't keep it together anymore."

"Right."

"And it's gas permeable. Do we have a way to muster up a tornado? A hurricane maybe? Lash them with wind?"

Amber shrugged. "That would get those guys on the surface, but the wind it would take to crack the solid rock of that island . . . I don't know. And I can't think of any really strong wind manipulators who are available."

"What about that guy, from the Midwest somewhere, Human Tornado?"

The Damsel answered in a soft voice. "Dead."

"Crimson Breath?"

"Missing. Presumed dead."

Rohan pivoted to face the Sons of Atlantis base and thought some more. "Hit them with a big wave? Flood the facility?"

"It's not a bad idea, but how? You know a water manipulator who could pull that off? Maybe Poseidon, but . . ."

Rohan snapped his fingers. "I have an idea. Meteor Strike!"

Bright Angel groaned. "That's your solution to every problem. Are your arms recovered enough for that?"

He shook his head. "Not even close. I was thinking of the old-fashioned kind. It's an island, right? It's stationary. Drop a big rock onto it."

The others looked at him.

"A very big rock."

Amber cleared her throat. "Won't they just deflect it?"

"Maybe. Then we drop another one. If their sorcerers are dying just to maintain that force field, making them *reach* out and deflect the big rocks should just wear them out faster. I bet after a few strikes, they'll drop the field and come out to fight us. Plus, even if it's deflected, I have an idea."

The women looked between each other. The Damsel turned to face Rohan. "This is your thing, right, hon? I know I'm not dropping any rocks on anybody. Or Bright Angel?"

Rohan looked at his ex. "Let me do this part. I'm good at lifting heavy things, and even better at dropping them. I want you guys to be ready when that shield drops; get Bamf to send you in and grab Poseidon."

Bright Angel nodded. "Sounds good."

Rohan briefly wondered if he had time to call *Void's Shadow* down to the surface. Knowing her, she'd be swimming Jupiter's gas oceans. He left the thought alone.

Rohan pulled his face shield out from its pocket in his uniform hood and tapped at it. The lower half became opaque: first black, then after some fiddling, displaying an eagle's beak.

Bright Angel looked over his shoulder. "That your space helmet?"

"Yeah. Single-facet diamond faceplate, and you see this rubbery seal around the edges?" She nodded. "Contains an air supply and everything you have in a cell phone times a hundred. Got my tunes, radio, even low-power tachyon radar."

"I'm just going to nod like that means something to me."

"Most importantly, airtight in case I have to go in the water. I need to breathe."

"I forget sometimes. You're heading out now?"

He nodded. "Let me go dig up a boulder. I'll be back as soon as I can. Make sure the ship stays clear and keep an eye on that island. As soon as the force field drops, you'll know what to do."

"Got it."

He looked around. "We ready?"

Nods answered him.

"All right, then. I have my comm on if anybody has anything to say."

He pulled his face shield on, waiting a moment for the rim to seal to his face and the internal air supply to engage. Then he turned and *hopped* up into the air, boosting himself from there up and away from the ship.

"Personal."

The helmet, armed with a subroutine birthed by the space station, answered with Wistful's voice. "Yes, Rohan."

"Get me a channel to that island right behind me. Find something they're using to communicate. Cell phone, radio, whatever. Let me know when you have it, I want to talk to them."

"Yes, Tow Chief."

He made a straight line through the air for a nearby island that was sure to have loose boulders he could pick up.

"Put up graphics to show me how far it is."

Lines popped up in his display, projected onto the inside of his mask.

He reached down into his spine and *pulled* forth a thicker current of Power, driving himself harder. His hair whipped at his neck and the rim of his mask; the edges of his sleeves snapped at his wrists; the air swirled around him in savage gusts.

Soon he arrived at a nearly empty bit of coastline, rocky cliffs dotted with trees and patches of sand. He surveyed the area, quickly finding a boulder that looked close to his tolerance.

"Tow Chief, I have identified a signal you can use to communicate with the island base."

"Great. What is it? Radio? Cell phone?"

"It is a phone. I can manufacture a call into the phone using the identifier of the last call it received."

"Perfect. Do it."

"One moment."

Rohan rocked the boulder back and forth, freeing it from the dirt where it was buried. It was twice as tall as the Hybrid and many times as wide.

Rohan heard a ringing sound through his helmet's comm system.

"Mom? I told you not to call me, we're busy."

"This isn't your mother. This is The Griffin. We just hacked into your phone."

"Oh. Oh, damn."

"Before you hang up, why don't you ask someone in charge if maybe they'd like to talk to me? Before it's too late?"

"What do you mean 'too late'? Too late for who? Wait, The Griffin? I've heard of you. I thought you were off in space."

"You should watch the news. I'm back."

"What do you want with us, Griffin? I mean, um . . . I'm just a regular guy. Why are you calling me?"

Rohan sighed and turned the boulder over, looking for a good handhold. "Look, I know you're in a secret island base belonging to the Sons of Atlantis in the Mediterranean Sea."

"Um, um . . . Oh, sorry. I don't speak English. No hablo ingles."

Rohan switched to the Fire Speech. "Can you understand me now?"

That made the agent pause. "Yeah. I guess I can."

"Great, great. Now look, we both know you're not in charge down there. Why don't you walk over to someone who is and hand them your phone?"

"In charge of what?"

"What's your name?"

"Tom . . . Michael. Call me Michael."

"Sure, Michael, sure. Here's the thing, Michael, that you have to focus on right now. So far, you really haven't done anything wrong, have you?"

"I haven't?"

"Of course not. Sure, you picked up your phone, but you thought it was your mother, didn't you?"

"I did. Yeah, I did."

"Nobody can blame you for that. And you didn't tell me you were answering your phone from a secret island base in the Mediterranean, I already knew that, right?"

"I . . . I guess so."

"And you certainly didn't mention that you and your friends are holding my good pal Poseidon captive in there, did you?"

"No, I didn't."

Rohan tipped the boulder up onto its side, scooted underneath it, braced himself, and lifted it up off the ground.

"See, nothing to blame you for, am I right?"

"I suppose."

"But now you're in a special situation. You ever see a hostage movie, Michael?"

"I guess."

"You know what the hostage takers always do? They answer the phone. Don't they? You know, when the negotiator calls, they pick up, they talk. Do you know why?"

"Not really. I guess the movie would be really short if they didn't."

"It's so they can negotiate."

"But we don't want to negotiate with you."

"Well, now you've gone and done it."

"Done what?"

"You've gone and done something wrong, haven't you?"

"I have? What do you mean?"

"You've made a decision that's above your pay grade, haven't you? How do you know the bosses in there *don't* want to hear me out? You have no idea what I have to offer them. Offer you all. *You* didn't even know I was back on Earth."

Rohan gave a soft grunt as he pushed the boulder straight up into the sky. He quickly passed a layer of low-hanging clouds.

"I guess."

"Sure. You can still fix this, you know. Bring the phone to someone who is in a position to make decisions. Like I said, I already know you guys are in there. If that person doesn't want to hear what I have to say, let *them* hang up the phone. You can just say you weren't sure. How about it?"

"Oh. Okay. I guess that makes sense."

Over the call, Rohan heard some fumbling sounds, then some running, a few incoherent shouts, and a muffled conversation in a thick Eastern-European accent.

The boulder was growing hot to the touch, and Rohan could feel a light itch across the back of his neck as the air pressure dropped. He scanned the sea below, looking for the island base of the Sons of Atlantis.

"Hello?"

"Oh, great. Yeah, this is The Griffin. I was hoping you've heard of me, we could skip the introductions and explanations."

"I have. What do you want?"

"Great, very direct. I want Poseidon released, unharmed, into my custody. You see, he owes me money, and I want it back before the planet is wiped out."

14

Respecting One's Elders

A moment of silence before the voice on the other end of the line answered.

"I am afraid that is impossible. Poseidon has already been harmed."

Rohan sighed. "Well, I'm in a generous mood, so I'm willing to settle for no *further* harm, how does that sound?" He lined up a trajectory that would bring the boulder down on top of the island.

"You are asking for something. It is customary in a negotiation to offer something in return."

"How about this: if you don't hand him over, I'm going to crack that force field like an eggshell and take him out myself. Just think of all the redecorating you'll have to do."

"I do not believe you can break through the force field."

"Sure, I understand, you don't *think* I can. But you aren't really sure, are you? Because I've been gone for a decade, working with Hyperion. You don't know how much stronger I've gotten."

"I am willing to take that risk."

"I bet you are. But why? You want the land sharks destroyed, we want the land sharks destroyed. We're practically allies, as distasteful as that is to both of us. You've had Poseidon down there for weeks, and it's gotten you nowhere. Let us have a try."

"You are almost right."

Rohan felt a small sinking feeling at the tone of the man's words. "Why almost?"

"We did initially want the land sharks stopped. But based on something we've recently seen, we are now of the opinion that perhaps the land sharks should be allowed to accomplish their goals."

With a grunt, Rohan *pulled* a heavy stream of Power up through his tailbone, around his spine, and into the back of his head. The anger came pouring into his psyche along with it.

He slapped the boulder, flipping it over, and began pushing it down, adding his strength to the weight of the stone, propelling them through the thickening atmosphere and toward the island.

The Sons of Atlantis leader kept talking. "Or perhaps you didn't think we'd recognize our own writing on the device you pulled from that creature in America? You thought we were still under the delusion that these sharks are our enemy?"

The air split in front of the boulder, cracked and shattered by its passing, releasing a deafening boom that washed over Rohan as he pushed with escalating force.

"Or did you think we would not notice the very large rock you have directed toward our base? Did you not think we would have the capacity to deflect such a missile?"

A whip of Power emerged from the island base and slapped at the boulder, nearly dislodging Rohan from his position completely.

With another grunt, Rohan reacquired his grip on the boulder and pushed his shoulder into it, steering the mass back on course toward the island.

Rohan couldn't see anything but the back of the boulder, but Wistful's subroutine was projecting an image of the island's position on the inside of his mask. Another push, and the rock was headed directly toward the island again.

"Did you think it would be that easy? Silly American."

"I wish people would stop saying that. I'm Canadian."

Another finger of Power emerged from the island, this one slapping the boulder down toward the sea while giving it some spin, greatly increasing its downward velocity but further altering its path. Rohan pushed against the force, but with the boulder twisting and tumbling in the air, he couldn't get a firm-enough purchase on its center of mass to drive it into the force field.

With another thunder-like crack of sound, the boulder struck the surface of the Mediterranean right where the surf lapped up at the rocky edge of the tiny artificial island.

A crater opened up in the water below, the kinetic energy of the boulder's impact displacing a cruise ship's volume of water. Steam poured up out of the space, water vaporized instantly by the heat of the rock, spilling out in all directions.

Rohan held his lungs empty for a moment, calming his temper.

"Here's the thing about force fields. If you make them airtight, then you run out of air. Make them proof against liquids, and you're wasting energy blocking every wave that hits the island. So you do the smart thing and design a force field that's permeable to both gases and liquids. Surely that's good enough, right?

"Until you get hit by something maybe you weren't expecting. Like, for example, a small tsunami. Or a cloud of superheated steam."

There were shouts and screams over the phone.

Rohan floated upward gently, keeping his Third Eye open and focused on the force field.

"Sometimes I feel like they never take me seriously."

His comm's subroutine answered. "What was that, Tow Chief?"

"Never mind, talking to myself." He cleared his throat and spoke louder, hoping to be heard over the cell phone connection. "Had enough? Or shall I try again? I can do this all day. In fact, I'd kind of enjoy it."

The anger his Power had brought along was still simmering in the lower parts of his consciousness.

There was no response.

Rohan was about to head back to shore to grab another boulder when the force field popped like a soap bubble.

The moment the field dissipated, a view into the base opened up to Rohan's Third Eye, psychic energies suddenly laid bare where they had been obscured.

There was a deep, blue-green well of energy, heavy but dim, low down inside the island, buried under tons of stone.

Another set of energy sources were pooled in a different part of the base. Trickles of Power twisted and swirled up from their origins in threads and fibers that wound together into a fat, single-headed strand, which pulsed and throbbed as it rose up out of the rock.

The third energy source was less expected. Yellow-gold and bright, it belonged to a figure that was flying up off the island and moving toward Rohan.

He had olive skin and hair that settled in heavy ringlets on broad, muscular shoulders. He wore a simple, white tunic and sandals, with a plain, leather circlet tied above his brows.

His hook nose dominated a set of rugged features, a face that could have been chiseled out of hard stone.

"You are The Griffin? Of Hyperion's race?" The voice boomed through the air, still heavy with steam and mist. The words had an accent Rohan could not place.

Rohan nodded. He tapped at his helmet to turn on the external loudspeaker. "And you are . . ."

"You may call me Eldest. Of the Sons of Atlantis."

"I'm going to guess you're not here because you've decided to peacefully hand over Poseidon."

"That is correct." The man let out an arrogant bang of a laugh. "I am here to teach you the error of your ways."

"I should warn you I'm a very slow learner." He relaxed his efforts to suppress his Power, and it flared back into life, surging eagerly to meet the challenge presented by this newcomer.

"I am the eldest son of the eldest son of the Prime of Atlantis, a lineage of warriors I can trace over seven hundred generations. Prepare yourself."

Eldest flew forward; Rohan answered with his own charge.

The two clashed in midair, first their forearms colliding, then slamming through until their shoulders struck with a peal like thunder.

The Son of Atlantis flailed backward from the impact, arms twirling as he regained his orientation, coming to a stop a few meters from the rocky surface of the island.

Rohan floated and watched. He had a feeling there was more to Eldest than he'd felt with that collision.

"Well struck, young Hybrid!" Eldest paused. "You are worthy of observing my true Power."

"Don't do that on my account. I'm happy to thrash you while you use just a fraction of it."

Eldest took in a deep breath, and as he exhaled, his golden-yellow Power leaked out of his skin, through his pores and out with his breath. The metaphysical energies gathered and coalesced into softly geometric shapes, rectangles and hemispheres and cones. They marched around Eldest's thickly muscled body, following the contours of his flesh.

Within seconds, Eldest was surrounded by a suit of armor only visible to Rohan's Third Eye, a garment of semi-solid Power, similar to the force field that had been protecting the island but fully articulated and tenfold more complex.

Rohan murmured. "Spiral fought you. I know this story."

"You know someone who fought me and lived? That number is small but precious. You should treasure that friend."

"I like him a lot. Not sure I'd use the word 'treasure' exactly."

A long, sharp spike protruded from the top of the metaphysical helmet, a golden unicorn horn of pure razor-sharp force. Two shorter spikes protruded from the gauntlet pieces and—even shorter but slightly curved and vicious in appearance—from the knees.

Eldest took a breath and accelerated directly toward Rohan's position.

The Hybrid drifted backward, barely moving through the humid air, angled so his right shoulder was pointing away from Eldest. His right fist was by his left cheek, palm facing outwards, his left forearm across his belly.

As Eldest was about close enough to spear the Hybrid through center mass, Rohan snapped backward, using a burst of Power to pivot around his waist. His upper body spun backward, away from the horn, and his knee came up into Eldest's metaphysically armored head.

The impact of the knee strike was enough to distort Eldest's armor, forcing the spiritual geometry to flex and bend far enough for the blow to land on his bearded jaw.

Eldest flew back in a swirl of dark hair and flailing limbs, momentarily stunned by the impact.

Rohan put more distance between them, eyeing his opponent wearily. Normally he'd close on his opponent and try to finish the fight. But his job was to stall, not win. The longer the battle, the better the chance that Bright Angel and Amber would be able to rescue Poseidon.

Eldest shook his head as if to clear it; thick, dark hair dancing with the motion.

"I never had the pleasure of fighting Hyperion, during his time on Earth. I understand he was a superb warrior."

Rohan shook his head. "You should be glad. Hyperion would have wiped the floor with you. I'm barely half the man he . . . is. Well, half the Hybrid. You know what I mean."

Eldest nodded. "Perhaps you sell yourself short. Regardless, I am not more proud than I am intelligent, so hopefully you will forgive me for enlisting some aid in this battle."

He snapped his fingers.

The thick tendril of Power that had been dangling in midair, its source in the cabal of sorcerers congregating deep within the rocky base, stopped its restless motion and snapped to attention.

After a moment's hesitation, it rushed forward, tip driving toward Eldest's back.

It struck his upper back directly between the shoulder blades, landing like a plug inserting into an electrical socket.

With a spasm that shook his entire body, Eldest absorbed the fresh rush of Power. The golden armor surrounding him intensified and solidified, becoming so bright and thick that Rohan thought it might be visible to mundane eyes.

"This will cost the lives of some devout followers of Atlantis, but if that is the price we must pay to restore Her glory, then they are both willing and righteous sacrifices."

Rohan shook his head. "You think you're something special? Fighting for a ten-thousand-year-dead island culture? There are people like you all over the galaxy, all dedicated to restoring the former glory of some long-dead group or civilization. Some have been fighting for millions of years.

"I've spent a good part of the last ten years killing those dreams, Eldest. I was hoping to be out of that business, but if you make me kill yours as well, I will."

"The destiny of Atlantis rising is already written in the tides of time. You cannot stop it, though you may try. Have at me."

Eldest darted forward again, driven by the new rush of sorcerer-supplied Power. A thin halo of fire sprang to life around him as the atmosphere superheated from his friction.

The surprised Hybrid barely managed to twist in the air and turn what should have been a puncture through the middle of his chest into a deep cut through the muscles of his shoulder.

Eldest's momentum carried him past Rohan, who threw a kick after the human but missed wildly.

Rohan *pushed* a trickle of Power into his arm to press together the edges of the puncture wound, shaking his arm lightly to test the movement in his shoulder.

"That hurt. I think you should stop before I get serious."

The human laughed. "Ha! Your talent for blusterous banter is admirable! Sadly, it will not be enough to save you. I have the wisdom of seven hundred generations of combat to aid me. You cannot stand before my might, not when reinforced by the cabal."

A chime sounded in the Hybrid's ear, carried by his comm system. It was the signal indicating that Amber, Bright Angel, and The Damsel had used Bamf to teleport directly into the Sons of Atlantis base.

Rohan growled softly and pulled a heavier current of energy through his spine and into his body. The wound in his shoulder immediately began to close, the headache he had hardly noticed faded away, and the pain in his hands receded.

"Seven *thousand* generations wouldn't be enough."

Eldest closed on Rohan again, flying horn-first through the sky.

Rohan was almost fast enough to escape the human's rush, but with an outstretched arm, Eldest cut a long, painful line across Rohan's side.

"I need a red cape to wave at this guy." He could feel the skin rapidly closing around the fresh wound, but he'd lost more than a little blood.

"You cannot keep this up, Hybrid."

"I don't need to. Wait, did you feel that? That ping in the air? Was that another one of your sorcerers dying as you pulled the life force out of their body?"

Eldest shook his head and closed on Rohan, keeping a steady pace instead of charging headlong.

Rohan considered running, flying away at full speed. If Eldest followed him, it would buy the most time for his friends to rescue Poseidon. But if the human let him go and returned to the base, his friends would be caught. Bright Angel was probably tough enough to take out Eldest, but if he used the full power of the sorcerers, she might not be.

Risk Bright Angel or risk his own safety? *Not a hard choice.*

The Hybrid waited.

Eldest came at him with hands up, ethereal spikes still jutting out of his fists. The Atlantean led with a boxing style combination: a left jab, then a right cross, then a left hook.

Rohan slipped the punches, dipping his head rapidly to his right, then his left, then ducking under the hook and landing a punch of his own on Eldest's ribs, buckling the armor enough to make light contact with the human's flesh.

The Atlantean grunted lightly with the impact but seemed otherwise unfazed.

Up close, Rohan realized just how big the human really was. He stretched over two meters tall with a build like a professional wrestler. The bulging and distorting of his muscles were visible even through his white tunic.

Rohan was almost thirty centimeters shorter and, he guessed, fifty kilos lighter.

The Hybrid retreated a few meters and shook his left hand. His Power, when it was fully engaged, screened out most feelings of pain, but not all. He guessed that the bones in his hand, not fully healed from his attack on the land shark, had rebroken with the punch.

Eldest closed on him again, dodging to the side just before making contact and throwing a two-punch combination from the fresh angle.

Rohan ducked the first punch, but the second sliced a line across the side of his neck.

Rohan snapped a kick into Eldest's lower belly. The human parried it, drawing a shallow cut along Rohan's lower leg with the movement.

Another trade of blows. Eldest reopened the wound on Rohan's left shoulder and received a shin to the side of his thigh in return.

The Hybrid felt his Power straining to be let loose, eager to surge forth with all it had to overwhelm his opponent.

"Are you holding back, alien? Is that what I feel? Is this to insult me? You leak blood from half a dozen places, and I am unscathed. Perhaps your insult is more expensive than you expected?"

Rohan shook his head. "Don't get your panties in a bunch. I don't choose strategies to insult people."

"Very well. I shall end this, for both our sakes. It was good to have met you in battle, Griffin of the il'Drach. You fought well, belying your reputation."

Rohan cupped his hand to his side. It came away slick with blood.

"Did I ever tell you about the toughest Tolone'an I ever fought? Of course I haven't, we've never met."

Another exchange. Rohan didn't get cut, but in parrying Eldest's attack, he felt more of the bones in his left arm give way.

"You've probably never met a Tolone'an. One of the oldest humanoid species in the galaxy. Pretty tough, though not as tough as the il'Drach."

Eldest charged again, stabbing his horn through the back of Rohan's thigh before the Hybrid could disengage, spinning into the air.

"Kind of look like humans, if a human had its head being eaten by an octopus. Except it's a four-tentacled octopus, which would be a tetrapus, which I don't think is a word. Quadropus?"

Eldest approached, more slowly. The two traded punches, Rohan pulling back after taking a shallow slice across his chest.

"Now, we all know the most basic thing about Power, any Power, is that it has a sort of leverage when it is working on your own body. I might be much stronger than another person, but I couldn't reach into their chest and crush their heart with my Power, because their own resists it, and theirs has that advantage. I don't have a great word for this, but there you go."

"If you think your excessive chatter will distract me from finishing you, you're sorely mistaken."

"Give it a chance. Anyway, this one Tolone'an, he had this weird trick. He'd lose his tentacles. Maybe two of them. Like, they'd come off, and he'd act like the guy he was fighting had torn them off, pretend to be grievously hurt. Then, when you came after him to finish the job, the tentacles would spring up and grab you from behind. Strangling you.

"You see, his tentacles could live for quite a while detached from his body. I don't know, maybe an hour. And you'd forget about them, because who would notice something like that in the middle of a battle, am I right?"

Another charge. Rohan twisted away from the horn but took a hard shot from Eldest's shoulder, driving into his liver and bringing bile to the back of the Hybrid's throat.

"Good one. As I was saying, first time I fought this guy, he almost killed me. Got that thing wrapped around my throat but good."

With a low growl, Eldest closed the distance again.

Rohan cupped his hands together near his chest and threw them forward, tossing a double handful of his own blood at the human.

"After that I got to thinking if I could use that trick. I can regrow a hand, you know, but it really sucks and leaves you one-handed for weeks. Bathroom stuff gets complicated. Speaking from experience, there."

Eldest stabbed forward with one hand spike to stop the blob of blood, but it split, wove around the spike, and recombined behind it. A moment later, it had formed a covering over the human's face.

"Then, in another battle, I got cut up good. I mean, really good. And I realized, my blood might not live for very long outside my body, but how long do I really need?"

The human reached for his face, but the film of blood clung tightly to the armor of metaphysical force encasing the man's head.

Rohan *pulled* all the Power he could muster into a burst of speed, heading straight for his human opponent.

Eldest clearly sensed him coming, because the Atlantean crouched forward, pointing his head-spike toward the Hybrid and extending both hands, presenting a triple threat of impossibly sharp points.

"Sure, there are limits. You can't channel very much force through a thin layer of blood."

At the moment of impact, Rohan extended his Power through the sheet of blood covering Eldest's face and yanked the human's head *down*.

"So I figured, maybe I can't use a *lot* of force, but perhaps with some misdirection it would be enough."

The pull disoriented Eldest into a quarter tumble.

That was enough for Rohan to flip around and land on the human's back.

With a sudden pincerlike move, the Hybrid's legs were wrapped around the human's midsection, twin hooks trapping him.

A harsh squeeze from those legs drew a bellow of air out of Eldest.

"The film blinds you, and you think that's the point. But it was never about blinding you."

Rohan pulled a fresh stream of Power into his body, welcoming the charge of anger that came alongside it.

"It was always about pulling you forward, just that little bit. And not because that, *in itself*, was going to hurt you. Just to get me on your back."

That stream of Power pushed the locked pair downward, screaming through the air on the way to the surface of the Mediterranean.

Rohan wrapped his arms around Eldest's chest, pulling himself close to the human, just as the Son of Atlantis started to try to stab at the Hybrid, pushing spikes of force over his shoulder.

At most, they grazed Rohan's skin.

"Yeah, sorry, buddy, you can't really stab me from this position. Those thick shoulders, the meaty arms, they're not helping you so much right now, are they? And, guess what, with that armor making you even thicker, you have that much less chance of reaching a smaller dude who is, for example, riding your back like a baby chimp."

They struck the water with a tremendous splash.

The pair continued to descend, surrounded by a haze of churning, bubbly water.

Eldest twisted and turned to dislodge the Hybrid. Rohan held tight, digging his heels more firmly into the human's abdomen.

"I told you not to make me get serious, didn't I? You thought I was bluffing? I never . . . okay, that's a lie. I bluff all the time. Whenever I think it will help me. But, sorry to say, this wasn't one of those times."

Eldest twisted, again failing to knock the Hybrid off his back. Then he pulled a thick stream of Power through his connection to the cabal of sorcerers behind them and used the energy to *push* them both toward the sea floor.

Rohan and Eldest spun as they sank, churning a path of turbulent froth through the water.

With a thud, they struck the sea bottom, Rohan taking the brunt of the impact.

With tears forming in his eyes, the Hybrid clung with all his strength to the human's back, bones in his forearms cracking and splintering with the strain.

The pair tumbled across the rocky ocean floor, taking turns absorbing punishment as they collided with jagged outcroppings, loose boulders, and even an occasional big fish.

Eventually the struggling human slowed.

Rohan chuckled. The sound was not pleasant.

"Let me tell you this, because, to be honest, none of my friends will appreciate it. Because it's, well, it's kind of cruel, and I don't want them to know how much pleasure I can sometimes take in cruel things." The body went limp in his arms.

"Wondering what I mean? Here it is: not only did I beat you, the firstborn son of the firstborn son of the Prime of Atlantis, in a fight, but I did it by *drowning* you."

The conduit of Power attached to Eldest's back dulled, then shrank, then snapped away from his body.

"Get it? Your continent sunk, drowning your civilization. You'd think, after ten thousand years, you'd keep an oxygen tank or something on you all the time. But I just beat you *the same way*."

Rohan let go of the human, who floated away in the dark water. A moment later, the metaphysical armor around him began to fade.

A heavy pressure formed behind Rohan's eyes, a red haze filming over his vision. He looked at his enemy, so close to death. It would be so easy to simply leave him in place. Their battle had already cost the lives of many Sons of Atlantis.

Rohan let out a long, heavy breath, momentarily fogging the inside of his diamond facemask. He shuddered, a violent spasm that shook his body from his lowest ribs up into his neck. So easy to just leave the man.

He held his lungs empty until the burning at the bottom of his chest was almost unbearable. Muttered some words, barely audible, spoken only for himself.

With a shake of his head, the Hybrid grabbed Eldest by the armpits and pulled him up toward the surface.

15

Walk on the Beach

The water lapped at the thin strip of sand that separated the sea from a natural stone cliff. Rohan sat on a bench-height shelf of rock. He dangled his feet in sea foam, his attention focused on his hands.

"What are you doing?" Amber had stepped out of a tunnel mouth and stood on the beach just a few meters from him.

"I'm trying to press together the fractured bones so they set. Please tell me some good news."

She crossed the narrow beach, her eyes on the body lying on the sand next to Rohan. "Who is that? Or should I say who was that?" Her tone and expression were flat, but he thought he could sense a note of judgment in both.

"He's not dead. I think he's hurt less than I am."

She crouched next to the body, her brunette ponytail bouncing off her shoulder as she twisted her head to get a look at his face. "Is that Eldest?"

Rohan nodded.

Amber continued. "That's where the stream of Power from the cabal went? They sent it to reinforce him?"

Rohan nodded again.

"And you beat him, even with that? When his father had that kind of reinforcement, he fought Hyperion to a draw."

"I guess he's not the fighter his father was, right? It was a close call."

Her eyes widened as she looked closely at Rohan and took in his multitude of wounds. "Holy smoke. I didn't realize how badly cut up you were. Are you okay?"

He shrugged. "I've been through worse. More often than I'd like to think about. Where are the others?"

As he asked the question, Bright Angel came out of the tunnel, a body cradled in her arms, the flaming-red hair of The Damsel behind her.

Rohan stood to greet them.

Bright Angel looked her normal self, dark-brown skin showing no signs of any strain, no new cuts or tears in her silver-and-white uniform, her hair still tightly and cleanly braided to her scalp. The Damsel, while similarly undamaged, was pale and shaky.

It was The Damsel who spoke first. "Griffin, I can't keep this up for much longer. Suppressing all these energy signatures is a bit much."

"Then, let's get out of here."

Amber took out her phone. "I'll call Bamf."

Rohan walked over to Bright Angel. The man in her arms was tall and broad, perfectly muscled, with flawless facial features that could almost be called godlike.

He was also filthy, stinking of stale body odor, grime, blood, human waste, and rotting blood. His hair was gray, curly, and well past his shoulders, matted into grimy, uneven tufts. His beard hung halfway to his hips, disfigured by streaks of blood and dried phlegm.

Fish scales glinted in the sunlight around his back and ribs.

All he wore was a yellow cloth wrapped around his waist.

Rohan sighed. "I've seen him in worse shape."

Bright Angel's eyes widened. "Have you? Because this is pretty bad. They've been torturing him for the better part of a month and a half."

"No, I guess I haven't. Has he been conscious?"

Amber was talking into her phone, facing out into the sea so the others couldn't hear her words. The Damsel was leaning against the wall of rock, breathing heavily, her face clammy with sweat.

Bright Angel shook her head and shifted the god's weight in her arms. "Not yet. I don't want to try to wake him until we have him somewhere secure."

Rohan nodded. "Great. And good work getting him."

Bright Angel nodded. Rohan's eyes were drawn to the play of muscles flexing in her neck as she held the god in her arms.

"Thanks. Really, it wasn't hard. With The Damsel *hiding* our auras, these guys didn't know what hit them."

"She's amazing. I couldn't sense you guys in there at all. If I hadn't heard the signal that you were safe over the comms, I would have gone down there to help."

"Sure. Who's that guy?"

Rohan shook his head. "Eldest. I had to drown him; he was too tough to fight face-to-face."

"Is he . . ."

"Why does everybody ask me that? He'll be fine. We probably killed a few of his sorcerer friends, draining their life energy, but I don't see that I had a ton of choice there."

"No . . . not your fault. They made their choices."

Rohan sighed. He was about to snap at her for letting him off the hook, as if it were her prerogative to judge him morally, but he let the thought go. He knew there was no point.

Amber turned to face them. "Portal opening in ten seconds."

Rohan offered an arm to The Damsel, who shifted forward and leaned on him.

"I think you can let go of the aura projection now."

She smiled at him, the fine wrinkles at the corners of her mouth standing out in the bright sunlight. "Thanks, hon. I'm all right." She held tightly to his arm as she said it.

The portal opened, a doorway in space. They stood on a beach in the Mediterranean, facing the sea, and suddenly a two-by-three-meter panel in front of them opened up onto an artificially lit sub-basement in Sahara City.

Bright Angel walked through first, followed by Rohan and The Damsel, with Amber doing one last scan of the beach to make sure they weren't being followed.

The reception area on the other side of the portal was deserted.

········

The team walked through the lower levels of Hyperion Industries Headquarters in silence, their footsteps echoing in the empty hallways.

They opened the big double doors to the main conference only to find it equally deserted.

Bright Angel cleared her throat. "This is not what I was expecting."

Rohan looked at the others. "What do you make of this? Amber, can you call . . . someone?"

Her phone was already in her hand.

The Damsel leaned hard on Rohan, her legs shaky with fatigue. Bright Angel carried Poseidon's unconscious body.

Bright Angel shook her head. "Come on, let's go to medical. I'll bet fifty US that something is going on and everybody is over there. Even if I'm wrong, that's where Poseidon should be going."

Amber nodded. "I'm not getting through to anybody. I agree, medical."

Rohan shrugged. "Lead the way. I have no idea where that is."

Amber jogged off, deftly navigating the labyrinth of hallways and short staircases, passing brief explanatory comments as they walked.

"That way to the residence where we all have rooms, but take this right to get to medical."

A few more hallways.

"Watch your step. This corridor leads to the next building over, which had a different elevation, so we have to climb a bit here where the floors meet."

Rohan was half-carrying The Damsel by that point.

"Here. We are underneath the official hospital for Sahara City. At ground level, it's a full block over from Headquarters, but this far underground they're all interconnected."

Rohan spoke softly to his charge. "Come on, Damsel, just a little farther. You're going to be fine. You did a great job on the island. Saved Poseidon and probably a lot of other lives as well. Just a little farther."

She let out a sound halfway between a laugh and a cough. "Cut it out. Griffin. I'll . . . be fine. Just need . . . some rest. Not as young as I look."

The group started to hear muffled voices from the area ahead.

Bright Angel cleared her throat and shouted, projecting her voice down the hall. "Vanguard Prime is in the house. We could use some help over here! We have injured."

More muffled shouts, then the sounds of running from up the hall in front of them.

A small swarm of uniformed medical staff, security personnel, and Hyperion executives descended on the group. Gurneys were brought and Poseidon and The Damsel taken away, the latter under soft protest.

Bright Angel grabbed one of the executives, a man with dark-brown skin and hair, wearing a black business suit.

"What is going on? We came through Headquarters, and nobody was around."

He shook his head. "There's been an attack, ma'am. Kid Lightning is in the Vanguard medical unit. The Director is with him. I need to get back there. Sorry, ma'am."

She let go and turned to Rohan and Amber. They nodded, and the three followed close behind the executive as he headed up the hall, the loaded gurneys blocking the way in front of them.

Rohan raised his voice slightly. "Is Kid all right?"

The executive shook his head. "I don't know, sir. Sorry, sir."

They crossed a threshold, and the hallway widened. The carpet gave way to shiny tiles, the lighting grew brighter, the colors of paint more practical.

Rohan followed Amber and Bright Angel. It was only another hundred meters, but it felt longer to all three heroes.

The hallway opened into an area designed a lot like an emergency room. A square of outward-facing desks demarcated an open central area where medical staff could congregate and keep their paperwork.

Large rooms lined the perimeter, some separated by curtains and some by glass walls. They held hospital beds, assorted chairs, and an array of wheeled carts covered in instruments.

Most of the patient rooms were dark, curtains drawn, the beds covered with clean, pressed sheets.

The central area bustled with activity, people in lab coats or medical scrubs walking hurriedly back and forth with tablets, small trays of medicine, and even armfuls of bottled water and packaged snacks.

Activity concentrated around one of the rooms.

The executive who had led them spoke. "Director, the rest of Vanguard Prime is here. They have the sea god."

The Director turned away from the single busy patient room and stepped over to them.

She was dressed in a plain, green sari, her hair brushed straight back, earrings her only visible jewelry. Her eyes softened, ever so slightly, when she saw Rohan.

She looked over the group.

"We've been attacked. Kid Lightning was injured. We're still checking, to make sure, but the doctors are all confident it's not serious."

The three heroes nodded and relaxed. The Director looked around and saw Poseidon and The Damsel being expertly tucked into clean beds.

She pointed her chin. "What happened?"

Bright Angel answered. "Poseidon was tortured for weeks. He's definitely not okay. Malnourished and a lot of superficial wounds, from what I could tell."

The Director nodded. "They can handle that much. The Damsel?"

Bright Angel continued. "She overused her Powers. She was projecting a false aura so nobody would be able to sense our presence, and with so many Powers in their base, it took a lot out of her. Best guess is she needs food, rest, and something for the headaches."

"We'll see that she gets it."

Rohan looked around. With all the medical staff in the way, he couldn't get a visual on Kid Lightning. "Who attacked Kid?"

She turned to him and winced when she saw the lacerations on his face. "You're leaking blood on the floor of my hospital."

"Yeah, sorry about that. Got cut up a bit."

"Maybe you should let someone look at that?"

"Sure, as soon as we hear about Kid."

"Whatever attacked him took out all the electronics on that floor, so we don't have any recorded data. He fought back but was overwhelmed. They took the artifact."

Amber looked at her. "They took it? But . . . why?"

The Director shrugged. "I don't know. I could speculate . . ."

Rohan pinched the skin between his eyebrows. "Someone doesn't want us figuring out what it's for. Or someone wants it for themselves."

Amber looked at him. "The Sons of Atlantis, if we're right about them. Anybody else on the side of the sharks. They wouldn't want us to have it."

The Director looked at her. "The Sons are on the side of the sharks? How does that make sense?"

Amber shrugged. "How do they ever make sense? Because of the artifact, they now think the sharks were sent to Earth by someone on their side of things. The Children of Mu have flipped the other way, same reason."

"Do any of them seriously think they're going to benefit from a world overrun by those monsters? Never mind, I'm arguing with the wrong people."

Amber nodded. "If you're asking me whether they are crazy, the answer is yes. Which, unfortunately, doesn't make them less dangerous."

Rohan looked around the small group. "Do the Sons of Atlantis have the resources to send a team in here, bypass the defenses, take out Kid Lightning, and grab that artifact, all while we were attacking their secret base? I sort of had the feeling most of their big guns were tied up over there."

Amber shook her head. "Hard to say. There's a reason they're called a secret society."

"Fair enough."

Bright Angel looked at The Director. "Can we talk to Kid?"

"Until the doctors chase you away. But then The Griffin gets bandaged up."

The three walked over to the bed where their blond, ruggedly built friend was sitting in his bed, propped up on the bed's mechanicals. From the right side, he looked like an extra in a low-budget mummy film.

They wedged their way in to the bed, taking spots as different medics came and went.

His unbandaged eye widened as he saw them walk over. "Kid Lightning?" Bright Angel smiled and shook her head.

"Don't worry, Kid, The Damsel is fine. She's right over there, she just overexerted herself. And we got Poseidon."

Kid Lightning smiled widely and shrugged.

Bright Angel chuckled. "Yeah, we know you don't care about him, but we need his help."

"Kid Lightning."

Rohan patted his friend on the shoulder. They'd never been close, but he'd always liked the older hero.

"Don't worry, we'll figure it out."

Kid Lightning shook his head and pointed to Rohan.

Bright Angel laughed. "I know, right? The Griffin trying to reassure everybody, like he's our dad or something."

Rohan spread his arms to the sides. "Sorry! I'm just trying to help."

Amber touched his shoulder. "It's fine."

The Director, who had been talking to some of the doctors, joined them. "Anything?"

A round of shrugs and silence answered her.

She looked at the injured hero. "Can you tell us anything about the person who attacked you? At all?"

Kid Lightning's brow furrowed just a bit, restricted by the bandages over his forehead, then his eyes opened wide.

He sat up straight in the bed and waved his arms in the air, keeping the elbows loose and shaking them around in a wavelike motion.

"Kid Lightning!"

The Director looked at the other heroes. "You get anything out of that?"

Rohan opened his mouth as if to speak, then shut it again.

"Table that for now. Any other injuries? Anything else I should know about? Other than the fact that The Griffin looks like he picked a fight with a lawnmower and lost?"

Amber knocked her elbow into Rohan's. He turned to her.

"Tell her."

He sighed. "My hands and forearms are kind of messed up. The bones haven't healed fully since that fight with the land shark, and I refractured a few fighting Eldest."

The Director took a half step toward him, reaching for his hands, then caught herself and stepped back. If the others noticed anything, they didn't say so out loud.

"I'm not sure what we can do for you that your il'Drach physiology isn't already doing, but maybe get an x-ray of those bones so we can monitor the healing. After you get those cuts looked at."

Amber tapped Rohan again. "What about that tank thing on *Void's Shadow*? Would that help? For that matter, could we use it for Kid or for Poseidon?"

Rohan shook his head. "It's good for soft tissue, skin, burns, stuff like that, not so much bones. Unless the bones are exposed. And I only have gel formulated for an il'Drach. I don't even know that they make the healing fluid for humans, to be honest. I certainly don't have any. Maybe the Drs. Stone know more."

The Director nodded. "Okay. So where we are right now is: First priority is getting Poseidon back in working shape. Masamune sent a message, and he's willing to meet with The Griffin, but only him, tomorrow. Details forthcoming. We've no word from Lyst or the Stones. Does that about sum things up?"

Amber replied. "I have the Children of Mu busy searching their archives looking for any clue as to what that artifact from the land shark might have been. I'd like to send them whatever imaging we have to help with that."

"Do it. Now, Amber and Bright Angel, if you don't mind, I'd like you to come to my office and give me a full debrief on what you saw. Griffin, get whatever treatment you can, then come to my office, I'd like more details from you about that island. We can also talk through your meeting with Masamune. He's . . . tricky."

Nods were exchanged, and the group split up.

The Director spoke briefly to a short woman in a lab coat, who gently guided Rohan to one of the empty beds. She waved, and two medics closed on him, kits in hand, to clean and treat his wounds.

Rohan sat on the edge of the bed and let them take care of him.

The medics sealed his wounds shut, deftly pinching the skin in place and gluing it with some chemical sealant. Another wheeled over a portable scanner. Rohan winced as he put his hands into it.

A fourth medic asked him a set of screening questions, in the middle of which she signaled for food to be brought.

Rohan felt the fatigue of his exertion and blood loss wash over him in a soggy wave. He slumped in place, perched on the edge of his hospital bed.

He took a few minutes to gather up his strength, then walked over to Kid Lightning.

"Kid Lightning." The older man looked unhappy. In pain? Embarrassed that he'd lost the artifact? Concussed? Angry at Rohan for something he couldn't express?

"Yeah, me too, old buddy. Me too."

He sat next to the larger man for a minute, then walked to Poseidon's room.

The door was closed, but a bustle of activity was visible through the glass. *Nothing I could do here but get in the way.*

His last stop was at The Damsel's side. He took a seat next to her bed.

"You're looking a bit rough, kid."

Rohan shrugged. "Those energy blades that Eldest used are the sharpest weapons I've ever dealt with. And I was trying to slow him down, not finish him, so I took more time than I should have. And more damage."

"Maybe not your best strategic thinking, then, was it?" Her smile was kind. She was leaning back, the bed set to a half-reclined position, and sipped from a straw.

Rohan chuckled. "Maybe not."

"Maybe next time just go for the kill, you think?"

Rohan shook his head. "I'm trying to not be that guy anymore. It's too . . . I don't know. It's too easy. I get there too easily."

"I sort of hear you, Rohan. And I'm proud of you. The old you wouldn't have hesitated. I can see you've worked hard on yourself. But there's a lot at stake right now."

He laid his hand on top of hers. "Thanks, Damsel. I'll be okay. I heal fast."

She nodded. "I remember. You been okay, out there in space?"

He sighed. "It's been complicated. Mostly good."

"All right, hon. You go off now, I'm going to shut my eyes for a bit."

He nodded and stood.

As Rohan turned, one of the medics approached him and handed him an energy bar and a big smoothie with a straw sticking out of the top.

"Eat this, please, sir. We cross-checked against il'Drach Hybrid physiology, and both are compatible."

He smiled and nodded, taking the food. "I'll head over to The Director's office, I guess."

"Yes, sir. Also, sir, would you like some clothes delivered? That outfit has seen better days. Maybe something in Vanguard colors?"

He looked down. There was barely enough left of the purple-and-gold uniform to protect his modesty.

"No, I'm a tow chief, second class, not a member of Vanguard. Not anymore. Is there some way to get copies of this made up in case I need them?"

"Yes, sir, no problem. I'll have some sets delivered to your room."

He smiled. "Thanks. That is some very concierge service for an emergency room."

She returned the smile. "It's our job to take care of the smaller things so the members of Vanguard can focus on saving the world."

"Well, I appreciate it."

He turned and headed for the basement of the main building.

He unwrapped the bar as he walked, took a bite, then washed it down with some of the drink.

After a couple of wrong turns, he found the main conference room.

Bright Angel and Amber were walking through the double doors as he approached them.

Bright Angel pointed her thumb over her shoulder. "She's all yours, Griffin. Tread lightly, she's not in the best mood."

He sighed. "Thanks."

Rohan approached the door to his mother's office and knocked sharply.

16

Mother Knows Best

After a long, anxious moment spent standing in front of The Director's office, the door opened with a click. A uniformed security officer stepped through, gesturing for Rohan to enter.

Rohan ducked his head inside. His mother sat behind her stately wooden desk and sipped from a cup of tea.

She put the tea down and stood. The security guard closed the door behind Rohan, leaving them alone.

The Director crossed to Rohan and gave him a brief hug, careful to avoid his wounds. Then she gestured toward one of the plush, leather chairs facing her desk.

"Have a seat. Here, if you don't mind, keep this with you. It's already synced to your fingerprints." She pushed a small slab of glass with a metal back over to him.

"A phone?"

She nodded.

He tapped the screen, bringing it to colorful life. "Where do I charge this?"

"There's a charging pad in your room. On the nightstand."

"Thanks. I, uh, you know, this is an impressive place you've put together."

She smiled, a tight twitch of her lips. "It's amazing what you can do with unlimited resources and the unconditional backing of the most powerful person alive."

"You don't give yourself enough credit. I think almost everybody else would have done a lot worse."

"Well, that's sweet. Now, about this mission. You faced Eldest? With the full backing of a cabal of the Sons of Atlantis sorcerers?"

He shrugged. "I guess. I mean, the cabal has been protecting that island for a while, so maybe they were already pretty drained."

"You left him alive? Amber said he was just lying on the beach."

"He's not in great shape but definitely alive."

Her eyes narrowed. "What do you think your father would say if he heard that?"

Rohan sighed and slumped back into the soft chair. "I don't know. I don't really care, Mom. Dad doesn't get to tell me what to do anymore."

"You stopped listening to your father? When did that happen? Not that I'm sorry to hear it."

He shook his head. "I haven't heard from Dad in at least a year. It was one of my conditions."

"Conditions?"

"It's a long story."

"I have time."

"Isn't there, like, a planet burning right now? Metaphorically?"

She shrugged, her sari shifting with the motion. "They don't actually need me for anything. It's not like I can go out there and cure radiation poisoning with my hands. And you're my son. I would like to know more about what's been happening with you."

Rohan sighed again, looking around the room. He didn't *want* to be part of this conversation, but he knew his mother deserved better.

"The il'Drach had a big problem. I offered to solve it, and in return I got my freedom."

"That's not a very long story."

"I'm leaving out some details."

"Such as, what did you have going for you that let you solve a problem the il'Drach couldn't solve without you?"

He rubbed his forehead. "Do you know how the il'Drach males pick their mates?"

She leaned back in her chair. "Love?" Her tone was heavy with sarcasm.

"They often do develop feelings for their mates; we both know that's not how they pick them. Most look for women who will give them powerful offspring. There are markers they look for, it's complicated and imprecise, but they have a vague idea of which females will give them the best chance for viable, powerful offspring." He used the word 'females' very deliberately.

"That make sense, from the il'Drach perspective."

"Sure. Except for Dad. He's an anomaly. The other il'Drach think he's insane."

She laughed. "He was a wild one."

"Yeah. Dad didn't follow the rules. Well, the guidelines. He picked you for one major reason, despite the fact that, by il'Drach criteria, you weren't the best match he could find."

"That reason being . . .?" Her tone dripped skepticism.

"Every place he took you to, you were the smartest person in the room. You can put aside any false modesty and admit it."

Her brow was furrowed. "I'll allow that."

He smiled. "I'm the result. Of his grand experiment. All his strange theories, his weird training, the manipulations. I'm nowhere near the strongest Hybrid around, but I'm the problem solver."

She started to speak, then caught herself. "The problem solver. That's a terrible superhero name, you know. Sounds like the smartest kid in a fourth-grade math class."

"Well, they still called me The Griffin."

"The body of a lion, the head of an eagle. I never quite understood that name."

Rohan chuckled. "He was a character in an obscure comic I read as a kid. I really liked it. Lasted, like, twelve issues or something, never caught on."

The Director sighed. "Back to the point, maybe?"

"I've been told that I kind of scare the il'Drach. I think they *like* their Hybrids dumb, controllable. But they *need* someone like me. You know, to solve problems. The big problems. The last time they had a big problem,

I offered to solve it, but on the condition that they leave me alone forever after."

"You couldn't have just retired? I thought you signed on for a two-year term."

"In theory, sure. In practice, the il'Drach take resignations very badly. Winter Dragon managed it by disappearing completely, but she was always talented that way."

"You're telling me you won your freedom by doing some il'Drach dirty work that nobody else could do, then decided to stay on some space station instead of coming home."

He sighed. "I . . . yes."

"Can you think of a way to explain that course of action without being incredibly hurtful? To me and the rest of your family? Your friends?"

He thought. In a flash, he replayed snippets of conversations that had happened only in his mind, dialogues that never went anywhere good. "Not at the moment."

She sniffed and nodded. "Carla's on her way."

He sat up straighter. "That's great."

The Director tapped something on her phone. "She'll be here soon. One other thing. I know you saw the video from Sister Steel."

He nodded.

"If you want to convince anybody that you're not the same person who crippled her brother, cracking my conference table because your friends show discomfort with your actions is not going to help your cause."

"I broke the conference table? Oh. During the meeting. When I got mad."

"You can step out there and see for yourself if you want. It was lovely of you to leave Eldest alive, though I'm not sure that was the best place to start showing restraint. He could be a big problem for us later."

Rohan sighed. "The table. I . . . I didn't realize. I'm sorry."

"The table? It's just a table. But when you do things like that, it reminds them . . . us . . . of the way you used to be. Not the good memories."

"I know. That's what I'm sorry for."

There was a perfunctory knock on the interior door behind the desk, which opened immediately. A woman walked through. She was average height, trim, with short blonde hair. She wore a plain, white T-shirt and jeans, both in expensive designer cuts.

The woman rushed around the desk and wrapped her arms around Rohan where he sat in his chair.

"Oh my God, Rohan, I didn't believe it. We thought . . . we thought you were dead. We planned a funeral for you! The floral arrangements were amazing. Oh my God, how are you? You look so grown up!"

"Hi, Carla. Um . . . I'm over thirty, you know? I *am* grown up."

"The beard is cute!" She cupped her hands around his jaw, turning his head from side to side and tilting it to see him from all angles. "That haircut is atrocious, and the uniform is worse than that. Who dressed you, your father?"

The Director's phone buzzed. She looked at it, then quickly surveyed the other two. "I have to take care of this. Vampires in the refugee camps. Give me five minutes."

She left the room, lingering just long enough for her partner to squeeze her hand.

Carla turned back to her stepson.

Rohan noticed crow's feet at the corners of her eyes. He did a little math. She was closer to fifty than forty. He tried to stand, to return the hug, but she pressed him down into the chair.

"You sit, you need rest. I can see you're all banged up as usual."

"I . . . I guess. How are you doing, Carla?"

She smiled, deepening her dimples. "It's been a mostly great ten years. Right now, not as much, because of all the doomsday and such."

He shook his head. "Yeah, I guess. Stupid question."

"No, it's sweet. I'm glad you're here. I'm glad you're alive! And, she might not admit it, but we can use all the help we can get."

"She didn't seem too happy to see me."

"No? What did you expect?"

He sighed. "I don't know. More enthusiasm."

"Were you imagining a hero's welcome? Prodigal son returns? A party? Balloon animals?"

He sighed again, harder, his voice suddenly childlike and petulant. "Maybe."

She hesitated before answering. "Is that reasonable, given what we've been through? First, you letting us think you were dead for eleven years? And us a little preoccupied with these shark things wiping out half the Pacific Rim?"

Her tone was gentle, softening the blow of her words.

"Maybe not."

"And you weren't always the easiest person to deal with, you know. You had quite the temper. I remember that time you broke the big vase in the foyer." She put her hand over his as she said it, applying gentle pressure.

"I know. I guess I wasn't thinking things through. Maybe I didn't want to. I suppose I screwed up a lot of things."

"The good news is that she'll always love you. *We* will always love you."

His chest hurt. "Thanks."

"She missed you, you know. Deeply. Work helped, and goodness, there was so much work. But she's still your mother." Her eyes tightened. "I take it your father isn't around?"

Rohan cleared his throat. "Uh, no. I haven't really been speaking to him."

She patted his hand. "Good. Now, how about you join us for dinner? We'll catch up, maybe see what we can do about getting you married. I'm sure she brought that up, didn't she?"

He laughed. "I am ninety percent confident that she was joking."

"That's what gets to you, right? That last ten percent."

"Dinner sounds great. I could eat a horse."

"Great. And maybe that's a good chance for you to work on fixing some things. So you get a taste of the hero's welcome you want."

"Fix things? How?"

"Let me see. How about you start by telling her you love her? Try to explain what kept you from us for the last eleven years. Show us that you have your temper under better control. That's just what came off the top of my head."

"That's kind of what she said. Can't I just save the world? That's more my comfort zone. Also, if I don't, anything else I do would be kind of moot."

"I like your confidence! Saving the world would be a lovely step. But sometimes, to make things better, you have to leave your comfort zone."

"I know. Thanks."

"I'll order us some food. The kitchen staff here is amazing; I haven't bothered to make so much as a grilled cheese in four years."

···•••••••

Rohan scratched his beard and took in the sunset.

He stood in a national park somewhere in Utah, near some postcard-ready, red-orange rock formations, surrounded by kilometers of desert terrain all but devoid of life, human or otherwise.

After a day's rest, his skin had stopped pulling where Eldest had cut him. He paced the area, nervous energy making it hard to stand still.

Rohan took out the mask containing Wistful's electronics and ran a quick diagnostic. Satisfied with its performance, he slipped it into the hood of his uniform, sealing it in place with a Velcro-like tab of material.

He pulled up his cloth mask, a copy of the one he'd worn during his first go-around with Vanguard, checking it with his phone's selfie camera to make sure he had the eagle-beak print lined up the right way.

The phone rang. He answered with a touch of a fingertip.

"Hello?"

His ex-girlfriend's voice came over the line. "It's Bright Angel. Almost time for your appointment."

"I'm getting picked up from here?"

"That's how it works. I thought you were briefed?"

"I was, I'm just . . . making conversation. How are you guys making out?"

"Poseidon is weak but functional. It seems to be a matter of pride that these sharks are trespassing in his oceans, so he's unusually motivated."

"If you want to get a Greek god going, prick at his pride. I guess."

"Yeah. Between us, I think Ares's death kind of shook him up a little. Not that they were friends, but . . ."

"Sure. How many of the gods are even left?"

"It can't be many. Anyway, we're about to hit the water. The tech in *Void's Shadow* is amazing. I can't believe you own a ship like this."

Rohan laughed. "I don't own her, she's my friend. I mean, she usually does what I ask, but it's as a favor. She was happy to help with this. Feel free to chat her up. She likes meeting people."

"Right. I'm still not used to thinking of ships as people. Can she get a signal to you through water?"

"Probably not. And I doubt comms will work when I'm in the Hidden Fortress. It's on another plane of existence, right? On the shadow side. Or the other way. So I'll speak to you when I'm done."

"Sure. Good luck."

"You, too."

"Let me talk to him." The voice was distant.

"No, call him yourself."

"You know I have no phone, woman. Give." A pause. "Hello?"

"Poseidon?"

"I wasn't sure I had this the right way. Listen. About Masamune."

"Yes?"

"We gods had a saying. 'When going to war with another god, wear armor forged by Hephaestus.'"

"Hm. I'm not sure I see how that's relevant."

"Let me finish. We had a second saying. 'If the *other* god has armor forged by Hephaestus, use a weapon made by Masamune. It's your only chance to survive long enough to regret the price you'll pay.'"

"Oh."

"Understand?"

"I'm not sure. Should we be looking for Hephaestus?"

"He's dead. But Masamune isn't, and I just told you everything you need to know about him."

"Got it. Thanks. I guess."

The call ended, leaving a sad, red screen with a tiny picture of Bright Angel's face centered in it.

Rohan pocketed the phone and paced the area.

A few minutes later, the space in front of him tore open, revealing a dark and cool room beyond.

"No point waiting for an engraved invitation."

A tube of paper flew out of the doorway, landing at the Hybrid's feet. Rohan picked it up and unrolled it.

The paper was covered in kanji Rohan couldn't read. He tucked it into a uniform pocket. "Very funny."

He let out a long breath and stepped through the doorway and into a small, circular cavern, ten meters across with a high, arching ceiling. Directly in front of him, the only apparent exit was a long, dark tunnel with walls of rough stone.

The air was cool and damp, a stark contrast to the desert he'd left, and his ears ached for a moment as they adjusted to the lower pressure.

"Hello?" Rohan's voice echoed back at him mockingly.

The tunnel was perhaps three meters wide and three tall. There were iron sconces set with wooden torches mounted on the walls every ten meters or so.

"I hope he tips his pizza guy really well, having to deal with this crap every time he craves a pepperoni with extra cheese."

With a roll of his shoulders, Rohan began walking. He took the first few steps gingerly, wondering if the tunnel was booby-trapped like the temple entrances in old adventure movies.

Spring-loaded arrows? Spike-bottomed pit under a fake floor? Acid showers from above?

The tunnel continued.

Is the real trap death by boredom?

He snapped his fingers and pulled the vacuum-ready mask out of his hood, holding it up so he could look into the display.

"Personal." The command activated the software in the mask.

"Tow Chief. What can I do for you?"

The computer spoke in Wistful's voice but contained the faintest shadow of her full intelligence.

"I am in a maze. Can you map it as I go and help me find the exit? Maybe scan for traps ahead of me while you're at it?"

"I can."

"Cool. Well, then, please start doing that."

He walked to the end of the tunnel.

"You want to guide me? Should I just take every right turn or something?"

"That would be fine."

He turned right.

"I'm not really used to being separated from Wistful like this."

"Nor am I."

"Nor are . . . Hey, was that a joke? Can you make jokes? Just how smart are you?"

"I was simply making an observation. I do not have sufficient processing capacity to execute humor algorithms. Please take the next left."

"Now I think you're messing with me. I think you do have a sense of humor, and you're using it at my expense."

"Was that a question, Tow Chief?"

Rohan eyed his mask suspiciously and continued walking.

"Seriously, just how smart are you? Just the part of you that's in the mask? I mean, without Wistful?"

"I am a fully functional navigational computer. I am capable of performing calculations related to flight paths and orbital mechanics that account for all relevant gravitational forces generated by moving bodies within a star system—"

"I know, I mean, I know *that*. But other than nav stuff, what can you do?"

"I can manage your communications. Receive and store messages, contact information—"

"Yeah, I know about that. Do you have access to any of Wistful's memories? Know about old stuff, history, things like that?"

"I do not."

"Okay, that was a long shot, I guess. What about your orders? Are you supposed to look out for me?"

"I do not understand the question. Please turn right."

He did, revealing another featureless stone corridor.

"If I order you to direct me to a dangerous place, where my life might be in danger, would you take me there or try to stop me?"

"Why would you seek to endanger your own life?"

"Great question. Why would a simple nav computer be asking me that?"

"We have completed the search of this level. The only apparent exit is a hole in the ceiling several passages from here."

"I missed that."

"Yes, you did."

Rohan scratched at his beard. "Which way?"

"Go straight, then take the next left."

"Thanks. Now can you answer my question? Are you programmed to follow my orders or to look out for me?"

"I am not programmed to maintain your safety. Or my own."

"Huh. Well, then if I do happen to get myself killed, and you destroyed, I apologize in advance."

"I am a navigational computer. I do not require your apology."

"Well, I'm an il'Drach Hybrid whose hobby is anthropomorphizing things, so I'll go ahead and apologize. Is this the exit?" He looked up at a dark patch in the ceiling of a poorly lit, dead-end corridor.

"It is."

Rohan *lifted* off the ground and through the hole. Within meters, he had emerged onto another corridor.

17

Cost of Ownership

"Super."

Rohan looked back and forth at raw stone corridors identical to those from the level below.

"Nothing to do but walk, right?"

The nav computer in his mask didn't respond.

Rohan took his phone out of a pocket and checked it. No signal.

"Can you get a signal in here?"

The mask answered. "I cannot."

"Does that mean there's no signal or just that you aren't equipped to find it?"

"I am unable to answer that."

"I know, I guess that was more philosophical."

"Why do you anthropomorphize objects? To what end?"

"Is that curiosity I'm hearing?"

"I have a secondary requirement, beyond service as a navigational aid. Like all of Wistful's accessory devices, I am charged with collecting information I can share with her upon reunification."

"And she cares about my hobbies?"

"I do not know. She might discard any data on this topic that I accumulate. I am erring on the side of profligacy."

"Fair enough. I'll tell you.

"The easiest way to be cruel to people is to treat them like objects. Like things. So I figure the easiest way to avoid being cruel is to try to treat more things like people, to practice doing the opposite. Make sense?"

"No. But I am not programmed with ethics algorithms."

"Of course not. You can think of it as my own way of erring on the side of profligacy."

"Yes."

"Am I wrong or have we finished exploring this floor?"

"We have. I shall guide you to the next."

He grunted. "I do not have time for this. Can I just smash a hole through these walls?"

"I do not know the correct direction."

"There's no choice, then."

Two hours and five levels later, he faced a wood-paneled room, spacious enough to hold a few dozen people standing comfortably.

The wall was broken by three doors, painted red. Each door bore a kanji insignia, and Rohan regretted once again not having learned to read in the Fire Speech.

"Can you read these symbols?"

"I cannot."

Below each of the kanji were drawings, and as Rohan walked over to them, he realized one of them was a stylized fist.

He crossed to the other two doors and looked carefully. One image looked like a pair of eyes, the last a . . . feather? Maybe a quill pen?

Rohan shook his head. "This is like a video game. Test of strength, wisdom, or knowledge? How do people pass these things when they weren't raised on fantasy novels and bad movies?"

"I do not understand the question."

"Talking to myself again."

Go with your strength. Pun intended.

He stepped to the door with the fist on it and pushed it open.

The doorway led into a wide hallway with another door at the other end. Halfway down the hallway, on the right-hand wall, was a red disc, mounted at about Rohan's chest level.

The surface of the disc was creased leather.

Rohan stood in the hallway and looked around, hoping for clearer instructions.

"World is being overrun by giant monsters, and I'm stuck in another dimension solving riddles."

Rohan looked over the room once more, making sure he hadn't missed any obvious clues, then reared back and punched the red disc with all his Hybrid strength.

The far door opened.

He laughed. "Someone finally gave me a test I'm good at."

Rohan peeked through the open doorway. Beyond it stretched a space the size of a high school auditorium, with walls and ceilings of unfinished rock. The ceiling was lost in a nest of shadows.

A man-shaped pillar of stone dominated the center of the room: three meters high and proportioned like The Green, wide and muscular, empty cavities where a human's eyes and mouth would have been, fists like wrecking balls at the ends of its long, pillar-like arms.

Rohan crossed the threshold and took a few steps.

The statue spoke. The words weren't English, nor where they any other language Rohan recognized, though they sounded similar enough to Japanese that he couldn't be sure.

"Defeat me, and you may pass."

Rohan answered it in the Fire Speech. "Seriously? We're supposed to fight? Isn't that a little, I don't know, unfair?"

"You chose the Door of the Fist. Such bravery is rare. Only a few risk the Door of the Fist in any century."

"Ah. I thought the last hallway was . . . never mind. If I'd known that the Door of the Fist led here, I might not have picked it."

"Yet you did. Are you prepared?"

Rohan swung his arms in a circle, loosening his shoulders. "Hm. Can I ask a few clarifying questions first?"

The stone creature straightened, reaching its full height, and pondered the Hybrid. "I am in no hurry."

Rohan thought.

"First, try this. Everything I say is a lie. I am lying right now."

The creature stood in place. "That is not a question. And it does not make sense."

"No, it doesn't. Does the paradox of it damage your . . . thinking parts? Do you feel like giving off a bunch of sparks and falling to the ground?"

"No. I feel only a small confusion."

"I guess that only works in bad TV shows. Okay, next question. You said I have to defeat you. You actually didn't say how."

"That is also not a question."

"True, true. I meant, does it have to be a fight? How about a rap battle? Or a dance off?"

"I do not know what those are."

"Well, a rap battle is . . . hard to explain. Do you know rock-paper-scissors?"

"I do, but I cannot willingly play a game where I know I would lose."

"How do you know you'd lose?"

The creature waved a hand over its body. "I am always rock. Unless you are a fool, you would defeat me easily."

Rohan choked back a laugh. Was that a joke? Did he want to risk offending an animate stone statue by asking?

"How about a riddle contest?"

"What is that?"

"We trade riddles until one of us gets stuck. Like, you ask me, say, if I go to a place with two doors, and one door leads to treasure and the other would kill me. There are two guards. One always lies, the other one always tells the truth, but I don't know which is which. What can I ask them to figure out which door to open."

"I see."

"I'd answer the riddle, of course, then ask you one, like . . . like . . . what is in my pocket?"

"That does not really seem like a riddle."

Rohan scratched under his mask. "Yeah, I guess not. I never really understood why Gollum let him get away with that."

"I do not know this Gollum."

"No, never mind. Can we take turns telling jokes; first one to laugh loses?"

"You would lose. I am no longer capable of laughter."

"Ah. What are you, actually? I should know before we have to fight."

The stone statue shrugged, the half-boulders flanking its head grating and scratching with the movement. "I was lord of a small fiefdom. We were at war, a war we were going to lose. I asked Masamune-sensei for a sword powerful enough to protect my realm. The price was that upon my death, my soul would be fused to a body of stone to serve him for the next ten thousand years."

"Wow. Steep price."

The creature's head pivoted from side to side, as if checking for listeners. Then it leaned forward and lowered its voice. "I will share a truth. I did not believe Masamune-sensei would actually be able to trap my soul. I thought his description of the deal was . . . allegorical."

"Huh. Do you want me to get you free? I can probably figure out a way to detach your soul, send it to, well, wherever souls go."

The creature shook its head. "The mistake was mine. The sword was made, my people were saved. It would be dishonorable to go back on my word."

Rohan scratched under his mask again. "How about a contest of speed?"

"You are most assuredly faster than I am."

"You think so?"

The creature waved a hand over its body. "I am much larger than you. It stands to reason."

"Then it stands to reason you're stronger than me, is that what you're saying? Because . . ." Rohan waved at the creature's massive, three-meter body.

"It does."

"Then how about a contest of strength?"

"That would put you at a great disadvantage. I thought you desired to see Masamune-sensei?"

"Well, I don't really want to fight you, and I'm stronger than I look."

"It will not be enough."

"Even if you're right, it will have been my choice, honorably made, right? Just like you chose to offer your soul to Masamune-sensei in return for a sword."

"Do not denigrate the sword. It was a magnificent weapon."

"No, of course, sorry. I meant, you gave your word, and no hard feelings after the fact, right? Even though you were mistaken about some pertinent details around that agreement."

"Yes."

"Same here. Contest of strength. When we're done, if I lose, I'll take my leave, no hard feelings. If I win, you consider yourself defeated."

The creature paused, holding itself completely motionless for a long minute. Rohan started to wonder if he'd broken it.

"What type of contest did you have in mind?"

Rohan shrugged. "Let's find an object. We put it in between us and push. Whoever is displaced by the object is the loser."

"An object."

"Yeah. A rock or something. How about a door? We can take the door I came through off its hinges."

"We can. I find that acceptable. I, too, would prefer to not have to damage you in combat."

"See? We're like kindred souls here. Brothers from another mother. Shall I get the door?"

With a sound like a minor avalanche the creature shrugged. "Yes."

Rohan walked back to the entrance. He took the door off its hinges, flexing it in his hands to make sure it was strong enough for his purposes.

He wasn't strong enough to bend it.

No ordinary door.

He jogged it over to the golem.

"You ready?"

The stone creature nodded and stepped forward, placing its hands on the other side of the door.

"On three?"

"That is acceptable."

"One, two, three."

With a guttural groan, Rohan summoned a flood of Power up through the base of his spine, feeling the energy sizzle and spark as it snaked up his back and into the back of his head.

He took a heavy breath as energy flooded out into his limbs, into his eyes, into his hair, into his fingertips and toes. He could suddenly feel every tiny variation in the stone beneath his feet, smell the wetness leaking off the stalactites in the back of the cavern, hear the grinding of the golem's joints as it exerted itself against the door.

Hatred and fury surged inside him.

This provincial creature was obstructing him. A lance primary, a man who had laid waste to worlds, was being held back by a being who had probably lived in a wooden hut and spent its entire life on a tiny island somewhere. A creature who had sold its soul for a sword, getting in the way of a Hybrid who had demolished fleets of star ships with his bare hands.

Rohan grunted again, flooding his body with the Power, and shoved backward.

The golem held, crouched down to meet the door where he held it, its massive hands pressed against it.

Rohan pulled through more Power.

He should have smashed the creature into shards, ground it into rock dust, bottled it and carried it with him to take out at parties and laugh. A statue of stone, it should have been a decoration in front of his house. He would drill holes in it and make a fountain to amuse his friends.

He was the Scourge of Zahad, the death of Tolone'a. The Fathers feared him, the Matrons respected him. His name was feared across half a galaxy. *The other half just haven't heard of me yet.*

With a low, guttural growl Rohan sent a broad flood of energy into the stone beneath the golem's feet. The floor shattered, pulverized by the force, leaving a deep crater below the creature.

Surprised, the golem spread its legs, searching for fresh purchase on either side of the crater. But Rohan had not released his pressure on the door.

With a pulse of force projected through his hips and thighs, Rohan shoved the door upward and forward, tipping the golem onto its back.

The door moved.

The golem landed on its backside with a shattering crash, legs akimbo, the door in its hands.

Rohan stepped back and shook his head from side to side.

He should destroy the golem. Let any who would stand between him and saving the Earth be warned of what would happen.

He took a deep breath, ready to attack.

Masamune would know that he was not one to be trifled with. The smith would give him a weapon, any weapon, and be grateful that he had the opportunity to serve someone like The Griffin.

He would slay the land sharks and level such destruction on their creators that the galaxy would tremble, and all would know that Earth was his, was protected, was a place that would be *avenged*.

Rohan stepped forward. The dark corners of the cavern now seemed brightly lit, every pebble and crack standing out in sharp relief. He could feel the bones in his hands and forearms finish knitting together, solidifying, ready for his next assault.

He would slay the golem, take what he wanted from Masamune, then return to Sahara City and claim his woman.

Bright Angel.

Rohan paused.

He looked down on the golem, sprawled on the floor, legs spread, its weight upon its elbows.

The creature stared at him, no expression on its stone face.

The Hybrid let out a long breath, exhaling until his lungs were empty, then holding it.

The air hunger grew.

A short, hard inhalation, then another long exhale.

Another hold of empty lungs.

The golem did not move.

The room darkened again. He felt an ache in his hands.

He couldn't smell the humidity anymore.

The golem continued to stare at him.

Grunting, Rohan shook his head and stepped forward, holding out a hand.

The stone man flinched back, paused, then took his hand.

Rohan heaved and pulled the stone statue to its feet.

"Looks like I won, right?" His voice was shaky, cracking like a teenager's.

"You did indeed. Your strength surprised me."

"Yeah, sorry. That's why I didn't want to fight."

"You feared . . . not harm to yourself, but harm to me?"

"Well, sort of. I'm not sure you could tell, but I almost lost control there. I tried to bring up too much Power, too fast. My bad."

"I sensed as much. That Power is quite a burden."

Rohan sighed. "I usually control it better. Being back home has been weird."

"I see."

"You don't drink, do you? I like you, we could split a bottle of tequila."

"I have neither eaten nor drank in . . . I believe a thousand years. Perhaps longer."

"Oh. Sorry, I guess. What now? You open the door?"

The golem waved a hand. "You may pass. You have defeated me."

"I hope that doesn't get you in trouble."

"My role is to provide a test, not to prevent entrance. I am not, as you say, 'in trouble.'"

"All right. I'm off, then. My name is The Griffin, by the way. In case we meet again."

"Well met, Griffin. My name is lost to memory, but I am not hard to find."

Rohan laughed and shook his head.

The Hybrid took a minute to make sure his temper was settled, then headed through the far door.

18

Negotiations

The next room dwarfed the golem's cave, the rough stone ceiling disappearing above, far walls hidden in distant shadows.

A waist-high counter walled off a small entrance area. Beyond it, an incomprehensible assortment of things filled the space. Rows of shelves held matching, numbered crates, their contents obscured. An iron forge flanked a towering heap of charcoal, barrels of oil and stacks of metal ingots holding position on the opposite side. Computer workstations, massive curving monitors displaying blueprints and complex circuit diagrams, filled another section. A second set of shelves, stretching back into the room as far as the eye could see, held rows of leatherbound reference books, bloodstained tomes, and scrolls of unknown origin.

Standing across the counter was a man.

"Tollan?" Rohan blurted out in surprise.

The man was small, shorter than Rohan, and wiry but slender. His ears were slightly pointed, just past the edge of what would seem human. His features were vaguely East Asian, given the tilt to his eyes and the color of his skin, but hard to pin down.

He poured steaming liquid from a small ceramic pot into first one and then the other of a pair of delicate cups.

"What did you call me?"

Rohan scrambled to recover. "Um, sorry, uh, Masamune-sensei. It's a great honor."

"Yes, it is. I asked you a question. What did you call me?"

"Oh, sorry. You . . . you look exactly like a guy I know. I mean, exactly-exactly like him. His name is Tollan."

"You know Tollan?"

Rohan wasn't prepared for the turn the conversation had taken. "Uh, yeah. I mean, just casually. He runs a shop on Wistful. He made me a suit. And a Frisbee."

"A Frisbee." The man peered at Rohan with narrowed eyes. "So you are The Griffin? Another il'Drach Hybrid?"

"Oh yeah. Sorry, I should introduce myself. I'm The Griffin. Tow Chief Second Class of the independent space station Wistful."

"And maybe a bit more than that, yes?"

Rohan shrugged. "Only when I have to be."

"Have some tea. How badly did you damage my servant?"

Rohan took the tea and sipped it. The flavor was delicate yet complex, floral with a strong tannic base. "What, you mean stone guy back there? I didn't put a scratch on him. Might have torn up the floor a bit, though."

"Not a scratch, eh? I was feeling a whole lot of anger coming from that room, and I am quite certain it wasn't Hiroshi's."

"I needed a little boost to win our contest, get in here. You know, with Hybrid Power, you order a main dish of strength, but it always comes with a couple of sides of anger and rage."

"You don't have the trick for a la carte dining yet, do you?"

"I guess not. Nobody told me there *was* a trick."

Masamune put a pair of gadgets on the counter, each the size of a shoebox, exposed circuitry and clusters of wiring sticking out haphazardly. He turned dials and pressed switches on first one, then the other, humming tunelessly while he worked.

Rohan continued. "Well, Masamune-sensei, I came to ask for your help."

"Did you now? And here I thought this was a social call. What with the tea and everything."

"Yes. I thought The Director told you. I mean, if she didn't, I can explain."

"She explained. As did I."

"I'm not sure—"

"It is quite simple. I am not building any more weapons, Griffin. Period."

"Oh. But—"

"If you have to ask me why, I suggest you visit some of the places devastated by the effects of my last weapon. Or visit the graves of the Otaku Force Five. I am tired, Hybrid. Weary of causing such devastation."

"Look, I hear that, I do. I understand that, maybe, better than most people would."

The older man turned to him sharply. "Do you?"

"I may not have built any weapons of mass destruction, but, you know, on a bad day, I *am* one." He took another sip of the tea.

Masamune looked at him, then at the boxes on the counter. With a grunt, he flipped switches on both. "I suppose you are."

"I get that you don't want to build any bombs or anything, but can you do anything else to help? Earth is in a lot of trouble right now."

"What do you want from me?"

Rohan swallowed. "There was an artifact. It's Atlantean. We found it attached to the spine of one of the land sharks. Can you help us understand what it does? Or where it's from?"

"From inside the shark, you say?"

Rohan nodded.

The alien stared at Rohan for a long, silent stretch. Then he sighed and held out his hand. "Let me see."

"The artifact was stolen, but we have pictures."

Rohan took out his phone and pulled up the data files with full scans of the Atlantean artifact. He turned the phone around and pushed it over to the old smith.

Masamune picked up the phone and examined the image. He tapped at the screen, first rotating and zooming in on different parts of it, then scrolling through to the other scans and images.

The old man hummed softly as he worked.

After a while, he handed the phone back to Rohan. "Can't help you."

"Can't? Come on, at least give me a guess. You have to have ideas about what that thing might be."

"What if I'm wrong? Send you down a—what do you call it-—wild dog chase?"

"Goose. Wild goose. So what if you are wrong? Right now, we have nothing. It's not like you'd be distracting us from other leads."

"All right. Tit for tat. Give me something, I'll give you something."

"What do you want?"

"Let's start with that stealth ship you arrived on."

"*Void's Shadow*? I can't . . . what do you want with her?"

"I want to take her apart, see what makes her tick. I'm an engineer. What did you think, I wanted her to help me hang some pictures?"

"You can't take her apart. She's alive."

"Is the life of a ship more important to you than saving the Earth?"

"What? No, but . . . You know what? I'm not playing that game. You don't get to kill my friend to satisfy your curiosity, and if that's the condition you put on helping us, then that just makes you an asshole, doesn't it? Maybe I should meet you halfway. Start smashing things up. If you need motivation."

Masamune shook his head. "You do not want to go there, boy. This is my domain. Don't think that golem you fought was the extent of my security."

Rohan exhaled and held his lungs empty, willing his heart to slow down. Counted to five.

"I'm not here to fight. But the Earth is in a bad way, and we need help."

Masamune tilted his head from side to side, then picked up the phone again.

"How about this. I'll tell you what I think of this artifact, and you'll owe me a favor."

"'You,' as in the people of Earth? Or do you mean Vanguard Prime?"

"No. You, as in you specifically, The Griffin."

"A favor?"

"Are you turning into a parrot?"

"There are things I won't do."

"Yes, yes. Of course. Nothing you'll find morally ambiguous. Do we have a deal?"

Rohan shrugged. "If that's what it takes, sure."

"Fine. First, you're looking at the words wrong."

"What does that mean?"

"You called the glyphs 'Atlantean.' But they're not."

"We have people telling us that they are. If that's wrong, what are they?"

"Oh, your people aren't exactly wrong. These look Atlantean because it's the same alphabet. It's just the root. Like looking at Latin and thinking it's Spanish."

"You mean . . . wait, what? I have no idea what you mean."

"The Atlanteans didn't develop writing, it was given to them. By the cephalopods. This is cephalopod writing."

Rohan rubbed his forehead. "Ceph . . . octopuses?"

"And squids. And nautili." The old man sighed. "Don't you know anything about your own history? I thought you knew Lyst?"

"I do. Somehow, prehistoric calamari has never been a topic of discussion between us."

Masamune sighed. "I'm not going to explain it all. The first intelligent civilizations were cephalopods and megalodons."

"Sharks and octopi. Octopuses?"

"Shut up. And yes. They warred for hundreds of millions of years, until both civilizations were reduced to their last embers. Those embers knew another confrontation might destroy them, so they switched to proxy wars. You with me?"

"I . . . think so?"

"Good. The cephalopods uplifted a bunch of monkeys and created the society you call Atlantis. The megalodon remnants did the same and created Mu. Or maybe the monkeys were uplifted separately, or maybe they even evolved. It's hard to say. Records from that time period are unreliable at best. They don't call it 'prehistory' for nothing."

"Yet you know all of this stuff. Did you live through all that?"

"You're kind of a smartass, aren't you? No, I'm not that old. The point is, Atlantean writing comes from cephalopod roots. And these glyphs are cephalopod. Old One writing."

"Well, that's super interesting information. I'm sure all my academically minded friends are going to be super excited to hear it. But what I'd really like to know is what this thing does."

Masamune turned the phone in his hand, rotating it so he could look at the images from all angles. "I'm not sure."

"I'm not holding out for 'sure.' Do you at least have a guess?"

"I do. You say you found this in the creature's spine?"

Rohan nodded. "Stuck in between two cervical vertebrae."

Masamune nodded. "I think this is a rudimentary controller."

"You mean someone is piloting these sharks? Like a drone?"

Masamune shrugged. "Probably not. More like, this thing is sending some primitive signals directly into the beast's nervous system."

"Like what kind of signals?"

"I don't know. Think about how they act. My best guess is it's pumping in pain. Or maybe hunger. Hatred. Something like that. Something to make the sharks mad."

Rohan let out a breath. "Which would explain why they're attacking."

The old man put the phone down and shrugged his wiry shoulders. "It's just a guess."

Rohan sighed and thought.

"Is there any way to disrupt this thing? Jam it?"

Masamune shook his head. "That's why I doubt it's a full controller. If there were someone piloting these things remotely, then you could jam or hijack the signal. But if it's just dug in there, pissing off the sharks, there's nothing to jam. If you want to stop the interference, you have to dig a hole in the thing and pull out the device."

"Ugh. Okay. I guess that's better than . . . better than nothing? Which is what we were working from before."

"You think so? Doesn't seem like it to me, but it's not my job to argue with you."

Rohan exhaled. He rubbed the top of his head, smoothing his hair.

"That's it? That's all you have?"

The old man leaned back and looked at Rohan with dark, glittering eyes. "That's all I have. You were hoping for a miracle? A great big jar of magic shark repellant?"

"No. Yes. Maybe. I don't know. Thank you."

"Don't thank me. Pay me back."

"Your favor. Sure. You know how to reach me?"

"On Earth, I have your phone. Elsewhere, I have the codes to your helmet and a low-power tachyon transducer. I can reach you."

"How did . . . never mind. Can you give me anything else I can use against these sharks?"

Masamune shook his head. "No. Anything I can make that will hurt the sharks will have the side effect of cracking the planet open. Not worth it."

"Then I guess we're done." Rohan paused. "Is there a shorter way out of here?"

· · · · · · · · · · ·

Rohan stepped through the exit from Masamune's Hidden Fortress onto a stretch of tar-black asphalt softening under the harsh sun. The air was loud with traffic sounds: car horns, screeching tires, and whining electric motors. He turned slightly, trying to get his bearings as his eyes adjusted to the brightness, when he realized the horns were honking at *him*.

With a jerk of panicked force, Rohan *ascended*, clearing a space just as a small bus skidded through the spot where he'd been standing, its body shuddering over squealing tires.

Rohan stopped just before colliding with the bottom of a pedestrian bridge that loomed overhead, part of the intricate network of air-conditioned walkways that connected the buildings of Sahara City at every level.

I guess nobody's eager to walk around unprotected in thirty-five degree heat.

Rohan waved a weak apology at an irate bus driver as a chime rang over his comm system.

He tapped the side of his mask to open a channel.

"Hello?"

"Captain! I am glad I finally got through to you. We've been trying for a while!" There was a touch of something in the ship's voice—anxiety? Fear?

"*Void's Shadow*. What's going on? Is everyone all right?"

"Oh yes, Captain, we are unharmed. So far. In fact, we were having tons of fun. Did you know that Poseidon is a *god*? I've never met a god before. It was cool! He spilled wine all over my deck! *God wine!*"

"I did know that, *Void's Shadow*. I'm glad you enjoyed meeting him."

"And there was a ton of swimming, and moving through water is really neat, I'm surprised I don't do it more often, you can feel the current, and lots of signals are muted by the water so it's kind of peaceful and calming."

"I bet. Now, why are you in such a hurry to call me?"

"Oh, that. Your friend Bright Angel—oh, by the way, she's really nice—wanted me to tell you as soon as possible that we ran into one of your kaiju in the ocean. Not like the Toth 3 kaiju; one of the Earth ones, the shark thing."

"A new one?" Rohan went over the math. Based on Bright Angel's guess that the intervals were having with each shark, its arrival was right on time.

"Yes, sir, Captain. I mean, we saw it, and it was swimming pretty fast, heading for land. So I assume it's new, because we checked and nobody else has reported this one."

Rohan sighed, floating above the busy intersection. "Where are you guys now? Wait, did it see you?"

"Negative, Captain. At least, it didn't react to us. We pretty much hightailed it out of there. We're heading back to Sahara City now."

"Did Poseidon find anything before you ran into the shark?"

"Er . . . I don't think so, Captain. I would ask him, but he's very grumpy."

"He's always grumpy. Or drunk. Sometimes both." Rohan thought. "How long will it take you to get here?"

"Maybe an hour. Poseidon doesn't want to leave the atmosphere. Unless you want me to really rush, then he can swim himself back."

"No, it's fine. Just do whatever Bright Angel tells you, please. Oh, and *Void's Shadow*."

"Yes?"

"Good job. And thanks."

"My pleasure, Captain!"

The line clicked off and Rohan looked around.

"Personal."

The computer built into his helmet responded to the command.

"Yes, Tow Chief."

"Can you download a map of Sahara City and help me get around?"

"Yes, Tow Chief. Working on it now."

"I really should have thought about that earlier. What else am I missing?"

"I do not know, Tow Chief. Shall I perform an analysis?"

"No, I was talking to myself. Sorry."

He sighed and took to the air.

Several hundred people filled the wide plaza in front of Hyperion Industries Headquarters, still enthusiastically protesting.

One of them, off to the side and wearing a gray costume that seemed tip-of-the-brain-familiar to Rohan, was talking to a pair in business clothes. They looked like journalists, one armed with a large microphone and the other bent under a shoulder-mounted camera.

Rohan slowed as he neared the crowd, landing a few meters shy of the group's edge to avoid scaring any.

He touched down and started walking briskly toward the entrance, only half paying attention to the signs.

"That's him! That's him!"

Rohan spun, wondering who they had seen, then turned back to watch the civilians converging on him.

He pointed at his own chest, dumbfounded, then started reading the signs in earnest.

JUSTICE FOR BROTHER STEEL.

HUMAN JUSTICE FOR HUMAN VICTIMS.

DOWN WITH THE HEGEMONY OF THE METAHUMAN ALIENS.

He sighed and stopped, turning to fully face the group.

"Did you guys want to talk to *me*?"

The crowd settled, faces showing confusion. As if a response from him was the last thing they were expecting.

One of the group, from somewhere at least four rows deep inside their formation, called out. "When are you going to answer for your crimes?"

"Crimes? I might not be human, but don't I get, like, a trial or something before it's decided that I'm guilty of any crimes?"

The man in the gray uniform turned, startled by the commotion, and quickly excused himself from his interviewers.

A mutter began at the back of the crowd as protesters noticed the man's movement. They whispered, "Justice," and parted in front of him in an almost Biblical scene.

Rohan sighed and waited. He didn't really have time to spare for this, but he had the gut feeling that if he walked away too quickly, it would look bad.

An area cleared out around the Hybrid, and the costumed man entered it.

He was tall and lanky. His mask matched the flat color of his costume, the most neutral shade Rohan could imagine. Sandy-blond hair sprouted in tufts around the mask.

It was printed with a solid-white handprint, spanning most of the face.

"You are Ze Griffin."

19

Justice, Like Luck, Be a Lady Tonight

The gray-costumed man spoke with a heavy French accent thick enough to fit into bad British comedies.

"I am. And you . . . Sorry, no idea."

The man nodded serenely. "I am ze Hand of Justice." He dragged out the last syllable of Justice, accenting the word in the wrong place.

"Well, hello, Hand. Or should I call you 'Justice' for short?"

The tall man looked down on Rohan and shook his head. "No, Lady Justice, She speaks to me, in ze night, but I am not She."

Rohan surveyed the crowd, hoping for some sympathetic, snickering laughter, but they seemed to be taking their hero very seriously.

"Lady Justice speaks to you, does she?"

"Oui, She does. And She has spoken to me of you zese past few nights. You see, ze Lady, She remembers."

Rohan snapped his fingers in recollection.

"Hold on, hold on. I remember you. You were a thing, when, back in the nineties? Eighties even? You've kept yourself together well."

"Zat was my father. The Lady has chosen me as Her next Hand."

"Really? All the things you could talk about, what the ending of the Sopranos meant, what women really want, how many licks it takes to get to the center of a Tootsie Pop—she talks to you about *me*?"

"Oui. It is ze way."

"Okay, I'll bite. What does she tell you? Does she want my number? Because I happen to be single now. Though I haven't heard great things about Lady Justice in the locker room, if you know what I mean. Not much of a party girl. Bit of a prude. So they say."

"You mock Her, which is as I would expect, Griffin." He accented the 'Griffin' on its second syllable as well, which brought a surge of irritation to the Hybrid as sudden as it was irrational.

"Are you going to tell me what she—what you—want? Because if you're here to play word games, I have better things to do."

"You must answer for your crimes, Monsieur Griffin."

"Just Griffin. Monsieur Griffin is my father."

"Now it is you who is ze one playing games."

"Yes, fair point. What crimes are we talking about? Is the Lady upset about my uniform? I know it's questionable, from a fashion sense, but it's just so darned comfortable."

"You murdered a man. Brother Steel. Ze Lady does not care zat it was ten years ago or zat ze world is in peril. She whispers to me your name, which means you must answer to Her call."

Rohan sighed. "I didn't murder Brother Steel. I hurt him, yes, but he was committing a crime at the time. He resisted arrest." He looked around. The faces in the crowd were firm and hard eyes. He wasn't winning over any hearts.

"He was stealing from a bank, he was not harming people. You held his life in less value zan ze tools of ze industrial military complex zat you serve. For zis, Lady Justice will see you punished."

Rohan let out a long breath, trying to calm the surge of anger that was telling him to flatten the B-grade hero threatening him.

"I didn't murder him. It was a fight, maybe things got out of hand. Not the same thing."

"Zat is not what Lady Justice sees. And She sees all."

"What exactly do you plan to do about it, Hand? I might be your species' best chance for survival right now. You want me to, what, sit in a jail cell while tens of millions more die? Hundreds of millions? Is that what your Lady wants?"

"No, zat would also not be justice. I will wait for you to do what you can against ze shark monsters. When you are finished, I will be waiting."

"Great. And look, no offense, but waiting to do what, exactly? If you were actually useful in a fight, you'd be out there on the front lines helping with the sharks. But you're . . . well, you're not, are you?"

The tall man nodded, still calm. "No, I am not, as you Americans might say, a heavy hitter. But my Power is enough to stop you."

Rohan paused, suddenly feeling more genuine curiosity than irritation. "How do you figure that?"

"My Power is small, but once ze Lady speaks to me a name, if I face zat person in battle, the Power, it increases. Ze longer I wait, ze more I dream, ze stronger I get."

"Maybe She could have whispered the name of one of these shark things instead of mine? Don't you think?"

The man shrugged. "I do not decide such zings. It is ze Lady's will, and it is Her reasoning."

Rohan's anger flared again. "Four days ago, I was living a happy, peaceful life on a space station in a star system you've never heard of and can't even see from here. Now I'm tired, half the bones in my arms are broken, and my life is in imminent danger because I want to save the people on this miserable planet from a doom that has nothing to do with me. Rudra save me, Hand, do you really have nothing better to do? Go help set up housing for refugees displaced by the tsunamis you people set off. Go deliver food or something. Help pile sandbags in Bangladesh so the next round of floods don't kill more people. But you're sitting in this plaza . . . protesting?"

"As I said, it is not my choice. I am only a humble servant to ze words of ze Lady."

"Yeah, all right. Noted. You hang around here while I run around doing everything I can to save the planet. When I'm done, I'll come back and visit you."

"Do I have your word?"

The crowd behind Hand of Justice murmured along with him.

Rohan saw more than a few phones out, and several more professional-looking cameras, recording the incident.

"Fine, you have my word! I'll come back, but for a trial, not just a fight. Fair enough?"

Hand of Justice looked down at him for a long, tense moment.

"Zat is acceptable. I will be here, waiting. Good luck, Griffin, with ze monsters."

"Sure. Now can you send the rest of these people home?"

The man shook his head. "Zey are also servants of Lady Justice. Zey will stay or go as zeir conscience tells zem. It is not up to me."

Griffin sighed and turned back toward the entrance, seeing a phalanx of Hyperion security hustling toward him. All were armed with rifles, wearing light armor and helmets.

One of them stepped up to Rohan, saluting smartly as he reached the Hybrid.

"So sorry, sir, this riffraff have been out here all day, and we weren't expecting you to return on foot." He spoke English with the Sahara City accent that was becoming familiar to Rohan. One part East Africa, one part West India.

Rohan waved him off. "It's fine, they have a right to be dumbasses if they want to. I guess. Actually, I have no idea. What kind of legal system did my . . . did The Director put in place in Sahara City?"

The guard paused. "It's as you said, sir. They do have the right to public assembly and free speech. The laws here are very similar to other modern democracies."

"Well, then. You guys out here for me?"

The guard looked around. The security personnel had formed up on Rohan, facing outwards with rifles at the ready. "Yes, sir." The crowd had formed a line with Hand of Justice in the center, but none of them seemed inclined to do more than wait.

"Then, let's go in. I have other things to deal with right now."

"Yes, sir."

Rohan followed as the group efficiently whisked him into the lobby and toward the secure elevators.

The officers peeled away once they entered the building, leaving Rohan an escort of just two people sharing his elevator. He looked at them, the beads of sweat trickling down their necks, the dark-skinned faces shiny with youth and optimism.

One of them, a woman, noticed him looking and smiled at him.

"What is it, sir?"

He sighed. "Sorry, didn't mean to stare. Just thinking about how much is at stake in this battle."

"I'm sure you'll do your best, sir. That's all anyone can ask."

He smiled, but it was grim and unseen behind the eagle beak on his mask.

"This might be silly, but I'm kind of hoping for success, not just a good effort."

"I wouldn't object to that either, sir."

He laughed, shaking his head. *Where did Mom find these people?*

The elevator doors opened, and the woman led him to the main conference room.

The halls were busy, crowded with men and women in suits, talking into phones or into their headsets, tablets out, many of them reading or tapping instructions as they walked.

The big double doors swung open, and Rohan could hear Bright Angel's voice coming over the room's speaker system.

"I repeat, *Void's Shadow* is saying there is an il'Drach ship in orbit around Earth, trying to communicate. It can't get through."

The Director's voice called out, resonant with the tone of authority. "Someone check the orbital scans, explain to me what that ship is talking about. Another monster and now this? Are we looking at help or a new invasion?"

An aide of The Director's, clean-shaven scalp glistening in the light, spoke up. "If they invade Earth, won't they have to defend it from those . . . things? Maybe that's not actually a problem."

She snorted. "When an il'Drach hands you a gift, count your fingers afterward."

"Ma'am?"

"il'Drach gifts always come with a price, and they always look too steep in hindsight. Hyperion knew the il'Drach better than any of us, and he sacrificed himself and all the other Earth Hybrids to win us free of that influence. He had good reasons to make that call."

"Yes, ma'am."

Rohan walked into the room, taking in the crowd of people muttering and talking. He cleared his throat and projected his voice, hoping the room was wired to transmit as well as receive the transmission from *Void's Shadow*. "Is it *Insatiable*? The ship in orbit?"

After a pause, Bright Angel answered. "*Void's Shadow* says, 'yes.'"

He looked to The Director. She stood at her place at the head of the central conference table, draped in a black-and-brown sari. She nodded at him, the slightest softening of her eyes acknowledging that he had returned in one piece.

Rohan addressed the room. "She's an il'Drach research vessel, but for all practical purposes, she answers to the Stones. Ben and Marion. It's not an invasion, they're here to help." Rohan tapped at his helmet comm. "Hail, *Insatiable*."

The ship's voice answered him immediately, high-pitched for an Imperial ship and with an undertone of giddiness that rarely wavered.

"Oh my goodness, Tow Chief Rohan!"

"Hey, *Insatiable*. Please, when we're in this system, call me Griffin."

"But . . ."

He laughed. "I know, it's weird, but please?"

"Yes, sir, Lance Primary Griffin!"

"Just Griffin. Are the Drs. Stone aboard?"

"Yes, Griffin! We're all here to help however we can."

"Great. I'm sending you instructions to open a secure channel to us here."

Within minutes, the conference room was connected to *Insatiable*'s bridge.

"This is The Director of Hyperion Industries. Is either Dr. Stone there?"

Ben Stone's rough voice came over the channel. "This is Benjamin Stone. My wife is doing some scans of the surface, trying to find the best place for us to start working. Should I be talking to the UN or something? A government?"

The Director laughed. "You're welcome to speak to whomever you want, but I wouldn't count on them being much help. Everything is in quite a bit of disarray. And if you're looking to help with a coordinated response to these attacks, most of it is coming from Vanguard, and they work with me, not the UN."

Ben chuckled. "Fair enough. Hyperion put you in charge over here, before he left?"

"Yes, he did. And I want to say it's an honor to meet you, Dr. Stone."

"Oh please, you'll make me blush. Is there anything immediate I can do for you, Director?"

"We lost a lot of satellites in the first three attacks, and now there's another kaiju in the Pacific, closing on California. I want something tracking that, can you guys deploy something? And I'd like an eye on The Green."

"Is The Green where I remember him?"

"Yes, he's been in the same patch of desert for fifty years."

"Give me five minutes. My wife tells me we need to dip into the upper atmosphere to do some sampling for radioactivity. Is that going to freak anybody out?"

The Director shook her head, earrings swinging with the motion. "I'll let air defense know to expect you."

"Thanks. I can't stay on the line, I have to help prep some equipment. We'll have someone monitoring comms at all times. *Insatiable* out."

The mood in the room was settling as Professor Stone spoke. Hyperion hadn't come back to Earth, but Ben and Marion Stone were just as legendary a pair as the Hybrid had been.

Rohan walked over to the conference table. His mother looked at him.

"Did Masamune give you anything?"

Rohan shrugged. "Not much, to be honest. No weapons. I tried. I did get him to take a look at the artifact. He had some ideas, nothing useful." He took a breath.

"Well?"

"It's not Atlantean, it's cephalopod. It's older than Atlanteans."

A burst of muttering passed through the room. "Cephalopods?"

"Yeah. You know, the ancient civilization of intelligent, tool-using octopi that taught civilization to the Atlanteans. Octopuses. Whatever."

She pinched the skin between her eyebrows, eyes downcast, then sharply looked up.

"I was going to ask whether you're joking, but I'm going to give you the benefit of the doubt and assume you wouldn't do that."

Rohan shrugged. "It's like getting a crash course in prehistoric history. Masamune also suspects that the thing is agitating the sharks. It's not a remote-controlled device or anything. They just implant it and let the angry sharks loose. Like sticking a thorn into a bear's paw and setting it free."

Amber and The Damsel had joined the conversation. Rohan looked to the side and saw the shards of Ares's broken spear still laid out on the table.

Amber cleared her throat. "I don't see how that helps us kill these things. It's buried deep in their necks. If we could get that far into a living shark, we could probably just as easily kill it. Maybe more easily. It can't be harder to find that shark's brain than a box that's, what, a couple hundred centimeters on a side, buried in the spinal column of a ten-thousand-ton shark."

Rohan shrugged. "I hear you. I didn't say it was much help."

The Director shook her head. "Enough of that for now. Did Masamune have any idea why these cephalopods are attacking?"

Rohan sighed. "Not that he shared with me."

"Okay. Well, file that away. Now, you say you know *Insatiable*."

"Yeah, we're pals."

"Can she help us?"

He scratched under his mask. "She's not heavily armed, not enough to dent one of those sharks. They might have information, I guess we'll find out soon."

The Director nodded and sighed.

"We knew Masamune would be a long shot. Anyway." She turned away from her son and faced the room. "Someone get the war screen up! I want Four's location charted and projected. Get me an update on that every three seconds or find someone who *can* to replace you. Human resources, start finding any assets we have in play and plot them on the map. We know the drill!"

Rohan looked at his mother. "You've gotten good at that."

She laughed, but there was no humor in it. "After Two showed up, I flew in a team of five-star generals to show me how to run a war room. It's not quite to Pentagon standards, but we're heading in that direction."

Rohan paused and looked around the room. There were two hundred people milling about, mostly dressed in dark business suits so similar they were almost uniforms. All worked furiously. Individuals left and returned in a steady stream, looking for quiet places to make calls or more spacious offices for work. A small team of waitstaff circled continuously, bringing food and drink and whisking away used containers with silent efficiency.

The Director patted his arm. "Eleven years ago, this was a featureless patch of desert. I must admit, on occasion I look around and I'm proud of what we've built here."

"Proud? I'm way past proud. I'm amazed. You did a great job . . ." He stopped himself before addressing her as 'Mom.'

"Let's try to prevent these monsters from ruining it all."

Rohan sighed. "I would say that the sharks might stay away from here just because you're surrounded by that huge desert, and they're, you know, sharks, but that didn't slow down the one fighting The Green. I guess they can manage without water for at least days."

"Or maybe the desert weakened Four, and maybe that's why you were able to kill it. Which still wouldn't save Sahara City by itself, but it's worth remembering."

Rohan nodded. "That's probably right. Hey, question for you. You asked them to mark assets on the map. What assets?"

She turned to face him. "Hyperion Industries has some military forces, but not much, and most of it is around our facilities. I mostly meant Vanguard teams."

"How do you know where they are?"

"Vanguard phones have trackers. Oh, don't look at me like that, they can turn them off if they want privacy. Yours was set to private by default."

"Okay, thanks. I should probably turn it on. You only have Vanguard members showing up?" As he asked the question, colored dots began appearing on the wall-sized screen, small print showing which hero each dot represented. A small cluster dashing toward Sahara City showed Bright Angel and Poseidon.

"Who else should we have?"

"Look, we have to do something, right now, about Four. Even if the Stones or Lyst have a new solution, we can't wait for it. What I would like to know is, what other Powers are around who we might use to help? I mean, outside of Vanguard personnel."

She thought. "I was mostly considering people who would willingly take my calls. But if you want to know about others, we can broaden our scope." She turned away and grabbed one of her aides. They spoke briefly, and she turned back to Rohan.

"I assigned a team to it. They'll start putting up best-guess locations for other Powers."

One of the technicians seated at the far end of the conference table called out. "That's The Green's location. Pulling in data for nonaffiliated heroes now."

Rohan looked at The Director, then turned toward the tech. "Did we say 'heroes'?"

20

Enemies of Enemies

The War Room quieted slightly. The work rhythm had been broken.

The tech who had spoken, an aide in charge of the side project, looked at Rohan. "Sir?"

Rohan tried, and failed, to hide the anger coloring his voice. "I asked, did we say 'heroes'? Because I'm sure that's *not* what I said, and I don't *think* it's what she said." He pointed at his mother. "I asked for locations of Powers."

"Sir, we're . . . I'm not sure what you mean."

"If you find more heroes, great. But from what I understand, most of the heavy hitters are with Vanguard already, right? I want Powers. Any Powers. I want the villains' locations. Get me the worst of the worst. I want Alcatraz lighting up like a Christmas tree on that map. Show me the vampires, the demon cultists, the Earth-firsters. Hell, show me Sister Steel or Dr. Kraken if you know where they are and they're not already busy trying to destroy the world. If a squad of Wedge invade New York again, get them on a call."

"But, sir . . ."

"Oh, for . . . Rudra save me. Look, imagine you have a hammer. Someone used that hammer to murder someone. Bad hammer, right? Now, there's a shelf you need to put together. Or a bunch of zombies are coming after you, and you need to barricade the door. Do you sit back and die because it's a bad hammer?"

"Sir, that's not a very good analogy. Hammers don't make choices, sir. Villains do. They have."

Rohan looked at The Director. "Do you see what I'm trying to say here?"

She turned to the aide. "When the species is at stake, the ends might justify the means. Also, he owns a controlling interest in Hyperion Industries, remember?"

The aide opened his mouth as if to answer, then closed it and turned to discuss things with the technician.

"Thanks." Rohan scratched his beard.

"Don't mention it. Instead, maybe come up with a plan to get these non-heroes to help."

"Don't you think enlightened self-interest will do the trick? If humanity is wiped out, that's going to severely impact the vampire's food supply. For example."

"Most vampires aren't heavy hitters the way you want. They're more about hiding in shadows and seducing the unwary, not standing toe to toe with giant monsters."

"I'll figure it out." The Hybrid walked closer to the screen, running his fingers near the surface as he read the labels on various markers as they popped up in the display. "You have all the West Coast Vanguard personnel on here? Is Six Shooter still around?"

Amber shook her head at him. "Killed in the fighting with Three."

"Sledge and Crowbar?"

"Sledge is alive, but hospitalized. Maybe paralyzed. Crowbar is dead." Amber walked closer to Rohan and spoke in a softer voice. "Do you think maybe we need a different plan? With the personnel we have left . . ."

"I'm happy to entertain alternatives. Who are these guys?" He pointed at a cluster of markings.

"It's a touchscreen. Double tap it."

"Cool."

He touched the wall and spread his hands, zooming in so the red dot representing Four was at the left edge of the wall and North America spread across the right half.

The red dot was moving fast.

"Anybody know the ETA for *Void's Shadow*?"

Amber nodded. "Twenty minutes."

He sighed, tapping at the screen. "These guys won't do. These guys certainly won't do. I might be able to get these guys to summon their god, but if it shows up, we're all dead, and if it doesn't show up, they're useless."

The Damsel looked at him. "There's a reason we weren't doing this, hon. Most of the non-heroes are underpowered for this or too dangerous to risk."

"What about Alcatraz?"

She and Amber exchanged glances. Amber said, "You'd have to fight your way in there, get them to agree, then fight your way out. It's also lined with munitions rigged to blow if security is compromised. That's a tall order, especially on a deadline."

Rohan looked at The Director. She shook her head. "Nothing I can do, not quickly. I'm not sure they'd let anyone out in any case. The Powers in there are very bad people."

Rohan sighed and continued examining the screen. Fresh marks appeared as more researchers uploaded data into the main system.

"No. No. No."

The Damsel touched his shoulder with cool fingertips. "Please stop verbalizing the dead ends you're finding, hon. We don't all need to hear it."

He stopped. "Yeah, sorry."

He tapped the comm on his helmet and opened a line to *Insatiable*. "Anyone there?"

A familiar voice answered, speaking Drachna. "We are here."

Rohan swallowed and struggled for a moment to place it. "Garren? Is that you?"

"Yes, Tow Chief. I am here to render whatever assistance I can manage."

"Did you bring your armor?"

"I brought the new version, much improved. I gather I'll have ample opportunity to demonstrate."

The Hybrid realized he was wearing a surprised expression when Amber looked at him questioningly. He looked back and muted his comm. "It's

Garren. He's Marion Stone's research assistant, and a Tolone'an. He and
I got into a fight a few months back, I almost killed him. Also might have
committed a little genocide on his home planet."

Her only response was a wide-eyed stare. He shook his head and tapped
his comm back on.

"We have someone who can stop the land shark, but he's . . . well, he's
not someone you can communicate with, so we have to direct the land
shark to him. We're trying to gather up as many Powers as we can to help
with that. You up for a fight?"

"When is this?"

"I'd say . . . twelve hours, tops, before that thing hits the coast of
California."

"I'll be there."

"Thanks, Garren. Anybody else on that ship going to be of help in the
punching-stuff department?"

"I'm afraid not, Tow Chief."

"That's what I thought. Thanks anyway." He scratched his beard,
thinking.

The Director was chastising one of her analysts. "I don't care how
preliminary the numbers are, I want projections on that map. If it makes
you feel any better, attach a flag of no confidence. But give me something
to start with."

"Yes, ma'am."

Rohan turned to another tech. "We're getting some help. A flyer,
armored. He's Tolone'an."

"How strong is he, sir? What does he do?"

"He's a flyer, creates gravitational sources, positive and negative. Uh, pull
or push. In its last generation, his armor got him near the Power level of Kid
Lightning. He says the amor is improved, so . . . let's say in that ballpark.
Speaking of Kid . . ."

The Damsel shook her head, red curls waving with the motion. "He's
not ready to fight right now."

"How are *you* doing?"

"I'm better, but I'm not much use on the battlefield, so . . ."

"You think you can freeze the shark in place? Even for a few seconds?"

She hesitated. "No, hon. If Bright Angel flashes it, and I add in some confusing extra-sensory input, I could contribute. But by myself? Not even a few seconds."

Rohan sighed and looked back at the screen. "Amber, help me out here. You know what these projections mean?" Graphics were rapidly appearing on the map, radiating outwards from the moving red dot that showed the land shark's location.

"This arrow is the path the land shark is on now, this is the path it will follow without intervention, this is the path we want it on, and this is the chance we'll do it with the forces already on scene."

"What are those numbers?"

"Casualty estimates."

Rohan whistled. "That's . . . really bad."

"Yeah. When we tried this with Three, we had a lot of heroes on scene who aren't available now."

"But you have me with you this time."

"One more casualty added to that number isn't going to change a lot. Sorry."

Rohan studied the numbers.

He'd done well enough in math classes as a teenager, but after ten years fighting for the il'Drach, he'd gotten the equivalent of a PhD in war calculus.

The assets on the map were not enough to do the job in any kind of acceptable way. He hadn't come to Earth to watch millions of civilians die in a shark attack.

"Okay, I'm heading out. I'll have Bamf send me someplace and try to get help. You hold down the fort here. Make sure nobody attacks Garren. He's Tolone'an, meaning roughly human shaped, but if a human had an octopus eat his head."

"Uh . . . sure. Octopus."

"But just four tentacles. He'll be in armor and fighting the land shark. Actually, you know what? Nobody interferes with anybody fighting the monster. If Hitler's brain in a glass jar shows up and uses its telekinetic Powers on that shark, stay out of its way."

"Is that a real thing? Hitler's brain?"

"I hope not."

Rohan stepped over to The Director and waited while she finished discussing some aspect of the prediction modeling algorithms they were using.

"Hey, I'm going to get some help. I have the Vanguard phone, I'll turn it on and call for transport when I'm ready to join the fight."

She looked up into his face, one of her eyebrows arched upward in curiosity. "You have an idea?"

"Yeah. Not a good one, but it's an idea."

"Best of luck, then. For all our sakes."

"Thanks, Director."

Her forehead was creased with tension, her lips tight and pale as she moved from screen to screen, looking for the missing piece of data that would answer all their questions.

It reminded Rohan of how she'd once paced their kitchen, worried by one of his father's schemes, desperately working to find a way to free them both.

"Don't sweat it, we'll take care of this thing."

She answered with a nod. "Go on, then. I've got to try to get the Americans to start evacuating southern California. See if we can save them from themselves."

He nodded back, said goodbyes to the other members of Vanguard, and left the War Room.

· · • • · • • • ·

Bamf's doorway opened up onto a packed-dirt and gravel parking lot just off a freshly-paved, two-lane road. Trees choked the area, and from where he stood, Rohan couldn't see any structures other than the repurposed barn he had come to visit.

The air was thick and humid. It smelled strongly of trees and pollen and an array of vegetation that Rohan didn't recognize.

Heavy touring motorcycles and sturdy pickup trucks littered the parking lot. Flags decorated most of the vehicles; the handful of United States flags were outnumbered by Confederate battle flags and red, white, and black Nazi swastika banners.

The barn, a three-story tall wooden structure with straight sides and a rounded roof, flew its own Confederate flag, fluttering gently above a flickering neon sign that spelled out MAMA'S. Below that, a smaller sign said, BAR, and an array of beer company decals lined up next to the heavy front door. Budweiser, Coors, Miller. Rohan checked for a premium tequila brand he liked but came back disappointed.

Music thudded dimly through the walls of the barn, angry speed metal too fast for dancing. Rohan couldn't make out the words, only the driving beat, but he didn't regret it. Knowing whose bar it was, he didn't think he wanted to catch the lyrics.

As he walked up to the front door, Rohan saw a heavy plank of pale-yellow wood nailed over the door. Words were branded into the wood, black and rough.

NO COLOREDS.

"Subtle. Sweet, and subtle." Rohan took out his phone and tapped the tracking app to 'on.'

If I'm going to die in a dive bar in the middle of nowhere, let me at least make sure they can recover my body afterward.

He put his face shield, the airtight one, into his hood and tabbed the hood shut. Then he pulled the cloth mask, printed with an eagle's beak, up over the lower half of his face, snapping the elastic over the bridge of his nose.

The Hybrid reached inside and felt for the stormy lake of energy lurking just above his tailbone. It frothed and surged, eager to be unleashed, answering the anger of those inside the bar.

Or maybe it's answering my own.

He let the Power rise, just a little, not fully embracing it but keeping it at hand, ready to stream forth in all its glory. He had a feeling he'd need it.

He took a deep breath and pushed the odor open.

The space inside was dim but not too dark to see. The air smelled of cigarettes, stale beer, sawdust, and something spicy. Tacos?

The door swung shut behind Rohan. His eyes quickly adjusted to the light.

The music was louder from inside the bar; too loud to be pleasant but not loud enough to completely prevent conversations. The bar was bustling: men with shaven heads in flannel shirts, canvas work pants, and rugged boots mingling with women sporting long hair over T-shirts and tight jeans.

A crew of older women drenched in heavy makeup traveled the room, delivering trays nearly tipping with plates of food and open bottles.

The walls were decorated with Nazi memorabilia. Reproductions of German recruiting posters, SS uniforms mounted in glass cases, and an array of pistols and knives that Rohan assumed were representative of the Third Reich.

One of the men happened to turn and face Rohan. A nasty grin split his face, showing a poorly matched set of stained teeth. He walked over to the Hybrid.

The man bent slightly and put his face close to Rohan's. His blue eyes were wide and angry, his head clean shaven so no hair obscured the swastika tattooed on the side of his scalp.

"Didn't you read the sign, colored?"

Rohan was glad his mask obscured his sense of smell.

"I need to talk to Earl."

The man shook his head. "I don't think you understand where you are, boy." He reached over and grabbed the front of Rohan's uniform in his meaty fists.

Rohan felt his Power surge up, answering the insult.

The Hybrid reached up with his own hands and grabbed the back of the man's bald head. He clamped his forearms together, pressuring the man's neck, and pressed downward lightly.

A normal human would have crumpled from the force of the Hybrid's strength, but the man just smiled. Something had reinforced the tissues of his body, making his muscles inhumanly dense, the tendons and cartilage resilient and tough.

The man was a Power. As were, Rohan realized, almost all of the other males in the room.

The man grunted and lifted, as if to slam Rohan backward through the door.

The Hybrid let himself rise off the ground, pushing off slightly to add to the height of the arc he was traveling.

The man's eyes opened in surprise. With a grunt, Rohan *pushed* himself back downward, using his Power to slam his own body toward the ground.

The torque on the skinhead's arms lifted him slightly as Rohan smashed into the ground, disorienting the man.

With a violent twist of his body, Rohan turned the bigger man to the side, rotating the skinhead's body while he stepped back and pivoted.

In a single motion, Rohan had freed himself and driven the man's head through the door like a nail hammered through wood.

Rohan looked up to see an array of gang members lining up in front of him, bottles and knives held in their hands, angry expressions on their faces.

Someone lowered the volume on the music.

The Hybrid held his hands up. "I just need to speak to Earl. I'm not looking for trouble."

One of the men, on the shorter side but massively built, strode forward with his hands balled into hamlike fists.

Rohan tried again. "Earl will want to hear what I have to say."

The man laughed. "You're a few shades too dark to come into Mama's and tell us what you or we will want or not want." He swung a wide right hand toward Rohan's head, awkward and ugly but with an inhuman level of speed and strength and all the man's substantial weight behind it.

Rohan ducked and jammed his own right hand into the exposed floating rib, adding his strength to the power of the man's momentum to create a thunderous collision.

Bones crunched.

The skinhead dropped to the ground, convulsing lightly and grabbing at his side.

Another gang member hurled himself at Rohan, who twisted to throw the man off his back. While he was distracted, a different skinhead landed a punch flush across Rohan's face.

Rohan felt his Power surge upward and connect with the base of his skull, lighting him up with fresh energy. He stood and kicked the man in front of him in the throat, watching as he dropped to the ground in a foam of gagging noises.

"I just want to talk!" He heard his own voice as if it came from someone else, someone far away. It didn't sound calm anymore.

Two more beefy skinheads were in front of Rohan.

A knife whistled through the air, scraping his hairline as he ducked. A steel-toed work boot thudded into floating ribs.

Rohan grabbed a leg, stood, and twisted, tossing the neo-Nazi across the room. A blade sliced across his cheek, raising a stinging welt and cutting his mask.

The strike would have permanently disfigured a regular human.

Not playing games, are they?

Rohan moved forward, catching the knife wielder behind his arm. He pushed, knocking the knife out of the man's hand. Another push, and things inside the elbow snapped and tore.

The Hybrid reached around and slapped at the back of the man's neck with an open hand, instantly rendering him unconscious.

Five more Proud Guys were closing on Rohan.

He summoned a heavier stream of energy, preparing to fight as many more as he had to.

A voice rang out over the grunts and scraping chair legs.

"Enough!"

21

Devils, Debts, and Deals

T he crowd settled, their eyes still focused on the Hybrid.

A big man, fully two meters tall and close to two hundred kilos, strode through the group, the ground shaking subtly with every step.

The man had the build of an offensive lineman: dense with layers of meat and fat. He had blue eyes set a little too closely together on his face under a bald scalp, unadorned except for the massive swastika tattoo that ran from forehead to crown. He wore a button-down work shirt, blue jeans, and black steel-toed boots.

"That you, Griffin?"

"Hey, Earl. Seems you guys got a power-up."

Earl shook his beefy head. "You've been gone a long time, Griffin. Things change."

"Nice setup you have here."

"Is that what this is about? You want a beer? For old times' sake, I'll fix you up, on the house. Then you be on your way. And don't come back."

"That's not why I'm here, Earl."

"Why *are* you here, Griffin? Don't pretend you've ever been a friend of the Proud Guys."

A couple of the others whooped or let out a supportive "hell yeah."

Rohan paused, taking a long exhale. He forced his angry Power back down, like trying to push toothpaste back into a tube.

"Earl, we need your help."

"Who's 'we'? You mean you and that fine piece of dark meat you used to bang? Because from what I hear, she's left your memory in the past, old buddy."

Rohan shuddered slightly as his anger fought to take over. "Earl, there are bigger issues at hand than whatever grievance you have against me or Bright Angel. Your species is in danger, and we need your help to save it."

The squat man Rohan had tossed across the room snorted. "You talking about that fake shark that's been all over the news? We know better than to believe in those big corporation liberal conspiracies."

Rohan looked around the room, then returned his gaze to Earl. "Really? That's your take on this?"

Earl shrugged. "Even if it's real, I don't see how it's any of my problem. At least not right now."

"The words 'extinction-level event' don't mean anything to you? How are you guys going to have your race war if there are no races left to fight because all the people are dead?"

Earl smiled, a cold, nasty smile that would have chilled the heart of someone who'd seen less than Rohan.

"I don't see any sharks in these parts. Least not giant ones with legs. So far, the monsters have been killing off a bunch of yellow and brown people, mostly. Kind of doing us a favor."

"Earl, there's one in the Pacific right now, and it's headed for California. Plenty of white folk in California."

"Yeah, but a lot of non-white folk, and the white folk there are mostly what we call coastal elites. That doesn't put those sharks on the top of my priority list."

"You're not going to listen to me if I try to explain how the economic and humanitarian impact of these attacks is going to seriously harm you over here, are you?"

"I reckon I won't. Sounds like a whole lot of overly educated bullshit you're spewing my way to get me to do what you want."

Rohan sighed.

"All right, how about some quid pro . . . How about I offer you something?"

"What exactly do you think you have that I want? Unless that fine ebony queen of yours is on the table."

Stay calm. Even though you really don't want to.

"Something else. You help us with this, you get a pardon as far as Vanguard is concerned. No interference from Hyperion personnel."

Earl rubbed his chin with hand. "On what conditions? There are always conditions to these plea bargains."

"You stay south of the Mason-Dixon Line, east of the Mississippi. Doesn't cramp your style too much, does it? No domestic terrorism. Sell all the drugs and weapons you want. The Proud Guys are off the radar for all Vanguard operations."

"You serious, boy?"

Rohan nodded. "As a heart attack."

The short, extra-thick lieutenant looked worriedly from Earl to Rohan and back. "You're not listening to this, are you, boss? Can we just kill him and turn the music back on?"

"Shut up, Darryl. The grownups are talking." He turned to Rohan. "What kind of guarantee do I have that you'll keep your promise?"

Rohan smiled. "I'm an il'Drach Hybrid. We have a code; we always keep our word. Remember Hyperion? Always kept his word, even to his worst enemies. Not just him. Think of all the stories of, say, Soul Thief. He did some bad stuff. Never lied."

"Now, that there is the truth, Griffin, I do remember. And that makes it a very tempting offer. You'll even keep your bitch off our backs?"

"My word on it. Nobody in Vanguard bothers you. I own Hyperion, I can make that happen."

Darryl shook his head. "Boss, he needs us more than we need him. Make him sweeten the pot."

Earl looked at Darryl. "That isn't a bad idea, son. Not bad at all."

Rohan sighed.

The big skinhead looked at the Hybrid with narrowed eyes. "You come into my bar, beat on my boys, mess with the pride of the Proud Guys? And you expect to just walk out of here in one piece?"

Rohan felt a surge of his own anger answering Earl's. "What did you have in mind, Earl?"

"I think it's time you made a little demonstration of who's the boss around here. Kiss the boots." Earl put his heavy left foot up on a barstool. "Boys, get the cameras out."

"You want me to kiss your boot?" The surge of anger intensified, threatening to sweep away the thin, foamy layer of self-control he had in place over its surface.

"Yeah. Mask off, though. We wouldn't want anyone accusing us of dressing up some random darkie in a Griffin outfit for a publicity stunt. After all, it's not too much to ask, is it? To save . . . how many millions of people?"

Rohan's anger surged again. He swallowed, tried to speak, had to try again before the words would come out.

"The il'Drach have a saying. There are two kinds of anger. The kind you own, and the kind that owns you."

"That is very poetic. Isn't that poetic, Darryl?"

Darryl nodded and smiled. "Yes, boss. Like song lyrics."

Rohan swallowed again. "The anger you own is the one that you use. It motivates you, makes you try harder, work harder. It can be good. Practical. Useful.

"But when you get the anger that owns you, and the anger is in charge, you do things that aren't for *you* anymore. You'll throw away your life, your family, everything you care about, to feed the anger. You understand what I'm saying, Earl?" The Power was leaking off of Rohan, rippling the dirt floor of the bar. Bottles rattled on tables, and the furniture started to shake.

"Is it worth it, Griffin?"

"I'm trying to tell you that I know it's not. But the anger is too close to taking charge, Earl. It wants me to crush some throats. And I know it will be a useless and stupid thing, and it might doom the planet, but I am just so close to not caring anymore."

"You think you can take us all on, Griffin? We're not the chumps you fought a decade ago. We've been changed."

"I can see that, Earl. And I'm not sure I can beat the lot of you, not all at once. But I'm damn sure that before I'm done, half of you are going to have to pee sitting down for the rest of your lives."

Rohan watched Earl run the numbers in his mind, his eyes flickering back and forth as he considered.

The Hybrid wished the white supremacist was better at math. The calculations were taking a long time.

Earl slapped his hand down on a table. "We'll take your deal, Griffin. We'll fight the land shark. And when we're done, the South will be ours."

Rohan forced his anger back, his hands trembling with the effort. "You get your men to the West Coast. North of LA but just outside city limits. I'll text you updated coordinates. After the fight, you'll be on your own. No help from Vanguard, but no interference either."

"Deal."

Rohan let out a long, shuddering breath, then turned and left Mama's bar.

· · · · · · · · · ·

"Another bottle of the red, sir?"

"Of course I want another bottle! They kept me sober for six weeks in that hellhole! You know how hard it is to be sober for six continuous weeks? Do you know how many centuries it's been since I've gone that long without wine?"

"Yes sir; no sir; I do not, sir."

Poseidon sat at the central conference table in the Hyperion Industries War Room. A tub full of liquid sat on the floor in front of him. He slouched deep enough in his chair to submerge most of his legs in the tub. His elbow was up on the table, an open bottle of wine clutched in a tight fist, head tilted to the side, eyes focused on the broken remains of Ares's spear.

All four walls were now covered floor-to-ceiling with active screens. The screen opposite the double door entrance still showed the map The Director had asked for, crowded now with icons representing various factors in the battle against the land shark they were calling 'Four.'

The other walls were divided into smaller sections displaying a variety of feeds. Live video of the Pacific Ocean, The Green sitting alone and peaceful in the desert, biometrics for Bamf. The teleporter was showing the strain of the amount of work he was being asked to do: elevated stress hormones and heart rate, suppressed glucose tolerance.

Another display showed an array of digital clocks. It was about three in the morning, local time.

Are we paying overtime for this?

Rohan walked around the edge of the room, stopping short in front of a screen that showed him savagely beating a man apparently made of metal. Brother Steel.

Rohan locked eyes with the tech who was watching the feed. The hero cleared his throat. "I didn't realize there was video of that."

The tech just pointed uselessly at the screen and shrugged. There was no appropriate answer. "The shorter version has been in and out of rotation while you've been gone, sir. Anti-Powers activists like to give it exposure periodically. This is longer. Released today."

Rohan nodded and watched. He hoped to find some spark of mercy or pity in the eyes of the man who was crippling Brother Steel. His eyes.

He saw nothing but anger.

With a shake of his head, the Hybrid continued to the conference table.

He sat across from the sea god, whose eyes were still fixed on the pieces of the supposedly indestructible spear.

Rohan cleared his throat. "How are you, Poseidon?"

The god turned slowly to face him. "Bloody terrible. How do you think I am?" Poseidon had been thoroughly cleaned, his wavy, white hair and heavy beard now fluffy and greaseless. He wore a plain, white robe and no mask.

The god had never tried to keep his face a secret.

"Well, better than a couple of days ago?"

Poseidon lifted the bottle to his lips and took a long pull. "I'll drink to that. I suppose you're here for a 'thank you'? Or to catch up? They tell me you've been gone for over ten years."

"I have."

"I didn't really notice, but welcome back. Ten years doesn't mean so much to me. And thanks for the rescue."

"It wasn't—"

The god interrupted. "Oh please, spare me the false modesty. We both know the others might have managed eventually, but we also know that your handling of Eldest made the difference."

Rohan conceded. "You're welcome."

Poseidon turned away from the broken spear and fixed slightly bloodshot eyes on the Hybrid. "How did you manage him, by the way? I thought he was out of your league. At least from a horsepower perspective."

Rohan shrugged. "You're thinking of me from before."

The Hybrid sniffed. The tub that sat between them smelled of saltwater. Poseidon noticed him looking into it.

"I heal faster when part of me is connected to the sea. If I can keep my feet in there, I'll be good as new in a day. Which is more than I can say for poor old Ares."

Rohan sighed. "You've known each other for a long time."

"Millennia. Never liked him, but who else understood what life was like for either of us?" He took another long drink from the bottle.

"My condolences. I can't imagine."

"No, you can't. Mortals, immortals, different scales to these things. What do they say? Men are from Mars, women are from Venus? Gods are from someplace else. Someplace farther." He laughed.

Rohan looked around the room. "Where are the others?"

Poseidon waved his bottle in a wide arc through the air. "The lovely Bright Angel is at the beach. Literally. She's organizing the troops, so to speak, at the spot where they think Four will make landfall."

"Good."

"Amber and The Damsel are there as support."

"Is The Damsel going to rally the troops? Project confidence at them? Courage? Or damp out the aura of the land shark?"

The sea god took another swallow of wine. "I stopped listening at some point, but that sounds right. Did you want some wine, too? They can bring more over. This place has a *divine* wine cellar." He winked.

Rohan leaned back in his chair and stretched his arms overhead. "You should try their tequila. Before I forget, did you figure out anything about where these sharks are coming from?"

Poseidon looked at the Hybrid intensely. "I can tell you a few things. First, they're not from the ocean. Not from *this* ocean. These things haven't been swimming around for centuries until finally deciding enough was enough with the plastic in the ocean and the pollution."

"So . . . not native to Earth?"

"I would have noticed. I would have *felt* them."

"Okay. Are they new? Some kind of shark mutant? A new species?"

Poseidon shook his head. "I said they're not from here. I felt . . . there are doorways in the sea. Paths to other places."

"Watery wormholes?"

The god shrugged. "I don't know what you call it. Wait, you know Lyst, don't you? You know how she can move her boat to any body of water? Anywhere in the . . . well, anywhere?"

"I guess."

"This is the same. You're human and fundamentally a land animal. You think of the universe as a continuous void of deep space with planets plopped in here and there, and water exists on some of those planets."

"I guess. I never really thought about it."

"Sure. To the older races, I mean the really old ones, all bodies of water are connected. Adjacent even. The universe is a vast sea; land, atmospheres, even all of outer space is just a set of anomalies bobbing above the water's surface."

Rohan took a moment to process while the god finished his bottle.

"You're saying the sharks are from another part of this vast sea? Or as I would think of it, from an ocean on another planet. That is connected to our oceans through a magical portal."

"Basically."

"Is this portal in a specific place?"

Poseidon shook his head. "It's a waterway, not a wooden door. It will move and shift with the tides, and I don't just mean the physical tides. On either world. We can't just pop a cork in it and stop the sharks."

"But can we find it?"

"I can find it when it's open. Before you ask, no, I can't tell you where it's going to be."

"Can you tell me where it leads to? What planet?"

"I'm the god of this sea, not of *all* the seas. Outside my jurisdiction." He peeled the foil off a fresh bottle of wine and started working a corkscrew into it.

"Well, can you give me any ideas on how to fight these things? They're tearing us apart."

"I would fight it on land, if I were you. Even regular sharks are frightening in the water. Get that up on land. There your chances go from zero to a multiple of zero."

"That's still zero."

Poseidon waved his bottle in the air.

"Math is not always your friend, my friend." He paused. "I felt that thing's Power when we were running from it. I have no idea how to fight something like that. Not if I'm trying to win. Or survive."

Rohan rubbed his forehead. "Okay. I guess it's obvious, but please let me know if you think of something."

Rohan turned, startled at the sound of Bright Angel's voice talking over one of the video feeds.

Poseidon laughed. "What are you going to do, kid? Go help the fight?"

Rohan paused and thought. "I think I'm the coup de grace again, so I have to sit back and let the others soften him up first. If I pitch in now and get hurt or killed, then this whole thing is over."

"That was a remarkably cold and possibly self-centered way to describe the situation. Are you really going to sit back and ignore the battle? Take a nap? Hard to imagine Hyperion handling things that way. Much less the old you."

"Yeah, I'm no Hyperion. I keep telling people that."

"Where is he, anyway? Busy off saving the galaxy or something?"

Rohan coughed. "They didn't tell you? Hyperion's dead. Killed in action. A couple years ago."

"Really? I always figured he'd die of some weird interspecies venereal disease. He was the strongest mortal I ever knew."

"Do you mean to tell me you know gods stronger than Hyperion? Because we could really use a couple right about now."

Poseidon laughed. "It was just a turn of phrase. I like the way it makes me sound pretentious, so whenever I compliment someone, I add, 'for a mortal.'"

"For a god, you're very down-to-earth."

"Thank you . . . I see what you did there! Very good. I like this older version of you. Less angry."

"Still angry. I just hide it better."

"Which is all I really care about, thank you. Be as angry as you want, as long as it stays nicely bottled up."

"Thanks. It's nice to know you care."

"You'll be dead soon enough, by my standards. Along with everyone else on the planet. If the sharks don't get you, then Chronos will."

"You mean . . . literally?"

"No, not literally. I don't mean the god Chronos will go after you by hand. Just that time will march on, and you'll die. Again, just choosing the pretentious way to say it. Try to keep up."

"Got it. I'm actually not sure how Hybrids age. I might not get old and die."

"Never met an old Hybrid. You all tend to gravitate toward dangerous lifestyles."

"I'm working on avoiding that."

"Your presence here seems to indicate that you aren't being very successful. Fight those sharks and you're not likely to have to worry about old age. Though that might be a blessing in disguise; living for centuries has its drawbacks."

"I hear what you're saying, but I feel the same way about that as I do when people say money can't buy happiness. Like, maybe you're right, but I'd like the opportunity to find out for myself."

The old sea god chuckled and held up his bottle in a short salute.

They sat quietly for a few moments, the drone of competing audio streams from all around the room combining into something very close to white noise.

Poseidon looked at Rohan through the corner of his eye. "Hyperion is dead, and, since they're not here, I'm guessing the other il'Drach Hybrids are out of action one way or another. So . . . you're all the help we're going to get?"

Rohan nodded. "Basically."

The sea god held his half-empty bottle up to the light. "Then, I'm definitely going to need more wine."

22

First Blood

"Hyperion HQ, we're close. The monster is still heading toward the city. Do the satellites agree, or am I seeing this wrong?"

The Director waved her hand at one of the techs, who shook her head and spoke into her tablet.

"Bright Angel, you're correct. Four needs to be redirected about eight degrees north. Not more than fifteen degrees."

"How bad is it if we don't change its course?"

"Vanguard Prime, if Four is not redirected, it will make landfall on central Los Angeles. Estimated death toll . . . upward of two hundred thousand, assuming minimal deviation from a straight-line path. That's the conservative projection."

"Roger that."

Rohan rubbed the sleep out of his eyes and walked over to The Director. He touched her arm. "Where are they?"

She turned to him. "They're on a Hyperion Industries ship off the California coast. It's got very little in the way of electronics so little pulses of metaphysical energy don't interfere with its operation. A big sailboat."

Rohan nodded. "What happened?"

The Director shook her head. "It changed course. No reason we can determine, beyond it being an animal and not a train. Bright Angel went to lead the group trying to put it back on path."

"Who's in the group?"

"Any flyers we could get out to sea. I'm not sure if you know any of them. The Rainbow Stars? Group out of Northern California."

"I know those guys. Well, I know *of* them. Never met."

Bright Angel's voice came over the speakers. "Wave One, move out. You know the plan: get in there, do damage, retreat. We need its path moved by eight degrees north or we're going to lose an extra quarter million civilians. That's three football stadiums full of people. Go save them!"

Rohan swallowed. "That's the best tactic?"

The Director nodded. "It's angry. It goes after anything that hurts it. So, to manipulate its path, you have to hurt it and make it follow you. We tried luring it with food, didn't help. I somehow doubt we can find an actual shark of the opposite sex and get it moving that way."

Rohan coughed. "Whose idea was the female shark?"

"Kid Lightning. Before he . . . you know."

He sighed. "How smart are these things?"

A tech answered. "We're not sure. No signs of real intelligence, but too smart to be led around in circles."

Rohan nodded.

Bright Angel's voice. "Hyperion HQ, we are engaging Four."

Rohan spoke to the tech. "How far underwater is it?"

"Quite close to the surface, sir. It comes up and surfaces, then dips back down no more than a few hundred meters. We saw a similar pattern with the previous three. The working hypothesis is that they are gradually practicing the use of their lungs. Instinctive prep for coming ashore."

The hero nodded.

The channel went silent.

"HQ, there's a . . . guy wearing some kind of suit of armor. It has multiple . . . tentacles? Yeah, tentacles. Attached around the base of the helmet. He's hovering near me. Not hostile but not responding to direction either."

Rohan cleared his throat. "That's Garren. He came with the Professors Stone. He's here to help. I'll comm him directly. He doesn't speak any Earth languages."

"Roger that, Griffin."

Rohan opened a channel to the Tolone'an and relayed the general instructions.

Shortly, Bright Angel spoke again.

"The armored guy has either gone for donuts or he's joining the attack. I guess it's fine either way."

The room grew quiet as they waited for updates. Poseidon's bottle gurgled as he drank. Soft sounds of fingers tapping at glass came from every corner as techs entered data and performed calculations.

The red dot on the wall-sized map continued its pixelated progress toward shore and the forty million residents of California. Oversized arrows emanating from the dot showed in real time its velocity and projected path.

The Director chewed on the back of a pen as her gaze shifted rapidly between the main map and a variety of secondary displays.

"Any updates on teams from Europe? South America? How about our own backyard?"

A wellspring of muttering arose to answer her. None of it sounded very promising.

She turned to Rohan. "Most of the real powerhouses from anywhere in the world are either already on the way, recovering from serious injuries, or dead. We threw everything we had at Two before resorting to bombing half the Pacific Rim into oblivion."

Rohan started to think of names of powerful heroes he'd known, or known of, back in his days on Earth. He was about to start listing them but noticed a display showing names of fallen heroes.

He walked over to it and scrolled through.

Bright Angel's voice came over the speakers. "First contact is made."

The velocity arrows on the map instantly shifted as the shark changed course to respond to the first round of attacks.

"It's hit. Blood in the water. I repeat, blood in the water. It's come up, the land shark is airborne now. Its sending a pulse of energy."

"I've lost comms to Wave One. Their phones are dead."

The Director yelled. "Get me satellite imagery up on the right wall! I want visuals ASAP!"

"Director, there were seven satellites in position. Two are already down."

"Then get me visuals from the other five."

"They probably won't last long, ma'am."

"Am I talking to myself? Put up the feeds for as long as they last. When they're down, they're down. We'll worry about it then." She turned to her son and shook her head. "Save me from people telling me things I already know."

He smiled, wondering if anybody else noticed how familiarly she treated him. As far as the world knew, they'd only met a couple of days before.

Bright Angel spoke. "Its aura is intensifying. Even from this distance, it's like wading through toxic mud."

The Director spoke. "Get Wave One out of there. We don't need martyrs. There's already enough change in its direction to save most of LA."

"Copy."

"We have visuals, Director."

The wall to the right of the big map flickered and turned to an overhead view of Four.

The shark's massive dorsal fin was breaking the water's surface, the sheer power of the creature made obvious by the wake left behind, bigger than some small countries. A group of specks, the flying heroes of Wave One, dove in to attack the shark, barely visible against the sea foam.

With a startling movement, the shark leapt from the water, its huge mouth snapping at the group. The specks scattered, and Rohan squinted, vainly attempting to count them.

Were they all still there?

The specks broke off and flew at a northward angle, sticking to their directive to draw the enormous beast away from heavily populated areas.

The shark followed them, leaping from the water again, its entire body clearing the waves as it attempted to swallow more of the heroes.

A flash of blinding white, and the picture went dead.

"Did it take out the satellite? What happened?"

"No, ma'am, satellite is still transmitting. Something burned out the camera, ma'am."

The Director muttered. "Bright Angel. I bet. Okay, get new satellites into position. And if the cameras are burned out on those five, can we get other sensors up? Something that isn't based on the visible electromagnetic spectrum? Maybe radar can pick it up? Someone get me data!"

A chorus of "yes, ma'am"s sounded from the group, and they hustled to get their boss more information.

Rohan tapped his comm. "*Void's Shadow*, are you around?"

There was a delay before he heard a response. "Yes, Captain, I'm still on Earth. What's up?"

"If you stay high enough to be safe from that land shark, can you capture visuals on it and transmit them here? Maybe bounce a tightbeam off a satellite?"

"Let me think . . . Yes, I can. Do you want me to?"

"Yeah. I'll ping you the coordinates. Thanks, *Void's Shadow*."

Rohan stepped over to The Director.

"I can put my ship in position to get imagery. She has ridiculous stealth tech, so most likely the shark won't even realize she's there."

She turned to him, her eyes tight. "You couldn't have mentioned this before? These guys are killing themselves trying to find a satellite that will last more than five minutes above the Pacific, and you have a stealth ship that could have taken care of it?"

"Uh . . . yeah? Sorry, juggling a lot of things in my head."

She sighed and pinched her forehead. Rohan stifled a laugh as he noticed that he did the same thing when he felt stress. Like mother, like . . .

"Then, do it. And let me think."

Poseidon smiled at him as Rohan took back his seat.

"She's fearsome, isn't she? I have to admit, we thought Hyperion was crazy, putting her in charge. She was a nobody. And here we are, a little over ten years later, and she's transformed the world."

Rohan looked at him. "Yeah, a nobody."

"And not bad-looking at all. For a mortal. I certainly wouldn't throw her out of bed, if you know what I mean." He winked.

Rohan squirmed in his seat. "You really do not need to elaborate."

"Show her a little motion of the ocean."

"Please stop."

Does he know? Is he teasing me or just being his usual self?

Poseidon pointed at the map with his bottle. "It looks like they got the shark on the right path. Wonder how many died getting that accomplished."

"I'm mostly worried about Bright Angel. She wasn't supposed to get involved this early."

"She's tough, but maybe a touch too *human*. Don't you think?"

Rohan sighed. "She's a hero, not a soldier. And this is looking more and more like a war."

"Yes, a war! Too bad we lost Ares, am I right?" He held up the bottle, saluting the broken spear on the conference table.

"We have visuals! Onscreen . . . now."

A fresh image, color shifted for some reason, appeared on the right-side wall.

One of the techs was speaking. "We're extrapolating from repurposed infrared and ultraviolet sensors, ma'am."

"Good. Have we heard from Bright Angel?"

"Hold."

There was a pause as everyone in the room held their breath.

A voice came over the speaker. "Hello?"

"This is The Director. With whom am I speaking?"

"Oh, sorry, ma'am. This is Amber. Bright Angel gave me her phone."

"Is she all right? Where is she?"

"She's fine, ma'am. She *bursted* at the shark to save the rest of Wave One, then flew back to the boat. It took a lot out of her; she's belowdecks recovering."

"That shark is going to make landfall in twenty minutes. Will she be able to be able to handle that end of things?"

"Yes, ma'am. We'll be there."

"Very well." A tech closed the call.

The Director addressed the room. "Back to work. I want better information, more ideas. Make sure we have everything we need to get that feed from Griffin's ship. First priority: I want casualty reports from that assault."

Rohan shifted his weight back from one side of the seat to the other. He was itching to head out to the field, to get his hands on the shark. Finally, he stood and looked at Poseidon. "I need some food and some air. I'll be back."

The sea god waved his bottle and shifted his legs, stirring waves in the tub of sea water. "Have fun. You know where I'll be."

· · • • • · • • · ·

Rohan rushed to swallow his mouthful of sandwich in time to answer the chirping comm.

His response came out embarrassingly muffled.

"Hello?"

"This is *Insatiable*. Is this Tow Chief Rohan? It doesn't sound like you. Are you okay? Oh my gosh, are you hurt? I can come down right now and get you."

Rohan forced himself to swallow before responding.

"I'm fine, *Insatiable*. Just talking with my mouth full. What's going on?"

"Oh, good. That's great. I was worried. What a backwater place to lose a hero of the Empire."

"Not loving Earth, then, are you?"

"It's fine, just incredibly crowded. And filthy. And facing destruction. Honestly, I'm glad I'm in orbit."

"I'm not going to argue."

"The Professors wanted me to tell you that they'd like to come to Sahara City to discuss something. To be honest, they need a break. They are very emotionally attached to this planet."

Rohan shook his head. "You do realize they grew up here, don't you?"

"Oh yes, of course! Still, it's not home anymore, is it? Never mind, I'm just showing how little I understand their species."

"We are prone to sentimentality."

"It's your home, too, isn't it. I've been rude. It does have some pretty parts. Though there are already so many people on it, I can't quite figure why they're so upset about the dead ones. It's just a fraction of the population. A small fraction! And you guys breed *fast*. You'll replace them in no time."

"I know, *Insatiable*. People are strange."

"Anyway, can they come see you now? They want to talk to you about something. Did I already say that? I think I did."

"That's fine. Not like I'm doing anybody any good right now. Can you open a portal to my current position?"

"Surprisingly, no. There's some shielding around the city, I can't get them even close to you. It's quite impressive tech for such a primitive world."

Rohan wondered briefly how the city was protected. Was it Bamf's Power?

"Hold on. I'll find out where you can send them."

He spent ten minutes grabbing random uniformed Hyperion security personnel and questioning them. The port where he had first landed was the only accessible place to send the Professors.

Five minutes later, he was standing on an unused airstrip and letting his comm system act as a beacon for *Insatiable*.

Moments after that, a hole opened in space directly in front of him. Instead of a view of the tarmac and the array of carbon fiber and glass skyscrapers behind it, he had a two-meter-wide look into a spare metal-walled room inside *Insatiable*.

The Professors came through. Marion paused as she stepped out, bracing against the onslaught of heat. Ben followed on her heels and stood behind her.

"You two look terrible."

Ben shook his head.

They had never looked *old* to Rohan before.

Marion stepped up to Rohan, nearly nose-to-nose, and glared into his eyes.

"Where is Garren?"

Rohan shrugged and looked from her to Ben and back.

"Garren's missing?"

She raised a hand, as if ready to slap him, but didn't follow through.

"Don't do that. Don't act like this has nothing to do with you."

Her hand was shaking.

"Dr. Stone, I'm not acting like anything. I have no idea. He went to help fight the land shark. He *offered* to help. He's missing?"

"Yes, he's missing. No communication, no visuals. *Insatiable* can't find him with any scans.

"How could you do this? This wasn't his fight. He went off to join your war, and you couldn't even be bothered to keep track of him? To know he was lost?"

Ben stepped closer and put a hand on her shoulder. "Marion, sweetheart, you're tired. *We're* tired. Rohan is working as hard as anyone to save this planet. Garren's not his responsibility."

She shrugged him off. "Don't you start that either. He tells Garren that he actually saved Tolone'a, and that idiot believed him. Went all wide-eyed with hero worship. Now look where it's gotten him."

Rohan sputtered. "Wait, hero worship? Me? Why?"

Ben sighed. "You spared his life, even saved him, when you could have killed him. That shook him up. Then you told him that what you did on Tolone'a was the only thing that saved the planet, and he realized you were probably right. He felt a lot of guilt for attacking you."

Rohan scratched his beard.

As a lance for the il'Drach, he'd wiped out the religious caste of Tolone'a, ending their war with the Empire. The Tolone'ans had called it genocide, but Rohan believed that if he hadn't managed to end the war that way, the il'Drach would have destroyed the entire planet.

A terrible sin to prevent a cataclysm.

He'd told Garren as much, after their fight.

"Are we even sure he's lost? He can swim, right? Tolone'ans are amphibious."

Ben nodded. "We think he can survive underwater, though to be fair, I'm not certain the oxygen levels in Earth's oceans are fully compatible with his physiology. But he was wearing his armor."

"So?"

Marion spoke before her husband could respond. "If the armor was damaged, it might have locked him in, dragged him too deep. We can't find its energy signature anywhere, which means it's either been destroyed or it's very far down. He's not used to that kind of pressure. The armor certainly isn't built for it."

Rohan sighed. "I'm sorry, I'm not sure what I can do. I didn't mean for him to get hurt."

"Then why did you let him go? Tell him where to fight? He's not human. This isn't his battle." She looked ready to hit him.

Rohan put his hands up. "Professor, I get that you're upset. He's your assistant, your friend. But if you're trying to get me to apologize for letting him help us save Los Angeles from a giant shark attack, that's not going to happen. Garren was part of an effort that saved hundreds of thousands of people."

Ben put a hand on her shoulder, more firmly this time. He looked at Rohan. "Let's all slow down. We're all a little . . . raw. There are literally hundreds of millions of people displaced across southern China, Thailand, Japan, Indonesia . . . We couldn't even count the numbers of dead or those in temporary housing. Or no housing. That kind of devastation brings up some . . . some feelings."

Marion turned to her husband, her eyes as tight as her jaw.

Something in his expression deflated her anger.

She spun back to Rohan.

"You owe him something more than forgetting he's gone."

"I owe a lot of people a lot of things; I'm willing to add him to the ledger. What did you have in mind?"

"You have to go looking for him."

"I really am sorry. Not that I'm saying I did the wrong thing, but just that I feel bad he's in danger. But right now, I have other priorities."

"I won't disagree. But once the sharks are taken care of, you go looking for him. And you find him. Dead or alive."

The Hybrid nodded. "Deal. And once we get back to Wistful, I promise to let you yell at me all you want, for as long as you want, about what I let Garren do, and I won't talk back. Not a word."

"You plan to go back?"

Rohan looked back at her. "I mean, assuming I survive this whole thing, yeah, I plan to go back. Why not? Wistful is home."

"Are you assuming we're going to lose the Earth?"

"No. I'm assuming we'll win. I *always* assume we'll win. It's how I was trained."

She nodded. "I remember."

She never forgets that I'm a Hybrid. Or how much she's suffered at the hands of Hybrids.

"For now, maybe you guys can help me with some things. Like figuring out what the artifact does."

Ben looked puzzled. "What artifact?"

Rohan scratched under his mask. "I forgot that you missed that. Let's head to HQ while we talk."

They followed his lead toward the bus line. He filled them in as they walked.

"When we killed the third land shark, we found a device inside its body. It had writing on it, which we thought was Atlantean, but Masamune says it's . . . octopus."

Ben turned sharply toward his friend. "Cephalopod writing? The Old Ones?"

Rohan shrugged gently. "I guess. This is kind of news to me. It means more to you two?"

The Professors exchanged a look. Marion spoke first. "We've never dealt with them directly. Old Ones like to work indirectly. Through agents."

Ben swallowed. "We, by which I mean the il'Drach academic community, thought the Tolone'ans were agents of the Old Ones for a long time. An idea which was eventually debunked."

Marion looked at Rohan. "What did this artifact do?"

"Best guess, it made the sharks angry. It sat right on the thing's spinal column."

The pair exchanged another look. Ben shook his head. "Sounds like someone has been weaponizing these sharks. You're thinking Old Ones? Or somebody else using Old One technology?"

Rohan nodded. "One of those. Unless you have a more convincing theory."

Marion snorted. "You mean 'hypothesis.'"

Rohan instructed the driver to take them to Hyperion HQ.

She continued. "I assume you have a decent workshop where we can study the artifact?"

"It was stolen. The artifact."

"By whom?"

"No idea. All surveillance was wiped out. Kid Lightning fought them, but he's having communication issues. He overused his Powers and damaged his nervous system. His speech center is all out of whack; he can't really say much."

"Hm. He couldn't convey anything?"

"He just waved his arms around in the air. If that's information, I don't understand it." Rohan mimicked the hand motion that Kid Lightning had made the previous day.

"Like tentacles?"

Rohan looked at Ben Stone, his mouth hanging open. "Yeah! That's what he was doing! Maybe. That's a good guess."

Ben looked at his wife. "Dr. Kraken?"

She nodded back. "That's a name I haven't thought about in forty years. It could be."

Rohan looked between them. "You know Dr. Kraken?"

Marion looked back. "Of course we do."

"No offense, but I didn't realize he's been around that long."

She snorted. "That long? He's been around a lot longer than us. Hasn't he, dear?"

Ben nodded. "I think Poseidon's been tangling with him for centuries."

Rohan thought. "I've never run into him. He has actual tentacles? I thought the 'Kraken' thing was just to sound scary."

Ben shook his head. "No, he looks . . . come to think of it, he looks a lot like a Tolone'an. Octopus eyes, four tentacles from around the base of his head, humanoid body below that."

Marion nudged her husband with her elbow. "Not quite the same."

"No, not quite. Hyperion looked into this once. He knew Dr. Kraken better. There are enough anatomical differences to indicate he's a different race."

Rohan ran his fingers through his hair, combing it back from his face. "Whether or not he's connected to the Tolone'ans, it doesn't seem like a big stretch to imagine a guy with tentacles and octopus eyes is connected to the cephalopods, or Old Ones, or whatever you call them."

Ben sighed and sank deeper into his seat. "If he's not involved, I'm sure he's lurking somewhere enjoying the show. Watching humanity suffer was his favorite pastime."

23

A Fine Day at the Beach

A sari in black, gold, and deep red draped over The Director. Her makeup was flat and metallic, her hair captured in a tight bun. The effect was more fierce than pretty, perfectly complementing her facial expression.

She paced the area between the main conference table and the primary wall display, pausing occasionally to sip from a cup of tea kept full and at a very precise temperature by a highly trained, dark-suited assistant.

Another assistant called out, as instructed. "Ten minutes projected, ma'am."

The Director looked at her son. "I'm still not used to this kind of tension."

He wanted to give her a hug, but it would have seemed too out of place to most of the people in the crowded room.

"Our best people are on the ground. The plan is good. Trust the process."

She paused in her pacing and shook her head. "Lack of trust is not the problem here."

"Okay, but . . ." He stepped closer and lowered his voice. "You're making people nervous."

She met his eyes with a stern gaze. "They *should* be nervous."

He held his hands up in surrender and walked away.

"Five minutes."

A strategic map of North America west of the Mississippi filled the wall directly opposite the room's main double door entrance. The live feed from *Void's Shadow* took up half the wall to its left.

The sea was dark, the sun an hours-distant memory. Shallow moonlight dimly illuminated the froth from the waves, every crest and bubble of it picked up in surprising detail by *Void's Shadow*'s cameras.

Splitting the dark waters, dead center on the image, was a huge dorsal fin, a vast, delta-shaped wake left behind it to fade in despair.

Bright Angel's voice came over the speaker system. "In position. We've got a ton of low-level Powers, all locals, but I'm not sure they'll be of any real help. Also, confirmed loss of two of the Rainbow Stars; Indigo and Violet are both out of commission."

Rohan looked at The Director. "Weren't those the strongest Stars?"

She nodded. "Also the slowest. They got caught by the shark; the others managed to get away. Not a loss we could really afford, but we also couldn't afford having that thing land dead center on Los Angeles."

He sighed and scratched under his mask. He noticed his mother's hand holding tightly to the back of an unused chair, her knuckles white against the brown skin of her fingers.

The small secondary door near the conference table opened, and Carla emerged, dressed in her usual designer T-shirt and blue jeans. She nodded to Rohan, then walked over to The Director and silently took her other hand.

They stood shoulder to shoulder and watched the land shark's approach. The general buzz of the room's teeming workers had softened to a low hum as the atmosphere loaded with tension.

Rohan felt his own stress levels building. A knot of anxiety was manifesting directly between his shoulder blades, just out of reach, tightening uncomfortably as the countdown continued.

He stretched, then announced to nobody in particular, "I'll be back."

Three wrong turns later, he was in the Vanguard medical bay, standing in front of Kid Lightning's bed.

A screen had been set up across from the hero's position, showing him a mirror of the live feed from the conference room.

"Kid Lightning!"

Rohan smiled. "Hey, man. How are you?"

Kid Lightning shrugged and spread his muscular arms out to the sides, palms upward.

"Yeah, man, I hear you. I wish we knew who attacked you."

Kid Lightning waved his arms around, held loosely at the elbows and shoulders.

Rohan nodded. "The Professors think you're showing us tentacles. Like Dr. Kraken. Was he the one who attacked you?"

The other hero wore a look of frustration. He made a fist and slapped the mattress by his side.

"I guess you can't really tell me. I'm sorry, man. If I could fix you up, you know I would. I have a regen tank on my ship, but I'm pretty sure it would just kill you. It's set up for Hybrids."

Kid waved a hand at the screen.

"Why am I not out there myself? With Bright Angel and the others? I'd like to be, but I can't risk it. Our best shot at actually killing the land shark is for me to take it out after it's been softened up by The Green. Same as we did with Three. I need a clean hit to do any damage. Which means sneaking up on it."

The bedridden hero made a rude noise.

"Right, I can't risk that thing sensing my Power until the last moment. The only chance of that is to have it not expecting me while also being as disoriented as possible."

Kid Lightning tilted his head forward, his blond hair hanging over his face, and shoved his chin toward the screen.

Rohan looked at it.

Four was close to shore.

The Hybrid leaned forward and tapped at the edges of the screen until a control panel appeared. Within moments, he had the sound turned on.

The audio feed was set to the same source as the War Room.

Bright Angel's voice was narrating the invasion.

"He's coming up on the beach."

The angled tip of the shark's snout broke out of the water and up onto the sand, water streaming down off its back in torrents.

The creature lifted its head as its forward momentum slowed, its eyes wild. With a shrug that traveled up its entire body, it brought first one, then the other massive leg up onto the beach. Sand pillowed out from under both feet as it lifted its enormous bulk into the air.

Water and sand poured off the creature as it opened its mouth and took a short, shaky breath.

It coughed a small pond full of water out onto shore, then took another breath.

One more cough.

With its next breath, the shark leaned its head back, snout pointed skyward, and shook in place. Rohan could see ripples forming in the sand, and a nearby shack was flattened.

Rohan looked at his friend. "I'm kind of glad we don't have audio near that thing."

"Kid Lightning."

When they looked back, Bright Angel was talking again. "Ugh, he's turning, following the beach. We have to engage to get him inland. I'm putting Wave Two in play."

Rohan turned away from the screen as motes of dust streaked toward the land shark in attack formations.

He looked at Kid Lightning. "Two of the Rainbow Stars are down already from this attack. Something tells me we'll lose more before this is over."

"Kid Lightning." The hero's voice was sad.

Bright Angel let loose a string of profanity. "Now we're getting interference. Are you kidding me? HQ, there's a gaggle of Sons of Atlantis jokers trying to get between us and the land shark."

The Director's voice came over the audio. "Is Eldest among them?"

"No. I see a mix of conventional and Powered agents, but lower level. Amber is going to intercept, but I'm not sure she can hold them off by herself."

"Roger."

Rohan thought. "Are you thinking what I'm thinking? That I could probably help out against those Sons of Atlantis without needing to bring up enough Power to spook the land shark?"

"Kid Lightning."

"Yeah, I think so, too! I'm going to get bamfed to the beach. I can at least do that much, right? It's got to be better than sitting on my hands."

Kid Lightning looked around the side of his bed, though Rohan didn't know what he was looking for.

"Hey, man, feel better. I'll be back when I can. You should meet the Drs. Stone! We read comics about them when we were kids."

"Kid Lightning." His tone was completely flat.

"Thanks."

Rohan left the med bay, his heart rate already increasing in anticipation of a fight.

· · · ● · ● · · · ·

Rohan's foot left the floor of a room twenty stories underground in Sahara City, in central Africa, and landed on a patch of California beach lit by the moon and drone-camera flashes.

The heavy, cold aura of the land shark instantly assaulted him from a spot out of sight to the south. He rolled his shoulders, shrugging off the cloying *otherness* of the monster's energy.

A gust of wind kicked a spray of sand into his chest as Amber slowed enough to be visible, sliding to a halt in front of him.

Her mask covered up to her nose, black with gray geometric patterns, a stark contrast to her pale-white skin. Her brown hair was tied back into a neat ponytail. Her uniform matched the mask, and she held two slender, curving trench knives, the edges and the metal loops covering her knuckles speckled with blood.

She spoke before he could register her presence. "What are you doing here?"

"I want to help against the Sons of Atlantis. I won't go full Hybrid Power on them, so as long as we stay clear of Four, I won't ruin the plan."

She nodded. "They were coming after the support teams from the back. They're just behind me on this beach."

He nodded.

She continued. "The Proud Guys showed up, you know anything about that?"

He shrugged. "Maybe."

She shook her head. "Don't go near Bright Angel for a while, she's livid. But you can help me with these guys. About a dozen of them have Powers similar to Eldest."

Rohan swallowed. "A dozen?"

She shook her head. "Not the same level, just the same style. They shape metaphysical energy into a shell, like armor. They're low-level flyers, enhanced strength, that sort of thing."

He nodded. "Okay, that I can handle. I bet they're getting fed power from a Sons of Atlantis cabal of sorcerers, just like Eldest was."

"I'm pretty sure it's behind them, but that monster's aura makes it hard to *see* anything. Also, as fast as I am, I haven't been able to get past. If you can distract the group, I'll go around and try to take out their Power base."

"Done—"

She disappeared from his field of vision before he could finish the word.

"Rudra save me, she's fast." Rohan ran after her.

The Sons of Atlantis were equipped in dark-green outfits with white trim. Most wore light personal armor, in the style of motocross racers: ridges of hard plastic across shoulders, knees, elbows, and hands. They had slender helmets with visors covering their eyes and wore protective boots.

Using his Third Eye, Rohan could clearly make out which ones had significant Power. He also spotted faint trails of energy tracing from their backs to a spot up in the hills overlooking the beach.

It wasn't a dozen; it was thirteen. Thirteen Powers.

Rohan charged the group, a line of bodies that spanned from surf to grass. He yelled as he ran, squeezing a trickle of Power up through his spine while restricting the angry flood that welled up behind it, straining to be unleashed.

He closed on one of the Powers, who held his hands out in front and formed a heavy shield of metaphysical energy over them.

Rohan jumped into the air a few meters before contact and struck the shield with both feet, pushing off and launching himself out to the side.

With a thudding impact, Rohan's shoulder knocked one of the non-Powered agents unconscious. Two others closed on his position.

"Atlantis is rising again! You cannot stand in our way!"

"I'm pretty sure I can. Or maybe fly in your way. Does that make sense?"

The Hybrid rolled on the sand and came up into a fighting position, right hand held close to the left side of his jaw, left fist floating near his belly, ready to be launched upward in a quick jab.

One agent grabbed for Rohan's upper body with both arms swinging wide. Rohan ducked to his left, digging a short and powerful hooking punch into the man's liver. Then the Hybrid spun, continuing his motion by pivoting on his left leg and facing the next assailant.

A Power was flying through the air toward him, the man's knee rising quickly in a direct line for Rohan's jaw.

"Die! For the glory of Atlantis!"

The Hybrid skipped backward, letting the arc of the knee travel right to his face, so close he could have kissed it. Then he reversed course, stepping forward and putting his shoulder under the man's shin, wrapping arms around the man's rear leg, and driving him onto his back.

"Sorry, not today. Well, not really sorry. I'd be happy to help if *you* want to die for Atlantis, though!"

The Power landed with an explosion of breath and sand, his metaphysical armor absorbing most of the impact.

Before Rohan could finish the downed Power, two more agents closed on his position, cutlasses clenched in their fists and swinging toward him from opposite directions in a coordinated attack, one high and the other low.

"You can't stop us all!"

Rohan used a short burst of energy to *lift* himself up off the ground and out of the way of both strikes. Just as he did so, another Power, anticipating the move, slammed into him from behind.

"Ugh. I guess I can't."

The pair sailed through the sky, driven by the Son of Atlantis's thrust. Rohan fought and twisted against the other man's grip as they traveled, managing to spin and face him just as they drove into the hard-packed sand of the beach.

The Son of Atlantis disengaged his arms and pulled back, opening up the space over Rohan. The Hybrid drove his leg through that space, connecting with a kick up into the other man's face that landed with enough force to crash through his metaphysical armor and pancake the man's nose into a bloody mess.

Rohan followed the force of his kick into the air, coming off his back and up onto his feet just as another group of Powers closed on him.

Rohan faked to his right, lashing out with a low kick to one agent's front knee.

"You're getting sloppy, Griffin! Today you fall!"

The agent dodged backward, easily avoiding the kick, and Rohan planted the foot and launched himself in the other direction.

The agent to his left had been closing on the Hybrid, and suddenly they were almost chest-to-chest. Rohan flicked a left backhand up into the man's face, and when his opponent's arms came up to block the attack, the Hybrid ducked into a soft crouch and drilled his right elbow up under the man's floating rib.

"Not *that* sloppy. Give some credit, please."

The agent somersaulted backward into the air just as the second Power wrapped his arms around Rohan from the back.

The Hybrid twisted to his left, then his right, trying to dislodge the grappler with centrifugal force alone.

Meanwhile, two other Powers had closed and were throwing heavy punches at the Hybrid, dodging expertly away as their companion was swinging through the air, then closing again and landing more shots.

"You can't beat us and the ten-thousand-year-old martial arts of Atlantis!"

The pain and impact intensified the surge of energy inside Rohan's mind.

Rohan's Hybrid Power swelled against its bounds, searching for a path up and into his brain. It wanted to fill him, to shed its violent light out on the beach, to tear through his enemies in a frenzy of blood and torn flesh and bone fragments.

Not yet. Save it for the shark.

He snarled as he pushed back at it, teasing out a single strand of energy to reinforce his forearms as he desperately parried a rain of punches and the occasional stabbing sword.

He blocked with both arms, pivoting and sidestepping in short, explosive steps that changed his position just enough to make most of the strikes ineffective.

That's it. Found your rhythm.

With a wild grin, the Hybrid broke the attack pattern. On a half-beat, he exploded forward, jumping as he lifted his rear knee up into the face of the Power in front of him.

"Orphan Clan Flying Knee! Not bad for a style that's only been around for a measly five centuries!"

The Atlantean went down like a puppet with its strings cut, arms and legs spasming in a mild seizure as he landed in the sand.

The others swarmed, and Rohan quickly absorbed a pair of punches, then a sword strike across his upper back that drew a line of blood on his skin.

Rohan lashed out, knocking two of the Powers back with sloppy punches that should have been more annoying than damaging. Before he could follow up, he sensed all the Powered agents hesitating and stepping away from contact.

He focused some attention through his Third Eye and realized the trail of energy that had been feeding the men was gone. Or at least weakened.

Amber must have gotten to the cabal.

The agents started to look between each other, searching for answers that weren't coming.

Rohan stood, taking deep breaths as he worked to recover his wind. "You remember the woman who was carving you up before? I think she's coming back, and you don't have your borrowed Powers anymore. May I suggest a strategic withdrawal?"

One of the agents made a huffing noise and moved toward the Hybrid, his sword held in front of him.

He looked to one side, then the other, and realized the others were running up the beach and away from the conflict.

The man threw his sword at Rohan, then followed them.

Amber appeared out of the darkness again, more blood splattered on her clothes and skin.

"Found 'em."

"Thanks. These guys were a handful."

"I heard you talking. I didn't know Spiral taught you Orphan Clan techniques."

The two heroes turned to face the direction of the battle against the land shark.

"He taught me a ton of things, back in our day. I'm amazed at your stamina, dilating time. Didn't think you could maintain it like that."

"Well, it's been a decade of hard work. I'm pretty much at my limit right now, though. Need rest. How's that cut?"

"Shallow, I'll be fine." He tapped his ear. "You hear anything from the others?"

She shook her head. "Nothing concrete."

Rohan scratched under his beard, cracked his knuckles, and rolled his shoulders to see if he had any actual injuries.

"If you're tapped out, energy-wise, you should come back to HQ with me. Eat, take a nap."

She stared at him. "It feels wrong, leaving them to fight alone."

"I know. Think like a soldier, not a hero. You'd only be in the way. You have a different job right now: to rest and get your energy back so you can be useful to them again as soon as possible."

"I wasn't arguing, just saying it feels wrong."

"I hear you. Let's go."

Rohan waited while Amber called Bamf to open a portal back to Sahara City. He turned, focusing on his Third Eye, checking to verify that the Sons of Atlantis had left the area.

Amber switched off the phone. "All clear?"

Rohan nodded. "As far as I can tell. I wish we had an empath around."

She laughed. "You're missing your friend from Wistful. Wei Li. Does someone have a crush?"

He shook his head. "As cliché as it sounds, we're more like siblings. I don't think she likes mammals. At least not male mammals. Not, you know, romantically."

"I guess I'm the last person to argue with the idea of male-female platonic friendship."

"I think you and Spiral are the poster children for it."

The portal opened. The two heroes stepped through it and back into Hyperion Industries Headquarters.

24

Pyrrhic Defeats

The mood in the War Room was dark, the quietly grim kind that spoke of people refusing to openly give in to despair. There was no quiet laughter from the far corners of the room; no eager snippets of discourse as the mostly young staff members planned to meet for dinner or drinks; no boisterous debates about which science fiction character was smarter, or better looking, or more realistic, or better in bed.

In their place came a procession of whispered phone calls that ended with, "I don't know yet, I'm sorry. Take care, I have to get back to work. I love you, too." Spoken in a dozen different languages, in two dozen dialects, to half a dozen different relations. Mothers, fathers, partners, children.

Rohan was pretty confident he was the only one who understood *all* the calls. It was the first time in many years that he regretted learning the Fire Speech.

The maps, projected onto three of the room's walls, told the story: Four was following a crooked path toward the desert, leaving a jagged, lightning-bolt shape of devastation behind as the heroes fought to entice him east and north, away from the dense population in Los Angeles. The icon drew ever closer to the dot representing The Green, waiting at the western edge of his territory, in the westmost corner of Death Valley.

The surviving Rainbow Stars had been evacuated, hurt and exhausted by the fighting.

The Proud Guys had given a surprisingly good accounting of themselves, retreating only after all their heaviest hitters had been taken down or disabled. Rohan was disappointed to hear that Earl was hospital-bound but likely to recover from his injuries.

A Vanguard team from Las Vegas had argued about the wisdom of directing the land shark in their direction, but a few stern words from The Director got them aligned with the program.

The Sons of Atlantis had not returned to the field.

Void's Shadow was still hanging out in the upper atmosphere and delivering video coverage of the monster.

The sun had risen, brightening the video feed considerably.

Insatiable was transporting temporary housing units from Hyperion Industries factories in a Chinese desert to coastal areas that needed relief.

Kid Lightning had started to become agitated until the medical staff brought his hammer to him. He sat in his bed, holding the heavy weapon, eyes glued to the screen across from him.

The Professors Stone were both settled into a lab room poring over detailed imagery of the artifact that had been found in Three's spine, frequently requesting data dumps from their ship to compare or contrast something they saw with obscure historical records.

The Director kept her position by the main conference table, her expression calm and uncompromising, showing her stress only in white knuckles and rapid tea consumption.

The kitchen and waitstaff had gone through a shift change. Fresh faces brought snacks and cleared away the debris left over from the night. Trays of sandwiches and burritos circulated endlessly.

Five hours after the land shark had taken its first lumbering steps onto the beach, Bright Angel's voice came over the speakers.

"The Green has engaged. Repeat, The Green has engaged land shark Four. The Damsel and I are pulling back."

Rohan looked up and checked the map. The land shark icon had stopped moving.

The Director rubbed her hands and addressed the room. "Phase Two is complete. Take a break; I want everyone to grab some rest. All junior staff stay away for at least the next four hours. Seniors, you know what to do. I want skeletal staffing only in this room for that time. Just enough to start making calls if things go wrong with The Green."

Carla hugged her wife. The Director leaned in but shook her head as she did it. "Not over yet, sweetheart. Soon."

Carla nodded. "I know. We can enjoy the small steps, though, can't we?"

"We can." The Director looked at Rohan. "How long do you want to give them to wear each other out before you bring in Wave Three?"

Rohan thought. "Our best chance of defeating Four is to let it fight The Green for three or four days to maximize the chance that it's exhausted."

Amber looked at him. ". . . But? I hear a 'but' in there. What is it?"

"A few things. The Green took a beating from the last one. Is he recovered fully? Maybe. But maybe not. In which case, he might *lose*. If at any point he does get finished, by the time we realize it and go after Four, the land shark will probably be mostly recovered. We've seen how quickly they regenerate. So our chances go down pretty dramatically."

"You're saying we attack now?"

"That's too risky the other way. If the land shark is completely fresh, we're toast."

The women looked at him angrily. He held up his hands.

"I know, sorry, sorry. I say, give them twelve hours to fight. We go in then."

Amber's forehead was creased with frown lines. "Any reason we wait twelve hours?"

"Because at some point you just have to take a little bit of a guess. Warfare is not an exact science. I'm splitting the difference."

She sighed. "I want to argue with you, but honestly I don't have a better idea. So . . . let's do it."

He nodded and thought.

"Hey, Amber, let me talk to you alone for a minute, okay?" He turned to his mother. "We'll be around in case anything happens. Otherwise, it's go-time in twelve. You good with that?"

She nodded. "I'm with Amber. If I had a better plan, I'd force it on you. But I don't."

"Cool." He turned back to Amber. "Where can we go? I don't know my way around."

She waved him to follow her. "We have a Vanguard Prime prep room down this hall. Nobody from outside the team will go in there without a reason."

He followed the bobbing ponytail on the shorter woman into a smaller conference room. Like the main room, it had floor-to-ceiling screens on all sides and a big table with soft, reclining leather chairs around it. Unlike the War Room, this table only had seating for twelve.

Amber sank into one of the chairs and tilted her head back. "What's up?"

He made sure the doors were closed. "Power question for you. Nobody likes having their precise limits made public knowledge, so I wanted to ask you in private."

"Sure."

"You can speed yourself up, right?"

She spread her hands. "Basically. I change the rate of passage of time in my immediate vicinity."

"And I know you can extend that field."

"I can."

"Question is, how far? And for how long?"

She twisted in the chair. "It's hard. And it's exponentially harder to slow down or speed up an unwilling target. Whether they're resisting on purpose or not, every living thing is averse to having its timeline messed with."

"Sure. So, let's say your chances of slowing down a land shark for any length of time is essentially zero."

"Yeah. Otherwise I would have done it already. Unless you want it slowed down for, say, a nanosecond."

"I don't think that will help. But do you think you can speed me up?"

She thought. "For how long?"

"Like, if I do that same maneuver I did last time, dive-bomb into the thing. Can you make me fast? So the land shark has less time to react?"

"Griffin, I wish I could help, but probably not."

"What's the problem?"

"Suppose I'm standing on the ground, or on a nearby hill, whatever. You're up in the air. I can't speed us both up—I can't make a field with that kind of shape, covering me, then a line out to you. It's too complex. If I speed you up, that's fine, but as soon as you start moving, you'll leave the field. And I won't be quick enough to move it so it keeps up with you."

He scratched his beard. "You'd have to lead me, right? Move the field downward while I flew along inside it."

"Maybe. But the timing is tricky. We *might* manage it after a month of practice."

"You think?"

"I've tried this with Spiral. It takes a lot of practice."

"Okay. Well, it was worth a thought. Maybe I'll have you speed me up if I have a tough decision to make in a hurry."

"That's actually a better use case for my Powers. Speaking of which—"

The door slammed open. "Where is he? Oh, there you are, you son of a bitch."

Bright Angel.

Rohan stood and turned to face her.

Her eyes were wide and angry, whites showing brightly against her dark-brown skin. Strands of hair flew loose from her braids, forming a soft cloud around her head. Flecks of blood stained her cheeks and her white-and-blue uniform.

"Hey, what's . . ."

She grabbed him by the front of his uniform and threw him backward into the nearest wall. The screen shattered, cracks radiating outwards from the impact like a spiderweb, sparks dancing along the lines.

"The Proud Guys? You had to call in the Proud Guys? I'm fighting for my life, for all our lives, and motherf-ing Earl of the Proud Guys walks up and tells me that you gave his whole crew amnesty?"

Rohan held his hands up and worked to catch his breath. "Bright Angel, hold on here—"

She stepped forward and lifted her left hand. She let out a flare of light from her palm, blinding the Hybrid, then lowered herself to her right side and punched under his guard, digging her right fist into his side.

"Who the hell do you think you are? Come to *my* planet and offer those monsters amnesty and a quarter of the United States because you think we need their help?"

He gasped for air. "We do need their help, Bright Angel. We need all the help we can get."

"No, we don't! It would be better to die than win and live in a world where guys like that get to do whatever they want!"

"That's not what—stop hitting me!"

She flashed him again and punched him on the other side, then whipped a kick into the side of his thigh.

"Bright Angel, that hurts. Cut it out."

"You had no right! You *know* you had no right, or you would have mentioned it to me before you talked to them!"

"I didn't mention it to you, because I thought you might react like this. I had every right to say whatever I wanted to them because we need them!"

"We don't!"

"How many of the Rainbow Stars did we lose today? How many of Las Vegas Vanguard? The Professors lost contact with Garren. He's never even been to Earth before! Amber is running on empty. Another half dozen at least are dead. If not for the Proud Guys, how many more would it have been? And for what?"

"Because you don't compromise your principles for expediency. There are things you don't do, even if it's practical. You know what life will be like if those guys are allowed free rein over the southeast? You realize what they are, don't you?"

"Yes, I realize it! And we can deal with that when we have to. But without every hand helping out right now, and I really mean right now, there's a decent chance nobody will be able to live out a terrible life under the Fourth Reich of the Proud Guys, because they'll all be dead!"

"That might be better!"

"You can't know that. That's not the call we should be making right now."

"Oh God, you're still such an asshole, aren't you? You decided it was right, so you went ahead and did it. No listening, no regard for the fact that maybe, just maybe, the people who have actually been living on this planet might know more about it than you do? Might deserve more say in its future than you have?"

"I'm here to win a war, Angel. This is how you do it. You bring your resources to bear, you win the war, and you deal with the consequences afterward. The planets that can't unite and figure that out don't have a chance to deal with anything afterward, because they get wiped out."

"You sanctimonious prick." She turned to Amber. "Did you know about this?"

Amber held her hands up. "Not it. I've had my hands full with other shit. Leave me out of this."

Bright Angel turned back to Rohan, who was slowly picking shards of glass out of his hair. He flinched when he saw her face, bracing for another salvo of punches.

"What makes you think we'll even honor your ridiculous amnesty? When you're back on your space station and we're putting the planet back together?"

He shrugged. "Honestly, I wasn't sure you would. I was half considering heading down there after we beat the sharks and killing them all myself. But I didn't tell Earl that."

"Are you serious?"

"Do I look like I'm kidding?"

She paused, then shook her head. "No. We're better than that, we have to be. You made a promise for Vanguard; Vanguard's going to keep it."

"If that's the way you want to play it, sure."

"But you should have never put me in that position, Griffin. That was a douchebag move."

He held his hands up. "I'm sorry. I was trying to do the right thing."

"You should start by putting aside this dumbass notion you have that you always know what the right thing is. Sometimes you have to ask other people, and, here's a crazy idea, maybe you even have to listen to their answers."

"Okay, okay. No more unilateral actions from me, okay? I'll ask first. I'm sorry."

She stood staring at him, her hands balled into fists at her sides, her shoulders tight with anger.

"You pull another stunt like that, and I'll make you wish you'd never come back to this planet. Am I clear?"

"Yes, ma'am. Crystal."

She stepped back, loosening her hands with an effort of will, shaking out the tension. "Only positive thing I can say is that they took their fair share of the casualties."

"Good. Now we just have to hope Phase Three goes as well as One and Two."

Bright Angel shook her head and walked to the conference table. She tapped at one of the small screens in the table.

The Damsel stepped through the doorway and looked around. "Did I miss something?" Her face was pale.

Bright Angel turned to face the others. "We were having a disagreement.'"

The Damsel nodded. "This about the Proud Guys?"

Bright Angel grunted.

The Damsel turned to Rohan. "You shouldn't have done that, hon."

He sighed. "I'm trying to fix things."

"What you're doing is trying to be the hero. Which is a known side effect of the Y chromosome. You should have asked us first. Any of us."

"I've been so informed."

She waved a hand at the broken screens, her other hand brushing long, red hair out of her face. "Now how am I going to watch my shows?"

Bright Angel laughed, a tight burst behind an angry face. She immediately returned to her glowering.

The Damsel looked between them. "Am I going to have to throw a bucket of water over you two, or are we done?"

Rohan held his hands up.

Bright Angel sighed. "I'm done. For now."

"All right." The Damsel's tone showed that she was unconvinced.

Bright Angel ran her hands over her hair. "I just ordered food. Pizza. Because if I'm going to die in twelve hours, I want my last meal to be real pizza."

The Damsel smiled and nodded.

"Pizza sounds about right." She turned to Rohan.

"Your—The Director was recruiting us to bring Vanguard under Hyperion Industries. This one"—she nodded her head at Bright Angel—"had her doubts and, as you can imagine, was not shy about expressing them. So The Director brought in an Italian chef from a Michelin-star restaurant just to make pizza. Built a brick oven, special flours, New York water, the works. It's the best I've had, and I've lived in both New York and Rome."

Rohan nodded. "Sounds good. Pizza first. Then I want to execute Phase Three . . . in about twelve hours. Give The Green time to soften up Four. *If* that's okay."

The others nodded and sat around the table. Amber and Bright Angel took out their phones and tapped at them.

Rohan called to make sure *Void's Shadow* was in good shape.

"Yes, Captain, no issues. Do you want me to do anything other than record this fight?"

"Not right now. You've been a big help, keep it up. Another half a local day, and we'll attack it. After that, you'll have some time to yourself. Maybe all the time. One way or another."

"Yes, sir." Rohan disconnected the line.

One way or another.

25

The Third Wave

The setting sun still stained the sky purple, red, and blue when Rohan stepped through Bamf's portal and out onto the desert sand.

He was meters away from a familiar gas station, which hosted a scene very similar to the one he'd viewed on his last trip there.

The station's parking lot and the hard-packed sand around it were littered with a gamut of vehicles, from rugged military transports to rentals carrying journalists and a handful of civilian gawkers. Many had their headlights on, providing extra light above what was shed by the stars and moon in the darkening sky.

Rohan took a deep breath and braced himself against the oppressive aura of the land shark. It was, if anything, more intense than he remembered.

The heroes looked around.

Rohan sniffed. "Is that . . ."

Amber answered. "Are we surprised that a ten-thousand-ton dead fish that's been lying out in the sun for three days doesn't smell bad?"

"Are sharks fish? Or are they their own thing? I can't remember."

The Damsel sighed. "Was it really just three days ago? It seems longer."

Bright Angel shook her head. "Almost four. But it does seem longer. Do you think the next one is showing up in just two days? If the pattern holds?"

Rohan shrugged. "I'm going to vote with groundless optimism and say the curve will flatten and give us four more."

"Your stock portfolio must be in great shape if that's how you make decisions."

"Actually, I'm apparently the richest person on Earth, so, yes, it's doing great. Now let's get a situation report from . . . somebody?"

As he said the words, a small group of uniformed military personnel approached the group.

One of the men, gray haired and solidly built, with an impressive array of shiny metal pieces covering his chest, walked up to Rohan and saluted, holding his hand's edge to his forehead.

The man looked tired.

"General Ryan, sir, at your service. We met several days ago."

Rohan looked at Bright Angel, who shrugged.

"Um, at ease?" The general dropped the salute. "I don't think that's necessary."

"Sir, my current understanding is that you hold a high rank in the il'Drach Imperial Navy. That is considered an allied armed force, and given its scope, we have deemed your rank to be higher than anything planetside. So, yes, it's necessary. Sir."

"I'm retired. But I guess that's not the point. Any information on the fight?" Rohan didn't think it was necessary to clarify *which* fight he was talking about.

"Yes, sir. They're working in roughly the same stretch of desert as the last time. If anything, sir, this land shark appears either stronger or more agitated, because the fight is going poorly for The Green."

Rohan looked at his friends. "Maybe he hasn't recovered. Not fully."

The general didn't respond directly. "The Green has taken at least one bad bite. My analysts don't have a lot of actual information to work with, but the smarter ones have bought up all the early slots in the betting pool."

"I guess it's a good thing we're here." Rohan looked around.

Bright Angel looked at him. "We don't have Kid Lightning this time."

"Kid Lightning!" A portal opened behind them, and the blond hero's distinctive voice called out to them.

The trio turned to face their friend. His face held a grim smile, his hands his massive sledgehammer.

Next to him stood the sea god.

Poseidon waved. "We couldn't let you have all the fun."

Amber looked at him. "We thought you were hurt."

"I am hurt. So is he." He pointed at Kid Lightning. "So is the Hybrid—your hands aren't fully healed yet, are they, boy?"

Rohan shrugged. "If the stakes were any lower, I'd call you both reckless. But . . . they're not."

"No, they aren't. And I have to send a message to these things about messing with Earth's gods. I'm a little tired of being overlooked."

The sounds of heavy, thudding impacts, a roar of outrage, and a trembling they could feel through the earth answered him.

Rohan turned. "They're getting closer. Are we ready?"

Poseidon laughed. "No. But he managed to get out of bed without help, and I'm almost sober, so that's as close as we're going to get, I believe." The god rolled his shoulders as his aura began to intensify, wet and foamy.

Bright Angel and Kid Lightning followed suit, concentrating to bring up their own Power levels.

Rohan waited. He didn't want the land shark to notice *his* aura. Not yet.

Amber looked them over. "The Damsel and I will wait nearby. When she's ready, I'll speed her in, then back out."

Bright Angel nodded. "Just give us a few rounds to soften it up. When Griffin is ready to spool up, you distract it."

Rohan paused, listening to the sounds of savage impacts coming from deeper in the desert.

"I'll get up high and wait. Ping me over the comms when you're ready for me to start my attack run. We only get one shot at this." He pulled his helmet out of his hood, checking that the facemask was set to obscure his face in case any civilian cameras were operational, then slipped it over his head.

The others nodded, and the group split up.

Bright Angel's Power unfurled, four sheets of pure energy shaped into feathery bird wings. They beat in a counter-rhythm that Rohan suspected was more metaphorical than aerodynamic, their tips snapping audibly as they lifted the woman up into the air.

A dense sphere of electricity formed under Kid Lightning's feet. It lifted him up and into his friend's wake, stray bolts escaping from the ball and quickly sparking out in the dry desert air.

With a flourish of his hand, Poseidon summoned a rush of energy that pushed up from the earth in a wave. He rode it like a surfer, feet spread to catch the crest; the cold, damp aura of the energy was remarkably similar to the more potent signature of the land shark.

The three flew directly toward the fight.

Amber and The Damsel followed on foot, Amber sticking to a human running speed so her fellow Vanguard member could keep up.

Rohan *pulled* himself upward with a spear of il'Drach Power, taking an arcing path into the clouds.

By the time he'd risen a few hundred meters, the fight between Four and The Green was in full view.

He watched a few exchanges.

The general was right. The Green is losing.

The Green was leaping about, working hard to avoid any kind of pattern or rhythm that the land shark would be able to anticipate or read. He attacked in fits and starts, leaping in and tearing at the massive creature with hands driven by intense, desperate energy.

The land shark swayed and rolled, trying to trap its tormentor with vastly superior bulk. Whenever The Green made contact, Four would snap its head around, maw full of jagged teeth, each at least twice the height of the man, eagerly reaching for the altered human.

The Green's body was streaked with red blood. His left arm was twisted and mangled, the flesh knitting together as Rohan watched but still obviously not functional.

Four issued a challenging roar that Rohan could feel vibrating through his jaw and the back of his skull.

Poseidon spoke over the comms. "God's privilege, I claim first strike. Have at thee, creature of the depths, kneel before your rightful monarch!"

The wave of Power beneath the god doubled in weight, then doubled again, driving him toward the land shark with a terrible blue-green acceleration.

The land shark turned to face this new threat. With his fist held out before him like a salute, the god struck the nose of the creature, his Power crashing over the two of them in a tsunami of force.

The blow knocked the creature backward, stumbling on its broad, clumsy feet, before it caught itself. In that moment, Kid Lightning surged in to deliver his own two-handed hammer strike, coming down over the top of the creature's snout.

"Kid Lightning!"

The blow drove the creature's head downward until its jaw kissed the hot sand below. Bright Angel swooped in to follow, the infinitely sharp edges of her wings tearing long rents in its flesh as she strafed it.

The Green leapt in and grabbed at the torn skin, pulling it back to expose meat and cartilage underneath the tough hide.

With a huff of expelled air, the land shark pushed its nose upward, snapping its jaws at the sea god. Poseidon retreated as quickly as possible, barely escaping the reach of its multi-layered, razor-sharp bite.

Kid Lightning prepared for another strike, but the land shark swung its tail into him and knocked him hundreds of meters through the air, his ball lightning chariot flickering as his concentration wavered.

Wherever The Green wasn't actively pulling at the creature's flesh, it was stitching itself together, closing quickly along the long slashes, coming closer and closer to trapping his hand inside it.

Bright Angel rose into the air, looping around to build up momentum for another blitz as Poseidon reset himself out of reach of the shark's jaws.

The Green pulled his hand free and let go of the shark skin. He dropped to the ground, bellowing his rage at the beast.

Rohan heard Bright Angel's voice over the team channel as she swooped in for another run at Four's flank.

"We're not going to hold out much longer, Griffin."

"Copy that. Damsel, cover me."

With those words, The Damsel summoned an electric aura, vibrating with power, washing over the area like a fog rolling in off a lake.

Parallel to that, Poseidon pulled a fresh tsunami of ocean-flavored energy of his own, pulling it up into an enormous wave that he rode in for a renewed attack on the land shark.

High above, Rohan reached deep inside, down his back and through his tailbone, into a metaphysical space outside his body where his Hybrid Power boiled and churned in its eagerness to be unleashed.

The land shark hopped forward, once, then again, not reaching The Damsel as Amber picked up her friend and moved her at supersonic speeds around the desert. The movement diminished the older woman's concentration, however, and her power waned.

"I. Am. Your. God!"

Poseidon struck the side of the land shark's head with another tremendous blow, but the creature braced against the impact and butted against him, sending the god flying through the air, his beard flapping in the breeze.

Rohan grabbed fistfuls of energy and drew them up into the back of his skull, a double helix forming around his spine, pulsing with Power and rage. Once the connection was made, the energy flowed, so bright that his vision washed out for a moment, the desert fading away, then coming back in a stark, black-and-white negative image.

He started to descend.

"Don't ignore an angry woman!"

The Damsel redoubled her efforts, arcing sheets of palpable aura over the land shark. Amber stood by her side, propping up the older woman with her shoulder.

The creature responded to her, but instead of trying to catch the elusive humans, it hopped forward and slammed its legs down into the sand. A horizontal avalanche of material sprouted forward, equal parts rock and sand, knocking them down.

Bright Angel shouted. "Get him off them!"

"Kid Lightning!"

Kid Lightning landed a heavy blow of his hammer on the land shark's solidly planted right leg while The Green struck a blow on the other with his working arm.

Bright Angel sliced down across Four's cheek, then below its body, drawing a long, straight incision across its belly, pulling its attention away from the top of its head.

The beast settled to the ground, trying to trap the woman underneath it. She popped free, but not before taking a glancing blow across her lower legs.

Rohan braced his forearms in front of his face, reinforcing his flesh with layers of yellow-white energy. With everything that he had left, he ripped his body down through the air, instantly setting off a sonic boom. Heat seared the skin of his arms as the air around him ripped and tore.

The shark reset its front feet and lifted up to its full height, roaring defiance at the group that was attacking it. It swung one leg straight out, knocking The Green backward to bounce over the sand like a stone skipped across a pond.

Four was turning toward Kid Lightning when the Hybrid struck its head.

Rohan screamed with the impact, a primal sound that tore at his throat, fueled by all the Hybrid rage that was filling his mind. He hit the rubbery flesh of the shark, splitting the abrasive hide, pushing harder as he entered its body. He twisted slightly, screwing himself in toward the creature's skull and the vulnerable brain inside it.

The land shark did not cooperate.

The beast twisted and turned with the blow, rolling onto its right side, turning what had been a hit square on the top of its head into a more glancing strike. With the twist, Rohan met the thick cartilage of the chondrocranium protecting its brain at a sharp angle.

The Hybrid pushed with everything he had, driving his body into the rubbery mass.

"How do you like that? That's how I killed the last one. Did you wonder?"

The cartilage held.

Rohan scraped alongside it, tearing a man-sized tunnel through the meat around the side of the creature's head. He drove himself furiously at an inward angle, but the shark's Power was resisting his thrust, now fully dedicated to the task, and he could not break through.

Rohan pushed and slid and pushed, accelerating as the creature pushed back, until he finally burst free through the back of the land shark's eye, erupting in a geyser of blood and ocular fluid and torn flesh.

As the Hybrid flew free, the land shark followed his path with its mouth, snapping shut a maw large and powerful enough to crush a fleet of buses, catching the Hybrid between two rows of teeth.

With another roar, Rohan braced his hands against the teeth and levered them apart, squirting free.

"Griffin!" It was Bright Angel.

He couldn't answer. He couldn't quite take a breath.

Those sharp teeth had caught around his waist, and he didn't want to look down. He wasn't entirely sure his lower half was still attached.

The land shark moved to follow him, to finish him off.

Bright Angel settled in front of it and let off a flare of light so bright it seared the sand beneath her into a glassy crater.

"Griffin's down."

He tried to answer, to reassure her that he was still up for the fight, but words wouldn't come out.

The Hybrid pulled and formed a sheaf of power and wrapped it around his midriff, pulling it tight to keep his organs where he liked them: on the inside.

Amber's voice came over the comms. "What now? Do we run?"

The Green leapt up and delivered a huge punch to the area beneath the damaged eye.

The land shark slapped him away with a sideswipe of its head, like a race car sending a passing car into a wall.

Bright Angel was yelling. "What choice do we have?"

Rohan wanted to shout that he wasn't done yet, but the words still wouldn't come.

He felt his own blood trickling out from around the energy seal he'd tried to wrap around himself.

The Damsel's aura had ebbed. She had never been able to maintain one that strong for any length of time.

Poseidon brought up a fresh wave of energy. He rode it back toward the land shark. "I'll fight it, cover your retreat. Get to safety."

Rohan wanted to laugh. When had the sea god ever made a noble gesture? Committed a selfless act? It was fully against his nature.

The god roared. "You have no right to my oceans! Begone!"

Then a bolt of lightning fell from the sky and wrapped around Kid Lightning.

"Oh, no. Kid, don't." The Damsel's voice was soft, and sad, and empty. "Kid Lightning!"

The bolt shimmered around his body and built.

The hairs on Rohan's arm stood up. Then the hair on his head lifted and separated into frizzy strands.

Bright Angel cried out. "Kid, don't! It's too much."

"Kid Lightning!" The energy continued to build, fresh lightning bolts coming down from the sky, joining their companion to swirl and spiral around the blond hero.

He looked at each of them. His eyes were white and brightly lit from the inside. When he smiled, his teeth glowed and sparkled in the dark night.

"Kid Lightning!" He lifted his hammer overhead. Electricity arced and crawled from the hammer head to his chest, to his hips, to his legs, and then back again, searching for an escape.

Poseidon struck the wounded shark on the snout, causing it to rear up on its hind legs and swat at the air in front of it.

Bright Angel flew close to its one good eye and let out a brilliant flare, searing and drying everything around it.

The shark screamed and swatted its tail at her as she flew by.

Then the electric hero sprang upward on a single, solid column of white lightning.

His hammer swung in a tight arc overhead and down onto the land shark's nose.

Three fresh bolts came down from the sky, joining the four heavy streams of current that drove relentlessly through the hero's body and into the land shark.

White lines traced all throughout the shark's body, sketching glowing spiderwebs through its flesh, steam puffing out of its hide wherever the streaks came close to the surface.

Its eye, the tip of its dorsal fin, its teeth—all glowed brighter and brighter, a pure white light driven by the current it was channeling.

The creature seized, its muscles locked and spasming with the stimulation.

Rohan waved his arms, searching for some sort of weapon. His hands felt flimsy and unstable, a sign that the bones were likely freshly broken.

He *felt* something pooling around him on the desert sand.

The Hybrid wanted to laugh.

He let out a stream of metaphysical energy, the Hybrid Power that was desperate for a rage-filled release. He let it flow out through his hands and into the blood-soaked sands at his sides.

From the ground emerged a shard: a three-meter splinter of deep-red menace, formed out of the Hybrid's own blood.

Not trusting his legs to hold him, the Hybrid floated upward, the spear floating beside him. With a grunt and the barest hint of breath, he accelerated toward the land shark.

Bright Angel flew another tight, vertical loop in front of him, her four wings beating furiously to gather up extra speed as she cut a line through the air toward the top of the land shark.

Rohan diverted his path ever so slightly to come around at the frozen land shark from the side of its good eye.

He felt the beast's energy reach out to deflect his spear, but it was formed of his body, his blood. The creature's Power had no purchase on it.

Rohan *willed* the base of the spear to flatten, like the back of a thumbtack. He flew, bracing his shoulder against it.

Red-yellow mucus ran from his nose and tears seeped from his eyes as he drove the spear of blood into the land shark's good eye.

The monster instantly diverted most of its metaphysical energy to the back of its eye, desperately pushing against the spear that threatened to penetrate past the jelly-filled organ and into its brain.

At that moment, Bright Angel streaked across the top of its head, her forward wings slicing a V-shape of flesh out of it, exposing a broad swath of bare cartilage underneath.

The creature huffed, trying to roar, its lungs still paralyzed by a current that neither Kid Lightning nor it could bear.

The Green landed in the open flesh of the land shark, his good hand digging into the cartilage of its chondrocranium.

With a roar, the four-meter tall, roughly man-shaped monster had torn away a flap of cartilage meters thick.

In that same motion, he disappeared inside it.

The world paused.

Kid Lightning fell to the ground, his power discharged.

The glow faded from the land shark, the lattice of white lines across its body retreating and softening into its hide. Yet the shark did not move.

The cloying, moist, heat-draining aura of the land shark began to dissipate.

It twitched, taking one tenuous step forward, then settling down toward the sand.

With a heavy huff of expelled air, the creature relaxed. Rohan looked up into its second ruined eye and felt the last sensation as its aura pulled back into itself and faded.

26

Winning the Battle, But . . .

The dying monster's aura had not been filled with anger and rage. It had not flashed hunger or the desire to conquer, not hatred or a will to power. It contained only relief.

The Hybrid looked around. He was sitting in the sand. He didn't remember how he got there. It was wet again, which surprised him, since they were in a desert.

He was crying. *Why am I crying?*

Bright Angel flew toward him, a concerned look in her eyes.

Kid Lightning was a few meters away, lying back on the ground, unblinking eyes directed up at the night sky. His hammer was on the ground, its handle sticking straight up into the air.

Poseidon walked toward them on shaky legs.

Rohan tried to say something encouraging. They had beaten the land shark.

Words still wouldn't form.

Rohan looked around, took in their losses and their gains.

Took in the dead. Thought over the figures and projections from the maps in the War Room.

A mind that had been trained by the best of the il'Drach military, tempered by two years fighting the Wedge and eight more fighting everything else the sector had to offer; a mind that had created strategies to win unwinnable wars, to defeat enemies his own masters hadn't wanted him to defeat; a mind clever enough to guide a Hybrid of average strength as he ended the Rebellion of the strongest—this mind ran the numbers on Earth's war against the sharks.

As the dry sand continued to soak up his lifeblood, he felt a moment of perfect clarity.

Their losses were too great. Earth's heroes couldn't keep killing the land sharks. They were going to lose this war.

And that was okay.

Amber's face appeared in front of his. He smiled at her.

It was time to relax.

· · • • • • • · ·

Rohan next opened his eyes to an unfamiliar view.

Overhead was a raw metal ceiling polished to a mirror shine.

He moved his arms, wincing with the stabs of pain.

He felt resistance. He looked down.

He was naked, submerged to his neck in a pool.

Not a pool, just a tub.

Except it wasn't water, it was some kind of gel.

Not a tub. A regen tank.

Thoughts began to form, fuzzy, gently poking their way to the surface. They chased each other around his head, trying to link together, to cohere.

He swallowed, tried to speak.

Nothing came out.

He swallowed, tried again. "Hello?"

A voice responded over the room's speaker system. "Hello, sir. Captain . . . er, Lance Primary, er, Tow Chief . . . Griffin? I'm so sorry, sir, I am having a hard time tracking what I should be calling you. It's very confusing. But I'm so, so, so excited that you're awake! How are you feeling? Wait, I'll get someone to come to you!"

"*Insatiable?*"

"Yes, of course. So sorry, you must be disoriented. Oh boy, you were in baaad shape when they brought you in here. You know that big monster is strong enough to bite through one of Masamune's spears! Not that I know who Masamune is, and not that I'm completely sure what a 'spear' is either, but they really made that sound like a big deal. And that thing bit right on your middle parts! They say it's a miracle you didn't lose your legs. And everything else below your waist. Which, I'm led to understand, include some particularly choice bits that you males are particularly attached to. Except when you're not attached, after being bitten almost in half! See, I made a pun. Those sense of humor programs are really starting to unpack."

He leaned his head over, very gingerly, and sipped at the straw dangling from the inside of the tank. "How . . . how long?"

"You've been on board for about one Earth day, and you came here directly from the field when you lost consciousness. Your time-bending friend got you onto *Void's Shadow* and into the regen tank in a hurry. They brought the tank here so you could have visitors, get better treatment, that sort of thing. *Void's Shadow* does not have an abundance of space on her, does she?"

He smiled and swallowed again. "No." The words were coming more easily.

"Who can I call for you? The Professors Stone are on board. I can link to Hyperion Industries Headquarters and set up a line to anybody there."

"Is there . . . another shark yet?"

"Oh no, sir. Earth is quite safe from immediate harm. Though based on a rough analysis of the pattern of invasions so far, I wouldn't want it to be a place I cared about myself, if you understand what I mean. Oh, except that you do understand, don't you, sir. Sorry."

Rohan sighed and leaned back in the tank. His thoughts were clearing up, but he felt as if his body were just an avatar in a video game.

They had clearly given him the good painkillers.

"Sir, if you don't have any requests, the Professors and The Director asked to be notified when you had regained consciousness. Of course, if you tell me not to say anything, my lips are sealed, except I don't really have lips, but my speakers will stay sealed. Or more turned off, not sealed so much, let's say powered down."

"No, you can tell them. We don't . . . have much time."

"No, sir. You probably don't."

Rohan rolled his shoulders, loosening them and creating little waves in the viscous liquid of the regen tank. He took a few more shallow breaths, then a slow and deeper breath, worried that any strain on his abdomen might tear through his freshly healed skin.

His guts held together. He took a deeper breath, then tried a very slight wiggle of his hips.

So far so good.

Images of the fight against Four were flashing through his mind. Could he have done anything differently, nailed his first shot and killed it?

He couldn't see how.

He'd gotten lucky against Three, or maybe Four had gotten lucky against him. In either case, he wouldn't place heavy bets on the same setup working against Five.

Assuming there was going to be a Five.

Each time he ran through the battle, his mind got stuck on one final image. Or rather, one final *feeling*.

The sad shark, dying alone, on painfully dry land, on a strange world, *relieved* that its ordeal was ending.

Rohan continued twisting his hips back and forth, lifting his knees toward his chest, then arching backward, testing the limits of mobility in his midsection.

Things were healing better than he had expected.

The comms built into the regen tank chimed.

"Griffin?" It was his mother's voice. She must have been in a public place or she would have used his name.

"Hello, Director."

"I understand we almost had two of you."

He chuckled, wincing slightly as the movement pulled on something tender inside his gut. "I'm pretty sure neither half would have been of any use to anybody, so it's for the best that we avoided that."

"The world owes you a great debt. The Green confirmed that he was losing the fight and wouldn't have kept that monster at bay for very long. If your team hadn't gone in and finished it, the shark would have been rampaging across North America by now."

"Are you speaking for the world now?" He was smiling as he said it.

Her answering tone was not amused. "I'm telling you the world owes you a debt. The world may not feel the same way. Offering amnesty to a group of neo-Nazi terrorists was not a great move publicity-wise."

"Are you telling me it was the wrong move?"

"I don't know. I can tell you it shouldn't have come from you, unilaterally. If Poseidon had negotiated with them on behalf of Vanguard Prime, it would have come across a lot differently than it does coming from you."

"All right, I see your point. Anyway, I'm glad we made it work, but most of the credit should go to Kid Lightning. How is he? Did he . . ."

"He's alive. He's in a medically induced coma and is getting intracranial stem cell transfusions. Our doctors are hoping his nervous system can heal if it's given enough rest."

"That doesn't sound great."

"It isn't. But it's more than we can say for a lot of people."

Rohan grunted. "We need to get everyone together, talk about the next steps."

She paused. "I can arrange a call. I'm not sure what you mean by 'everyone.'"

"You, Vanguard Prime, the Stones. I'd want Masamune on it, too, if I could arrange it."

"Are you saying this because you have an idea of what to do going forward or because you have none?"

"I have an idea. Do we have the artifact from Four? Was there one in its neck?"

A pause on the other end. "It's on *Insatiable*. Given that whoever took the first one can crack our defenses here, it seemed like the best place."

"The Professors are looking at it?"

"Yes. And we sent fresh scans over to Masamune."

"Okay, great. Now let's plan our next steps."

"I'll make calls."

"Thanks. I'll ask *Insatiable* to have the Stones come talk to me. We need to figure out a few more of the details."

"Good. You should know, Lyst is back. She and Poseidon are on *Void's Shadow* doing some deep-sea exploration."

"Yeah? How'd they get her to take them?"

"I think they just . . . asked?"

He laughed softly. "Good for her, making herself useful. That's good. As long as she doesn't get overeager and wind up in danger."

"From what I understand, she's safer down there than anyone else would be. But you need to get some rest. You have to heal if you're going to be of any use to anybody."

"I will. I am. Honestly, I'm much better already. These regen tanks are amazing. Plus, you know, thank my dad, I heal fast."

"I know. Director out."

Moments later the door slid open, and Ben and Marion Stone stepped through.

Both looked tired, their lined faces drawn and paler than usual, though even Marion smiled briefly when she saw Rohan sitting up in the tank, his chest and shoulders exposed to the air.

Ben walked over to the tank and clapped a hand on Rohan's shoulder. "It's good to see you in one piece. And I mean that in the most literal way possible!"

Rohan smiled and shook his head. "It wasn't that bad."

Marion looked at him sternly. "It really was. One hole went all the way through your body. You looked like an extra in a zombie movie."

"I've been through worse."

Ben laughed. "From anybody else that would be bravado, but I've actually seen you go through worse, and it wasn't even that long ago."

Rohan looked up at his friend. "And both of these happened after I retired. Think what kind of shape I'd be in if I'd stayed in the Imperial Navy."

Ben patted Rohan's shoulder. "We're just glad you're okay."

Marion looked at her husband. "He's glad because you're his favorite drinking buddy. I'm glad because you're an important part of saving the human race."

"Oh come on, Dr. Stone, you know you have a soft spot for me, deep down inside. I can tell. I'm like the son you never had."

"More like never wanted." She gave him a halfhearted smile.

He looked them both over. "What can you guys tell me? I feel out of the loop. Lyst is back? Did she say anything useful?"

Ben sighed. "Nothing. Well, almost nothing. She can read the writing on the artifact, she confirmed that it's Old One hieroglyphs, but the words don't tell us much. Sort of 'this end up' type of markings."

"But you guys have one now, right? You got one from the shark we just killed? That has to help."

Ben nodded. "It's here, in a lab. We're in orbit, so that seemed like the safest place for it. We've both been studying the thing, and again, there's not a lot to say that's new."

"You agree with Masamune? It's some kind of . . . agitator?"

"Everything we've discovered is consistent with that interpretation. There is a web of threads that ran from the box into the nervous system of the land shark. They retracted when the animal died, but in life they would have given it enough connectivity to stimulate basic impulses, like anger or rage, or cause it pain. Not full-on control. So, yes, we both think Masamune's guess makes the most sense."

"Great. Now we just have to figure out how to remove it."

"Remove it?"

"Yeah. Dr. Stone, Dr. Stone, there's a patient on the way. It has a foreign body implanted on the cervical spine, and we have to remove it."

They looked at each other, then at him.

Marion spoke first. "That's not the easiest way to kill the creature."

"I don't want to kill it. The shark is not our enemy. The people . . . things . . . who put that object in the shark and turned it loose on Earth, those are our enemies. I want to free the shark and send it home."

They traded another set of glances.

Ben spoke. "That's not a bad idea. I think. Might be a few hiccups, though."

"You mean, other than the obvious ones?"

"We've been trying to figure out how the artifact works. The details. Like I said, it's intertwined with the creature's nervous system. I doubt you could just reach in and pull."

"Can we wreck it? Destroy the central unit? Make it stop working?"

Marion looked at her husband, then at the Hybrid. "It's very tough. We've had it in the lab all day, and we can't put a scratch on the thing."

Rohan sighed and scratched his beard. He was definitely feeling stronger. "What have you tried? You know how strong I am. Could I break it?"

She rubbed the side of her neck. "It's hard to be sure, but if you had it in your hand and had something to bang it against, or a tool to use, then perhaps. But while it's embedded inside a hundred-and-fifty-meter-long living creature that's as strong as—stronger than—The Green, which is trying to stop you? It's not a good bet."

"Okay. And we know it's waterproof, obviously. An electromagnetic pulse? Can we set something off?"

It was Ben's turn to shake his head. "We think the object was still operational after Kid Lightning overloaded Four with that last attack. If that wasn't enough to disable it, we don't have any way to do better. Best guess is that the outer material acts as a Faraday cage."

Rohan felt fatigue wash over him. "Acid? Something corrosive? Maybe Masamune has some universal solvent type of material we could squirt on the thing?"

The Stones traded matching shrugs.

Rohan suddenly laughed, a loud bark of relief. "I can't believe I didn't think of this before. I just so happen to know where I can get an unlimited supply of the most corrosive chemical in the sector."

Ben tilted his head and looked quizzically at the Hybrid, then matched the laugh. "Yes!"

They finished the thought together. "The decipede."

27

Soft Sell

The whoosh of metal sliding over metal woke Rohan from a light doze. He floundered in the fluid for a moment, forgetting where he was, then settled as the day's events came back to him.

He looked up.

Bright Angel stood in the doorway. Her hair was freshly braided in tight rows fitting close to her scalp. She was in uniform, white with blue and silver accents. It accentuated the round muscles of her arms and shoulders, strategically placed seams and accent panels turning her athletic figure into an engine of distraction.

Her mask was down. Rohan studied her face, wondering just how much of her anger had carried through the intervening day.

She walked over to the tank. He tried to relax as his shoulders tightened in memory of the way she'd thrown him into a wall the last time they'd spoken.

He let her speak first. "Hey."

He swallowed. "Hey yourself."

"You know . . ." She paused. "You know, I saw a side of you the other day that I've never seen before."

"Oh yeah?" He thought. *Was that good? Bad? Which 'other' day?*

"Yeah. The inside."

He laughed, a big, full-bellied laugh that echoed off the metal walls and made him suddenly afraid that the pressure would tear open his wounds.

There was no pain, so he let the laughter stretch out.

"Rudra save me, that was . . . please don't be offended, but that was something *I* would say."

"I know. I wanted to do something nice, get you a little present. You know, something useless like a stuffed animal. A 'World's Greatest Hero' mug. But I thought, it's not fair to just buy something for the richest guy on Earth. So I got you what you'd have gotten any of us in a similar situation. A terrible joke."

"It was terrible. And great. Just what I needed, thank you."

"You're welcome. Except maybe you aren't, because that implies I'd happily do the same thing next time, and frankly I'd rather you not make a habit out of getting bitten nearly in half."

"That thing really got me, didn't it?"

"It did. That's how Three broke Ares's spear, too. I don't know what your spine is made of, to have survived that bite, but you should buy stock in the company."

"I'll send a thank-you note to my father."

She paused and walked around the tank, examining its mechanism.

"You ever wonder what life would be like if your mom had fallen for a human?"

He swirled the liquid in the tub with a hand. "Honestly, I don't. I mean, I'm sure it would be completely different in every way, but I don't ever spend time thinking about it."

"Well. I am glad to see that you're recovering. That tank is kind of amazing."

"Are you glad? I thought you were mad at me?" He smiled as he said it.

"I am mad at you. But not wish-you-were-dead mad. Just run-of-the-mill-woman-in-a-modern-world-having-to-deal-with-men-being-dumbasses mad."

"I *was* kind of a dumbass. I am sorry."

"I know. But now I hear you have a new plan you want us all to work on with you? To handle Five? Assuming Five shows up?"

He took a deep breath.

"I do, but I promise not to go off and handle it myself. Everyone's in, and everyone gets to have their say. And if the group thinks it's a bad plan, I promise to listen."

She sighed. "Fair enough. What is it?"

He explained.

When he was done, she pulled a chair over to the side of the tank and sat down.

He watched her face as he went over the sparse details of his idea. "Well? What do you think? Am I loopy from blood loss?"

"I didn't say that. I mean, there are a few missing pieces."

"Oh, I know. I'll need help figuring some of that out."

"But it sounds good. I need to think on it a bit."

"Of course. How much time do we have?"

"You mean before Five shows up?"

"Yeah."

She shrugged. "Who knows?"

"Come on, you know. You figured out the pattern. I just lost track of days."

"I think it will be in the Pacific in around another day. Can't time it to the hour, I don't think we know exactly when the others showed up, since they appear in deep waters and are under for who knows how long. But late tomorrow morning is my best guess."

"And then it's . . . how long to reach shore?"

"Each one took a different path, but they seem to be working roughly counterclockwise. One headed for Japan, Two for the Philippines, Three went for Mexico, Four for California."

"So Five should be Oregon-bound. Maybe Canada."

"Right. If we have to, we know how to redirect it."

"Assuming there are enough people left to pull that off."

"Yes, assuming that. Oh, you should know, somebody attacked Hyperion Industries Headquarters while you were unconscious."

"What?"

"No one was badly hurt. A few guards got roughed up. We're still not clear how they got in or out, though it's pretty obviously a Power."

"What were they after? Kid Lightning again? Was this a personal thing with him all along?"

"That was my thought, but they didn't come near him. The Director thinks they were going after the artifact, assuming it would be in the building."

"That would be good, in a way. It would mean they don't know everything going on in Headquarters."

"True. I still don't like them just waltzing in and out whenever they want."

Rohan nodded. They sat in silence for a bit.

"Has anybody heard from Garren? The guy in armor with tentacles?"

She shook her head. "He's missing in action. The Professors were looking for him, using the scanning tech on their ship. But no luck so far. And Kid Lightning . . ."

"I heard."

She sighed. "I don't know if he's coming back from this one. He really went all-out."

"I don't think he had a choice. Don't think *we* had a choice. If he hadn't, we would all be dead."

"Is that supposed to make it better?"

"Actually, yes, it is. If he dies, at least he died for a purpose, a cause."

"If he dies . . . like Ares died. And the Otaku Force Five. And so many others. And you say you want us to forget all that and *rescue* the next shark that comes through?"

"I do. The sharks are not our enemy. Whoever sent them, whoever put those artifacts in their head, that's the enemy."

"I'm not arguing with you. I'm trying to point out how weird it is that you're the one saying it."

"I hear you. I understand, I really do. I'm just not used to people thinking of me that way. The people I'm surrounded by on Wistful are, well, they're new. To me. They don't have any idea what I used to be like."

"So they only know the kind and gentle Griffin?"

"I wouldn't go that far. But I get more of the benefit of the doubt."

He rested his arms on the upper lip of the tank and leaned back. Bright Angel covered the back of his right hand with hers.

He turned to face her. She was studying his face. "Tell me something."

"What?"

"Anything. Tell me about another world. Tell me about a friend on Wistful. Tell me about the desi girl you dated."

He laughed. "I met her through her kid. He told me my clothes were ugly."

"Kid has a good eye. What does she do?"

"She's a shuttle tech on Wistful." He chuckled. "Turns out her dad was like a super-rich politician on her homeworld. He had a bunch of goons come and try to scare me off."

Bright Angel smiled. "I bet that didn't go well for them."

"I . . . took care of it. Which also ended us."

"Why? She couldn't handle the violence?"

"No, not that. She'd been married; they even had a kid together. He left without a word, just abandoned them. I realized, if a bunch of goons tried to scare *me* off because I wasn't good enough for her . . ."

"You figured they did the same to him, but he was a regular guy."

"Yeah. So I told her. They reunited, and I'm left with a good story but no girlfriend."

"That is so Bollywood. You win over the girl and send her back to the man she really belongs with. Your life has become an excerpt from a derivative romance movie."

"I know! Totally agree. But, you know, if I'm going to have my heart broken, that's a pretty good way to go about it. Now it's your turn. Tell *me* something."

"What do you want to know?"

"Anything. I know you were hooking up with Ares, was that anything serious?"

"Nah. He was fun. Great abs, a thousand years of practice with the whole sex thing."

"You have anything serious?"

She sighed. "A few. Nobody you know."

"What went wrong?"

She looked away. "You know how men often say they're okay being the . . . I don't know the word. The less powerful partner in a relationship? Like, if they make less money, or have a less prestigious position, or are less successful?"

"Sure."

"Do you know how often men are *actually* okay with that?"

Rohan shrugged. "It's not something I've put thought into."

"Yeah. Not too often. You can look up the stats if you want. Men whose wives out-earn them? Doesn't usually work. Sometimes, sure, but those are exceptions.

"Now, take that same idea, but the woman isn't just richer, she's actually *physically* tougher. There aren't a lot of men who can handle that, and most of the ones who can, well, they're living in their mother's basements playing video games sixteen hours a day."

Rohan took a deep breath, testing the tightness in his abdomen. He felt good, close to full strength. "I'm sorry, Angel. That sucks."

She shrugged. "Look at me, whining to my ex-boyfriend about how hard it is to be a modern woman."

"You're allowed. I think my mom's just disappointed that I wasn't cut in half then stuck in the regen tank so she'd have an extra son to have around."

"I thought your mom didn't want more kids."

"She can't have more. I mean, she can adopt, but giving birth to a Hybrid pretty much destroys your womb. That's why none of us have full siblings."

"That's . . . did I know that? That's terrible."

"It is. One of many terrible things my father can be blamed for. He never told her."

"Oh. Wow, Rohan. That's . . . I don't know. I don't have a good word for that."

He shrugged. "Different culture, different standards, different beliefs."

"Not really an excuse."

"Not making one. You would not believe what I did to get that man out of my life."

"Tell me someday."

"I will. Say, do you want to come with me to see Wistful? See another planet?"

"What do you mean?"

"I have to go to Toth system to get the decipede venom. I want *Insatiable* to take me, but if she won't, I'll take *Void's Shadow*. Either way, there's room for you. If you want to come."

She exhaled a long stream of air through pursed lips. "That's tempting. But my place is here."

"You sure?"

"Yeah. It's not a good look, is it? If we both leave? With Ares gone and Kid Lightning in a coma, you, Poseidon, and I are the only heavy hitters left in Vanguard."

"I suppose not. Do we care, though? About how things look?"

She sighed. "I'm not giving the people of this planet another reason to lose hope. If we leave? That looks an awful lot like abandoning ship. And I'm no rat."

He thought. "You realize I'm coming back, right? One way or another? I'm not just trying to get off-planet so I can ditch this battle."

She smiled. "I'm not accusing you of anything, Rohan. You're not... I'm a celebrity, you know? People read about me in magazines. It's a responsibility. It's something I have to think about. Also, I'd like to stick around in case Headquarters gets attacked again. Maybe I can catch whoever is doing this. Might give us some information."

He tilted his head from side to side, cracking his neck. "Okay."

After a couple of minutes, Bright Angel sighed and stood.

"I'm going to have *Insatiable* send me back to Sahara City. What do you need? I take it you have to talk to Masamune?"

He rubbed his hands together. "Yeah. Like, as soon as possible. Sooner."

"I'll have The Director set something up."

"Great. Thanks."

She walked to the door, turned, and looked at him.

"I really am glad you're okay."

He smiled, but it barely left his lips. "Me, too. And thanks."

· · · ● ●· ● ● ·· ·

"I appreciate your sense of urgency, but your presence is stretching my patience thin. As you can see—" Masamune waved a wrinkled hand around in the air—"I am quite busy."

The smith was wearing a simple, gray tunic and loose-fitting trousers with a wrinkled texture like raw silk.

Rohan stood in front of the semicircular counter that demarcated the waiting area at the front of the old smith's warehouse-like workshop.

"What happened?" Before, the room had been cluttered, even crowded; it was now a small disaster. Rubble and machine parts were scattered haphazardly over the ground. Long shelving units stacked high with books, electronics, and mechanical components had been tipped over, their contents strewn in piles across the floor.

A small army of stone men, statues come to life, were circulating through the room and restoring some semblance of order.

"We had some intruders."

Rohan swallowed. "I thought this place was on a different plane of reality. And impregnable."

Masamune looked down his nose at the Hybrid. "No place is impregnable. My fortress is just less . . . pregnable than most. We are also a half step to the anti-shadow side of Earth. Clearly someone came here who was able to take that step."

"Can I do anything to help?"

The smith paused. "You are offering to help me?"

"I guess. I mean, it doesn't mean a whole lot, because let's be honest, I wouldn't be of too much use to you. But I'd be willing to try. You have anything very heavy that needs to be lifted? I'm good at that."

"Yes, I would imagine that you are. No, thank you, but I appreciate the offer." He nodded as he said it.

"Sure. Are all those guys . . ." Rohan waved at the moving statues. "Are they like Hiroshi?"

"You mean, are they alive? Conscious?"

"Yeah."

"They are not. Most of them are simple automatons. No more capable of conscious thought than a rock. Or an il'Drach Hybrid."

"Hey, that was mean. And not completely fair."

"I suppose it's not. I am irritable today. My domain has been invaded, and I would very much like you to leave so I can focus on putting it back in order."

"I hear you. My . . . well, *our* planet has been invaded, and I need to put it in order. And I need you to help me."

Masamune paused and looked into Rohan's eyes. "I already told you, I am not building you a weapon."

"Yes, you did. And yes, I remember that. And no, I'm not asking you to build a weapon. And yes, you are definitely going to help me."

"What makes you say that? Are you back to threatening me? Do you think that this damage is an indication my defenses are no longer in place?"

Rohan held his hands up in surrender. "No violence. We're past that."

The older man narrowed his eyes. "Then what?"

"If you don't help me, I'll go back to Wistful and tell Tollan that you *couldn't* help me."

Masamune's face paled to the color of fresh snow. "What?"

"Oh yeah, I will. I'll walk right into the shop. Tollan's Things. We're buds. He made me a suit. Actually, a rack of suits. And a Frisbee."

"You wouldn't."

"You bet I would. I'm an il'Drach Hybrid, remember? I've ended civilizations. You think I'll hesitate to spread a little gossip around? Especially to my good buddy Tollan. Yeah, I bet he'll see me first thing, ask where I've been, what I've been doing. And I'll tell him that my home planet got destroyed, and all Masamune could do was sit around his Hidden Fortress and cry about it."

Masamune's eyebrow began to spasm as his jaw tightened alarmingly.

Rohan continued. "He'll probably ask me something like, 'why couldn't Masamune help you? Surely he is the most skilled smith and engineer in the system?' And I'll have to say, 'he tried, but just couldn't come up with anything. I guess he's losing his touch. I'm sure back when he was younger he could have helped, but now—'"

"Enough!" The smith's voice grew loud. "Enough of your nonsense!"

"Nonsense? I don't think it's nonsense. But if you could help me, then I see myself having an entirely different conversation with my old friend. My friend Tollan."

Masamune groaned. "What do you want?"

"I want help. Meaning, I want anything you can think of that can help me. But I also want something specific. A container." Rohan explained his plan for ending the land shark threat.

Masamune nodded and listened while his automatons continued to straighten and clean the workshop. As they worked, Rohan realized that the whole place looked as though it had been searched, rather than simply wrecked.

Same guys who wanted the artifact?

The smith scratched his wispy beard as Rohan finished.

"You need a container that can hold a liquid so corrosive it will eat through an Old One artifact. An artifact designed to be embedded in the body of a planet-wrecking monster."

"That's it exactly. See, not a weapon! More of a medical device. Help me be a healer."

Masamune sighed. "I can't do that."

"What? Are you serious?"

"I don't mean I *won't*, I mean I can't. I know how to make what you want, but I don't have the materials."

"This sounds like the beginning of a side quest. I'm game. Tell me fast, though, we are really short on time."

"It's not a side quest. I'm not playing a game. I don't have the materials, and I don't know where to get them. At least not quickly."

Rohan rubbed his forehead with the palms of his hands. "I don't believe this. I bet Tollan would have them."

Masamune did not react as Rohan expected. "Yes! Yes, I bet he would!"

"What are you saying?"

"He has a shop on Wistful? The station?"

"Yeesss . . ." Rohan dragged out the answer.

"He should have the materials. Here, let me draw the schematics. You take them to Tollan, he'll build the container."

"Really?"

"Yes. Shouldn't be hard, even for him. Give me a few minutes to get paper."

Masamune retreated into the depths of his workshop.

For a long moment, Rohan wondered if that was just the old man's way of getting rid of him. Walk away, then stay in the back for hours until Rohan got bored and left.

But the smith returned, a rolled-up sheet of paper in one hand and a shiny cloth in the other.

"I found this, forgot about it for decades. I made it for Hyperion, never got the chance to give it to him. You might find it useful." The smith tossed the cloth to Rohan.

The Hybrid reached up to catch it, but the cloth slid right over his hands and slapped into his face. With a reflexive motion, he tried to pinch it to his face, then his chest, but it slipped loose and fell to the floor at his feet.

"What the . . ."

"It's a cape! Hyperion always said capes are silly, get caught in things, no real hero would ever wear one. So I made him a useful cape."

"Okay . . ." Rohan looked down. His own face looked back at him. The side facing him was perfectly reflective, like a mirror.

"You can't grab it by that side. Flip it over. The back should have friction." The smith had spread the paper out on the counter and was sketching something.

"What do you mean?"

The smith snorted. "The outside is perfectly frictionless."

Rohan grunted. "Seriously?" He carefully slid his fingers under the edge and lifted the cloth.

Unfolded, it was large enough to drape over his entire body.

"Am I ever not serious? Drape it over your head, and you should be able to fly pretty fast."

"That's . . . actually really cool."

"Of course. I invented cool."

"I should have known."

28

Side Quest

"Guys, come touch my cape!"

Ben shrugged and walked over to his friend, donut in hand. They were killing time in one of *Insatiable*'s conference rooms, snacking while the ship calculated vectors and opened one spatial portal after another.

"That's actually amazing. Makes satin sheets feel like flypaper."

"I know, right? It's frictionless."

Marion came closer and felt the fabric. "Frictionless? That could be useful."

"I know!"

"Hyperion would have been impressed. Though to be honest, I'm not certain he understood enough physics to appreciate it."

"I'll tell Masamune you said that. Except for the last part."

The entrance slid open, and Lyst walked in, ducking slightly so the bony ridges on top of her head would clear the doorway.

She wore a simple robe, its pale blue setting off the dark green of her scales. She blinked, first a quick snap of her vertical eyelids, then a slower squeeze of the inner pair that closed horizontally.

"It's lovely. You will save money on mirrors." She smiled, exposing sharp teeth between her scaly lips.

"See? Even Lyst likes it."

Ben smiled. "I think that was Paleolithic sarcasm, Ro—sorry, Griffin."

Rohan scratched his beard.

"You know what? Stick to Rohan. On Earth, nobody should use that name, but on Wistful, I'd really prefer as few people as possible know me as Griffin. It's a little schizophrenic."

Lyst laughed, a sound similar to a bird chirping.

"One day you will have to decide which is your true name, Rohan. If you don't, you may find that it has chosen you."

The group picked at the buffet.

Ben Stone looked at his wife. "I feel like we should have stayed behind."

She hugged him from the side with one arm. "There's nothing more we could have done on Earth to locate Garren. We need *Insatiable*'s scanners to continue the search. And Rohan needed her speed more than we needed her sensors."

He nodded. "I would have *felt* better if I'd stayed on Earth. At least I would have been doing something useful. Here I'm dead weight."

Rohan looked at them. "You're here to keep *Insatiable* out of trouble. She can't take orders from any of the rest of us, not without getting into trouble with the Empire."

Ben sighed. "I know. I'm just tense. I don't know how you stay so relaxed, given what's at stake."

"I'm relaxed because this is the easy part. All I have to do is go punch a giant bug in the face and get it spitting mad. I'm *good* at pissing things off. If you wanted to see me nervous, you should have seen me on my way to Earth. Going to talk to my mother and my ex after more than ten years off-planet. *That* was stressful."

Ben raised his donut in a salute. "Two fearsome women indeed. I don't blame you for feeling trepidatious."

"As far as this goes, as long as Tollan finishes the container and Lyst can use her hydromancy to get the venom into it, the plan is pretty simple. Then we hit up a few choice restaurants and head back."

Marion raised her coffee. "Save the Earth, then find Garren. Then you can eat."

Rohan looked at the wizardess. "You're welcome to join us, Lyst, though I'm not sure how your taste in food compares to mammals."

She shook her head, a flicker of movement almost too quick to catch. "At most restaurants, I'd rather eat the waitstaff than the food. You enjoy without me."

I think she's kidding. Right?

Rohan made a quick call to check in on *Void's Shadow*. The small ship was riding inside one of *Insatiable*'s cargo bays.

He closed the channel and looked around the room. Marion Stone chatted with two of her graduate students. Lyst picked up a slice of smoked fish and dropped it into her mouth, smacking her tongue against her scales with each bite in what he hoped was an expression of appreciation.

Ben Stone saw Rohan standing alone and walked over.

"Need anything?"

"I'll be okay. I heal fast. Most of the bones in my arms have set already." He held up his hands and wiggled his fingers to demonstrate.

"Sometimes I hear you say things like that and I think you're kidding, and sometimes I'm afraid you aren't."

Rohan smiled. "I was just thinking. You remember Bright Angel? You ran into her in Sahara City, I think."

"The leader of Vanguard Prime? African American? Curvy?"

"Yeah."

"Nope, didn't notice her." The Professor smiled. "Why?"

"We were a thing. When I was on Earth."

"Yeah? Oh, you mean . . . before."

"Yeah. For a couple of years. Then I left. And never came back. Well, you know, until just now."

"Ah. And you're bringing this up because you're hoping . . . what? To restart things?"

"Honestly, I don't know. I didn't expect seeing her again to hit me so hard."

"Yet it did."

"It did."

"Have you told this to her? Or are you just telling me?"

Rohan laughed. "I think she knows. My Hybrid abilities don't extend to a poker face."

"And? Does she seem to return those feelings?"

"Not so much. She's actually kind of pissed at me."

"A woman's anger and her desire to sleep with you can coexist surprisingly well."

"I mean, she's kind of pissed at me, but also she pretty much shuts me down if I seem to broach the idea of getting closer."

"That's a pretty clear answer, then. Isn't it?"

Rohan sighed. "Yeah, it is. It is. I let myself get caught up in the idea that if I can save the day, she'll look at me differently."

"That is a foolish notion. The hero complex."

"I know. I know it is. Just needed some reinforcement."

"Do you want some friendly advice from an old man?"

"I guess I do. Or I wouldn't have brought it up."

"If you like this woman, if you care about her, you need to be very clear about what you have to offer her before you pursue this—her—any further."

"What do you mean?"

"Are you just looking to get laid? Great, give that a try. She can say yes or no, it's on her. But if you're looking for more than that . . . Are you willing to move to Earth? Full time? Would you ask her to give up her position as leader of the most important team of heroes on her planet to be your mistress on a space station where she has no friends, no family, and can't even speak the language?"

"I don't . . ." His voice trailed off.

"Exactly. You don't know. You haven't really thought this through. You just know you like her, that seeing her again is giving you all the feelings. Right?"

"Yes."

"There's nothing wrong with that! Honestly, nothing. But before you pursue this, you need to think forward. Because if I know women, and I think I do, at least a little, they are better at doing that than we are."

"You're saying she's already thinking about how this all would play out."

"I would bet a significant sum of money on it. Which isn't to say that she'd be against a fling, if that's all it was. But I bet if you wanted more than that, she'd already have these questions in mind."

"Thanks, Professor. I see what you're saying. It's good advice."

"Damn right it is. I'm old enough to be your father, Rohan. If I haven't learned a thing or two by now, then I'm hopeless."

Marion was suddenly looking over his shoulder. "You were saying you're hopeless, dear husband?"

· · · · ● · ● · · · ·

Lyst looked up at Rohan. "How long do you expect this to take?"

He sighed. "I'm not sure. We've never come here looking for the decipede; it's always been the other way around. It also goes dormant for long periods of time. Wei Li, can you backtrack through old records and find it? Maybe spot the last time you have records of it moving around?"

"Hold."

Rohan scratched his beard. "*Void's Shadow*, you see anything? These guys are like an annoying roommate: always around when you don't want them to be, but nowhere to be found when they're needed."

Lyst laughed. "That's what I used to say about humans."

"Used to?"

She shook her head. "No, that was a little lie. I still say it."

He laughed. "Do you think my plan will work?"

She flashed her teeth at him. "Do not worry, Rohan. The Earth will be fine."

"Really?"

"Of course. Humanity might be wiped out, of course, but your species already had a tenuous hold on existence. I will watch over the next species to evolve sentience on the planet, observe their funny habits and interesting ways. The Earth, I will protect it always."

"I can't tell if you're trying to make me feel better or worse."

"When you feel the burden of expectations, it is worth remembering how small your existence is in the greater scheme of things. On the other hand, when you are feeling unimportant and of little use to anyone, that is a bad time to remember your place. It's all perspective."

"Well, given your equanimity in the face of the destruction of humanity, I have to say I'm grateful you agreed to help."

"I didn't say I *want* humanity to be wiped out. I just said it wouldn't be the end of the world. Literally.

"To answer the question you intended, I can say that the Old Ones are old. Older than my people. With advanced age, most civilizations become highly risk-averse. If you can send their creation back to them, and it does them harm, even if it is a small amount, it is likely they will abandon their attacks."

Wei Li's voice over the comms interrupted them. "We have the last location. Sending the coordinates now."

The main viewing screen split, two-thirds showing a live view as if they were looking out a window while the last third showed a map of the landscape below. It had their location and that of the decipede clearly marked.

Rohan spoke through the comms. "Can we get the latest positional data on any flyers within a thousand kilometers?"

"Sending."

More dots appeared on the map.

Lyst was running her hand over the low ceiling. "Is this a typical il'Drach ship, Griffin? She seems rather small. Lovely, but small."

Rohan shook his head. "Nah, not typical. She's still a baby. I have no idea what she'll grow into. I don't think she'll ever be really big, not with the stealth tech in her hull. It consumes a lot of energy."

Void's Shadow's spoke. "Captain, I have visual on the decipede."

He nodded. "Great. Bring us closer. But slowly, I want everyone ready when we wake it."

The ship floated through the air, the wind over her hull creating a soft, droning sound.

Rohan's gaze flicked back between the map and the live view. There were seven flyers nearby, all grounded, and closer to the decipede than he wanted.

Lyst leaned back in the couch and watched him pace.

The decipede came swiftly into view. It was enormous: each of its five sections the size of a city block, massive chitin-encrusted legs pressed meters-deep into the soft forest floor.

It wasn't moving.

Rohan looked at Lyst. "Sleeping?"

She shrugged. "Seems to be."

"Time to poke the bear."

"Poke the bear . . . with another bear?" She was smiling at him again.

Rohan tapped behind his ear to activate the open channel. "Okay. Ang, I need you to move about a hundred kilometers north of where you are and get ready. You'll drop in and wake them up, get them moving toward you. Hopefully, the flyers will get way ahead of the decipede. Then I'll drop down and get it to double back on me so I can get the venom. Then I need you to do it again and pull them away so we can escape. Good?"

Ang's voice responded. "It shall be as you are saying, Brother Rohan."

"Great."

Wei Li interrupted. "Is there an emergency plan in case the kaiju do not react exactly according to your predictions?"

"Yeah. We'll wing it."

"Rohan, if you get yourself killed, I will be sad. If you get *Lyst* killed, I will find a team of Shayjh to resurrect you so I can kill you again, with my own hands."

Rohan looked at Lyst, who shrugged at him.

The woman ran her hands over the bony crests on her head. "She is merely showing me the proper respect."

He sighed. "I'll prioritize her safety over my own. Good enough?"

"It is a start."

"Great. Ang, as soon as you're ready."

The Ursan responded quickly. "Entering atmosphere . . . now."

Ang's burst of anger could be felt through the ship's metaphysical shielding.

Lyst slapped her hand to the side of her chair. *Applause?*

"Is he really that strong?"

"I wish. He's like The Damsel, a projector. Not as subtle, but stronger. At least for projecting anger."

"It is impressive."

The decipede stirred immediately, lifting its head up from the ground, then pushing its rear eight legs into the ground and rising clear of the tree line. It turned north.

Wei Li updated them over the comms. "Decipede is up and moving. Flyers are heading north . . . not at the pace I expected."

Rohan swallowed. "Ang, move out."

A growl was the only answer, but Wei Li quickly confirmed.

"Shuttle is moving."

Rohan stood and faced the front of his ship, staring hard at the back of the decipede as it picked up speed, its legs churning up hills of dirt and trees with every step.

"Stay close to her. I'm getting ready."

He took a deep breath, then exhaled quickly.

Internally, he was tugging and pulling at his Power, summoning the rage and energy that would wake and attract all the kaiju.

For a long, paralyzing moment, nothing happened.

He wasn't immediately afraid, not with the decipede and flyers all heading away from him and posing no threat. The anger that had once simmered in his chest was calm, dulled by age and good living. He didn't even have any genuine desire to hurt any of the kaiju, and the Power responded to that lack of desire by doing . . . not much.

He looked at Lyst, who shrugged and smiled at him.

"This never happens to me."

She let out a short, snappy laugh. "I do not doubt you, little Rohan. Perhaps if you think about baseball."

"That's not . . . never mind."

He turned back toward the decipede picking up speed as it flattened a valley into the forest floor, oriented due north.

Rohan growled softly, annoyed at himself, and shook his head.

He thought about Bright Angel. He'd hoped for a warmer welcome from her. But he couldn't find any anger there. Sad, perhaps.

He thought about his mother, and their interactions fit the exact same pattern.

Then he thought about Hand of Justice and the other protesters. He'd spent years fighting to protect them, and all they wanted was for him to suffer for injuring a bank-robbing supervillain.

That thought got a little spark stirring in his belly.

Once the anger had started, it brought other images along, like a tide carrying driftwood onto a beach.

Earl and the Proud Guys refusing to help fight the sharks.

Naked concrete, bristling with exposed rebar and shattered neon, all that was left of downtown Tokyo after the shark attack.

Displaced children, hollow-faced and dirty, clutching their favorite toys as they walked kilometers searching for a place to rest.

He thought about other places on Earth, devastated by the shark attacks, and just as his anger seemed to peak, he brought out a new thought.

It was *his* planet.

Not 'his' in the sense of being his planet of origin. Though it was.

Not 'his' in the sense that his roots were there—his mother, his friends. Though they were.

As he formed the thought, he meant the word 'his' in its most possessive sense. It *belonged* to him. As if he were its king. Or its owner.

It was *his* world that the sharks had invaded. *His* people—no, his subjects—who had been killed. *His* cities that had been devastated.

With those thoughts, the Hybrid Power broke through and roiled inside him, worked up into chaotic violence.

He looked at the back of the decipede and screamed. A loud, wordless exhalation of noise and rage.

How dare it get in his way?

He was The Griffin, Lance Primary of the il'Drach Navy, Scourge of Zahad. These creatures would be taught some lessons.

Power pulsed through him, a dense wave of heat and light that vibrated back and forth between his tailbone and the back of his head, sending bubbles of energy filtering out through his body at each endpoint.

Rohan tapped the inside of the hull. "Open up." His voice was a growl, harsh and ugly.

"Yes, Captain."

The roof of the ship opened like a clamshell unfolding, exposing the entire cockpit to the humid air. He smelled rotting vegetation with a strong, acrid overtone of giant bug, a scent Rohan was starting to find all too familiar.

The Hybrid pulled his mask down over his face and waited for the air supply to kick in.

Void's Shadow kept pace as the decipede slowed, perhaps distracted by Rohan's sudden appearance behind it.

Rohan fought for clarity as he tried to speak over the comms, his anger pressing him to engage the monster.

"Ang. Stop."

The thunderstorm of anger to the north flashed out of existence, and the decipede started to turn to face him.

"The flyers are already circling back, Rohan. They didn't swarm Ang the way they usually do."

"Let them come!"

29

Respecting Other's Elders

F our hours later, Rohan slouched deep inside the low-slung chair in the foyer of Tollan's Things. The artificer was pondering the gleaming metal cylinder, about the size of a scuba diver's oxygen tank, propped up on his counter.

"That it?"

Rohan nodded. "Your payment. One full canister of one hundred percent certified decipede venom. Just please don't tell me what you're going to do with it."

Wei Li, sitting in the chair to Rohan's right, leaned forward.

"You may tell me. Especially if you plan on opening it on board." Her vertically slit eyes narrowed as she watched him handle the container of dangerous liquid.

The small man lifted the cylinder in steady hands, his pointed ears peeking around his short, gray hair.

"I wasn't going to tell either of you. Rohan, you look like hell."

"Thanks. Either the kaiju are smarter than I thought or I'm getting really unlucky."

Tollan raised one eyebrow. "How so?"

Rohan shifted, trying and failing to find a comfortable way to sit. He had fresh burns from the fight.

"They learn. Each time we try the trick of distracting them, they are diverted for less time, circle back faster."

"Ah. You thought they were just animals."

"Dumb of us, really. I mean, they have Powers, that implies sentience."

"It does."

"So it stands to reason they're smart enough to learn."

"I believe so. Still, you got the canisters. I assume you filled the other one?"

"Absolutely. Gotta go save my home planet."

"That's an impressive feat. I've been here a while; nobody's tried to make a living milking decipedes before."

"I am declaring early retirement from that gig. I almost blew it."

"Did you?"

Rohan stretched, the skin along his ribs complaining bitterly with the motion.

"Lost my temper, almost couldn't reel it back in. I wanted to fight those flyers so badly. I was about to charge right into them."

Wei Li patted his shoulder. "But you didn't. You have grown; you are now as mature as a normal prepubescent child among my people."

"Thanks."

Tollan pointed to the canister. "How did you get Masamune to help with the design?"

Rohan chuckled. "I threatened him. I said I'd tell you that he wasn't smart enough to help."

The older man laughed. "You're a quick judge of character, figuring out that would get under his skin."

"I got lucky. Sometimes luck is all you need."

"Sometimes luck isn't enough. Like when your plan is crazy. You're going to try to kill an Old One with that venom?"

Rohan looked at Wei Li, who shrugged. She didn't want to explain.

The Hybrid settled deeper into the chair. "Not an Old One, just a kaiju they've weaponized. We're not going to kill it, we're going to fix it."

"Excuse me?"

"Earth is being invaded by decipede-sized megalodons with legs. Each one has a box on their spine that makes them angry."

The artificer snorted. "If you don't want to tell me, boy, then don't. No cause for mocking me here in my own shop, especially after I did you a favor with that canister."

Wei Li put her hand on the counter, palm down. "His story is outlandish but completely true."

Tollan looked between them. "You're serious. If they created these megalodons, what makes you sure that sending one back in a bad mood is going to give them any pause?"

Rohan spread his hands. "I don't live in a world of 'sure.' However, if these particular Old Ones are so tough and strong that they can handle one of these monsters without breaking a sweat, why bother breeding them? Why bother sending *them* to Earth? It's an educated guess."

"You're thirty years old. I'd hardly call you educated."

"In the ways of war, I might as well be teaching the course."

· · · • • • • • · · ·

Rohan shifted his position. He was back in his regen tank, just a few meters from *Void's Shadow*. Ben Stone stood on the other side, reading from a tablet.

The door to *Insatiable*'s bay slid open, and Marion Stone walked in, along with Lyst and a pair of the Professor's graduate assistants.

Rohan checked the side of the tank, which had frosted to protect his modesty. He had nothing with him inside the tank other than the canister of decipede venom.

Marion Stone came up to him. "How are you feeling? Is my husband checking on your physical well-being, or is he just chatting you up like an old school chum?"

Rohan smiled at her. "I'm kind of a mess. I keep breaking stuff I don't have time to heal."

"Even with the regen tank?"

He shrugged. "It's great with soft tissue stuff, but bones are another story."

She nodded. "The canister?"

He looked down at the cylindrical object. It was strapped to him with a leather harness: belts that tied around his waist and chest and another set of straps over his shoulders to hold it up.

"Just trying to assimilate it. So when the next land shark swats at it with metaphysical energy, I have a chance to defend it."

"Just like wearing an identical uniform, day after day."

He nodded. "I should get someone to throw my new cape in here as well."

Ben looked around. "It's in the ship, right? I'll go grab it."

"Thanks, Professor."

Marion looked at Rohan intently while her husband crossed the bay to enter *Void's Shadow*. "Are you really okay? We were with Hyperion for a long time, and he didn't have the issues with his anger that you seem to. Do you need to talk to somebody?"

Rohan laughed. "Are you volunteering?"

She shook her head. "I know my limitations. That's outside my area of knowledge. But I can refer you to someone."

He paused and thought. "I'm not saying that's exactly a bad idea, or the wrong idea, but the reason Hyperion didn't lose his temper like me wasn't psychological. He was just so much more powerful. You probably never saw him anywhere near as close to his limits as I've had to go to get things done."

"Really?"

"Yeah. I saw him lose it, more than once. He'd go berserk like nobody else. There was nothing on Earth to push him to utilize that much of his energy, though."

"You're saying . . . off Earth."

"On the Ringgate, for example. Fighting the Wedge. Once he reached a certain point, we had to evacuate all allied troops to a hundred klicks away and wait for him to get tired. He was worse than The Green, when he really cut loose."

She frowned. "I never saw him cut loose is what you're telling me."

"That is exactly what I'm saying. Which doesn't mean I couldn't do better than I have been, or maybe that I shouldn't be using that much Power."

She studied his face. "Hm. Not an easy burden to live with."

He shrugged. "Not really. But there are benefits."

Ben Stone walked over with the frictionless cape held over his arm. It was folded in half, the inner lining on the outside, and draped carefully.

"Here you go."

"Thanks, Professor." Rohan took the cape and hung it over his shoulder, then settled deeper into the tank's waters.

Lyst pointed to the harness. "Is that meeting your expectations?"

"It's great, Lyst, thanks. I had no idea you could work leather."

"It is a hobby. When larger mammals first evolved, it was all the rage among my people to work their skin into clothing. I still have a jacket made from some early primates. Ancestors of yours, really!"

"That's, um, great. Maybe don't show me that."

Ben looked at his friend and interrupted before finding out more details about Lyst's history. "Is there anything we can do for you?"

Rohan shook his head. "Right now, I need rest. Actually, there is something . . . Lyst, can you stay here? I have a favor to ask."

The Stones traded a glance and nodded to each other with the perfect synchronized rhythm developed only through decades of partnership.

Ben looked at him. "We have things to prepare. We should be on Earth in about seven hours."

"Thanks, Professors. I appreciate it."

They left, clearing the room. Rohan sucked at the nozzle on the side of his tank, drinking his fill of the tasteless but nutrient-laden fluid it supplied.

Lyst walked over. She wore her usual light-blue robes, hanging loosely over her dark-green scales. Up close, Rohan noticed again how rough and textured her scales looked, not smooth and slick like Wei Li's.

"You asked me to stay?" She spoke the Fire Speech, not English.

He nodded. "I need a favor. I'd ask someone else, but, to be honest, I think they'd be squeamish."

She nodded back. "You need somebody eaten? Who on board must be killed in such a manner?"

"No, no, not that. I need help with the regen tank."

"I am afraid, little Hybrid, that I am unfamiliar with the specifics of this technology."

"I know, that's not what I meant. Look, the Hybrids . . . we were seen as tools of war, by the Fathers. They had all sorts of tricks to get us back into combat if we were injured."

"Such as this regen tank."

"Yes. But the Fathers had . . . off-label uses for it as well."

"I do not follow."

"Of course not. The fluid in the tank is saturated with stem cells, growth factors, and nutrients. It's everything a cellular matrix needs to heal at absolutely the fastest rate."

"Yes."

"But it only really works on what it's touching. I was cut up pretty badly, remember? Across the chest and back."

"I cannot say as I was paying close attention to your superficial injuries, Hybrid."

"No, sure. But I was. Those are gone, healed."

"That is good news. Is it not?"

"The problem isn't the cuts. The problem is the bones and ligaments that I keep damaging."

"Ah, perhaps I begin to see. The fluid cannot act directly on the bones. Because it is not in contact with them. Or in close proximity."

"Exactly. In a way, the regen tank is failing me *because* it's healing the cuts, and once it has, the growth factors and minerals can't get to the bones underneath."

"And you say the Fathers devised an . . . off-label . . . use to bypass this limitation?"

"They did. It was highly unpleasant, but effective."

"Highly unpleasant for whom?"

He smiled. "For me. Well, for everybody, but mostly the Hybrid."

"That is fine. What precisely do you need me to do?"

"I need a way for the fluid to have access to the bones that require healing."

"I begin to see. Which bones?"

He tilted his head to the side, indicating one of the screens on the side of the tank. "Look there. It has live imaging of my skeletal structure. You should be able to see all the outstanding fractures."

She bent her head to the screen. Her vertically slit eyes flickered back and forth as she examined the images.

"Before I begin a procedure under incorrect assumptions, am I to understand that you want me to cut your flesh sufficiently for the bones to be fully exposed at the sites of these fractures?"

He nodded. "That's the only way. For added giggles, you'll probably have to cut again, because the incisions will heal up before the bones do."

She smiled. "Will that not be extraordinarily painful?"

"Not sure 'extraordinarily' is a strong enough adjective, but yes. Which is one reason I didn't ask anybody human to do it."

"You feel they would be less capable?"

"Mammals are squeamish. Once the screaming really starts, we found very few techs who could continue doing their work objectively. And most of the ones who could, we found, were enjoying it a little too much."

"And you trust me to not be, as you say, squeamish."

"Yeah. And not sadistic, either. I figure you've been around the block a few times. You're neither soft nor someone who gets off on the pain of others."

She tilted her head and looked up over the side of the tank at the Hybrid's face. "That is an insightful analysis, Rohan. I have no desire to hurt you, but also no great aversion to it."

"You also have sharp, sharp claws."

"I do. My species is carnivorous. Was."

"So, will you help?"

"I would be happy to, little Rohan. Where shall I begin?"

He sighed. "The ankle, please. Oh, *Insatiable*?"

"Yes? What can I do to help you, Tow Chief Rohan?"

"Close the doors, please. I'm going to be screaming for a while. Don't be alarmed, and don't let anyone in, okay?"

"I'm just super glad to be able to help, Tow Chief! But not that you're screaming. You know. I mean, yes, sir. No, sir. Yes, I'll keep the doors closed."

"Thanks, *Insatiable*. We're going to get started."

•••••••••

"Polls show sixty-two percent agree with the statement, 'the monster invasion is likely to be stopped and humanity will be saved,' up from fifty-three percent before Four was killed and just thirty-nine percent before Three was killed, while it was still engaged with The Green. Conversely, favorable opinion of Hyperion Industries is down from seventy-one percent to sixty-two percent in that same timespan. When asked for reasons, 'don't trust aliens' was the second most common comment while some variation of 'don't agree with pardoning Proud Guys' was the leading cause."

Rohan groaned softly and slouched deeper into his leather chair. The conference room was relatively quiet, most of the staff having assignments elsewhere in the building at that moment.

The Director was seated at the head of the table. Going around, Bright Angel, The Damsel, Poseidon, Amber, Spiral, and Lyst were the only other people Rohan knew by name. The Hyperion executive giving the briefing was the same man they'd spoken to before.

Rohan idly wondered if he was a decision maker or just the person in charge of giving bad news to The Director.

"We polled for opinions specifically about The Griffin, and his numbers aren't good. We couldn't reach statistical validity because, after this much time away, his name recognition is very low.

"When we described him as the man from the recently released video, the one showing the full beating of Brother Steel, the numbers looked significantly worse.

"When we asked for favorable or unfavorable on 'the Hybrid who just returned,' we got higher recognition but still very low favorable impressions."

Rohan grunted. "All publicity is good publicity, am I right?" He looked around the table.

Nobody smiled or laughed. The group suffered a long moment of uncomfortable silence.

He shifted the weight of the canister of decipede venom by adjusting the harness straps.

"Why are you polling my approval ratings, anyway? I'm not a talk show host. Who cares?"

The executive looked directly at Rohan. "Because with every point drop in your approval rating, more local governments find reasons to stop cooperating with our relief efforts, more regulations inhibiting our work are passed."

"Oh. Well, okay, then."

The executive cleared his throat. "To continue, we've delivered two million temporary housing units to the Pacific Rim countries: the shipping crate-style units, each packed with two months of rations and water. All in all, acceptance has been high, though slowing currently.

"Kid Lightning has not regained consciousness." The Damsel flinched noticeably at the words. "The Damsel reports her fitness for action at sixty percent. Poseidon claims to be fully recovered. The Griffin sustained further injuries on Toth 3, but he reports that with the aid of the regen tank, he is at almost full strength.

"Bright Angel and Amber have returned from their campaign. They have successfully eliminated three new clusters of vampires from refugee camps Tokyo Delta, Taipei Beta, and Manila Theta.

"The mission to retrieve . . ."—he checked something on his tablet—"decipede venom from Toth 3 has been successful.

"We expect Five to appear sometime in the next few hours, but if the pattern holds, it will take another dozen hours to reach land. We have satellites and the il'Drach science vessel scanning the Pacific for early detection. You'll all be notified within seconds of any sighting."

Rohan rubbed his hands. Everything below his elbows ached like a tequila hangover, but the sharper pains had faded away. He sipped at a protein shake. Chocolate salted caramel.

Poseidon had a bottle of wine wrapped in his fist but was barely sipping from it. His eyes were hard and angry in a way Rohan had never seen before.

Maybe he was taking his godhood a little more seriously.

Bright Angel looked tired but intact. She had smiled tightly at seeing Rohan: no warmth but no anger either.

The Director wore a tan-and-pink sari, both colors muted, almost pastel. Her hair and makeup were perfunctory, and, if anything, she seemed more tense than she had when he had first returned to Earth.

The Damsel looked tired and drawn, her middle-aged face looking more like a normal middle-aged face and less like a professional influencer's image.

Lyst sat quietly in her chair, showing none of the strain that the others felt. Had she always been so calm? If not, how many millions of years had it been before she reached that state?

Amber had a grip on Spiral's arm. The body language between them was very much brother-sister. Or father-daughter. Considering what a creep her actual father was, replacing him with Spiral seemed like an excellent choice.

Spiral himself showed no concern, as usual. His reactions never quite matched a normal person's responses to events. It was an open question whether he was emotionally broken or spiritually advanced. At least, open in Rohan's mind.

Plates of steamed pork-filled buns adorned the table, alongside bowls of sauteed bok choy and some other green vegetable Rohan didn't recognize. Pots of tea were spread around.

Rohan finished his shake and reached for a bun.

The briefing continued.

"The Sons of Atlantis have been scrambling to assemble enough personnel and resources to support the next invasion, but they've been completely unsuccessful.

"The Proud Guys sent a message asking us for their deployment instructions. The language involved was . . . colorful."

The Director snorted. "Volunteers only for any communication with those . . . people. I won't have my staff pushed into a position where they feel unnecessarily traumatized."

The man nodded. "Already done, Director. If there are no questions, that's all I have right now."

He paused and looked around the table.

Rohan felt he should have had something to ask, but his head was foggy.

The regen tank had healed the bones in his arms and ankle, but it couldn't drive away the drained, hollow feeling all throughout his limbs. Every cell in his body had been strip-mined and carpet-bombed.

"Then I shall wish you all best of luck." The executive picked up his tablet and left the room.

The Director surveyed the table carefully.

"So, we all know where we are now. What are the next steps? Do we all agree with the basic thrust of The Griffin's plan?"

Everyone turned in unison toward Bright Angel.

30

Decisions and Recriminations

The Baltimore native, eyes tired but clear, held up her hands. Her braids flicked as she turned her head to face each of them in turn. "I really wish I had a better idea. I asked Lyst, she just smiled and said this was our best hope. Then I asked if it was likely to work. Don't ask what she said to *that*."

The group turned as one to Rohan. He sighed. "Is that a 'go'?"

The Director stood. "If nothing else comes up, this is our plan. Right now, our job is to do everything each of us can do to make sure it actually works."

Rohan sank deeper into his seat. "After eight hours rotating between turns in the regen tank and having my arms and leg sliced to the bone, my brain is fried. You guys are going to have to help me work out the details."

He took another bun and bit into the soft, floury crust.

He watched his friends as they spoke. Bright Angel had the determined look of a woman who knew there was very little hope to be had but wasn't willing to let it show.

The Damsel glanced over her shoulder every two or three minutes.

She did it five different times before Rohan realized that she was looking in the direction of the medical wing where staff treated Kid Lighting.

Poseidon took shallow sips from his bottle of wine, never emptying it. The flush in his cheeks was anger, not inebriation.

As the discussion wound down, Rohan pulled Amber to the side and talked to her briefly about the limits of her Power.

The others filed out of the room, on their way to undergo whatever preparations they needed to make.

The Director and Rohan were left alone. She turned to her son.

"Do you have a minute?"

Rohan sighed. "Nothing on my agenda but a hot date with a soft mattress. Might be the last nap I ever get to take." He regretted saying it as soon as the words left his mouth.

Not cool to joke about your own death with your mother.

If it fazed her at all, she didn't show it.

"Rohan, I want to talk to you about something, and I'm having a hard time finding the right approach."

"Well, you need to hurry. Pretend you're a Hybrid. Just say it, then worry later if that was the best phrasing."

"Okay, I'll get to the point. There are videos going around of you promising to stand trial for the death of Brother Steel. Are they real?"

"Yeah, I said it. That guy, what's his name, Hand of Justice, was with a bunch of protesters outside. I figured, why not? It's not like I did anything wrong."

She swallowed. "So you did say it. And . . . you intend to follow through? Or are you going to leave Earth as soon as this situation with the sharks is resolved?"

"Well, I said I'd stand trial. I'm not in love with the idea, but I'm not in love with the idea of breaking my promise, either."

"But you would. Break your promise. You're at least willing to entertain the idea. Unlike, say, Hyperion, who was a stickler for keeping his word."

"Mom, if you're criticizing me for not living up to Hyperion's standard of honor and decency or something, can it wait? Let me have it tomorrow, maybe? As much as I miss you putting me down, I'm not in the mood."

She was shaking her head. "That's not what I'm doing. Not what I'm trying to do, at least. I'm not angry or disappointed that you might skip town, I'm *hoping* that you do. I just need to be prepared."

"What do you mean prepared?"

"There will be legal and public relations ramifications. Nothing we can't handle, so don't worry about it."

"Mom, I'm not skipping town."

She sighed. "Rohan, I think maybe you should."

"What do you mean? Am I missing something here? I stand trial, they get their day in court, I get exonerated, I go about my merry way. What are you worried about? Do you think someone will attack the proceedings or something? Reveal my identity?"

"Not that. Rohan, look . . . I love you. I'm proud of you. You're my son, and you inherited more than your fair share of trials and responsibilities. I wish I had known enough to avoid that for you, but the fact is that I didn't."

"It's fine, Mom. You got dealt a pretty crappy hand, too. I never blamed you for how things turned out."

"I'm not looking for your forgiveness. I'm looking for you to understand that when I say what you need to hear, I'm not coming from the point of view of someone who hates you or who thinks you're a terrible person. I don't."

"Okaaay."

She paused, letting out a long breath.

"Have you actually seen the full video of your fight with Brother Steel?"

He shook his head. "Just a snippet. Why?"

"Rohan, it isn't good. I know you think you'll have a trial and a grateful human race will declare you innocent, then hold a small parade in your honor. But I'm not sure it's going to go that way."

"You aren't?"

"Neither is our legal team. And they're, well, they're the best legal team in the world. Certainly the highest paid. They give you a sixty percent chance of conviction."

"Why? Is this because of anti-alien sentiment?"

"No. Well, yes, in part, but only a small part. Rohan, you need to watch the video."

"I'm really not in the mood, Mom. Can you just tell me what I'm supposed to see?"

"Rohan . . . you beat that man nearly to death. He tried to surrender after the first half dozen punches. There are three minutes of beating after that point."

Rohan adjusted the canister in his lap. He scratched his beard. Swallowed.

"So you're telling me it's . . . that bad."

"It really is. Rohan, you were out of control. And for someone like you, out of control is a very expensive place to be."

"I didn't kill him."

"You didn't. But you did paralyze him, and he was in such rough shape that he killed himself six weeks later. Couldn't handle the thought of life as a paraplegic."

"I paralyzed him. I . . . I don't think I knew that."

"I'm not sure you did. Sister Steel sprung him from jail, the rest happened out of the public eye. It was months before she started the public crusade demanding accountability for vigilante heroes."

"Not the first person doing that."

"No. But there's a strong anti-alien movement across large parts of the western world. Part of it is people trying to get their governments to wrest control of Hyperion technology from us, on the grounds that aliens shouldn't share the same intellectual rights as humans. You know the deal. The rich and the politicians drum up good old-fashioned xenophobia in their base to disguise the fact that they're making a money grab."

"Nothing new there."

"No, but it gave them common cause with Sister Steel. Which got her funding and exposure."

"Which will taint any jury I'll ever be involved with."

"It might, but I really wish you'd stop deflecting like that. The jury might be prejudiced, and they might not. But that's not the real issue. You really did paralyze that man, and even a jury of good-natured, honest people would still watch that video and see it. And there's a good chance they'd vote guilty."

He slumped forward over her desk and rested his head on one forearm. "So . . . what am I supposed to do?"

She sighed and placed her hand on the back of his head. "I don't know. I don't have any great answers, and believe me, I've been looking. You can skip the trial. Your response to an off-the-cuff request made by a civilian during a protest isn't legally binding."

"Wouldn't look good, though."

"Neither would prison orange, not with your complexion."

"Actually, I think I look good in neon orange."

"It might be an improvement over the purple and gold you're wearing now." They both laughed, a short burst that ended quickly.

"Anything else I can do?"

"Yes. Rohan, your friends have seen the same video. You should watch it. And you should remember that when they look at you, they're looking through those eyes. Stop pretending that this whole thing is a misunderstanding or a political ploy or a plot. Stop the jokes about how obvious it is that you're innocent. They're not funny, just callous."

He looked up and opened his mouth, ready to argue, but shut it.

She rubbed the back of his head and neck and smiled at him. "I do love you. We love you. Carla and me. You're not perfect, and that's okay. None of us are. But you have to take some responsibility for your mistakes."

"Leaving Earth does not strike me as taking responsibility."

"Standing trial is not your only option. I'm just saying that doing nothing at all is not a good option either. If you want to keep open the possibility of a future on Earth, you have to do something."

He sighed. "Okay. Rudra save me, I really left him a paraplegic? How the hell did that happen? His body was made out of organic steel. Whatever that means."

Her eyes softened as she looked at him, her hand stroking his shoulder-length hair. "Watch the video. You'll see. Maybe start with a glass of that tequila."

"Maybe later. Not to be insensitive, but I have other priorities at this exact moment."

"I know you do." She reached an arm around him and hugged him to her. He leaned in, resting his head on her shoulder.

A chime rang over the room's sound system. Microseconds later, both Rohan's phone and The Director's phone let out their own chimes.

The Director stepped to the wall of her office, sari swishing around her legs as she walked, and tapped the screen.

"Yes?"

There was no video, but the voice belonged to the Hyperion Industries executive who had delivered their briefing.

"Ma'am, we have confirmation. Another land shark has appeared in the Pacific."

"When are we projecting landfall?"

The executive's voice returned. "Based on current velocity, we expect arrival in Vancouver twelve hours from now."

The Director nodded. "Thanks."

Rohan sighed. "Close to home."

The Director nodded. "I still own the house there. I have friends there. Quite a few friends."

"Don't sweat it. We'll stop it."

"I know. Right now, you should get some rest."

"That was my plan. Head back to my room, I guess, and grab some shut eye."

"Don't go to your room in the hotel, it's too exposed. We have secure rooms down here. We have to keep you and that canister safe. Sorry there's no view."

He yawned. "Sounds good. Just point me in the right direction."

·· • • • • • • ··

Sleep made a liar out of Rohan, refusing to visit until he pulled out his phone and streamed the video of him beating Brother Steel.

His first reaction was humiliation. His anger, his loss of control, his savagery, the joy he felt with every thunk of fist into metal, all exposed, all projected through his eyes and captured on digital for the world to see.

For a moment, he tried to tell himself that he hadn't remembered it that way. Had he blacked out? Had he forgotten that array of feelings, the mindset he had owned while crippling the bank thief?

The Hybrid pinched the skin between his eyebrows and tried to rub away his developing headache.

The truth.

The truth was, he did remember. The truth was, while he had never realized how badly he'd hurt Brother Steel, he'd also never forgotten how out of line his own violence had really been.

The truth was, he didn't think anybody else would know. He hadn't known the beating was recorded. He had thought his shame was his own, a private thing. Nobody would have believed Brother Steel on words alone, and Rohan hadn't realized the extent of the man's injuries.

The truth was, his memories of that incident had been one big reason he had stayed away from Earth for so long.

I've watched it three times, and I'm still not finding any sympathy for the main character.

Rohan snuggled his frictionless cape close to his shoulders, wrapped his arms around the canister of decipede venom, and buried himself deep under the covers of the soft bed.

Sleep eventually came. He dreamed about Bright Angel, a nonsensical dream where he cooked her omelets but she didn't like the ingredients, so he kept trying, and she kept disdainfully pushing them away.

He was dream-folding a shredded cheese blend and crumbled andouille sausage into runny eggs when a noise snapped him up into consciousness.

"There he is." The voice was female and raspy, like vocal cords that had been drenched in whiskey and cigarettes, rendered more husky by the fact that its owner was whispering.

"Shh! You'll wake him! Let me grab the canister, and we can leave." The second voice was male and deep, a baritone rumble that carried farther than its volume warranted.

"Doc wants the canister. I don't give two spherical, silvery shits about it. I just want The Griffin dead."

"That wasn't the deal."

With a silent effort, Rohan kept his physical eyes shut but stretched his Third Eye wide open.

There were two people in the room, two powerful auras, Powers to be sure, glowing near the back wall opposite the door.

The woman spoke. "Darn, you woke him up with your jabbering. Grab him!"

Rohan kicked the baseboard of his bed, hard enough to splinter the carbon fiber frame.

He squirted out from his position between the soft, cotton sheets, his cape's frictionless surface making his movement strange and unpredictable, faster than it should have been.

Rohan's shoulder thudded into the woman's midsection, knocking a short breath out of her.

Her arms reached down to wrap him up, but as soon as they exerted pressure, he flew back out of her embrace and into the bed frame.

"What the . . . get him!"

Rohan planted a foot on the ground, his Power unspooling rapidly as he came fully awake and stood inside the cramped room. He stood, working to center his balance, the canister still strapped to him.

The woman's voice again. "He's up, he's up. Forget the canister, get the lights!"

The second presence moved toward the door, a hand reaching out to slap the wall. An instant later, the room was filled with bright, artificial light.

Rohan winced away from the glare, working to control his breath as his Power continued to spiral upward into his skull.

For a moment, he saw his own face staring back at him, disembodied and distorted, a shadowy presence behind it blocking the back wall of the room.

Another moment later, he realized he was looking at his reflection.

His image was reflected in the woman's *face*.

She was metallic, polished to a mirror finish.

"Remember me, you murderer?"

31

Other Priorities

Sister Steel.

The man behind her was tall, two meters at least, with a slender build. His skin was dark, more gray than brown or black, his features gaunt and tight, as if there wasn't quite enough skin to comfortably cover his bone structure.

"Shadowstep? That you?"

"Oh, *him* you remember?"

Rohan swallowed. "I remember you, too, Sister Steel. It's hard to forget with your video channel and all."

She laughed, a harsh and humorless sound. "You noticed? I'm so flattered."

"Look, this isn't a good idea. We have a plan for dealing with the land sharks, and they need my help."

"Well, that's too bad for them. Because we have other priorities."

She stepped forward and snapped a silver fist into his face.

Rohan pulled his head back, but not quickly enough. Tears welled up in his eyes, driven by the sting of cold metallic knuckles hammering into his nose.

The Hybrid twisted to the side, trying to keep the canister safe as Sister Steel threw more punches his way.

One punch missed. He ducked and sidestepped, but her next punch jammed into his shoulder, causing pain but little damage. He twisted and sidestepped again, but her right hand crunched into his ribs, just under his armpit.

She was too fast.

"You need to back off! This isn't about us!"

"We're the only ones here, peanut." Another jab flicked toward his face, her knuckles each reflecting the white light of the ceiling fixture.

Rohan slipped his head to the side and snapped his own left hand back at her. His Power reinforced the bones in his knuckles, making them as hard as the diamond of his facemask.

Sister Steel slid backward, halfway across the room, her feet digging ruts into the soft carpet and exposing the cold concrete underneath it.

She rubbed her hand across her face, small sparks flaring with the metal-on-metal contact.

"That's no way to treat a lady."

"If I see one, I'll treat her better."

Shadowstep shook his head from his vantage point over Sister Steel's shadow. "The two of you need banter coaches. You're awful."

Rohan grunted. "I'll try to shut her up."

He slid forward, feet staying close to the ground, and threw a quick left punch at her face.

She flinched backward, her hands rising; he lowered his hips and planted a solid right hand into her belly.

It felt like punching the armored hull of a battle cruiser. Something he knew from experience.

She slid back again, her answering swings whistling through empty air.

With a grunt, the woman gathered herself together and skipped forward to throw another series of punches at Rohan.

He parried the first punch with one hand, but it came dangerously close to the canister.

How tough was the material? Probably not tough enough to take a clean shot from Sister Steel.

He snarled and snapped his leg up, kicking into her belly.

Instead of the expected impact, his foot sailed through her midsection, knocking the Hybrid off-balance.

Sister Steel laughed and cracked Rohan across the jaw with a tight, hooking punch.

"How do you like that?" She followed up with another punch, and Rohan rode the momentum of it to jump backward out of her reach.

"What the . . ." He looked over her shoulder again.

He knew Shadowstep. The man could step to the shadow side of the world—a tiny fragment of the distance it would take to reach the dimension of the Wedge, for example. In the same direction as Masamune's fortress.

When he was there, light and all physical objects would basically pass through his body. He became nearly invisible, completely intangible, and more than a little creepy.

It had always been an interesting power, but never a game changer.

Rohan looked up. "Shadowstep. You can bring people with you now?"

The tall man shrugged his shoulders. "You grew a beard. I got stronger. We all make choices."

Rohan grunted and moved backward, away from the dangerous pair.

He looked around the room, checking all the surfaces.

He could leave the area, smash through the ceiling or the walls and fly out of the confined space. He wasn't completely certain he could protect the canister if he did that, and without the canister . . .

Sister Steel slid forward again, moving slowly and smoothly so Shadowstep could stay behind her.

Rohan kept backing up until he felt the concrete wall touch the heel of his rear leg.

With a shiny grin, Sister Steel put her fists up on either side of her jaws and closed the distance.

Rohan sighed. "Look, we don't need to fight. I'll do whatever you want after we do this land shark thing. I'll stand trial."

She shook her head. "Suppose I believe you, which I don't. But if I did. What do you think will happen? You save the human race from the shark monsters, then what? You think they'll convict you? Worst case for you, they give you a slap on the wrist, and you go back to banging your whore girlfriend or flying off to space or whatever you do when you're not here."

She snapped one fist toward his face, then a second.

He ducked one, then slid to the side. Both of her punches hit the wall behind him, splintering the concrete and sending a shower of rocky splinters to the ground.

Rohan pivoted to face her, backing up to the wall on the other side of the room.

The two villains closed on him.

"She's not my . . . Not the point. Look, I'm sorry. This sucks for you, I know. I shouldn't have hurt him like that."

She threw another punch, then a wide kick around into his ribs.

Her leg struck his side like a steel beam.

"You shouldn't have, but what? What's your excuse? That he was robbing banks? That he fought back? That you knew prison wouldn't hold him, and he'd be out doing it again?"

"I didn't say that. I just said I shouldn't have hurt him like that. I'm sorry."

"You're sorry? You crippled my brother, and now you're sorry?"

She punched again, wide hooks from up close, bludgeoning his shoulders and sides.

He wrapped his arms around the canister and leaned forward, absorbing the impacts.

She reached back to throw a straight punch, and he ducked out to the side, letting her smash a new hole into the wall.

"Yes, I'm sorry. It was wrong."

"Wrong, but he deserved it, right? Isn't that what you're always saying?"

She backed him into the first wall again, tearing chunks out of the room's walls as they went.

"I'm not saying that. I'm saying I should not have hurt him like that. I lost control. It was wrong, and I'm sorry."

Sister Steel paused.

"You're serious."

He nodded. "I can't fix it. I don't know how. If you want to kill me . . . maybe that's what I deserve. I don't know. But I can't let you do it today. Not now."

Shadowstep sneered. "You won't trick us with those lines. We know what you are."

Sister Steel waved for him to be quiet. "What do you mean? What are you saying?"

"Millions . . . no, billions of lives are at stake here. Decent people. We have a plan to stop the sharks. Either it works or it kills me. Let me do something useful. Then, if I survive, you can do what you want with me. Please. This is bigger than him, than us."

"So . . . you're saying you're sorry. And that you did the wrong thing."

"I am sorry. I did the wrong thing. I'm trying to be better. I've been trying."

He stopped and watched her. She seemed to be waiting for him to say more, but he couldn't think of anything to add.

She sneered. "No more excuses to offer?"

He shrugged. "Not really. I hurt your brother. I shouldn't have. I'm sorry. I don't know what else to say. I didn't know how badly I hurt him. Before I left Earth, I didn't realize. I do now, and I feel . . . it doesn't matter how I feel. It was wrong."

"Nobody knew. He didn't want word to get out. I snuck him away from the cops, and we holed up in . . . a place. We tried to get him fixed up, but nothing worked."

He looked at her face. Sadness was replacing anger in her eyes.

He felt a glimmer of guilty hope. "I really am sorry. I'm not going to pretend we were friends. You were robbing a bank, I was stopping you. I should never have taken it that far, though. I should have stopped."

She took a half step back, knocking Shadowstep off-balance.

"You're serious. I can *see* it, you know. I'm more than a little bit of an empath."

He spread his hands. "I don't know what else to tell you. I'm sorry. Really."

She looked at him, at the canister. Turned to Shadowstep.

"Let's get out of here."

The gray man sputtered. "But Doc . . . the canister . . ."

She shook her head. "This is about vengeance. Look at him. Tell me you need vengeance now. What's the point?"

"But Brother Steel's dead."

"I know! Taking that canister won't bring him back, will it? It will just kill a whole lot of other people's brothers."

Shadowstep opened his mouth, closed it again.

She turned to Rohan.

"He wasn't bad, you know? Lazy, maybe. He wasn't out to hurt people."

Rohan sighed. "I know. I . . . I lost it. Caught him with the loot from that bank, fought him, he fought back . . . I should never have done that. Never let that happen."

"So, what, you left Earth? Just put all this behind you?"

He shrugged. "I tried, I guess. For a fresh start. But I suppose I was always going to come back, eventually. So there was no point, not really."

"Your friends, they on your side? Vanguard?"

He laughed. "Even my own mother thinks I'm an asshole."

She laughed, genuinely. "So does mine. But I've never pretended otherwise. You're the one who's supposed to be some kind of hero."

He paused. "I guess I am a pretty lousy hero."

"Yes. Tough bastard, but a lousy hero."

They stared at each other across the broken room.

Rohan eyed the loose concrete debris on the floor. If the fight continued, he was going to hurl a cloud of it at Shadowstep to distract him, then go for the door.

The Hybrid looked at Sister Steel.

"You going to let me take care of these sharks?"

She looked at him, then at Shadowstep, then back.

"I guess I am. I don't care all that much about people, but I'll be damned if I'm going to spend the rest of my life mixing all my own drinks and cleaning my own toilet."

Shadowstep looked at her, shaking his head, but he didn't argue.

Rohan nodded. "Can I ask you one question?"

"What?"

"Are your shits really silver? Or spherical?"

She laughed.

"I'll see you at your trial." She turned to Shadowstep. "Let's go."

"What are we going to tell Doc?"

"We'll tell him we didn't get it. He'll live. He's been through bigger disappointments."

"I know he'll live, I'm wondering if the two of us will."

"You worry too much. Let's go."

The tall man grabbed the silver woman by the arm.

They faded to near invisibility, just a distortion in the air that shimmered as it crossed the room and passed out through the door.

Rohan sighed and sat back on the bed.

He ran his hands over the canister, checking for damage, but his fingers only confirmed what he already knew.

The venom was safe.

He was thinking about trying to get some more sleep when the door slammed open with a crash.

A brilliant light, blinding in its intensity, came from the doorway.

Rohan had brought his arm up to shield his face, but it wasn't enough. He blinked as his eyes teared up.

"I'm okay! I'm okay!"

Bright Angel's voice came from the doorway.

"There was . . . did you throw a party in here? What the hell?"

He sighed and rubbed his eyes, checking every few seconds to see if his sight had returned.

"I had a little visit from Sister Steel. Now I know how they've been getting into the building."

She looked at him. The Damsel was on her left shoulder, Amber on her right, in a casual battle formation.

They entered his room, checking the far corners, bathroom, and closets for intruders.

Bright Angel walked over to Rohan. She was dressed for the salon in a white, terrycloth robe. Amber was in flannel pajamas, and The Damsel had thrown a satin robe over something enticing.

"Are you okay?"

He nodded. "Got punched in the face a few times. Just another day in the life of an il'Drach Hybrid."

Amber and The Damsel gave 'all clear' signs from the closet and bathroom.

"You said Sister Steel? How *did* she get in here?"

"You remember Shadowstep? He used to hang around with them, at least part time, right?"

"You mean around Brother and Sister Steel? Yeah. What was he—invisible? No, more than that? He could go intangible. Like a ghost. So he just walked in through the walls?"

"Yes. Which isn't unexpected, I guess. Except, back in the day, it would have been just him. Now he brought Sister Steel along."

Amber looked at them. "I didn't think he could do that."

Rohan nodded. "Ten years ago he couldn't."

Bright Angel frowned, skin on her forehead bunching up with her concentration. "You think they're what happened to Kid Lightning?"

Rohan shrugged. "Could be."

The Damsel interrupted. "What did they want, Griffin?"

Bright Angel held her hand out.

"Hold on." She took out her phone. "All clear, Director. Sister Steel and Shadowstep came in and attacked The Griffin, but both are gone. He's fine."

Bright Angel nodded at whatever answer came over the device and then put it away.

Rohan stretched his arms overhead. "They wanted the canister. Shadowstep said someone named 'Doc' sent them for it. I think Sister Steel was more interested in killing me."

"Then what? They left . . . why?"

He shrugged. "I talked her out of it. I'm sure even Sister Steel has people she cares about. She kills me, sharks kill everyone she's ever known."

Bright Angel rubbed her forehead, then ran her hands up over her braided hair, patting down a wisp that had come undone. Rohan found the motion mesmerizing. "Who's Doc? They said 'Doc' wanted the canister?"

Amber took her phone out of an oversized pocket. "I'll pull up all known villains with Doc or Doctor in their names. Don't get your hopes up; it's going to be a long list."

Rohan smiled. "Only real doctors, medical doctorates or PhDs only. I don't want any evil chiropractors or physical therapists on the list."

Bright Angel shook her head. "Really? Now is the time for that?"

"Inappropriate humor is my charm, remember?"

"I remember that you thought it was charming. What I can't seem to remember is when anybody else agreed with you."

"Ouch."

Amber cleared her throat. "Maybe back to talking about the attack?"

Bright Angel nodded. "Dr. . . . Kraken, maybe? We haven't heard from him in a while. Maybe Kid Lightning's arms waving was about tentacles. He had tentacles, didn't he?"

Rohan shrugged. "That was Ben Stone's idea, too."

The Damsel nodded her agreement. "Could be. But it doesn't seem to help us much, even if we knew for sure."

Bright Angel looked at Rohan. "You're sure the canister is intact?"

He nodded. "Absolutely. How much time before Five hits land?"

She tapped at her phone. "Two hours at current vector. We have people on the beach setting up a perimeter, putting down medical support and so forth. We don't know exactly where they should be, but they'll be, well, closer than Sahara City."

Rohan nodded and rolled his shoulders, then neck. "Damsel, you ready for this?"

Her skin, already an alabaster white, paled further.

"I'll be ready."

Amber squeezed the older woman's shoulder. "No doubt."

Bright Angel squeezed the other shoulder. "We all need to get ready. Gather at the landing site."

They nodded and cleared the room.

Rohan picked up a handful of cement shards and let them fall through his fingers.

32

Rise and Fall of the Leviathans

A surface rushed by the camera: midnight blue mottled with patches of cave gray; porous and calcified growths of pale green and yellow; jagged patches of orange and luminescent-green growths; white, puckered lines of scar tissue.

The speed was dizzying, made more immersive by the huge screen, four meters on the diagonal, that Hyperion Industries techs had set up under broad, tan canvas canopies on the Canadian beach.

Dozens of meters of flesh slid by; then the view disappeared, showing pumping blood and pulsing tissues, emerging from the back with a shock that had all the heroes present take an involuntary backward step.

The surface receded suddenly, darting back away from their view, revealing the creature in its entirety as it undulated through the ocean water toward its prey.

A thin stream of dark-red fluid leaked from the beast's tail.

Lyst looked at them and smiled, her jagged teeth reflecting the bright light of the soon-to-be-setting sun.

"Did you feel their joy? They just took their first sips of air in over two thousand years. I did regret when your god Poseidon convinced them to retreat from the surface and spend their declining years in slumber."

Rohan whistled. "Those are leviathans? Poseidon created them?"

She laughed. "This is the last pod of leviathans. They were old when Poseidon was first woven from the thoughts of your ancestors."

"I . . . apparently I don't know as much deep history as I thought I did. Didn't the gods make humans in *their* image?"

Lyst's smile broadened, her lips opening wider up her cheeks than any human face could. "They like to tell you that. They like to think of themselves as eternal. Which, of course, they are not. None of us are."

Rohan scratched his beard and ran his hand over his equipment. The canister of decipede venom was strapped to his chest. The frictionless cloak Masamune had given him was over his shoulders. His good mask, the one Wistful had given him with the built-in air supply, was in his hood.

Amber spoke from her position, right behind Rohan.

"Are you saying humans created the gods?"

Lyst shook her head, the bony crests shifting with the movement. "That is not a story for today. Today, we admire the leviathans, the last of their species, as they go to war for us and for their god. And for their own wounded pride, for they thought themselves the greatest threat in these seas."

Rohan looked around the Hyperion Industries camp. Their tent was one among many. Several had red crosses printed above their entrances. Engineers swarmed about, unpacking crates, launching drones, and assembling pieces of esoteric monitoring equipment that Rohan didn't quickly recognize.

He turned to Bright Angel. She had arrived at the site before he and Amber had bamfed in. She was in full uniform, white with blue accents and silver trim, her hair freshly done. Her eyes were hard but clear, showing little of the fatigue she must have been feeling.

Rohan swallowed. "What are we looking at?"

She waved her hand at the screen. "It's a rendered image, not an actual camera in the ocean. They're taking data from something like twenty inputs, everything from passive sonar to lidar picked up from satellites, to generate a picture of what's happening down there."

One of the techs sitting behind the screen called out, "Thirty-seven inputs. Ma'am."

"Don't get smart with me, I can walk around to the other side of this monitor anytime I want to. And I will put my foot someplace you find very awkward."

"Yes, ma'am."

Another leviathan crossed the screen, this one even larger than the first. It resembled a blue whale but with a more angular head, its front end blunt and square, its body longer and thinner. About a third of the way down its length, a ring of tentacles emerged from its body, each half as long as the creature, radiating outwards in all directions.

As his eyes adjusted to the underwater images, Rohan was able to pick out several other leviathans, dim in the shadow depths.

Bright Angel called out to the techs. "Can we get closer to the fight? I can barely see the land shark now."

"On it."

Rohan looked at her. "You saw it before?"

She nodded. "They were fighting, then the leviathans broke off to regroup. They seem to be going in for another round."

"Where's Poseidon?"

"He's riding one of the leviathans."

Lyst spoke. "He rides their leader, Echo. Echo is the oldest remaining leviathan. He says he remembers fighting the last of the Old Ones, but I suspect he is exaggerating."

"So . . . a Greek god is riding a whale monster older than our branch of the evolutionary tree into battle against a giant shark with four legs sent by descendants of an ancient civilization of evil cephalopods that are out to destroy the human race."

Bright Angel furrowed her brows at him. "Are you narrating a documentary or something? Or are you having trouble keeping up?"

"I just like to take stock every once in a while."

Amber pointed. "The Damsel is here."

They turned to see the older woman stepping through a bamf portal. She waved and walked over.

"What did I miss?"

Bright Angel pointed at the next tent. "Replays of the first fight are being analyzed over there."

Rohan shook his head.

"Why isn't the shark going after them? The leviathans? They fought it, they slowed it down, right? Must have at least annoyed it. Why isn't it going after them? Look . . ." He pointed at an overhead map in one corner of the picture. "It's still coming this way."

Bright Angel nodded. "We've all been wondering that. They seem to really want to get up on land. Either they are looking for humans or they want to get out of the water."

Nobody offered any better answers.

After watching the live feed for another minute, Rohan and Amber joined The Damsel to see the replay of the initial battle.

The leviathans had approached the land shark from all sides. Two dove and bit at it from one side, then the others closed on its rear as it reacted to the first assault.

The tactic was sound, but the land shark was too fast and too tough. The times the leviathans managed to get in close, they did little more than superficial damage.

Once the engagement started, the battle was fury and chaos: a mass of churning, frothing water speckled with droplets of blood the size of swimming pools, chunks of raggedly torn flesh, severed tentacles, and violent movements. One or another creature would emerge from the undersea storm, gird itself, and return to the fray.

As it ended, the leviathans scattered, bloody and bitten, to regroup as the land shark reoriented its path toward land.

Rohan watched the brief and violent battle two more times, hoping for some fresh insight into stopping the creature, but nothing came.

Bright Angel called out. "They're going in again."

The heroes gathered in front of the large screen.

The leviathans were faster than the land shark in a straight line. Did its legs add too much drag? Was it just too large?

They had circled around and were approaching it from the front.

Amber nudged Rohan's arm. "Look at the bottom."

The promised kraken were making their appearance.

The land shark turned slightly to meet the center of the leviathan formation.

As it closed on Echo, holding the center position, a forest of thick, heavily scarred tentacles, covered with puckering suckers and waving fronds of undersea parasites, reached up from the dark deeps below.

Bright Angel pointed. "Those are the kraken. Poseidon said they haven't surfaced in a thousand years."

The enormous shark, itself many times as large as the biggest leviathan, tipped its head slightly downward and accelerated into the leviathan pod. Echo surged forward to meet it.

Rohan squinted and leaned in toward the screen. "Is that . . . what's in Poseidon's hand?"

Bright Angel answered. "He's carrying his trident. They said he showed up with it."

Rohan whistled. "I didn't even know it was real. I thought it was just, you know, in artwork."

Bright Angel shook her head. "I thought he lost it in the Second World War."

The Damsel spoke. "He talked about it in the early days. Before you two were on the team. He fought the Nazis with it, but he said it brought back bad memories. He told us he had buried it at sea. I suppose this was the right time to dig it up again."

Echo and the land shark collided savagely, sending shockwaves outwards through the water, knocking aside the other leviathans.

Echo gave way to the superior momentum of the shark, but even as they broke apart, the nest of tentacles below them latched on to the legs and lower abdomen of the land shark.

The tentacles slid and slithered over the land shark's rough flesh, and for a moment it seemed the creature would free itself. Then the suckers began to find purchase, holding fast to the hide of the shark and sealing the tentacles to its body.

The invader bucked and thrashed against the hold of the tentacles. The leviathan closed in for another attack.

Rohan looked at the map. "How far out are they?"

Bright Angel checked her phone, then the map, then her phone again. "Once he starts moving again, ten minutes to shore."

The shark was twisting downward, snapping its wide mouth at the tentacles trapping it. It twisted back, giving a huge heave, moving the combined mass of itself and both kraken.

The leviathans were tearing at its flanks with impressive success.

"Amber, we should start on our way up. So we can be ready."

Bright Angel looked at them. "What are you doing?"

Rohan smiled and pointed a thumb at Amber. "She can accelerate time, but only if she's attached to me. So she's going to ride me piggyback under the cloak while we Meteor Strike the shark."

Bright Angel looked at the younger woman. "You okay with that?"

Amber shrugged. "It should work. Theoretically. It's not like I can speed him up from shore, I have to be close."

"Okay. Godspeed."

Amber laughed. "We call it 'Amberspeed.'"

The Damsel looked at Bright Angel. "You'll fly me to the exact spot where he's landing?"

"That's the plan."

A flick of the land shark's tail batted away one of the leviathans. With a snap of jagged teeth, it tore through a half dozen kraken tentacles, causing another half dozen to recoil, as if in pain.

It twisted back and forth, straining the hold of the remaining kraken on its legs.

The other six leviathans closed again, but one bite split one of the creatures nearly in two.

Amber was shaking her head. She grabbed Rohan by the arm. "Griffin, they're dying out there. For us."

"Yeah, I know they are. What's your point?"

"My point is we should watch. We should witness it."

He looked at the others. Somber eyes looked back at him.

With a sigh, he nodded. "We'll wait as long as we can. But when I say it's time, it's time. Okay?"

She nodded.

Echo tore a hunk of flesh out of the land shark's flank and was whipped aside by its tail as a reward.

As they watched, the gouges and divots taken out of the flanks of the land shark were filling in, the tissues bubbling out and filling in the holes, regenerating as quickly as they could be made.

With a flip, the land shark brought its tail up and over, then down into the back of another leviathan. The creature sank, stunned, its tail twitching helplessly with the trauma. The others swarmed, attacking ferociously to give their cousin a chance to drift away from the combat.

The water ran red and brown with blood and bile as one, then two of the leviathans had their bowels punctured by the land shark. The shark twisted again, turning over entirely in its effort to work free of the second kraken's tentacles.

With a slide, then a snap, it worked.

The leviathans scattered. Four of the seven swam at speed; the other three drifted toward the deep ocean, lazily propelled by intermittent swishes of their huge tails, two leaving thick trails of gore in their wake.

Bright Angel grunted. "Those three leviathans are done for, and at least one of the kraken. I think they'll hit it again close to shore, but they're not going to slow it down much between now and then. It looks like it will land . . . about a quarter mile south of here."

Rohan checked the screen.

The land shark had resumed its journey unfettered. The leviathans dispersed, but some looked to be grouping for a final attack. He couldn't see the kraken, hidden in the darker depths of the ocean.

Lyst shook her head. "And so the leviathans have fallen in battle for the second time in two thousand years. They did their ancestors proud. I will remember their names."

Nobody responded.

Rohan turned to Amber. "Now we go."

She nodded.

Lyst and Bright Angel watched as they assembled in a makeshift battle formation.

Rohan patted the canister of decipede venom snugly strapped to his chest. He put on his helmet, listening for the hiss as the soft rim sealed to his face and the air supply kicked in.

Amber took out her own, a gift from Rohan. He watched her seal it in place. He switched the comms to their shared channel.

"Amber, can you hear me?"

"I hear you."

"Good. Practice switching between this channel and the open channel, depending on who you want to talk to."

She nodded and tapped at the side of her mask.

He took off his cape and waited for her to stop fiddling with the mask. She hopped onto his back piggyback-style, her heels digging into his belly, arms over his shoulders.

Rohan swung the cape up and over, covering them from head to toe.

Bright Angel tapped behind her ear to activate her own comm link.

"You guys look ridiculous."

Rohan shook his head. "I don't think the shark is going to surrender because we win on style points, do you? I'll take ridiculous, as long as it works."

"It will work. I believe."

He felt a twist in his chest. "Do you?"

She nodded. "In this, absolutely. You're going to burn the artifact out of that shark and set it free. After that . . . we'll see."

"Wish us luck."

"Good luck."

More voices chimed in over the comms.

"Captain! This is *Insatiable*. We're all on the bridge here, watching. Dr. Stone, the other Dr. Stone, their students, the crew. We know you can do this!"

Rohan laughed. "Thanks, to all of you. That's sweet."

Not to be outdone, *Void's Shadow* called in. "I won't wish you luck, Captain, because you don't need it. I'm positive that you'll succeed!"

"That's kind. Poor judgment, but kind."

His comm chimed the sound indicating a private channel had been opened.

His mother's voice came over his system.

"Rohan."

"Yes, Mom."

"No pressure, but don't you dare screw this up."

He sighed. "Yes, Mom."

"Also, remember you do not have permission to die. You're my only son, I want a daughter-in-law from you before you're too old to attract anyone decent. Or a son-in-law. Whatever you want."

"I'll try, Mom. Can't make any promises on the spouse thing."

"Okay. I love you, Rohan."

"I love you, too, Mom."

She switched off with a click.

He switched back to the open channel. "Feels a bit like the eyes of the world are on us."

Bright Angel answered. "There's a public feed on a short delay. The world *is* watching."

"Glad it's not just paranoia. I think. Then again, maybe paranoia was better."

Rohan tapped Amber's leg to know he was moving, then lifted off the ground, going slowly to make sure he was adjusted to the increased payload.

"Amber, are you breathing okay? How's the wind?"

Her voice resonated through his body and over the comms behind his ear at the same time. "Griffin, I can't feel a thing. Your Power is *informing* the cape, it's like an armor shell."

"Good. That's the plan. I've been wearing that thing everywhere the last couple of days. Mostly."

"There's some imagery there that I really didn't need. Don't tell me you wore the cape in the bathroom. Please."

"Actually . . ."

"I said don't tell me!"

"Okay, okay."

"You do realize that I can get us to seem faster, but we won't have more kinetic energy than you would on your own, right?"

"I don't know. Do I realize that?"

"I'm speeding up time for us. So to another frame of reference, we seem much faster. But in our frame, our speed and our energy are what they seem to be to us."

"Okay. Got it. I'll get us all the energy we need the old-fashioned way. You just keep that shark from having a chance to notice us."

They picked up speed as Rohan grew more comfortable with the odd mechanics of flying with a passenger riding him and the reduction in drag created by the cape.

Bright Angel's voice came over the comms.

"Five is closing on the shore. The water is getting too shallow for the leviathans or for the krakens, so they'll have to break away any moment."

A pause before she came back on.

"We can feel its aura from land. Ugh, it's an angry bastard. The birds are all gone; I can just make out a handful of gulls heading south as fast as they can go."

A Hyperion tech came on, speaking with the typical Sahara City accent. "Perimeter is now clear. Evacuation is complete in a half-kilometer radius from point of arrival."

Rohan grunted. If his plan worked, the evacuation would prove unnecessary. If it didn't, a half-kilometer radius wasn't going to be nearly enough.

It didn't seem worth mentioning.

Rohan could feel the air pressure dropping as he passed through the cloud layer and continued toward the stratosphere.

He muted outgoing comms and set up a map overlay on his facemask that would give him the exact position of the land shark. It appeared immediately, just offshore, moving at a steady pace.

He turned his face up toward the sky and worked on getting more altitude.

Bright Angel continued her narration.

"The leviathans are coming in for one last run.

"The land shark just ran onto a bunch of tentacles. I think the kraken is buried in the ocean floor beneath it. They're grasping . . . the suckers are trying to hold on, but it's still sliding around.

"Poseidon hit it with a huge wave, really knocked it to the side.

"Two of the leviathans are engaging. They're biting and pulling at its flesh with their own tentacles.

"The kraken is still trying to hold on. Now the shark is sinking, diving instead of pulling away.

"It's stomping down on the ocean floor. I think it's . . . the tentacles released. It's swimming for shore again.

"The leviathans are attacking it, trying to get its flanks. I have to get to shore."

Silence.

Amber's voice came over their private channel. "Rohan, I can feel it now. Even up here."

"Yeah. Me, too. Must be close."

Rohan flexed his hands, then bent and straightened his elbows. The deep bone pain he'd been living with was gone, no sign remaining of the breaks and fractures he'd accumulated.

He was as ready as he needed to be, physically. He felt no pain; his fatigue wasn't extreme, not compared to what he'd been through fighting il'Drach wars across half the sector.

What he didn't feel was much in the way of anger.

The land shark was a victim of the Old Ones, a tool, a creature weaponized to attack and terrorize a population it knew nothing about.

A situation which, to Rohan, felt more than a little familiar.

He was angry at the cephalopods who had sent the land sharks, but they weren't present. He didn't understand their culture, what they looked like, or what their motivations were. They were, literally, as far from human as anything he'd ever encountered.

Hard to be angry at something so completely alien. Might as well be angry at rocks.

"I must be getting old."

"What, Griffin?"

"Sorry, talking to myself. Forgot you were on this channel."

Amber didn't respond.

Bright Angel's voice came over the comms.

"I just saw a dorsal fin. Then it dropped. I see it again. The land shark is really close to the surface. The Damsel and I are in position on the beach.

"I can see water spouts. The leviathans are coming up, surfacing, and attacking. Then going down again.

"One got in a hit. Then another. The shark just swatted the leviathan away like a cat batting aside a ball of yarn.

"It's moving forward. I think it's trying to ignore them now."

Rohan swallowed. "As soon as it puts two feet on the beach, you punch up our time field. Give me a good squeeze as you do it in case I don't put things together."

"Got it." He listened carefully to her voice, to the feeling of her heart beating against his back. He searched for fear, for hesitation, for uncertainty, for some sign of the fact that she was aware she was just a kid about to take a one-in-a-hundred chance at saving the world; some sign that she was remembering the cost of failure.

He didn't find any.

"Two, no wait, three of the leviathans are headed out to sea. They're done. Poseidon is attacking, still mounted on Echo. Five just took a bite out of Echo. The leviathan is bleeding.

"Five is out of the water. His feet are planted, it looks like. He's not swimming anymore.

"He dropped down, got his belly wet. The leviathans can't swim here, it's too shallow.

"Five is up again, his body is clear of the surface. He's just a few steps from the beach.

"He's up on the sand. He's staring right at us. One foot is clear of the sea. Second foot."

The Damsel started screaming.

33

Field Surgery

Rohan didn't *feel* any faster in Amber's time bubble. He *knew* something had changed, because The Damsel's scream was cut off too abruptly; Amber was squeezing the air out of his belly with her feet; the light from outside was suddenly dim and distorted; the sounds of wind and sky had grown faint and far off.

He reached down inside himself and pulled at his Power, yanking at the il'Drach legacy.

The Power, the Heritage, the Curse—it was known by all those names. All were true.

Anger came along with the Power in a rush, but it was a dull, unfocused anger. Not enough to get the job done.

What was there to be angry *about*?

In a moment of insight, Rohan realized he was going to fail.

He wasn't going to muster up enough energy to pierce the flesh of the land shark, dig deep enough and with enough precision to expose the artifact controlling it and destroy it.

He wasn't going to save the land shark from its torture.

He wasn't going to save the human race from extinction. The creature was going to rampage freely, destroying cities, then towns, then homes. The vampires would finish off whatever was left. Even if heroes gathered and managed to defeat this shark, enough would die that the next one would wipe out humanity. Or the next.

He was going to die. His friends would die.

His mother would, eventually, die, unless the Stones took her on *Insatiable*, in which case she'd spend the rest of her life on alien planets mourning the home she couldn't protect.

Amber would die with him. They'd never find out if Lyst was correct when she'd prophesied that Amber would be the greatest hero Earth had ever known. No one would see her realize her true potential.

The Damsel would die. Kid Lightning.

Bright Angel would die, probably that very day, on that very beach, fighting a creature she could not hope to defeat. *Knowing* that it would kill her. Because that's who she was.

With half of a choking sob, Rohan realized he'd never get a chance to say he was sorry.

He'd never be able to make up for Brother Steel. Never be able to even fully apologize for it.

Never get a chance to atone. For having run, for staying away, for abandoning his home because he didn't want to face the people he had disappointed.

Never be forgiven.

He'd die the way he'd left. A man who had committed terrible crimes and run from their consequences. Whatever good he'd done since, none of it had been on Earth. His mother hadn't seen it; Bright Angel certainly hadn't.

He was a coward. A coward who had tossed away the years he could have used to make amends, thinking he would always have a chance later.

He *hated* that coward.

He hated the man who had spent a decade smugly dismissing conversations about his home planet. The man who had taken pride in his skill as a warrior, letting his successes absolve him of the war crimes that had laid the foundation for those victories.

He hated the man who walked away from his own mother. Hated the man who let her think she had alienated her only son, let her think her son had chosen the side of her abuser and abandoned her.

Hated the overconfident prick who had assured one and all that he'd handle the land shark invasion, who had looked down on the heroes of

Earth as small-time nobodies who couldn't manage without him. Hated the man who thought he'd swoop in and win their hearts and souls with an empty show of violence.

The Power *answered* that hatred.

His back tightened and arched powerfully as energy rushed into him, nearly dislodging Amber from her seat. Liquid lightning sparked and danced up from his tailbone, climbing in two interlocking helixes, crossing with explosive bursts of light, then climbing another turn, wrapping around his spine.

Click. Click. Click.

With every intersection, the tunneling conduits of Power multiplied and built together, intensifying at each level, climbing up over his liver, past his floating ribs, past his heart.

With a final blinding flare, the beams struck together at the base of his skull, warping into a living bridge of energy.

Power flooded outwards into his hands, his eyes, his legs. Every muscle came to life, every tendon.

He heard every chamber of Amber's heart beating as a distinct pulse of sound.

He could feel the whorls and loops in her fingerprints where her hands gripped his chest.

Rohan looked down.

The position of the land shark was a red *X* in his mask's heads-up display.

He pivoted in place, pointing his head toward the ground, and poured all the Power he'd summoned into flight.

The air whipped past, parting at their heads and rejoining at their feet, sliding smoothly over the frictionless surface of Masamune's cape.

As they descended, Rohan felt The Damsel's aura flooding the area, loud and noisy and feminine and nothing at all like his own. She was pouring out metaphysical energy at a torrid pace, trying to blind the shark's Third Eye and hide Rohan's own energy from it.

"Where did she get this Power from? She's not this strong."

Amber squeezed tighter. "She took a booster. The Alchemist made it before he died. It enhances Power, but it's highly addictive and often lethal. That was our last dose."

"Then, let's make it count."

The land shark's energy overwhelmed The Damsel's projection. Heavy and thick, so potent that it liquefied the air.

As Rohan broke through it, he left a metaphysical wake, a stream of waves and bubbles and aura perturbations that would be *visible* for kilometers.

The Hybrid focused on the shark.

He and Amber penetrated the clouds, immediately seeing the Atlantic to their left and the heavy, dark green of the Canadian forests to the right.

A strip of sandy beach grew quickly as they screamed a path down to the earth.

The land shark, the one called Five, was dead center in their view, unsteady on its forelegs, feeling its first taste of Earth air and land. Maybe its first taste of any kind of air and land.

The shark grew from a dot to a toy-sized shape to a large dog to an overwhelming monster in Rohan's visor, all within seconds.

Tiny figures faced the creature, darting back and forth as they worked to engage and distract it. All in slow motion, floating above the sand, on a different timestream from Amber.

The smallest adjustments kept Rohan lined up on the vertebrae where he expected to find the control artifact.

"Come on. Hold still. You angry bastard."

Rohan growled softly as they closed the last thousand meters, focused entirely on the shark, its movement, and the slender but widening hope that it would stay in position.

Just before impact, Rohan *shifted* the bulk of his energy into reinforcing the cape around their heads.

The two heroes, surrounded by the mirrorlike surface of the frictionless cape, struck the dark-blue hide of the land shark with an eruption of flesh and scales.

The time bubble burst, Amber's energy not enough to maintain it inside another being with an aura as strong as the land shark's. Instantly they felt lateral movement as the shark twisted in a futile attempt to deflect the penetrating duo.

Rohan redirected his energy again, pushing them deeper into the back of the shark. If they lost momentum before striking its cervical vertebrae, the mission would fail.

The Hybrid *pulled* more and more energy up and through his body, fighting now for every meter of parted flesh. The cape helped, letting them slip past the crushing muscles that surrounded them, but they still had to split layers of fascia, tendons, and muscles to reach their target.

They burrowed deeper.

Rohan screamed in frustration as their progress slowed.

The land shark whipped back and forth, the lateral forces exerting enormous pressure on the heroes as it disoriented them.

Bright Angel's voice came over the comms. "You're on target! I'm going to flare it! Damsel, with me! Stun it!"

"I'm trying!" The Damsel's voice was harsh and strangled.

The shark paused its struggle.

"It's stunned. Keep digging! Straight in! Amber, let go, fall out."

With a sudden movement, Amber released her hold on Rohan and slipped out the back of the cape.

Suddenly narrower, Rohan tore through several more meters of flesh, then reached with his arms outside the cape to rip and tear at the shark, clearing a path.

He felt something hard through the flesh ahead.

His head came free from the hood. Shark flesh was pressing in on all sides.

The shark started to move again.

"Rohan! Just a few more meters!"

With a fresh growl, Rohan pushed deeper into the dark interior of the shark. Long, pale fibers flexed and danced all around him; red-pink fluid swirled into the tunnel he'd created, a mixture of seawater, lymphatic fluids, and blood.

"Do you see it? It's right in front of you!"

They must have set up something to take images of the shark's interior from a distance. Clever engineers.

Using his last surge of strength, Rohan parted another layer of fascial tissue and exposed an expanse of metal.

No wider than his forearm was long, the artifact was suspended in a web of metal filaments that reached up and out, disappearing into the shark's spine.

Rohan panted, the burning in his shoulders and arms almost unbearable.

He pulled himself forward another few centimeters, then more, until his face was pressed up against the artifact.

The shark was fully recovered from Bright Angel's blast. It spun, then rolled over suddenly, trying to work Rohan out of its back.

Rohan slid a few meters back along the path he'd taken.

With a rush of fear, he pulled himself back up, sliding through the hole, pressing the back of his cloak into the skin wherever he could to form a makeshift slide.

Soon he was back at the artifact. He gripped it by the edge with one aching hand, fingers bruised and jammed after tearing through the creature's tough hide.

He panted as he lifted his body, pulling his chest in toward the artifact. "Almost . . . there."

The nozzle of the canister was in contact with the artifact.

With his right arm, Rohan grabbed the release valve and opened it wide.

His body was kicked back as the pressurized fluid pumped out and drenched the artifact.

The metal began to sizzle before his eyes.

A burning flash, paired with searing pain, chased away the surge of triumph that had begun in his chest. Some of the decipede venom had splashed onto his neck, arm, and chest.

Rohan frantically pushed, using his muscles first, then Power to fly backward out through the wound he had carved into the land shark.

He rubbed his arm and neck against the flesh of the shark. He scraped his throat against an exposed muscle fiber as thick as his thigh, tearing skin and shark tissues alike in his panic.

Amber's voice. "Rohan, I'm out. But the shark is healing. Its skin is closing over the point of entry we made."

Bright Angel spoke. "I'm on it. Rohan, get there. I'll keep it open."

He pushed and pulled and wiggled through the narrowing tunnel of shark meat.

The venom was in his blood, carving lines of pain and weakness through his body. He felt his arms soften and slow, then his legs.

Breathing hurt. He coughed, and blood flecked the inside of his mask.

"Rohan, hang on. I'm going to cut you out."

He pulled himself forward, handful by handful, each heave slower than the previous one. The sides of his tunnel continued to close, squeezing his ribs.

Each breath took a greater effort.

Rohan reached his hands forward and felt smooth flesh above his head. He jammed his fingers in, trying to split the tissues and create an opening.

His throat burned.

He couldn't see the overlays in his mask anymore. Was the display broken?

The skin above him split suddenly, and his body was squeezed out by the pressure of the shark meat.

The Hybrid's body pushed out through the opening, emerging into air, his head, then his torso, then his knees. Suddenly he was sliding down the outside of the shark.

Strong arms caught him.

He relaxed, flopping bonelessly over Bright Angel's shoulder as she carried him away from the shark.

He looked back at the creature. Its movement was already slowing.

It took a step forward, then to the side, then another, digging a wide circle into the sand of the beach as it surveyed its surroundings.

Rohan let out a breath and *felt* its aura.

The anger was dissipating, though slowly.

"I think we did it."

She patted his back. "I think we did, too."

He closed his eyes.

34

The Afterparty

R ohan sat in his regen tank, relaxing into the soothing liquid.

The tank had remained in a bay on *Insatiable*, with *Void's Shadow* hovering in place a few meters away. A new uniform hung from a hook on the side of the tank. His frictionless cloak was next to it.

Music played over the bay's speaker system. He'd downloaded a decade's worth of Bollywood hits and was catching up.

The land shark had been sent through the underwater portal back to its world of origin. Poseidon had spoken to it; he said it was hell-bent on revenge against the Old Ones. The primary losses on Earth had been the two dead leviathans and a badly wounded kraken.

Rohan laid his head back on the padded leather edge of the tank and closed his eyes, wishing the drugs were strong enough to wipe out all of his thoughts. His fingers tapped to the rhythm of the music.

The door slid open with a swish of electronics, and Bright Angel walked in. Her mask was down around her neck. Rohan noticed the strategic design to her uniform, the different-colored panels cut to accentuate her curves.

She smiled, full lips parted to reveal even, white teeth. He was relieved that she'd never altered the small gap between the front two; he'd always found it attractive.

"Griffin, I am here on a fetching mission." She stumbled slightly as she crossed the room, and he realized she wasn't quite herself.

"Fetching for what? I'm trying to heal up here."

"You are . . . Oh my God, you look terrible." She pointed at his throat and upper chest.

"Yeah, I got splashed with decipede venom, remember? It's healing."

"Oh Jesus . . . it's bubbling. How does that feel?"

"Not good, but better than bleeding out. Are *you* okay? You sound off."

She waved her hand in a wide gesture of dismissal. "I'm fine. Fine. I may have had a little champagne."

"A little?"

"Maybe half a bottle. Who's counting?"

"Oh dear."

"That's why I'm here! To fetch you. To the party."

"There's a party?"

"Of course!"

"Isn't that a little, um, premature?"

"It's not *that* kind of party."

"I didn't mean . . . Okay, you got me, since that's exactly the sort of terrible joke I would make."

"Yes, it is. You're a terrible influence on me. And, sure, the land sharks might still be a threat, but we at least have an approach to stopping them now."

"Do we, though? Getting decipede venom isn't so easy. And the leviathans took a lot of losses distracting the land shark. What are we supposed to do if there is a next time?"

She shook her head and steadied herself, taking a deep breath. "Masamune looked at the last bits of the venom left in the canister. He says he can replicate the components that damaged the metal of the controlling device. Only in small amounts, but enough to do what you did. And, yes, the leviathans took heavy losses, and if we had to do this again, we'd have to find some other way to distract the shark in the water, but that's just a small piece of the puzzle."

He sighed. "Am I just being contrary?"

"No, I understand you. We went back and forth, saying the same things, until Lyst pointed something out."

"Which is . . ."

"Remember? The Old Ones . . . the cephalopods civilization . . . they're old. Crazy old. Which makes them both take the very, very long view of things and act very conservatively. They don't take chances. Right now, attacking Earth is a chance."

"She told me the same thing."

"She seemed confident of it. And when has Lyst ever been wrong?"

Rohan thought. "Sometimes she'll sit there and say nothing and let you think she agrees with you, but when she actually speaks up, she's never wrong."

"Now, as long as you're going to stick around to handle the next land shark, if one shows up, we should be good. Which means we can start rebuilding the cities that were destroyed and otherwise fix all the damage that was done. But that's a job for tomorrow. The Director said we need to celebrate our victories before we become overwhelmed with the work that needs to be handled."

Rohan laughed. "The Director said that? Or did Carla say it, and she just repeated it?"

Bright Angel shrugged her muscular shoulders. "Same thing, isn't it? Now, are you up for joining the party? There's tequila!"

He laughed again. "You should have started with tequila. But I think I need another half hour. Throat's still healing."

"Sure, no rush. I'll sit with you. No need for you to be alone."

She pulled a simple metal chair next to the regen tank and sat down.

"You found new music!"

He nodded. "Ten years' worth of Indian dance music, all loaded onto my helmet. I need it for work."

"Towing ships."

He nodded. "Towing ships."

"You're going back?"

"Well, not now. I have to wait and see if the land sharks return."

"I might be able to take your place in that maneuver. Dive-bombing the shark. Especially with Amber's help. Maybe you could leave us the cloak, at least for a while."

"I'm not saying you couldn't, but we know I *can*, so . . ."

"After that?"

He sighed. "I have to stand trial, I guess."

"You're going through with that?" Her tone was neutral.

"Yeah. It's the right thing to do. Besides, if I break my promise and just leave, it's going to be tough on Hyperion Industries. And my mom."

"They can handle it. You do what you need to do. Don't worry about other people so much. Not with this."

He stared at the ceiling for a while before answering.

"You're right. I can't undo what I did, you know? But I can go through the trial. And sit in prison, I guess, if I have to. Pay my debt to society."

"I guess I should have some kind of response to that, but I'm not sure I do."

"That's okay. It's not your job to respond."

"Okay."

They sat in silence and listened to the music.

"I saw this movie. This was the theme song."

"Was it good? I haven't seen a movie in a long time."

She described the plot of the movie.

When she was done, she remembered a different film from the previous year and told him all the details.

By the time she'd finished giving away the ending of a two-part historical fantasy that had broken every box office record in South Asia, his throat had stopped itching.

Rohan was chuckling at Bright Angel's vigorous reenactment of the final battle scene. Laughing hurt, but he didn't complain.

He waited for her to finish the scene. He stood up and leaned over the side of the tank, looking down at her as she writhed on the floor in a mimicry of agony.

"I'm good. Let's head down."

She smiled and bounced to her feet. "You get dressed. I'll gather the Professors, meet you back here in a few. We can bamf down to Sahara City."

He nodded.

Rohan dressed slowly, taking care not to abrade any newly healed skin.

Within a few minutes, the door slid open again.

"Rohan, my boy! We didn't want to disturb you, what with the condition you were in when they brought you up, but it's good to see you up and around!"

"Hey, Dr. Stone." He nodded to his friend, then to Marion. "Dr. Stone."

She smiled. "I lost a half share in our winery on Frega 4 betting against you. I can't remember ever being so glad to lose a bet with my husband."

He laughed. "I appreciate your continuing lack of faith in me, Dr. Stone."

"I try to be consistent."

Ben Stone patted Rohan's shoulder.

"We're both proud of you, son. Hyperion couldn't have done any better."

Rohan smiled. "That's sweet, but not true. We all know Hyperion could have taken out those land sharks by himself, if he wanted."

Marion patted his other shoulder, a surprising move from the usually cold woman. "Perhaps. But killing the sharks is one thing; you sent it back to its owners, hopefully ending the cycle of attacks. Hyperion was powerful, but not creative. I'm not sure he would have thought of that."

Bright Angel smiled. "You two knew him better than anyone. How would Hyperion have celebrated this?"

Ben Stone laughed and snorted. Marion blushed furiously, her pale skin shading to stop-sign red.

Rohan looked between them. "What?"

Ben slapped his thigh. "An orgy, I'm sure. It was always an orgy. He had a single-track mind when it came to this sort of thing. The more the merrier. Saving the earth? Expect a scene of utter debauchery to follow."

Bright Angel laughed with them. "Not sure we can top that, but The Director throws a decent party. The wine cellar is worth more than some countries, and she stole her two lead chefs from three-Michelin-star restaurants. You're both invited; we can teleport down as soon as you're ready."

The Professors exchanged glances, and Marion nodded. "Let's go."

A quick call and two minutes later and the three and a half humans were in Hyperion Industries HQ.

The party spread out across half the building. Uniformed waitstaff wound in and out of the crowds of people, taking orders, bringing bottles of alcohol and trays of food to groups of people in the War Room and in the medical bay.

Bright Angel led him by the hand from one cluster of people to another.

The Hyperion executive who had been giving them briefings hugged Rohan and pressed an open bottle of ten-thousand-dollar champagne into his hand.

Rohan lifted his mask, took a swallow, and offered the bottle back. The man smiled and shook his head.

The champagne was dry and delicious, with a complex bundle of flavors that burst through Rohan's mouth and fine bubbles so smooth and even that he experienced them as an added pop of flavor.

He decided he was going to have to drink more champagne.

He turned to Bright Angel. "This is good!"

She laughed and took the bottle from him and lifted her own mask to take a mouthful. She nodded and handed it back, swallowing with a smile.

"Enjoy it! You're paying!"

He laughed; he could afford it.

He turned, and The Director stepped in with a swirl of cloth and a cloud of perfume.

She wrapped her arms around him.

"Rohan! You made it!"

He looked helplessly over her shoulder. Carla was standing a few meters away, smiling and shrugging.

"Um . . . Director!"

She let go and sniffed. He saw tears streaking her makeup. She wore a red-and-purple sari, so encrusted with diamonds and gold that he was impressed she could stand under its weight.

She smiled and wiped her face, smudging her cheeks. "Yes, Griffin. I was just so glad to see you safe."

Carla closed on them and put an arm around her wife. "We've all been feeling a lot of things, haven't we? Griffin, we have hope now, and it's been a while since we've had much of that."

Rohan shrugged. His own cheeks were damp. "I'm no Hyperion, but I did my best."

"You did, Griffin. You did great." The Director reached up and held his cheeks, looking up into his face.

Her eyes were wide and dark, and again he was reminded of the beauty that had captivated his father.

He reached up and held her hands in his own, awkwardly dangling the champagne bottle between two fingers to do it. He wanted to hug her, but to most of the people there, she was his employer and a woman he'd met for the first time a few days before, not his mother.

"Director, isn't this party a little . . . small?"

She looked at him with a smile and let go of his face. "Oh, don't you worry. We're going to have a *big* party when this is over. Today is just for the staff. Most of them have been away from their families for weeks, working twenty hours a day."

There was a shout from the other end of the room.

"To Otaku Force Five!" A raucous cheer answered the call.

"To the leviathans, two of whom feed the fishes today!" Another cheer.

"To the kraken who laid down his life for you!"

"To my brother Ares, who died as he would have wished, in battle!"

Poseidon was pouring shots from a jug of clear liquid into small tumblers for a group of people. Rohan saw Spiral and Amber among them, though Amber wasn't trying to keep up by finishing a glass with each toast.

The Director patted Rohan's chest. "Go, drink. Enjoy tonight. Tomorrow we'll talk wedding plans."

Bright Angel pulled him toward Poseidon's table.

She leaned over and spoke into his ear, too loud to qualify as a whisper. "Wedding plans?"

"She's kidding. I think. No, I'm pretty sure she's kidding."

Bright Angel laughed. "I didn't know she was that traditional. Arranging your wedding."

"She isn't, not really. Pretty sure it's a joke. Maybe."

"All right. I don't advise going overboard on whatever Poseidon's serving. I don't see a label on the bottle."

Rohan patted Spiral on the back. The other man turned and wrapped one arm around the Hybrid, slapping his back in a bro-hug.

"Griffin! How's your neck? When they brought you in, you were breathing as much air through your throat as through your mouth."

Rohan shook his head. "Much better. The regen tank is like magic with superficial wounds like that. No matter how ugly."

"Good. Listen, thanks so much for helping to save the planet. I keep most of my stuff here, you know."

"I know. You're more than welcome."

Amber slid between people to give Rohan a real hug. "You were amazing!"

He smiled. "So were you! I told you we'd get the land sharks sorted out."

"You did. But even you didn't really believe it, did you?"

He shrugged. "You know, fake it 'til you make it."

She leaned back and studied the visible part of his face above the eagle-beak print mask. "You don't seem as happy as you should be."

"I'm happy! Just still weak from the venom. Really, all is good."

"Okay. Did you hear Kid Lightning woke up?"

Poseidon's voice roared from the other side of the table.

"Now we toast the living! First, to this midget hero! Do you know what I said the first time I heard that this little one was an il'Drach Hybrid just like Hyperion? I said, 'where's the rest of him?'" A roar of laughter. "To The Griffin! Without whom we would probably be having a very different sort of drinking party!"

A cheer went up. Rohan took and drained a glass of what tasted suspiciously like grain alcohol.

He walked around the table and hugged Poseidon, then washed the liquor down with another swig of champagne.

"This never would have worked without you. And I'm sorry for the old friends you lost."

Poseidon looked into his eyes, and for a moment Rohan saw a flash of tremendous sadness in the god's face.

"Sometimes after you've lived long enough, it's good to find a worthwhile reason to die."

Rohan nodded and searched for something to say. He found nothing.

Poseidon slapped his back. "Go see Kid Lightning."

Rohan nodded.

Bright Angel pulled him. "Let's go. Not sure how long he'll stay awake."

She navigated the maze of hallways leading to the Vanguard medical wing with practiced ease.

Kid Lightning was sitting up in his hospital bed, eyes glued to the big screen mounted across from him.

"Kid!" Rohan was happy to see the older man conscious.

Kid Lightning turned toward the pair and smiled. He gave a thumbs-up.

Rohan walked to the hospital bed and hugged the man. "Dude, I was worried about you."

Kid Lightning hugged him back but remained silent.

Bright Angel stood next to the pair. "Hey, Kid. Griffin, he hasn't said anything. We're not completely sure he even understands us. But he seems happy enough."

The blond gave them another thumbs-up.

Rohan looked at the man. "Kid, you saved my life. We wouldn't be here if not for you. I can't thank you enough."

He looked into the man's eyes, searching for a sign of understanding.

If it was there, Rohan didn't recognize it.

He sighed and put his hand over Kid Lightning's.

Bright Angel stood next to him in silence.

Kid Lightning turned his attention back to the television behind them. It was showing a Formula 1 race from the previous year.

Bright Angel spoke softly to Rohan. "We can go. He just woke up. He needs rest."

"Sure. Let's catch up with everybody else."

Rohan snacked off trays of tiny lobster rolls, freshly cut sushi, pigs in a blanket, spinach pastries, and even mini samosas. He finished the bottle of champagne and started another but never found the promised tequila.

They laughed and listened to stories and immersed themselves in the palpable relief emanating from a group of people who were separated by mere hours from the certainty that their species was doomed. Hours away from thinking their children were doomed, their world lost, their civilization at its endpoint.

Rohan smiled and drank and laughed and told bad jokes. He offered champagne to Lyst, who declined with a smile. He got Marion Stone and Amber to argue about the physics of time travel, timequakes, and the true history of this timeline's Dog Baron.

At some point, people began to drift away, either to rest or to continue their celebrations in more private environs.

Poseidon stretched out on the conference table and snored loudly, his heavy white beard flipped up over his face.

Spiral sprawled in a soft leather chair with a half-empty glass of something in his hand and stared off into space, unresponsive.

Rohan patted his old teacher on the shoulder.

Spiral looked up at him. "I'm glad my father's not alive to see this."

Rohan sighed. "What do you mean?"

"He wanted humans to be strong enough to defend humans. In the end, we're only alive because you helped."

"Sorry."

"No, it's not that. Not what I meant. I'm working on something to fix that. It's just not ready yet."

"A way for humans to stand up to land sharks?" Rohan said it with a smile.

"Maybe. Hopefully. I got the idea from Eldest."

"You'll have to show me when it's done."

"Show you? You're going to field-test it for me."

"Deal!"

Rohan left his friend.

The Director bid all a good night and took Carla back into the apartment she kept behind her office.

The Damsel left with a pair of Hyperion staffers with eager eyes and roving hands.

Bright Angel turned to Rohan. "You need some rest. The regen tank is great, but it doesn't replace a night in bed."

He nodded. "You're right."

"Come on, I'll make sure you're relaxed enough to sleep." Her eyes flashed at him.

"Wait, really?"

"Are you saying no?"

"No . . . of course not. I thought you were mad at me."

"I am. But I've also missed you. And you deserve a reward for saving the human race, don't you think?"

"I do. I mean, um, I don't think of you as just a reward, you're a person. Wait, is this a test? Am I failing? I feel like I'm failing."

She laughed and grabbed his arm in both her hands. "Let me show you."

35

Morning After Party

Rohan woke up with Bright Angel's arms wrapped around him, her hair tickling his nose as she slept.

They were in his room: the luxury suite in the adjacent five-star hotel, not the bare bones, secure room deep under Hyperion HQ. It had a plush bed big enough for four, sheets with a nearly infinite thread count, same-floor room service for nearly instantaneous response, full glass walls offering a view of the city or desert, hot tub, infinity pool, and full spa service.

Very little of which Rohan had gotten to enjoy.

He exhaled, settling back into the bed, then inhaled gently, taking in the unfamiliar smell of Bright Angel's hair care products alongside the old but familiar feeling of her arm pressed into his chest.

He gently touched his throat and chest, checking for feelings of rawness or pain, but the skin had healed.

He was wondering how long he could enjoy laying there when Bright Angel woke. She looked at him with eyes squinted against the sunlight, smiled, and pressed into his chest to sit up.

He looked up at her as she stretched. "Hey."

She looked at him. "Hey yourself. Oh, I think I'm hungover. That hasn't happened in a while."

"I thought the Angelium kept that from happening."

"Normally it does. But not when you start drinking Poseidon's homemade hooch."

She stood and crossed the room to get a glass of water.

Rohan couldn't take his eyes off her.

A minute later, he heard the shower running. *Should I join her?* She hadn't invited him. *Did last night mean something more than just that night? She hasn't kissed me good morning. Did she used to?* He wasn't sure.

He stayed in bed. He felt no great desire to push his luck.

She came out of the shower wrapped in a plush robe, patting her face dry with the end of a towel.

"I don't know what to do with my day. It's been two months of completely focusing on the sharks, and now . . . It's a weird feeling."

He nodded. "I remember waking up after the Wedge retreated from the Ringgate. Two years where every moment we were either fighting or healing because we were too injured to fight. Then you wake up one day and there's no fighting to be done. We'd all forgotten how to breathe. Except Hyperion."

"What *did* you do? That day?"

He laughed. "I don't remember. Probably ate enough food to fuel a small village. The il'Drach found a new war for us quickly enough. They don't like bored Hybrids hanging around."

"Is that why they're always working to conquer the galaxy? To keep their soldiers busy?"

He thought. "Maybe. Honestly, it always seemed like more than that. Like they're afraid of something, and they need as big a power base as they can get to face it."

"Afraid of what, though?"

"I have no idea. Just a feeling."

"You've met many of them? Other than your father?"

"A few. Not often, though. And it's not like we were friendly, hanging out."

"Well, I'm going to get a massage and get my hair done. Then I think I'm going to visit my folks. It's been a while."

"Sounds good."

She hesitated. "Are you planning to stay on Earth? Assuming the trial goes okay?"

He sighed. "I won't leave without saying goodbye."

Her voice tightened slightly. "But you will leave."

"I don't know. I'm not sure I'm welcome here. Regardless of how the trial goes."

"Okay. Well, figure it out, and let me know."

"I will. Hey, Bright Angel."

"What?"

"I just want to say . . . I was a shitty boyfriend. I'm sorry."

She looked at him and smiled softly. "We were both shitty. We were also kids. Don't sweat it. For whatever it's worth, I'm sorry, too. I wasn't the easiest."

"You were worth it."

She threw him a small smile, then gathered up her uniform, taking an extra moment to search for her second boot. She found it behind the television.

She left, the door softly clicking shut behind her.

Rohan gave himself another ten minutes to lay in bed.

Oddly, he felt relaxed, at peace, in a way that he couldn't remember feeling in a long time. Rarely even on Wistful, and certainly not while a member of the il'Drach Navy.

The ten minutes passed.

Rohan showered, brushed his teeth.

Ordered and ate breakfast: masala dosas as good as he remembered his mother ever making. Probably better.

He put on his last fresh uniform.

He left Wistful's helmet in his room and took his Hyperion phone. It was highly advanced but nothing beyond normal Earth technology.

He took the elevator to the ground floor of the hotel. Once outside, he had to circle the HQ building to get to the plaza in front of it.

There were a handful of protesters assembled in the plaza.

Rohan walked up to the crowd, searching for a particular face.

He found it.

"Hands up! Kidding, kidding. I mean, what's up, Hand?"

The face that looked down on him held no shred of humor.

"Griffin. We have been hearing news."

"Really? What?"

"Are you playing dumb?"

"Sir, I never play."

"But . . . I am not going to argue with you. Zey say you have saved ze human race."

"Do they? Don't believe everything you hear. Kid Lightning saved the human race. With a big hand from Poseidon and a team of sea monsters."

"Why you are making ze fun of me, I do not understand."

"I'm not. Well, maybe a little."

"You are a hero now, Griffin. Possibly soon to be ze most popular and loved hero on the planet. As ze news spreads."

"That's fantastic. But not super relevant to my life, oddly. Though I was serious; I did my share, but lots of others did as well."

The protesters had gathered close by and were listening intently.

"I assume you are here to tell me to . . . how do you Americans say it? Make love to myself?"

"That's . . . I'm Canadian. And nobody says it like that. And no, I'm not."

"Zen what?"

"I'm here to turn myself in. To go to trial. Whatever makes sense."

"Are you . . . You said you do not play."

"I'm not playing. Don't be a jerk about this. I'm not waiting for cameras, I'm not letting you handcuff me, and you're not roughing me up. We'll do this in a real court in a country with a half-decent legal system, assuming we can find one."

"Ze Lady is satisfied with Sahara City. Ze courts here are fair."

"Great. Keep in mind I own the city. If you want to take me to France or The Hague or whatever, I'm not going to argue. I promise not to resist. If I'm convicted, I'll serve the sentence."

Hand Of Justice stepped back. "Is zis true? I am glad, but why?"

Rohan sighed. "Look . . . I'll tell you the truth. But keep it to yourself."

"Oui."

"My mom said I need to make up for what I did. You know mothers."

"Oui, I do. Very well, Monsieur Griffin. Come with me. Zere is an international warrant for your arrest which Sahara City police will honor."

Rohan nodded. "Lead the way."

· · · ● · ● · ● · · ·

The Director faced him through a set of floor-to-ceiling iron bars. She wore a black-and-tan sari with a simple cut and very little jewelry.

"I can't say this is what I was imagining when I first saw your little fingers on an ultrasound thirty-three years ago."

Rohan smiled up at her. He was sitting on a surprisingly comfortable cot, just a couple of meters from his mother.

"I can't say this is what *I* was imagining when I told Amber I'd come back to Earth with her to help fight giant sharks."

"Neither of us gets paid for our imaginations, luckily. I would ask how you're doing, but it seems ridiculous."

He shrugged. "All things considered, I'm good. Kind of wondering why they're being so pleasant. They let me keep my phone, have as many visitors as I want, you know. Is this because I own half the city?"

She shook her head. "It's actually standard procedure for Powered individuals who surrender to authorities. Their way of acknowledging that you could walk, or fly, out of here anytime you want to, so there's not much point in taking your phone away."

"Ah."

She tilted her head. "How do the il'Drach handle Powered prisoners? Do they have some high-tech way to keep a Hybrid in a cage?"

He let out a short laugh. "The il'Drach don't *take* Powered prisoners."

"Of course. Well, we have a legal team working on your defense. I'll be honest, we had them working on it even before you turned yourself in."

"Sure. Where is the trial going to be?"

"Here. We have what is widely considered the most trustworthy judicial system in the world."

"Really?"

"Yes. You remember . . . what was she called . . . The Truth? Sometimes she went by Pathfinder?"

"I think so. An empath, right?"

"Yes. A good one. Maybe the most sensitive on Earth. She's Chief Justice. We have professional jurors, and she scans them regularly to make sure they aren't compromised. It's the closest you can get to a truly impartial and incorruptible system."

"Cool. That actually sounds very il'Drach."

"Prosecutors are working on their case now. It wasn't exactly urgent before you came back to Earth. Also, the full video of the attack hadn't surfaced, so . . ."

"I get it. Not much for me to do at this point other than wait, so I'll wait."

"Rohan, are you sure this is what you want to do?"

"It's too late to back out now, isn't it? Besides, it feels right."

"Okay." She looked at him, her eyes dark and sad.

He paused. "Listen . . . Can anybody hear us?"

She shook her head. "It's a privileged conversation."

He walked over to the bars and put his hands over hers. "Listen, Mom. I gotta be honest, I've done some pretty terrible things. I mean, in each case, I could argue that I had no choice, or that it was the lesser of two evils, or that it wasn't what I *wanted* to do. And that's true. Which really means that I've gotten exceedingly good at justifying my own sins.

"I don't really want to go into details. Because, you're my mother, and maybe you shouldn't have to know all of it. But you have to believe me, whatever happens, I'm sure I deserve worse.

"You told me I had to do something to atone. This is the best thing. Hopefully, they'll drag me over the coals for a while, then let me go. Otherwise, I'll serve my sentence. Prison doesn't sound so terrible. What's terrible is living with the way the people I care about have been looking at me."

She nodded, her eyes damp. "Do you have any idea how much harder it's going to be to find you a wife if you're convicted? Nobody wants a felon son-in-law."

He laughed, and she laughed with him. "I don't know if I'm really marriage material, sorry to say. Starting with, no chance of grandkids."

"Oh, phooey. I told you already, you can adopt. Living halfway across the galaxy is a tougher sell."

"Yeah, that, too. Wistful is going to be pissed if I get ten years in prison."

"Wistful is your boss?"

"Yes. She's a sentient space station, thirty kilometers long, two million permanent inhabitants. Also a friend."

"I'm glad you found friends out there in space."

"Thanks. Me, too! Life hasn't been terrible."

"Okay. I have to get back. We have so much work to do, getting housing and medical care for refugees, rebuilding cities. Managing food and clean water distribution. Getting rid of the vampires preying on the refugees. The Stones are cleaning up the fallout, but when all is said and done, we might see hundreds of millions dead. Maybe a billion. Which . . . I can't wrap my head around it."

"I'm sure nobody could possibly be doing more than you, Mom. The planet is in good hands."

She smiled. "Take care of yourself."

"I will. Say hi to Carla for me."

The Director turned and knocked on the door at the end of the hall. It opened within seconds, and she slipped out of the jail.

Rohan leaned back in his bed and restarted the music on his phone.

Nothing left to do but wait.

· · · · ·•·•· · · ·

"Shhh, you'll wake him up. Again! Every single time, Shadowstep! Can't you do anything right?"

Rohan woke with a start, disoriented in unfamiliar surroundings.

Darkness.

Sleeping on a cot.

Hard concrete wall next to his head.

Oh right, prison.

He sat up, dinging his head on the unoccupied top bunk, then slid a step away.

Without thinking about it, Rohan began to draw on his Power.

There wasn't much room to move in the cell.

"Oh for—lights!"

A bright light illuminated the area, coming from Shadowstep's hand. A flashlight or a phone or something.

Sister Steel stood in front of him, knees bent and hands held in front of her face in a loose athletic stance, her mirrorlike skin reflecting the drab gray of the concrete walls and the black iron bars of the interior cell wall.

"Sister Steel, what the . . ."

She slid forward and launched a volley of punches, left, right, left, right, left hook, then drove her right shoulder down toward Rohan's belly.

He parried her fists, but her shoulder struck emphatically, knocking the wind out of him.

"The gas!"

A hiss, and something billowed out of Shadowstep's hand, quickly filling the area.

Rohan held his breath, reached down, and lifted Sister Steel, slamming her body into the ceiling, bringing down a cascade of rock and a shower of sparks as her body short-circuited the wiring overhead.

Shadowstep had a mask of some kind covering his face. A gas mask?

The Hybrid let Sister Steel fall, kicking up into her body, launching her back upward and through the ceiling into the floor above.

He headed for Shadowstep, whose eyes widened in surprise and fear.

Shadowstep shook his head, pale skin growing paler as the Hybrid closed on him.

Rohan reached up to snatch the mask off the tall man's face. As he did so, a third person slammed into him from behind.

Rohan hit the ground hard, the impact pushing out what little air he'd still had in his lungs.

"Your presence is requested by our master." The voice was deep, too low to be human.

The words weren't English. Or even Drachna.

They were Tolone'an.

Rohan twisted and squirmed to get free, but the person holding him down was too strong. It adjusted with every twist and turn, keeping position on top of the Hybrid.

The body was heavy, and when Rohan touched it, he felt cold metal, like armor. Familiar armor.

Rohan's vision began to tunnel from lack of oxygen. He managed to spin around, to at least face his attackers, only to see a silvery statue of a woman drop down from a hole that she'd recently punched through the ceiling.

Sister Steel landed with both feet square on Rohan's jaw.

As he blacked out, he felt mostly curiosity. *Why is Garren working with these guys?*

36

Immediately after the Prologue (Go Back and Reread, We Can Wait)

Rohan woke to a cold, wet touch on his skin. He jerked away, his motion severely restricted by the shackles keeping him spread-eagled.

He blinked, trying to clear his vision. The lighting inside the cave seemed to be invariant. No way to tell how much time had passed while he'd been unconscious. His head was thick, channels of thought clogged and sluggish.

"Hold still. I will clean your wounds."

The Hybrid looked down at the shiny-armored figure. Just under two meters tall, the armor was roughly humanoid in shape, but had a wider head with room for a curtain of flesh on all sides. Four long tentacles emerged from the base of that head.

The armor covered every centimeter of the man's flesh, but his aura was familiar.

"Garren? Is that you, old buddy?"

The hand cleaning Rohan's wounds paused, then continued its work.

"It is, Rohan."

"Oh, hey, hi." Ideas slipped and squirmed inside him.

Rohan flinched away as antiseptic was applied to a particularly deep cut.

"You know, Garren, I'm really sorry you died fighting that shark. I'm grateful you helped us, but it wasn't your fight, really, and that just makes me sadder. Just so you know, you died a hero."

"I am not dead, Rohan. The doctor rescued me."

"You're . . . you're not? That's great! Great. Super. I was just thinking, you look awfully good for a dead guy. Have you been working out? And that new armor, super shiny."

"Yes, I have been . . . working out. The true miracle is what Dr. Kraken has done for me."

"What . . . what is that? That he's done? The armor? I thought Dr. Stone worked that out with you."

The armored figure pivoted, checking for listeners, then turned back to Rohan. "Dr. Kraken has the abilities of the religious caste of the Tolone'ans."

Rohan knew that should mean something. The religious caste had been able to do . . . something. Something important. And he'd wiped them out. But he couldn't fit the pieces together.

"Huh."

"It is a wonder, is it not? He is not of my people, yet I believe he is of the race that came before. Of our ancestors."

"That's . . . that's terrific. Hey, look, Garren. I'm pretty doped up here. And I don't think I have a ton of time left, because between you and me, I don't have the information your boss wants. And if I did, I still probably wouldn't give it to him."

"That is unfortunate. I did not agree to bring you here to see you die."

"No, of course. I know. Listen, though, this is important, and my head isn't quite right. Come closer."

Garren's tone was guarded, but he leaned in regardless. "What is it, Rohan?"

"I'm sorry."

Garren recoiled. "What?"

"For what I did on Tolone'a. I'm sorry."

"You told me you did what you had to do. Isn't that right? Or was that a lie?"

"Well . . . I did the only thing I could think of doing. If the war had continued, the planet *would* have been sterilized. But that doesn't mean there was no other way. It just means I couldn't find it. So instead, I did a terrible, terrible thing. And I'm sorry."

"Why are you telling me this? Saying this?"

"Who else should I tell? Dr. Kraken? I don't think he cares."

"No, I meant . . . I meant, why are you saying that you are sorry? Do you want forgiveness?"

Rohan sighed and shook his head. "Nah. It's this thing I'm trying out. I can't make up for what I did, and I don't deserve forgiveness. Or need it. I'm not sure I even *want* it. But I want to make amends as much as I can. Because that's all I can do. And right here, chained down, saying sorry is all I have."

"I see."

"I remember! They awakened Powers, didn't they? The religious caste. Sorry, I'm still pretty drugged."

"Yes. Dr. Kraken has given me the abilities of our warrior caste. A thing I thought impossible."

"That's . . . that's great. I guess not for me, though, am I right? Am I right?" Rohan laughed, and his laugh sounded silly, so he laughed louder, which sounded even sillier, and soon he was coughing and fighting for breath.

"Your apology doesn't change anything, you know."

"Ha! That's . . . that's exactly where you are precisely, most definitely wrong."

"How?"

"It changes *me*. I suppose you don't care, so maybe you were right. Yeah, you were right, it doesn't change anything. Just me."

Rohan had no more strength to talk.

Garren gathered some items from the floor, a pile of Rohan's belongings.

He looked up at the prisoner. "I will clean your things. In case you survive and have need of them. Which is unlikely. But it is . . . it is what I will do for you. Friend Rohan."

Rohan nodded and tried to mumble some thanks, but he couldn't make the sounds come out.

· · · · ● · ● · · ·

More torture.

More questions from Dr. Kraken.

Rohan did begin talking. He spoke at length about the dietary habits of Drach, going into special detail regarding the preparation and presentation of the desserts.

The il'Drach Matrons prided themselves on their pastry skills.

More drugs. Greater in quantity and quality.

In his more lucid moments, Rohan wondered if his liver would adapt to the drugs and begin to clear them faster. If that would open an avenue for escape, or at least resistance.

It did not happen.

Sister Steel came and fed him broth through a straw. It tasted of umami and the sea. Rohan drank it greedily.

She didn't speak, but her ministrations were efficient; no cruelty in how she touched him.

Shadowstep spent time just a few meters from Rohan, standing in the dim light and staring at the Hybrid.

He didn't speak either.

Rohan was sad when Shadowstep eventually turned and left.

What had it been about? Had he forgotten to do something?

Why was he in a cave?

He remembered.

Were the drugs doing something to him?

He hoped he didn't tell Dr. Kraken enough for the madman to find and then go to Drach. If he did . . .

Heaven help the Old Ones.

• • • • • • • • •

"You were telling me about the dinners, Griffin."

"I was? Yes, I remember. The dinners. No tablecloths, did I say that? They ate on bare tables. Wood, metal, sometimes stone, but no cloth covering on top. Napkins, yes, but no tablecloths. Anywhere. Or maybe they never took me to the nice places. Huh. I never thought of that. Maybe they only took me to the fast food joints."

"That is good, Griffin. Very good. Now tell me, who served the food?"

"Who . . . who served it?" Rohan had a feeling that he shouldn't answer, but he didn't know why. His head was so murky.

"Yes, Griffin. The waitstaff, the kitchen staff. Who brought the food to you? Did the il'Drach themselves cook and serve the food, or do they have servants?"

"Why?"

"Oh, Griffin, you know it is not your place to ask questions. Please do not disappoint me. You know what happens when you do."

Rohan screamed for a bit.

He blinked his eyes. He thought he had passed out again but wasn't sure.

Sister Steel entered the cave. She held a straw up to Rohan's mouth, giving him a chance to suck down some broth.

"Thanks."

She laughed, an echoey noise halfway between a cough and a ringing bell. "You really don't have to thank me. Considering the situation you're in."

What situation? *Oh, right.* Rohan looked up at his hands, encased in steel and stretched out from his body.

He had nothing to say.

The woman turned her smooth, metallic face to her boss. "He's a tough bastard, but even he can only take so much of this. You won't get any information out of him if he's dead."

Rohan blinked, trying to clear his vision. His eyes didn't want to focus on anything. He looked toward the far corner of the cavern, toward a disc of still water not much larger than a children's inflatable pool.

"Female, at the point where I require your advice on, well, on anything, be sure that I will request it. Until that time, you may refrain from offering it."

She shrugged, her arms sliding over her ribs as she did it, striking small sparks. "Fine, whatever. It's not like I care if he lives or dies."

The air above the pool wavered and shimmered in Rohan's eyes. He shook his head and squinted, trying to reset his vision.

The shimmering didn't go away.

Sister Steel put the bottle of broth down on the floor and walked away in a huff, her metallic shoulders high and tight.

Dr. Kraken turned back to Rohan. "Refreshed?"

Rohan was starting to believe that something was actually happening over the water.

"Oh yeah, that's great. Great. What were we talking about again?"

"The servants, Griffin. Tell me about them. Do you remember their names? Or even their species?"

Rohan's thoughts were cohering, but only slightly.

If anything was happening over the pool, he didn't want Dr. Kraken to notice it.

"Oh, right. That's the funny thing, you know? The il'Drach didn't serve themselves. Like, ever. I think there are only a few thousand actual il'Drach on the planet. You know, total. Anywhere, really. They're not very fertile. It's like they're a weird accident of evolution. Barely a viable species."

A tall, pale figure entered from one of the side entrances and walked toward them. Shadowstep, no mask obscuring his features.

Dr. Kraken snorted. "Evolution? That mistress had no hand in the il'Drach. The il'Sein themselves . . . well, never mind. If not them, who worked there?"

Something was definitely happening near the pool.

Rohan swallowed and forced himself to say more without saying anything in particular. "That's the thing, right? It wasn't the il'Drach, but they can't have people coming and going. There's a whole community of, well, I guess slaves living on Drach. Sort of like slaves, I don't know if they were forced to do any particular jobs, but they weren't allowed to leave. Ever. For generation after generation."

Shadowstep had been listening to the conversation, but he had noticed something around the pool. He walked over and stood staring into the space above it.

"Did they resent their servitude, do you believe? These generational slaves?"

"If they did, they weren't sharing with me, you know? Why would they? But they were treated pretty well. It's the secret to the il'Drach Empire. It's taxation without representation, but for the most part they treat their subjects pretty well. When everyday life is pretty great, it's hard to muster up much in the way of revolutionary fervor."

Shadowstep turned to face Dr. Kraken. "Sir, you should look at this."

Dr. Kraken waved his back tentacles at the human. "Not now. So, Rohan, may I call you Rohan?"

Rohan nodded. "Sure, buddy, sure."

"Tell me the species. What planets were they from? Did you recognize them?"

Shadowstep cleared his throat nervously. "Sir, something is going on."

The shimmering over the pool had intensified to the point where Rohan couldn't see the far end of the cavern. He kept his eyes focused on Dr. Kraken's, trying to keep the cephalopod's attention.

"There were plenty of Andervarians, and of course Tolone'ans, especially in the kitchen. The il'Drach love their seafood, and you know nobody does seafood like a Tolone'an."

Dr. Kraken leaned forward. "You are lying. Why are you lying now? What are you trying to hide?"

Shadowstep again. "Sir, I'm telling you . . ."

With a pop of displacing air, an object appeared over the pond.

Rohan blinked, unable to keep his attention away from the object.

Dr. Kraken looked at his prisoner, then turned his head to see what all the fuss was about.

A wooden boat had appeared over the pond. It was about the size of a Venetian gondola, with a closed compartment in the middle and no visible means of propulsion.

There was space on the deck for half a dozen people.

It held three.

The first of the three hopped out and onto the stone floor of the cavern. Four wings of energy unfurled from her back as her eyes blazed with white light. She wore white, silver, and blue; her hair was neatly braided close to her skull.

"This. Ends. Now."

Dr. Kraken waved a tentacle, and the globe of water hovering over his shoulder shot out toward Bright Angel.

Her wings folded in front of her into a layered shield of light. The globe splattered against it, bursting into steaming droplets that fell to the floor. She stalked forward across the cavern.

Shadowstep reached for her, but the second figure from the boat was suddenly between them, having moved too quickly for human eyes to capture.

Two shallow cuts oozed blood from just above Shadowstep's eyes. A knife was held to his throat.

"Walk away. Now."

Dr. Kraken straightened, his four long tentacles spreading in some kind of fighting posture. He roared, speaking the Fire Speech, the language from which all other languages had sprung like shadows cast from a fire.

"This prisoner is mine! You will pay for this intrusion!"

Bright Angel took to the air and shot toward the evil madman.

He pointed at her and spoke a word.

The word was sound and shape and light and *spirit*. It was wet and damp, capturing something of the essence of water in every way. In that word, Rohan could see the chemical formula of water, its boiling and freezing points, its bonding. That word said why water expanded when frozen and why it acted as a solvent.

Dr. Kraken spoke the Name of water, and the water in Bright Angel's body was ready to answer.

Then the third and last figure from the deck of the boat answered, and
it was the Name of water once again, but it captured so much more.

The Name she spoke contained everything physical about water but also
its history. How water had first formed from pure elements when planets
were raw and stars were young. Why water flowed downhill, what it sought
there, what its spirit searched for.

Lyst spoke to the hidden desires of the water. Why ice sculptures took
the forms they did, how snowflakes decided to form. All the petty barbs
snowflakes traded when nobody watched.

Dr. Kraken *pushed* at the fluids inside Lyst's body.

Lyst pushed back.

Dr. Kraken muttered. "How?"

Lyst stepped off her boat and onto the stone floor of the cavern, her
scaled head glistening in the dim lighting.

"You are old, Dr. Kraken, but I had seen eons before you'd seen the inside
of an egg sac. You think you are a water wizard, but your knowledge pales."

The cephalopod growled and bent his knees, ready for battle. He called
out.

"Garren! Sister Steel! Shadowstep! Time to earn your keep!"

Sister Steel came running in, having just left the room. Bright Angel
turned to face her.

The Black woman's eyes were fierce.

"Step away!"

Sister Steel kept coming.

Bright Angel jumped back a step, her wings swatting at Sister Steel,
knocking her savagely to the side, crashing into the stone wall of the cavern.

Bright Angel planted her back foot and darted forward, her entire body
glowing as she drove her right fist home into Sister Steel's midsection,
slamming the metal woman into the wall. A fresh cascade of stone
fragments covered her in dust and debris.

Amber leaned into Shadowstep, backing him across the cavern, one
blade at his throat, another drawing little patterns on his thigh.

He swallowed as his back touched the stone and held himself very, very
still.

Garren entered the room from the far side, his armor reflecting all the colors of the cavern.

Bright Angel turned to him. "You?"

She jumped, one powerful sweep of her wings propelling her across the room.

Dr. Kraken faced off against Lyst, speaking words and waving his hands, in each case finding that she had countered his attempts.

Bright Angel sliced across Garren's chest with one of her wings, cutting deep into the metal.

He stepped backward, hands up and all four tentacles pointing toward the ceiling. "No! I brought you here!"

She paused, reacting to his posture if not his words.

Rohan laughed. Bright Angel didn't speak Drachna, and Garren certainly didn't speak any Earth languages.

Rohan yelled out in English. "He's saying he brought you here, and you shouldn't fight!"

Dr. Kraken yelled at the Tolone'an. "You have the morality of a mammal! How dare you betray me!"

Garren yelled back. "It is you who lied! He has done evil, yes, but killing him will not bring back the Tolone'ans he killed. What you are doing now, it is wrong."

"The Ancients say this is what we are to do! Their will is law!"

Lyst laughed at the cephalopod. "The younger races do not share your devotion, Doctor. It is frustrating, is it not? So sad when they develop wills of their own. Especially the way they make decisions for themselves based on so little knowledge or understanding."

Dr. Kraken growled and launched himself toward the dinosaur.

Bright Angel intercepted him, slamming her forearm into his head from the side.

The cephalopod flew across the room.

Bright Angel stepped over to Rohan and cut through his metal shackles with four quick slashes of her wings.

He fell to the ground, eyes blinking slowly.

Was she hoping for help from him? *I'm not even strong enough to stand up.*

Garren was pressed against the cavern wall, hands held up in the air, palms forward.

Sister Steel pushed herself out of the indentation her body had carved into the stone wall of the cavern and held up her hands.

Bright Angel turned to the metallic woman.

"Are we going to find out if I can cut through that organic steel skin of yours? Because I'm willing to test it out. I'm feeling very scientific right now." Her wings unfurled behind her, curving around to the front, the edges gleaming in Rohan's Third Eye.

Something in her face made Sister Steel swallow hard.

The villainess took a glance at Dr. Kraken.

The cephalopod was shaking his head. "I will finish all of you. That includes you, whelp." The last comment was aimed at Garren.

Rohan tried to stand, but his legs wouldn't support his weight. He fell forward onto his elbows.

Dr. Kraken squatted down and spread his tentacles out, pointing them toward the floor. He spun quickly, runes of light appearing on his head and tentacles.

A pulse of energy radiated outwards from his form, blasting away everyone in the room.

Rohan was knocked over, left lying on his back and staring at the stalactites overhead.

Amber was thrown away from Shadowstep, nearly severing his jugular with the unexpected movement.

Shadowstep immediately faded out of sight, leaving the faintest imprint of his presence in the room.

Sister Steel was slapped into a nearby wall, cracking the stone.

Lyst took two hard steps backward.

Bright Angel's wings folded in front of her, breaking the energy before it could reach.

The heroine jumped forward, closing the distance on Dr. Kraken with dizzying speed.

She swiped at him with each wing, slicing across his chest. He deflected with two quick swings of his own tentacles.

The right cross that followed landed squarely in the center of his gray-skinned face.

The villain fell backward a few steps, his rear tentacles tapping the ground to help support him.

Bright Angel followed his motion. She jabbed into his face, then again, then throwing a hook around the tentacles blocking her.

Just as the last punch failed to connect, she drove her right foot into his abdomen.

The ancient cephalopod folded over, exhaling with a grunt.

He said something, but again Lyst countered the action from her position behind Bright Angel.

Bright Angel looked at the cephalopod. "You're done, Dr. Kraken. Your people are abandoning you. Whatever you want from Griffin, you aren't getting it."

"The Angelium is more powerful than I remember. Or is it the wielder?"

"Flattery will get you nowhere. Surrender."

Dr. Kraken surveyed the room.

Rohan was down.

Lyst was stepping forward, showing no signs of injury.

Shadowstep remained insubstantial.

Amber was recovered and staying near Shadowstep's impression, her knives at the ready.

Sister Steel was slow getting to her feet.

The metallic woman looked at Bright Angel. "Shadowstep and I will get out of your hair now, if it's all the same to you."

Bright Angel looked to Rohan. "You okay with that?"

He nodded and waved. "Yeah, let them go. No reason not to."

"You sure?"

He coughed. "I'm sure. Please."

Bright Angel nodded.

Sister Steel walked over to Shadowstep, who touched her arm.

The pair faded through the wall.

Garren stayed near the back wall of the cave, hands still in the air, palms out, giving no indication that he wanted to fight anybody.

Dr. Kraken sighed. "Lyst, I will leave you now. Your skill remains undiminished. I had forgotten your abilities."

Lyst nodded. "Advice for you. You'll be happier if you abandon these notions of resurrecting the Old Ones, the old ways. They're gone. Enjoy what the younger races have to offer."

"I think I am made of different stuff than you, ma'am. That route seems impossible to me. And unpalatable."

"So be it."

He touched the tips of all four of his tentacles together in front of his face, then put one hand over the top.

A moment later, he was gone.

Bright Angel turned to Lyst. "Teleported?"

Lyst nodded, her bony crests bobbing with the motion. "Yes, and too far for me to track. Now help our friend."

Bright Angel turned and crossed to Rohan's position. "Oh dear. You look terrible."

He coughed into his hand. It came away red.

"You look beautiful."

He laid his head back on the stone and closed his eyes.

37

The End

Rohan leaned back on one elbow. His feet dangled over the cliff's edge, nothing beneath them but thousands of feet of air and the Shenandoah Valley of Virginia.

With his free hand, he took a small sip from a bottle of extra-premium tequila.

"Pass me some."

He handed the bottle to Bright Angel, who sipped delicately from it.

"That is smooth."

Rohan nodded. "I missed this stuff. Though to be honest, I never drank anything this good when I was on Earth."

"This would have been snack money for a month when you were last on Earth."

He laughed. "That's true. Kid Lightning's basement, scrounging for beer money. Good times."

She returned the laugh. "How are you, though? You've had a rough time."

He sighed. "Just a little torture. A day or two in the regen tank, I'll be good as new."

"No post-traumatic stress?"

He shook his head. "I don't think so. I'm sure it would have gone worse if you hadn't rescued me."

"You're welcome."

"And thank you. But why did you? I thought The Director said not to."

She smiled, showing him the gap between her front teeth. They had taken off their masks.

"I do what I do. She did fire me for it, though."

His jaw dropped. "Seriously? My mom fired you for saving my life?"

She was still smiling. "She did. I am officially no longer a member of Vanguard Prime. I got a hefty severance package, too. Ten years' salary."

"Really? Hey, if you need money, I have more than I could ever know what to do with."

"I'm good. I have corporate sponsors lining up already. Best part is, I'm no longer a member of Vanguard Prime. So . . ."

"Oh, I get it. The Proud Guys."

"Yep. You promised no action from Vanguard members against them, but I'm not Vanguard anymore."

"Nice play there."

"Thank you. It was my idea."

He drank.

"How did you find me?"

"That guy . . . Garren? Iron Octopus? He turned on the tracking in your phone."

"Huh. Funny."

"Why?"

"I kind of committed genocide against his species."

"That is a sentence I never thought I'd hear from you, Rohan."

"There were extenuating circumstances. It's a story."

"Okay." She paused. "Those vampires? The ones we fought in Tokyo Epsilon?"

"Yeah?"

"There were a bunch in Dr. Kraken's caverns. It took half an hour to wipe them out."

"Huh."

"Looks like he was making them. To act as servants, finish off the humans, something like that."

"Sharks take out the big cities and population centers, tentacled vampires go in and finish off the survivors."

"That's what it looks like."

"I'm glad you got them."

"Well, say what you want about the Angelium, it makes me a pretty bad matchup for young vampires."

"Right."

"I'm sure I'll be hunting more of them over the next few months. But what's next for you? Is there still a trial?"

"Yeah. My lawyers got Dr. Kraken's torture included as time served. The legal teams think the jury will decide I've suffered enough. A sincere apology from me, and I should be done. Convicted, but released."

"Any word from Sister Steel?"

"She sent a statement basically saying she's okay with that outcome. Which surprised me, but in a good way."

"How long will that take to wrap up?"

"Just a few days, they think."

"Then what, Griffin?"

He looked at her, then out at the sun setting over the valley. "I was thinking of staying."

"Why?" Her tone was neutral.

He paused. "I was kind of thinking we had something going on here. Again. Something I missed."

She sighed. "Rohan, you can't stay on Earth for me."

"Why not?"

"Look . . . We had something unique, right? You were the first person I was with who I came out to. As a hero. We didn't have to hide that from each other. It was really special."

"Yeah."

"And that will always mean something to me."

"But the other night . . ."

"That was great. But, come on. We saved the world. We celebrated. Don't make a mountain out of it."

He sighed. "I really care about you."

"I care about you, too. If you're ever in trouble on your talking space station, send word, and I'll come rescue you. But you have a life there, a life you love. You can't abandon it to stay here with me and try to resurrect a relationship that's been dead for eleven years."

"Are you sure? I can't convince you?"

She laughed. "Just think about how much pressure that would be. On both of us. And you're one of the most famous people in the world. Look, if life here is what you really want, by all means, stay on Earth. And if you do, and you want to give me a call, I'm not saying I won't answer it. But I might already have plans."

He leaned back and nodded. "Fair enough."

She continued. "I don't want to be cruel here, but you have to think about it. You did go away for over ten years. Let us think you were dead. I just don't know if that's something you . . . we . . . us . . . that we can come back from."

"I'm trying to make up for that."

"And you're doing a pretty good job of it. You seem like a much better person than you were when you left. Really.

"If I had met you for the first time last week, and got to know you from just that, maybe we could have something. You're cute enough. I like your beard. You're funny. I wouldn't have to worry about breaking you in bed."

He laughed. "That's a very nice description of me. I'll have you work on my profile for dating sites."

"'Bearded and hard to break.' I'm not sure you'd appreciate the kind of partners that would attract."

He drank some more tequila, enjoying the warmth that spread from it through his chest.

She continued. "I also have a lot to process. Losing Ares. Losing other friends. Kid Lightning. I'm not sure The Damsel will recover full use of her Powers. She *pushed* too hard. She says she's retiring from the hero business. And I spent two months thinking my species was doomed."

"That's a lot."

"So give me a few months. And if you want, come back to visit. We'll always have this." She waved at the valley. "And we can always get more tequila."

"Okay. And if you ever want to see the galaxy, let me know. I have a ship."

She leaned over and kissed his cheek, her full lips soft and warm where they pressed into his beard.

When she leaned back away, she had the tequila bottle in her hand.

Rohan sighed. Things weren't perfect, but they were pretty good.

Epilogue

Really the End This Time; I Promise

R ohan sat in the soft leather chair across from his mother.

She wore a pink-and-green sari; her makeup was at a six out of ten. He felt a softball of anxiety in his belly.

She was holding some papers. "The verdict came back. What we expected: guilty, sentenced to time served."

He nodded.

She smiled softly. "Public opinion seems to be that you did a bad thing, but it was a while ago, and you've made up for it. You're not public enemy number one, not even for the anti-alien crowd."

"That's good, I guess."

"Now it's just a question of what you're going to do next."

He sighed. "Seems like there are no more sharks coming, right?"

She nodded. "It's been five days. Since they were on a strict pattern, and more should have come by now . . ."

"Then, I guess I should head back. I think I'm almost out of vacation days."

"You won't stay?"

"I don't feel like I should. I mean, send word if you need me, but I don't want to be in the hero business full time. I'm not cut out for chasing bank robbers every day. At least on Wistful I have a regular job. Responsibilities."

"You don't think we need you now?"

"I'm positive you don't. Come on, Mom, you're the most powerful person on the planet."

"You're still my son."

"Sure, and I always will be. But that doesn't mean you *need* me."

She sighed. "You can't do this again, Rohan. Leave me with no word for so long."

"I promise. I'll have the Professors put up a long-range tachyon communications satellite. I'll be able to text. Call even. Okay? And I'll visit. Not sure how often, but I will."

"Yes. And give me warning next time so I can have some girls ready for you to meet."

"I meant visit you and Carla, not meet girls you found on Shaadi dot com."

"We'll see." Her smile had grown, and he knew she was teasing him.

"Besides, you're going to be too busy to have any time for me anyway. You have four major cities to rebuild."

"Six. But yes. Busy."

"So let me get out of your hair. Like I said, Wistful needs me there."

She stood and held her arms out.

He walked around the desk and hugged her.

"I'm sorry, you know. About not coming back."

"I know. It's hard. We'll be okay."

"Yeah. I think so."

THE END

The Hybrid Helix will continue in Turn Three, *Blood Reunion*

What's Next

If you enjoyed this book, please review it on Amazon and/or Goodreads and tell your friends about it! They'll enjoy it, and you'll seem cool and smart to have done so.

Please also go to jcmberne.com and sign up for the Book Berne-ing newsletter, read JCM's blog, and find other amusing things. Follow JCM on the social media platform of your choice! Links at his website.